Princess Charming

Princess Charming

Jane Heller

k

Kensington Books
http://www.kensingtonbooks.com

KENSINGTON BOOKS are published by

Kensington Publishing Corp.
850 Third Avenue
New York, NY 10022

Library of Congress Card Catalog Number: 96-079084
ISBN 1-57566-148-9

First Printing: April, 1997
10 9 8 7 6 5 4 3 2 1

Printed in the United States of America

Design by Eric Elias

PRINCESS CHARMING is the story of three women who take a vacation together. Writing the novel wasn't exactly a vacation for me, but the following women did make the voyage a lot smoother: my editor, Ann LaFarge; Kensington publisher, Lynn Brown; the publicity/promotion team of Laura Shatzkin and Deborah Broide; my literary agent, Ellen Levine; and my friend and mentor, Ruth Harris.

Special thanks, as always, to my husband, Michael Forester, my fellow sea cruiser.

For John Jakes, cruise ship aficionado

O Captain! my Captain! our fearful trip is done,
The ship has weathered every rack, the prize we sought is won.
—Walt Whitman, "O Captain! My Captain!"

Won't you let me take you on a sea cruise?
Oo wee, oo wee baby.
—Frankie Ford, "Sea Cruise"

Prologue

At six o'clock in the morning on a snowless, frigidly cold day in January, a man stood at a pay phone at the corner of Seventy-first Street and Lexington Avenue in Manhattan. He looked to his left, then to his right, and when he was sure he would not be overheard by passersby, he stepped closer to the phone and picked up the receiver.

He listened for a dial tone and nodded with relief when he heard one. He knew how rare it was to find a public phone that worked. That was the irony of the "high-tech" nineties. You could reach out and touch Sharon Stone on the Internet, but you couldn't call your goddamn mother from a pay phone.

The man took a deep breath and punched in the numbers he'd written on a small scrap of paper. He pressed his ear to the phone and waited. After only one ring, someone answered.

"I'm here," said a man who sounded as if he was expecting the call but dreading it. "What is it?"

"You're going to do something for me," said the caller.

The man on the other end of the phone was silent for a moment. "What's the 'something'?"

The caller cupped his hand around the mouthpiece and said in a hoarse whisper, "You're going to kill my ex-wife."

"Kill your ex-wife?" The man was dumbfounded, nonplussed.

"Yeah, why did you think I was calling you at six o'clock in the morning? To hire you to mow my lawn?"

"No, but I didn't think we were talking about a hit here. That's out of the question."

"There's always the alternative," the caller taunted.

The other man was speechless.

"So. Here's the plan," the caller said when there seemed to be no real resistance. "My ex-wife is taking a cruise next month. One of those seven-day trips to the Caribbean with her two girlfriends. The Three Blond Mice, they call themselves." He smirked as he pondered the nickname. Sure, all three women had blond hair, but the mousy part was debatable. The Three Blond Barracudas would be more accurate. "The name of the ship is the *Princess Charming,*" he continued. "It leaves Miami at five P.M. on Sunday, February tenth and returns there the following Sunday at seven A.M. I want you to take that cruise and kill her before the ship is back in Miami."

"You want me to kill her while she's on the ship?"

"You'll probably have to use a cover with the other passengers," said the caller, ignoring the man's question. "Hand them a line about why you're taking the cruise. But you're a good liar. I ought to know, huh?"

"Look, I–"

"The main thing is, do it and don't get caught," the caller interrupted. "Now. What do you say?"

Say? What could the man say?

"She deserves to be killed," said the caller, as if reading the man's mind. "You'll be performing a public service, believe me. Besides, killing her won't take up *all* your time on that cruise. You'll be in the Caribbean in the middle of winter, the envy of all your friends. You can hang out at the pool, eat as much as you want, do the shows, the casino, the disco scene. It'll be a goddamn *vacation.*"

There was another moment of silence while the man contemplated the unfortunate situation in which he found himself; he wasn't exactly flush with options.

"I'll do the job," he said finally. He did hate cold weather and he did need some sun. So he'd have to kill the woman. At least he'd get a tan while he was at it.

Day One:

Sunday, February 10

1

"**H**ow are you today, Mrs. Zimmerman?" asked the ticket agent for Sea Swan Cruises as he examined the small packet containing my tickets, passport, and Customs forms. He couldn't have been more than twenty; he looked callow, unripe.

"I'm fine, thank you," I said, mildly irritated that he had referred to me as *Mrs.* Zimmerman. There was nothing in my documents indicating that I was married, nor was I wearing a wedding band, and yet—

Well, he wasn't the first one to make the mistake. If you're a woman of a certain age, it probably hasn't escaped you that men—particularly but not exclusively *young* men—automatically call you "Mrs.," whether you're married or not. It comes with the territory, like receding gums.

"Sorry to keep you waiting, Mrs. Zimmerman," he said as he continued to inspect my papers.

"Take your time. I'm not in any big hurry." I sighed, wondering what on earth I was doing in the Sea Swan Cruises terminal in the first place.

Actually, I knew full well what I was doing there. I was embarking on a seven-day cruise to the Caribbean aboard the *Princess Charming*, the crown jewel in Sea Swan's line of 75,000-ton "megaships," because my best friends, Jackie Gault and Pat Kovecky, had talked me into it. The three of us had taken a week's vacation together every year since we were all divorced. We'd gotten herbally wrapped at Canyon Ranch and gone white-water rafting on the Colorado River and run with wolves at some New Age place in the Catskills whose name I've completely blocked out. We'd been skiing in Telluride, sunning in Anguilla, shopping in Santa Fe, you name it. The expression "Been there, done that" just about summed it up—except for a cruise. We'd never done *that*. Until Jackie suggested it back in October, while the three of us were discussing our vacation options.

"Well, why not?" she said when I didn't look especially enthusiastic. "Cruises are supposed to be incredibly relaxing."

"Not if you get seasick," I said.

"You won't get seasick, Elaine," Jackie said. "The ships come with stabilizers now. And even if you did get seasick, they'd give you a pill or something. They do everything for you on cruises. You don't have to lift a finger."

In her professional life, Jackie lifted more than her fingers; she lifted pots of geraniums and bags of fertilizer and saplings of various species. She was partners with her ex-husband, Peter, in "J&P Nursery," a landscaping and garden center in Bedford, New York, a tony Manhattan suburb that was all the rage with upwardly mobile corporate executives, Martha Stewart acolytes, and deer. Jackie spent her days knee deep in dirt—pardon me, *soil*—planting flowers and shrubs for newly minted thirtysomethings who had houses the size of Versailles and didn't know a Venus' flytrap from a pussy willow. As a result of the hard, physically punishing work she did, she always lobbied for the sort of vacation that involved no labor whatsoever—an environment where *she* would be ministered to.

I turned to Pat. "What do you think? Are you in favor of spending a week on a boat with the Great Unwashed?"

She considered the question. For what seemed like an eternity. Far be it from Pat to act impulsively. She weighed every decision as if it were momentous, irrevocable, her last, which could be painfully frustrating if all you wanted to do was pick a movie or settle on a restaurant.

"Jackie's right," she said finally, nodding her head for emphasis. "Cruises offer their passengers complete spoilage."

Pat was the queen of malapropisms as well as the slowest decision maker on record. In this case, what she'd meant, of course, was that cruises spoiled you. Pampered you.

"They look after your every need," she said. "Diana and her husband take cruises and seem to enjoy themselves very much."

Diana was Pat's younger sister. Her much more socially active younger sister. When they were babies, their parents had labeled Diana "the outgoing one" and Pat "the shy one," and the labels proved self-fulfilling and next to impossible to shed. But Pat's shyness was deceptive; she didn't say much, but she was unwavering in her decisions, once she made them. For example, it had taken her ex-husband, Bill Kovecky, their entire four years of college to convince her to marry him. Yet once she'd agreed, she was his forever. Through his stint in medical school, his internship, his residency. Through the births of their five children. Through his metamorphosis into Dr. William Kovecky, the God of Gastroenterology. Through his speaking engagements and television appearances and trips to exotic foreign countries to deliver speeches on ileitis. Through his self-absorption and withdrawal from his family. Even through the divorce. Pat remained loyal to Bill through it all, was still deeply in love with him. She may have been "the shy one," but she had a steely determination, and one of the things she was determined about was winning Bill back. Jackie and I shrugged whenever the subject came up. We weren't exactly experts on winning back ex-husbands, since neither of us wanted ours back. Besides, Bill hadn't married anybody else in six years, so maybe Pat wasn't in total denial. "Yes," she said again. "I think a cruise is a fine idea. Just what the doctor ordered." Since Bill was a doctor, she liked dragging the word "doctor" into as many conversations as possible.

"A cruise?" I groaned. "I really don't think I'm the type, you two." I had nothing against being pampered or spoiled or ministered to. I just didn't want the ministering to take place on an oceanic vessel from which I couldn't escape, should I not be enjoying myself.

"Not the type? What type?" Jackie protested. "From what I've read, there really is no stereotype when it comes to the passengers. Cruises attract a broad cross-section of people."

" 'Broad' is the operative word," I said. "You take a cruise and you're stuck on a floating cafeteria for seven days. The food they throw away could feed a small country."

"All right, let me put it another way," said Jackie, in her husky, ex-smoker's voice. "I haven't gotten laid since George Bush was President. I would like to end the drought before one of George Bush's *sons* is President. Now, I happen to know that single men take cruises. I would, therefore, like to take a cruise. Am I making myself clear?"

"Crystal," I said. Jackie was so earthy. "But you're forgetting something. The single men who take cruises wear jewelry."

"There you go again with your stereotyping," she said.

"And black socks with brown sandals," I said.

"Elaine," she sighed, rolling her eyes.

"And they look like Rodney Dangerfield," I added for good measure.

"Perfect. I could use a good laugh when I'm having sex for the first time in years. I've probably forgotten how to do it," said Jackie. "Look, I think we'd have a great time if we took a cruise, I really do."

"According to Diana, there's a lot to do on a ship," Pat stated, then launched into a laundry list of the activities they offered on cruises. "You wouldn't be bored, Elaine. I'm quite sure of it."

The debate had lumbered on for another hour or so. Jackie and Pat insisted we'd have the time of our lives and I anticipated everything that could go wrong the minute we left dry land. I was a creative, imaginative thinker, which came in handy in my career as a public relations executive but wreaked havoc with my emotional life. You see, my creative, imaginative thinking all too often took the form of what my ex-husband, Eric, used to call my "bogeyman obsession"—incessant forebodings of disaster. What Eric didn't realize was that I was right to be obsessed by the bogeyman because *he* turned out to be one. But more on that later.

In the end, I'd been outnumbered. I'd come to the conclusion that the only way to shut my dear friends up about taking a cruise—they were dangerously close to sounding like a Kathie Lee Gifford commercial—was to say I'd take one.

"It'll be a kick, lying around the pool, not a care in the world, having handsome young studs fetch us piña coladas," Jackie said.

"I suppose I could catch up on my reading," I said, caving in. "And I could jog around the ship's Promenade Deck every morning–unless, of course, the guard rails aren't high or sturdy enough and I fall overboard."

"Oh, Elaine. Get real," she said. "Nothing's going to happen to you on the cruise. It'll be fun. Something different for us."

"Yes, something different," Pat agreed.

How different, they had no idea.

So there I was in Miami that Sunday afternoon in February, standing at the ticket counter inside the Sea Swan Cruises terminal. The *Princess Charming* wasn't shoving off until five o'clock, but our non-stop Delta flight from LaGuardia and shuttle bus ride from Miami International Airport had deposited us at the Sea Swan terminal at twelve-thirty.

"My God. Would you look at that," I'd said when we stepped out of the van and caught our first glimpse of the ship. The brochure had said she was fourteen stories high and nearly three football fields long, but nothing had prepared me for the sight of her as she rose out of the water like a Ritz Carlton with an outboard. The thing was spectacular looking, its white facade and Windexed portholes glistening in the afternoon sun.

"It's majestic," Pat whispered, gazing up at the ship with genuine awe. "And so state of the artist."

After spending a few more minutes gawking at the *Princess Charming,* we'd gone inside the terminal, walked through the same kind of security x-ray machine they have at airports, taken our place on line, and waited. And waited. Ordinarily, I like arriving early for things. When you arrive early, there's no chance of missing the boat, so to speak. But now that I had finally advanced from the line to the ticket counter and was *still* waiting while the agent examined every comma on my Customs form, I was growing restless, grouchy, grim. There was nothing to do but stare at the 2,500 people with whom I would be trapped for a week, searching their faces as they stood in line, wondering which of them–if any–I would befriend over the course of the trip. They came in all shapes and sizes, colors and creeds, ages and affects, the only common denominator being that the vast majority of them were wearing polyester warm-up suits. I wondered what they were warming up for, and then I remembered the ship's fabled midnight buffets and guessed they were warming up for those.

I checked my watch as the ticket agent continued to pore over my documents. I was itching to ship out, get under way, get the whole business over with. Truthfully, I was already thinking ahead to the vacation we would take the following year, the destination *I* would suggest. A theater trip to London, perhaps. Or a week in Key West. Or maybe a trek through Costa Rica. Yes, that was it. Costa Rica. Everyone was going there now. It was a country that was said to be so . . . so . . . *real.*

I closed my eyes and pictured myself on the patio of some rustic yet terribly posh Costa Rican inn, mingling with sophisticated foreigners, trading smart little anecdotes, exploring–

"Next!" the ticket agent called out, bringing my reverie to an abrupt end. He handed me back my papers and motioned for Jackie, who was next in line, to approach the counter.

"Good afternoon, Mrs. Gault," he greeted her after glancing at her passport.

"The name's Jackie," she said. I couldn't tell by her tone if she was scolding him for the "Mrs." bit or trying to pick him up.

After what seemed like a lifetime, she, too, was checked in and then Pat took her turn. And while things were at yet another standstill, *I* stood still and observed my friends, shaking my head at the illogicalness of our friendship, at what an unlikely threesome we made.

We had met on the day of our respective divorces, a rainy morning in March of '91 in a sterile Manhattan courthouse. I don't remember who made the first move, but I do remember that Pat was sobbing, that at some point both Jackie and I were consoling her, and that once we determined that we had each come to court to Dump the Husband, we bonded instantly. We sat through all three hearings together, offered each other words of encouragement, and completely ignored our attorneys, who were getting their $250 an hour for showing up at the courthouse so what did they care? By the time the three divorces were final, we had shared intimate details of our marriages, wept, hugged, vowed to be friends forever.

"The Three Blond Mice," I had dubbed us that day, and the nickname had stuck.

We three did, indeed, have blond hair—mine, shoulder-length, blow-dried, and streaked; Jackie's very short and utilitarian and strawberry; Pat's wild and frizzy and wheat-colored. And we were about the same age—a year or two on either side of forty-five.

But there were more differences between us than there were similarities, starting with our sizes. I was extremely tall and thin, Pat was squat and chunky, and Jackie was somewhere in between. Consequently, we could never walk in lockstep and were always bumping into each other and mumbling "Sorry." Then, there were the differences in our attitudes toward men. Jackie was always lusting after them, Pat was always comparing them to her God-almighty ex-husband, and I was always wondering how I'd been deluded enough to marry one at all. And then, there were the differences in our personalities and life experiences.

I, for example, was the quintessential neurotic New York City career woman. More specifically, I was an account executive at Pearson & Strulley, the international public relations firm, and except for my annual vacations with Jackie and Pat and my regular visits to New Rochelle to see my mother, my job was my life. I was deeply devoted to burnishing the images of my clients, which included a chain of cappuccino bars, a manufacturer of novelty sunglasses, and an over-the-hill movie actress with an unfortunate habit of breaking the law. I lived in an antiseptically clean, one-bedroom Upper East Side apartment that was guarded by three Medeco locks, two dead bolts, and a lobby filled with a battalion of doormen. I ran four miles a day, rarely allowed high-cholesterol foods to pass my lips, never ventured out in the sun without at least a No. 15 screen, and fearing I might sprout a dowager's hump in my advancing years, had recently tripled my calcium intake. I was a careful, watchful person— a control freak, my ex-husband used to call me—and the aspect of life about which I was most careful was romance. I shunned it the same way I shunned mayonnaise. In other words, if I wasn't working late at the office, I was home alone at night, picking at a Healthy Choice entrée and then watching one of those interchangeable magazine shows like "Dateline." *Dat*eline. Who wanted a date? Not me, no sir. Not after the two most important men in my life had proven to be lying, cheating sons of bitches. I was twelve when I found out about the little popsy my father, Fred Zimmerman, was putting away. Fred had a lot of little popsies, it turned out, and one of them, a redhead with large eyes and large breasts, was so diverting that he left my mother and me for her. Needless to say, I haven't seen his traitorous ass since. My mother got on with her life, marrying Mr. Schecter, our next-door neighbor, a scant seven months after Fred's defection. I, however, was left not only with a desperate fear of abandonment but with a very sizable chip on my shoulder when it came to men. I vowed that I would never be suckered in by a man, never buy into the whole love-and-romance bullshit, never even read mushy novels or sing along with overwrought ballads. When I was thirty-six, I broke two of those pledges. In a moment of abject weakness, I not only went out and bought a Michael Bolton tape; I decided to marry Eric Zucker, who was thirty-eight and, like me, had never taken the plunge. I wasn't in love with Eric, but he seemed like a reasonable antidote to my loneliness and a fairly decent catch, all things considered. His family owned several funeral homes in the Tri-State Area, which meant that he was in a business that would never become obsolete and would relieve me of the unpleasantness of ever having to go funeral home shopping, when the need arose. Eric was nice looking in a brown sort of way brown hair, brown eyes, brown suits—and he was even more compulsively organized than I was. He actually alphabetized the prescription drugs in his medicine cabinet! What's more, he had the same initials as I did—E.Z.—so there was no need to invest in a new set of monogrammed anything. Best of all, Eric was as uninterested in mawkish emotions and overheated sex as I was—or so I thought. Six months into the marriage, he had an affair with the improbably named Lola, the makeup artist who applied lipstick, eye shadow, and blusher to the embalmed corpses at the family's funeral parlors. I wanted to kill Eric, but I was not a violent person. My lawyer wanted me to take Eric to the cleaners, but I was not a greedy person. My mother wanted me to sully Eric's reputation in the press, but I was not a stupid person. "You're in public relations," she said. "You know how to plant stories about people. Don't take him to the cleaners; just air his dirty laundry in all the gossip columns." I explained to my mother that since Eric was not a celebrity of even minor consequence, the gossip columns would not be receptive to an item about him or Lola. No, I decided to pay Eric Zucker back *my* way. His company's most feared competitor was another chain in the area called Copley's Funeral Homes. So I went after Copley's business with a vengeance, and after two months of groveling, I convinced them to let Pearson & Strulley handle their PR account. I got such positive media coverage for Copley's Funeral Homes that Zucker Funeral Homes lost visibility and customers. A lot of customers. They lost so many customers that poor Lola had to be downsized. "You ruined me and my family, you bitch!" Eric shouted at me during his most recent, verbally abusive phone call. "That's what you get for exchanging bodily fluids with Lola," I said sweetly, hoping Eric would feel at least *some* remorse for what he had done to me.

While I was positively undone by Eric's betrayal when I first found out about it, Jackie acted remarkably nonchalant when she learned that Peter wanted out of their marriage. After their divorce, it was strictly business as usual between them; she never missed a day at the nursery, went right on working side by side with Peter as if nothing had happened, didn't even flinch when his new wife, Trish, who taught first grade at the elementary school around the corner, stopped in to pick up precious little flowering plants for her centerpieces. But Jackie was one tough cookie. She and Peter had started the business right after they were married, and she wasn't about to bow out *or* buy him out, just because he had suddenly decided he was more attracted to a woman who had polish on her fingernails than dirt underneath them. Peter had liked the tomboy in Jackie once, the short, pixie haircut, the athletic body, the salty language, the hoarse, whiskey voice. But as the years went by, his taste changed, and one day he announced that she just didn't "do it for him, sexually." Personally, I thought Peter's rejection of her as a woman was the reason behind her constant chatter about sex –the reason she flirted and undulated and talked about wanting to get laid. It was all talk, as she, herself, admitted, but it was her way of showing the world she *was* sexy, no matter what Peter thought. We all have our shtiks, so who was I to judge? *She* came on to men to ease her hurt; *I* avoided men to ease mine. Jackie was Jackie, and I'd never met a woman like her. She could shoot pool, throw back shots of tequila like one of the boys, and of course, transform people's backyards into pieces of paradise. Ironically, the latest wedge between her and Peter was the very thing that had once bonded them: the nursery. Peter had recently revealed that he wanted to expand the business and sell not only trees and shrubs and landscaping services but vegetables and produce and dairy items. "So you want to turn J&P's into A&P's, is that it?" Jackie had said sarcastically. She was an expert in rhododendron, not goat cheese. There were plenty of places where the yuppies of Bedford could purchase their baby eggplant. What's more, J&P's was doing fine as a nursery. Why tamper with success? Nevertheless, Peter kept telling Jackie that she was holding him back professionally by not going along with his plans. He begged her to let him buy her out of the business, and she told him to go fuck himself. Currently, they were not speaking, except when it was absolutely necessary.

Rounding out our little trio was Pat, the roundest of the three of us. A full-time and very devoted mother, she and her five children and their aging cocker spaniel lived in a rambling white colonial in Weston, Connecticut—a homey, cheerful place where I spent occasional weekends in the summer. I would go to visit Pat, of course, and to get away from the fetidness of the city in August, but a major attraction of the Kovecky household was Lucy, the youngest of Pat's brood and the only girl. She was a nine-year-old with Pat's chubbiness and quiet demeanor, and I, who was not the least bit sticky or sentimental where children were concerned, was mad about her, doted on her, felt a powerful kinship with her. After all, I understood what it was like to have your daddy leave you. Oh, the other kids were nice, too. For males. It was a revelation to me how, in this age of children murdering their parents or, at the very least, toting guns to school, the Kovecky children managed to be good kids who were not nerds. Especially since they were products of divorce. Perhaps it was because Pat never uttered an unkind word about their father, never poisoned them against Bill. And it wasn't as if the children were left destitute. Bill may have turned into a big-shot gastroenterologist who spent more time palpating strangers' abdomens than he did helping Pat with the dishes, but he wasn't one of those deadbeat dads. No way. He made Pat a very generous divorce settlement, and grumble though he did to anyone who would listen, he never missed a payment, even though it meant scaling back his own lifestyle. The reason he and Pat didn't work out was that, somewhere between his first appearance on "Good Morning, America" and the birth of his third child, he decided he wasn't a mere doctor but a healer, a scientist, a saver of the world's collective digestive system. The other problem was that Pat was too shy, too constrained, too afraid of offending him to tell him he was being an asshole. Even her clothes were intended not to offend or call attention to themselves. She wore lacy, frilly dresses that made her look like an English milkmaid in one of those Merchant Ivory movies. She was so shy and self-effacing that her idea of a four-letter word was "oops." She had no self-confidence—at least, until recently. As part of her campaign to win Bill back, she had started seeing a therapist and was adding words such as "empowerment," "needs," and "me" to her vocabulary. She could be a little sanctimonious at times, and I often gave myself a laugh by picturing her locked in a room with Howard Stern, but I adored her. Everyone did. Except Bill, I guess. Although, according to Pat, he had telephoned her just the week before, saying he wanted to see her when she got back from the cruise. Jackie and I prayed it was because he had come to his senses and realized what a decent, loving person she was, not that he wanted to tell her he was cutting back her alimony and child support.

So there the three of us were, bosom buddies in spite of our differences. Three-women friendships can be tough to sustain, given that two are bound to talk behind the third's back and the third inevitably feels left out. But Jackie, Pat, and I were a team, a triumvirate, the Three Blond Mice. Nothing could come between us.

Of course, we'd never been cooped up on a boat together for seven days.

"All set?" I asked when the Sea Swan ticket agent had returned Pat's documents to her.

"All set," she nodded.

"Then it's show time," Jackie declared.

"We're sure we want to do this?" I asked, still feeling curmudgeonly about the cruise. I really would have preferred that Costa Rican inn.

"We're sure," said Jackie, taking me by the shoulders and literally

pointing me in the direction of the sign at the other end of the terminal that read TO THE SHIP.

We were walking toward the sign when I suddenly decided to call
my answering machine one last time. Yes, it was a Sunday, but public relations disasters could and did happen on Sundays. There was
always the chance that one of my clients needed me, that Pearson
& Strulley needed me, and that I would be duty bound to heed the
call.

We stopped at a bank of phone booths. I called my answering machine. There were no messages, but I tried not to take it personally.

As I emerged from the phone booth to join my friends, the man
who'd been using the phone next to mine finished his call and spoke
to us.

"Hey! Are you ladies sailing on the *Princess Charming* today?" he
said in a loud voice, made even louder by the echo-chamber-like
acoustics in the terminal.

"Yeah, how about you?" asked Jackie.

"Sure am," he said, then introduced himself as Henry Prichard of
Altoona, Pennsylvania. He was in his late thirties or early forties, I
guessed, but once men hit middle age these days, there's no way to
tell how old they really are. So many of them are having cosmetic
work done now—face lifts, collagen injections, chemical peels, you
name it. For another thing, they don't permit themselves to look bald
anymore, what with plugs and weaves and baseball caps that cover
a multitude of sins. This man wore a Pittsburgh Pirates cap, along
with tan shorts, a denim work shirt, and penny loafers. He had a
hefty, beefy build and ruddy, chipmunk cheeks. I deduced, from the
baseball cap, plus the golf bag and the diving equipment, that he was
the athletic type. Jackie liked athletic types. "I won the cruise in the
company contest. Best numbers in my district," he added, clearly
proud of his achievement.

"You're a salesmen?" Jackie asked, as she ran her eyes over him,
no doubt assessing his potential in the sex object department. God,
this is going to be a long cruise, I thought, worried that Jackie might
actually sleep with a man on this trip and that, once her notorious
dry spell was over, she'd have nothing else to live for.

"Yup. I'm with Peterson Chevrolet," said Henry.

"Was your prize a trip for two?" Jackie asked, cutting right to the chase.

"Oh, sure. They would've let me take my wife. If I *had* a wife." Henry scoffed at the very notion. "But what kind of woman would put up with a jock? A die-hard Pirates fan like me, huh?"

I looked at Jackie, expecting her to raise her hand, as she was quite a Pirates fan herself, having been born in Pittsburgh. She loved sports, especially baseball, and knew things like batting averages and on-base percentages and which players chewed tobacco and which went for the sunflower seeds. But she restrained herself and said instead, "You must have been in mourning when the Pirates traded Bonds and Bonilla. I know I was."

Henry Prichard's eyes widened and he gazed at Jackie with an almost shimmering respect.

"I *was* in mourning," he said. "But I'm looking ahead to this season. We've got a lot of young kids coming up from the minors, and I'm pretty optimistic about the future."

"Me too," said Jackie, and I could tell she wasn't just talking about the fate of the Pirates. "By the way, I'm Jackie Gault," she said and shook hands with him. Then, almost as an afterthought, she told him Pat's name and mine and explained that we were taking our first cruise.

"Same here," he said. "Which floor are you ladies on? I mean, which deck?"

"Deck 8," Jackie blurted out before I could stop her. Henry Prichard seemed harmless, but you never could tell with people, especially men, many of whom seemed harmless until they landed on the "Six O'clock News," in handcuffs.

"Aw, that's a darn shame," he said. "I'm on Deck 7."

"Well, maybe we'll run into each other at dinner," Jackie said hopefully. "Which seating did you get?"

Henry checked his ticket, then said, "The one that starts at six-thirty. How about you?"

"We got the six-thirty too," I sighed. I'd been crushed when the tickets had arrived in the mail and I saw that we'd been assigned the unspeakable Early Bird Special instead of the more civilized eight-thirty seating our travel agent had assured us she'd arrange. Now we

were certain to be stuck at a table with either octagenarians or howl-
ing children.

We chatted with Henry for a few more minutes—I had to admit,
he was an affable fellow and I could easily see why he had sold the
most Chevrolets in his district—but at some point he cut the conversation short.

"Gosh, I sure can get to talking once I start, but I really do need
to make another phone call," he said with a touching, gosh-shucks-
heck provincialism about him that people from Manhattan simply
don't have. "Why don't you all go on ahead and I'll catch up to you
later?"

"Great," said Jackie. "We'll look for you on board."

"Oh, I'll find *you,*" he smiled. "Don't you worry."

While Henry and Jackie gave each other a final and rather
provocative once-over, I stole a glance at Pat, who was staring primly
at her shoes.

Henry went back to the phone booth, while the three of us turned
in the opposite direction.

"He doesn't look a thing like Rodney Dangerfield," Jackie said,
elbowing me in the ribs.

"Congratulations," I said. "I hope you two will be very happy together."

"Actually, he looks very much like a cousin of Bill's," said Pat with
complete seriousness.

"The hell with Bill," Jackie announced. "The hell with all our exes.
Once we're on that ship, they can't touch us."

She cast one more glance back at Henry, who was deep in conversation with the person on the other end of the phone. Then she
linked her arms through Pat's and mine.

"Let's cruise," she said, and together we headed for the gangway.

2

"**S**mile, ladies," said the photographer as we stood at the threshold of the *Princess Charming,* waiting for the crush of passengers to thin out so we could finally board the ship. Strains of calypso music filtered out to us from inside. Steel drums. Maracas. All day, all night, Mary Ann. If you've been on a Caribbean cruise, you know the drill.

"Come on, smile, ladies," the photographer coaxed again. I assumed he was Australian, as "ladies" came out "lie-deez."

"No, thanks," I said, waving the guy away. I remembered what the travel agent had told us about ships' photographers—that they're like roaches in a New York City kitchen. Every time you turn around, there they are, capturing moment after photogenic moment of your cruise whether you like it or not.

"It's only six dollars and you don't have to pay until you've seen how it comes out," he hondled. "We develop the photographs right away and then display them outside the main dining room every night."

"Oh, come on, Elaine. It's his job. Let him take one of us," said Jackie, grabbing Pat and me around our waists and pulling us into a tight group shot.

Pat whispered to me. "I was hoping the ship would have a photographer. I forgot my camera and I really want to bring home pictures for the children."

The children. My heart lurched as it always did when I thought of little Lucy Kovecky. Of her wary brown eyes and curly blond hair and hesitant, poignant expression. Of whether she was happy to be spending the week with her father while her mother was away or whether it hurt too much to see him at all. I ached when I imagined how ambivalent she must be. Or was I projecting? Was I imagining how *I* would feel if my mother had left me in the custody of my adulterous, no-account father for a week so she could go sailing off to the Caribbean with her friends? Then I quickly reminded myself that Bill Kovecky was no Fred Zimmerman; Bill may have allowed his medical career to come before his family, but he was no philanderer, just another doctor with an ego that needed lancing.

"On second thought, go ahead and take the picture," I told the photographer. "Take a couple." Maybe I'd get one especially for Lucy, I decided. From her Aunt Elaine.

We said "Cheese," the photographer got his shots, and we finally made our way onto the ship, only to be nearly trampled by phalanxes of waiters carrying trays of complimentary "Welcome Drinks"—foamy, yellow concoctions adorned with pink umbrellas and maraschino cherries.

"How about a nice cool Miami Whammy?" one of the waiters offered.

"What's in it?" I asked, forever on the alert for egg yolks, heavy cream, and other agents of death.

"What's the difference? It's on the house," said Jackie, snatching one off the tray and belting it down.

"The *drink* is on the house. The *glass* isn't," the waiter explained. "It's our special souvenir glass. Only five dollars."

Five dollars? The glass was strictly hotel bar stuff, except that it bore the *Princess Charming's* tacky logo: a red, high-heeled shoe perched atop a gold crown.

"Want a drink, Pat?" Jackie asked before the waiter disappeared. She could tell by the look on my face that I was taking a pass.

Pat waited her customary ten seconds before making her decision.

"Yes," she said, and the waiter handed her a Miami Whammy. She thanked him and said appreciatively, "The glass will make a wonderful souvenir for the children." Pat's rule of thumb when it came to our vacations was that everything that wasn't nailed down was souvenir material for the children—photographs, glasses, cocktail napkins, plastic drink stirrers, notepads, menus, and especially those chocolate mints that the better hotels leave on your pillow at night. I often wondered what the kids actually did with the stuff once Pat shlepped it home.

She was about to take her first sip of her Miami Whammy when a man walking hurriedly past us whammed into her, causing her to spill most of her drink on herself.

"Oops," she said, embarrassed, as though it were somehow her fault. She reached into her purse for a tissue and began blotting the soiled spot on her blouse when the man who'd committed the offense realized what he'd done, came running back, and started apologizing profusely.

"Please, forgive me," he said to Pat, practically getting down on his knees and beseeching her. "I'm so clumsy sometimes. I'm profoundly sorry."

"Oh, that's quite all right," said Pat, flushing slightly. "I'm sure you didn't mean it."

"I *didn't* mean it. Not at all," he rushed on, speaking so fast he gave me palpitations and rubbing his hands together in true Uriah Heep fashion. "I don't go around knocking women—or their drinks—over. It's just that I've never been on a cruise before and so when they said we were supposed to board the ship by one o'clock, I took them at their word and didn't want to be late. So you see, I wasn't trying to barrel into you or do you any harm. Please, believe me."

What a speech, I thought. The man was positively breathless with remorse. And how terribly hot he must be, what with that dark, three-piece suit he had on. He was dressed like a banker, not a cruise ship passenger.

He was short and wiry, with thin lips and a thin mustache. His hair was shoe-polish-black and blunt-cut, with bangs: the "Buster Brown" look. Fortysomething, I guessed. Or maybe early fifties.

"I'm Albert Mullins," he said as Pat continued to dab at her ample, Miami Whammy—soaked bosom. "Why don't you let me help—"

Completely unthinking, he reached out and nearly placed his hand on Pat's breast in an effort to be of some assistance, then realized he was about to do something socially unacceptable and turned crimson, which, in turn, made Pat turn crimson.

"I'll have the blouse dry-cleaned," she said, recovering. "Please don't worry about it." She took a deep breath and told him her name and then Jackie's and mine.

He nodded. "Pleasure to meet all of you, although I would have preferred for you to meet me when I wasn't at my most boorish."

Albert then glanced down at his own clothes and remarked, apropos of nothing, "I'm terribly overdressed, aren't I?"

"We hadn't noticed," Jackie said with a touch of sarcasm.

"It was just that the *Princess Charming* seemed so formal from the brochures," he explained. "I felt I should wear my Sunday best."

"You look great, honey. Just great," Jackie said, rolling her eyes when he turned his head. Apparently, he didn't stir her passion the way Henry Prichard had. He was too fussy for her, too fey, too lightweight. She preferred big, brawny types—men whose size, power, and authority rivaled those of a backhoe.

"Where are you from?" I asked Albert.

"Manhattan," he replied. "Although I have a weekend house in Connecticut."

"Connecticut? Where?" Pat piped up.

"Ridgefield," he said.

"Oh, goodness!" she fluttered. "I'm from Weston! Only twenty minutes from you!"

Such talk was bold, for Pat. Positively brazen.

"What do you do, Albert?" I asked. My interest in the man was strictly career-motivated. Perhaps he was in a field that required public relations.

"I write books," he said.

"Really," I said with growing respect for Albert. "Novels?"

"No," he said. "Field guides. To bird watching."

Bird watching. I doubted that I could get him on a "Barbara Walters Special," but there were other network outlets. That Sunday morning show on CBS was always doing nature stuff. "Who's your publisher?" I asked.

"I don't have one, I'm afraid," he said. "I write for myself. I love birds, so I keep little journals full of notes about the species I see in Connecticut and elsewhere."

So the guy was an eccentric. Probably had a trust fund too, if he had places in Manhattan and Ridgefield and could still afford to take this cruise.

"I booked passage on the *Princess Charming* in the hope of seeing a lot of tropical birds during the trip," Albert continued.

"What a lovely idea," said Pat, who had given up on her blouse and was now sipping what was left of her Miami Whammy. "My children and their father often go bird watching in the summer. When he takes time off from his medical practice, that is."

"Your husband is a doctor?" asked Albert.

"My ex-husband. Yes, he's a gastroenterologist."

"Ex-husband. I see." Albert turned crimson again, as if he had just uncovered some intensely personal piece of information. But Pat's revelation must have liberated him because he then revealed, "I, myself, have never endured a divorce, although I did live through an annulment." He paused to collect himself. "I've been traveling alone ever since."

"Tell you what, Al. We've got seven whole days to trade war stories, right?" Jackie said, giving Albert what was meant to be a parting pat on the back but was more like a karate chop. She was as obvious when she wasn't interested in a man as she was when she was.

Albert got the point. It was time to wind things up.

"Yes, absolutely," he said. "I propose that we move along so we can all get settled in our staterooms."

I was aching to get settled in my stateroom. I hadn't gotten much sleep, what with all the last-minute, pre-vacation, middle-of-the-night memos I kept E-mailing to my assistant at Pearson & Strulley, and I was running out of gas.

"And once again, Mrs. Kovecky—may I call you Pat?" Albert interrupted himself to ask permission.

"Yes, of course," she said after a second or two, in what was, for her, a snap decision.

"Good. Then, Pat, won't you please accept my apologies about spilling the drink?" Albert asked. "One more time?"

Ye Gods, you two. Enough already, I thought, feeling as if I'd stepped into a Jane Austen novel, what with all the apologizing and demuring and May-I-call-you-by-your-first-name posturing. I assumed we were finished with Albert when he said suddenly, to Pat, "You know, it's only right that I pay for the dry cleaning of your blouse. It's such a lovely blouse. It certainly does become you."

Pat flushed again and looked down at the ground. "Thanks for the compliment but I'm really not one to tout my own horn." She paused. "I mean, toot. My own horn, that is." She giggled.

"Well, as I was saying, the moment I'm in my cabin, I'll call and have them pick up the blouse and dry-clean it," Albert pledged. "What did you say your cabin number was?"

"She didn't say," I said quickly.

"I'm in Cabin 8022," said Pat, in spite of my blinking and throat clearing and other attempts at catching her eye. I did not like the idea of my friends giving out our cabin numbers or even our deck numbers to men they knew little about. In Manhattan, you didn't give a man your home address unless he was a bona fide cable TV repairman.

"Excellent," said Albert. "I'll take care of everything. At once."

We said goodbye to Albert Mullins and entered the ship's dramatic, four-story atrium—a dazzling, chrome-and-glass affair, reminiscent of a hotel lobby. A member of the *Princess Charming*'s staff welcomed us on board, glanced at our tickets, and pointed us in the direction of the elevator. We rode up another six floors and got off at Deck 8, where a dark-skinned man in a starched gold uniform was waiting for us.

"Welcome to the M/S *Princess Charming,*" he said in a lilting Jamaican accent. "I'm Kingsley, your cabin steward, and I'll be taking care of you this week. Anything you want, no problem."

We all smiled and nodded and placed ourselves in Kingsley's hands as he walked us to our staterooms, where our luggage was waiting outside the cabin doors. At least, *some* of our luggage was.

"My suitcase isn't here," I said with dread. In all my years of traveling, I had never lost my luggage. I knew my streak had to end sometime, but did it have to end now? In only a matter of hours, I'd be smack in the middle of the Atlantic Ocean, where there wasn't exactly a Bloomingdale's on every corner.

Kingsley shared my pain, shaking his head and saying, *"Tsk tsk."*

"I came down to Miami on your air/sea package, so I assume the airline must have lost my bag," I said.

Kingsley nodded wearily as if he'd seen this all before. "No problem. We'll find it and fly it to San Juan. You'll get it back when we dock there."

"But Puerto Rico is our second port of call. We're not due there until Wednesday," I pointed out. "Today is Sunday. What am I supposed to wear for the next three days?"

Jackie and Pat looked at me helplessly. They knew better than to offer me their own clothes. I was a positive giantess compared to them. A giantess and a beanpole. What's more, my taste in clothes was far more tailored than theirs, far more designer-driven. No, I was too tall, too thin, too Nancy Kissinger to borrow from my friends.

"What will you wear? That's no problem," said Kingsley. Everything that *was* a problem was "no problem," according to him. "There's a boutique on Deck 2 of the ship. Right off the atrium where you first came on board. They sell beautiful clothes for the ladies."

Kingsley added that I should telephone the purser, who would probably give me a cash allowance toward whatever clothes I bought in the ship's boutique. Then he handed each of us our keys and showed us our cabins.

When he opened the door to mine, I stood there, appraising No. 8024 and wondering how the travel agent had conned us into paying for rooms the size of phone booths. Oh, 8024 was an outside cabin, all right. If you're going to take a cruise, you might as well have a view of the ocean, we'd all decided. The problem was that there *was* no view. Not much of one, anyway.

I trudged over to the measly porthole, a pathetic little round window that was no bigger than the one on the door of my Maytag dryer, and fingered the glass. Then I turned and surveyed the dated, mauve-and-turquoise decor of the stateroom, the FTD-looking arrangement of flowers on the dresser, the little white card next to the flowers with the sweet but impersonal message whose sole purpose was to elicit a tip—*Have a pleasant cruise. I'm at your service. [Signed] Kingsley, your cabin steward*—and heaved a deep sigh. All I'd really wanted from the room, from the cruise, was a soothing look at the sea. Sea? What sea? Not only was my porthole the size of a buttonhole, it looked right out onto the lifeboat that was mounted directly in front of it, obstructing whatever ocean view I might have had.

"I hate to trouble you, Kingsley, but I'd like to change staterooms," I told him as he was filling my ice bucket.

"Your friends seem satisfied with theirs," he said a bit defensively.

"My friends probably don't plan to spend as much time in their rooms as I do," I said. "Besides, they don't have to look out at an emergency vessel that conjures up images of the *Titanic.*"

Jackie's and Pat's cabins had the same puny porthole as mine, but they could actually see out of theirs.

"Look, Kingsley," I said. "This is no reflection on you, believe me. The room is spotless, very nice. It's just that I was counting on a view and my travel agent promised that–"

"You can call the purser," he nodded as if this, too, had come up before in his career as a cabin steward. He pointed to the mauve phone that hung on the wall near the dresser along with a ship-to-ship directory. There were also instructions for making ship-to-shore calls–at a cost of ten dollars per minute.

While Kingsley looked on, I dialed the extension of the purser and spoke to a woman with a clipped British accent. I told her about my missing luggage, and she promised I'd have it when we got to Puerto Rico. She said nothing about a clothes allowance. When I complained about my stateroom, she explained that the rest of the ship's outside cabins were sold out.

"I could downgrade you to one of the smaller, inside cabins," she offered.

Now, *there* was an option.

"I guess I'll stay where I am," I told her.

Kingsley beamed, walked over to the offending porthole, and pulled the drapes closed. "No problem now, right?"

"No problem," I said and handed him the aforementioned tip as he walked out the door.

Alone at last, I sank onto the couch that for the next seven nights Kingsley would be making up as my bed and tried not to sulk, tried not to be a washout when it came to life's little adversities. I yearned to be someone who rolled with the punches, looked on the bright side of things, made cheery remarks like: "Oh, well. At least I have my health." But it was hard for me to see the glass as half full. Very hard. I tended to dwell on the negative side of things, tended to see the danger, the evil that lurked. The expression "pleasant surprise" was an oxymoron, as far as I was concerned. The day my father walked out of our house was the day it dawned on me not only that disaster *could* strike if you weren't careful, but that it *did* strike if you weren't careful. I had evolved from a trusting child who believed in Santa Claus and the Tooth Fairy and parents who would love each other forever and ever into a woman who believed in very little, a woman who viewed life as something to be feared, a woman who couldn't distinguish between minor problems and genuine calamities. After Eric turned out to be the lying bastard my father was–and history, therefore, repeated itself–I came to the conclusion that it's best to expect calamities, rehearse for them. That way, you're never caught off guard, never disappointed. Unfortunately, the strategy doesn't work, I thought as I listened to the ocean lapping against our mighty, stationary ship. You can't stave off calamity any more than you can hold back the tide. I understood the concept, intellectually. I just wasn't so hot at living it.

Since I had nothing to unpack except the contents of my carry-on bag, I poked around the cabin. On my dresser was the week's schedule of activities. I kicked off my shoes and lay down on the bed to read it.

Let's see, there were movies, all of which I'd seen. There was bingo, bridge, basketball, none of which I played. There were lectures on napkin folding, perfume appreciation, baton twirling, and the Macarena. And then there were contests, lots of contests: the International Beer-Chugging Contest, the Bad Hair Day Contest, the Male Bellyflop Contest, among others.

I tried not to panic, I really did, but I felt as if I'd wandered onto the set of some horribly low-brow game show. I mean, why draw the line at the Male Bellyflop Contest? What about a Seasick Passengers' Puking Contest? What on earth was I supposed to *do* for seven days?

Calm down, I told myself. You brought plenty of books, so you'll find a nice, quiet lounge chair and read. And you'll jog around the Promenade Deck every morning and spend time with your friends.

I sighed with relief until I remembered that my books, running clothes, and sneakers were in my suitcase, which was probably on its way to Alaska.

Thank God, I have Jackie and Pat to keep me company, I thought, knowing what a good time we ended up having on our vacations, even the ones I hadn't been especially looking forward to. Jackie's unhysterical, just-do-it style was a tonic for me, always nudging me back to reality whenever my neurotic nature got the best of me. And Pat's giggly innocence and wholesome values were such a breath of fresh air; nobody I worked with at Pearson & Strulley had giggly innocence *or* wholesome values. What did *I* bring to the table when the three of us were together? I really couldn't say, but Jackie and Pat kept taking trips with me, so I must have contributed *something*.

I flipped on the TV set that was mounted on the wall across from my bed. There were two channels, I discovered: CNN and the *Princess Charming* Channel. CNN, you know about. The *Princess Charming* Channel, you had to see to believe. Basically, it was a low-budget, twenty-four-hour-a-day infomercial hyping the amenities of the ship. When I happened to tune in that first time, they were broadcasting an interview with Captain Svein Solberg, a sturdy, blond man of Norwegian descent.

"She is vithout qvestion da most beautiful ship on da seas," Captain Solberg was saying of the *Princess Charming* without even a trace of a smile. "She has four main engines, mounted on rubber mountings for very little vibration. She also has six additional engines. Vhen she is at maximum speed at approximately tventy-von knots, she burns about eighty tons of fuel in tventy-four hours. The four main engines vere built in France, while the six auxiliary . . ."

I know Scandinavians can be a touch on the unexpressive side, but this guy gave new meaning to the word "deadpan." His delivery was so wooden, he could have been a ventriloquist's dummy, filling in for the *real* Captain Solberg, who was, hopefully, much too busy maneuvering our vessel out of the path of sharks, leaky oil tankers, and flotillas of fleeing Haitians to sit and be videotaped for our in-room diversion.

"I vill be announcing our position and da veather report tvice a day," he continued. "Over da public address system. From da Bridge Deck. First, at noon. Den, at nine o'clock in da evening. Passengers are velcome to listen."

If you're coming over the PA system, buddy, we won't have a choice, I thought.

And speaking of the PA system, just then, a voice came on advising us that, at four o'clock, we would hear the sound of the ship's whistle—seven short blasts followed by one long blast—and would then be required to report to our "Muster Stations," whatever they were.

I searched the activities sheet, hoping for an explanation.

"All guests should take the lifejacket out of their closet, put it on, and proceed to their assigned station for the compulsory mustering," it read. I gleaned that this was some sort of safety drill.

I got up off the bed, found my lifejacket, put it on, and modeled it in front of the full-length mirror on the back of the cabin door. It was a high-tech Mae West—the good old orange job but with a fancy inflating device.

I suddenly remembered the lifeboat sitting outside my porthole and wondered whether any of the *Princess Charming*'s passengers had ever drowned during the voyage.

No, I would have read about it, I reminded myself, being the media-obsessed public relations person I was. If a passenger had died of anything but natural causes, I would certainly have read about it in at least one of the six newspapers that were delivered to my apartment door by six o'clock every morning.

I tried to laugh off my paranoia, just as Jackie would have. "Elaine, get real," she would surely have said with an impatient but affectionate sigh, rolling her eyes. "Nobody gets killed on one of these things, except maybe at the blackjack table. Ha ha."

She and Pat showed up at my cabin in their lifejackets just after the whistle sounded over the PA system. We were informed by Kingsley that our Muster Station was the Crown Room on Deck 5, one of nine—count 'em, nine—cocktail lounges on the ship. (I'm telling you: if your idea of a good time is getting and staying drunk, the *Princess Charming* is for you! They serve alcoholic beverages twenty-four hours a day. Between drinks, you can hang out at one of the ship's daily AA meetings!)

The actual mustering took ten minutes. About two hundred of us sat there in the Crown Room as a crew member spoke of what to do in case of an emergency. Nobody paid any attention, just like on airplanes. People were too busy flagging down waiters armed with trays of banana daiquiris.

"Oh, look. There's Henry Prichard," Jackie said, poking me. "The car salesman from Altoona, remember?"

"Sure, I remember." Henry was standing by the door of the Crown Room, talking animatedly to three elderly couples, presumably pushing one of Chevrolet's new, hot-off-the-assembly-line models. He looked as foolish as the rest of us did in our orange lifejackets.

Jackie was in the midst of getting up to invite Henry over to our table-for-four when another man claimed the empty chair.

"This seat taken or is this my lucky day?"

I smelled the man before I actually saw him—he was soggy with some ghastly cologne. He was exactly what I had envisioned when Jackie first suggested we take a cruise—a man old enough to be my father with teeth to match. You know what kind of teeth I'm talking about: the kind that make clicking noises; the improbably white, straight kind that sit in a glass at night.

"So? How 'bout it? Am I joining you lovelies?" he said, even though he had already made himself quite comfortable. His eyes darted from me to Pat to Jackie, as if he were waiting for one of us to act overjoyed to see him. But we were merely wondering why he was the only one in the Crown Room who wasn't wearing his lifejacket.

"What do I need a lifejacket for? I swim like a fish," he bragged when Jackie posed the question. After getting a whiff of his breath, I had a hunch that he drank like one too. "Anyhow, the orange didn't click with my outfit."

No, but it certainly would have "clicked" with his hair, which was a shade I would call Strom Thurmond Orange and was held in place with enough spray to paralyze a small animal. As for the "outfit," it consisted of white loafers, white slacks, and a pale blue silk shirt unbuttoned to his navel to expose a thicket of gray hair and a half-dozen gold chains on which hung several religious amulets. He was a cruise ship cliché. I was sure he was oblivious to the image he projected. As I cared deeply how people perceived me and was in a profession in which image was everything, I envied him to a certain extent.

"Lenny Lubin," he introduced himself. "Of Lubin's Lube Jobs."

He said he was in the automotive business and told us that if we were ever in Massapequa, Long Island, and needed an oil change, we should stop in.

"You ladies alone?" he asked suggestively.

"No, we're together," I said matter-of-factly. What is it with men anyway?

Lenny Lubin snickered, the way my ex-husband used to whenever I'd suggest we rent *Thelma and Louise*.

"I meant, no husbands or boyfriends?" said Lenny. "Three lovelies like you?"

Jackie laughed. "You want to know if any of us is available, is that it, Lenny?"

He wagged an arthritic finger at her. "You're the little vixen in the group, huh?" He smiled, showing us his Chiclets.

"That's me. The little vixen," Jackie snorted.

"What about you, Lenny?" Pat said, dipping her toe in the conversation for the first time. "Are you traveling alone on the cruise?"

"As alone as a man can be," he said, hanging his head in a pathetic attempt to elicit our sympathy. "My wife threw me out about two months ago."

"She did?" I said, feeling an immediate sisterhood with the estranged Mrs. Lubin.

"You got it," said Lenny. "I make a mistake—one tiny mistake—and you know what she does? She tosses me out like so much garbage."

"What was the one tiny mistake?" I asked, secure in the knowledge that, when you go on vacation, perfect strangers very often feel compelled to volunteer their whole life stories, particularly the more sordid chapters.

"You wanna know? You really wanna know?" asked Lenny, looking each one of us in the eye. It was a rhetorical question. We all knew he was going to tell us no matter what we said.

I glanced at my friends at that moment and sighed. There we were in the Crown Room of the *Princess Charming*, stuffed into our lifejackets, tired, hungry, hot. I didn't really want to sit and listen to some drunken old blowhard's sob story and I assumed that Jackie and Pat didn't either. Personally, I wished Lenny had done us all a favor and chosen to play golf in Palm Springs instead of taking a cruise to the Caribbean.

"Yes, we'd really like to know about the one tiny mistake that drove your wife to ask you to leave," said Pat, surprising me. Perhaps her therapy really was emboldening her, since she was not only shedding her shyness but drawing another person out. Unfortunately, what her therapist had neglected to tell her was that some people don't warrant drawing out.

"My one tiny mistake was that I slept with my wife's sister," Lenny confessed, looking not the least bit penitent.

"You call that a *tiny* mistake?" I asked.

"You should see the sister," he said. "Not even five feet tall."

Lenny laughed so hard he began to wheeze, but when none of us even cracked a smile, he said, "Hey, that was a joke! A bit! A setup! Whattsamatter with you lovelies? You leave your funny bones at home or something?"

"Or something," I said.

"Well, then it's time to lighten up. How about some drinks, huh?" Lenny snapped his fingers, which were as bejeweled as his neck, wrists, and chest, and when the waiter didn't drop everything and rush right over, Lenny tried whistling at him. I nearly died.

Eventually, the waiter made it over to our table, and before we could beg off, Lenny had signed for a round of daiquiris.

"This is cozy, huh?" he said, downing his drink in one gulp, which left him with a yellowish, thoroughly unappetizing milk mustache. "Now, I told you lovelies my name. How 'bout telling me yours?" he slurred.

Jackie did the honors. Then Lenny played a little game. He pointed at each one of us and tried to remember which name went with which face, finally getting it right on the fourth or fifth try. He then explained, unsolicited this time, that he and his wife *were* separated but that it was he who had done the throwing out. "She was getting on my nerves," was the reason he gave. "Once a nag, always a nag, ya know?"

He reached up to pat his orange hair, which had hardened to the texture of cotton candy, and as he did, the gold bracelets on his wrist clanged together like wind chimes.

"She never stopped ranting and raving about money," he ranted and raved as we tried to look riveted. "I didn't make enough, not for her. So one day, I says to myself, 'That's it.' I drove over to the neighborhood bar, had a couple of drinks, came home, and told her to pack up and get out if she didn't like what was in my wallet."

A couple of drinks, I thought. It was probably more like a couple of dozen and, from the look of things, poor Lenny hadn't stopped since.

"So—how about another round?" he said after glancing at the empty glass in his hand. He failed to notice that we'd barely touched our drinks.

"Can't," said Jackie, getting up from the table. "It's almost time for this baby to shove off. We want to watch the departure from upstairs on Deck 8."

Bless you, Jackie, I said silently, until I realized what was coming next.

"Why Deck 8?" Lenny asked.

"Our cabins are on Deck 8," Jackie and Pat said simultaneously. I would have to have a talk with them, I vowed. They were as good as handing our room keys out to every Tom, Dick, and Horny on the ship.

"Deck 8, huh? Too bad," Lenny leered. "I'm on Deck 9, the Commodore Deck. In a *suite.*" Deck 9 was where the really big, expensive staterooms were located. Either Lenny Lubin's wife was mistaken about his lack of funds or he wasn't being completely forthcoming with her—or us.

Pat and I rose from the table, Pat tucking a Crown Room cocktail napkin into her purse. For the kids.

"How about later, you lovelies?" Lenny said, his mouth forming a mock pout at the mere thought of being left alone. "After dinner? The four of us could have a couple of nightcaps in the disco, huh? I'm some dancer. I can do a helluva Hustle."

I loathed discos, but even *I* knew that the Hustle was about as in vogue as men who called women "lovelies."

"Didn't you hear what I said?" he asked as we gathered our things and began to waddle away from the table in our lifejackets. "I said, you should see me do the Hustle."

"We already have," I said, and we all bid Lenny farewell.

3

I felt the ship move.

I was standing in one of four dressing rooms in the Perky Princess, the women's boutique Kingsley had told me about, when the *Princess Charming* pulled away from the pier and began her voyage to the Caribbean.

I checked my watch. It was five o'clock. We were right on schedule.

As the ship chugged gently onward, I said a silent goodbye to terra firma and prayed the trip would turn out better than I feared.

"How are we doing in there?" the saleswoman shouted to me from the other side of the curtain.

"We're doing just fine," I lied. I had just tried on my eleventh dress. It, like the ten before it, did not fit.

"Let me know if you need another size," she said and disappeared.

Another size, I thought as I stared at my reflection in the mirror. I don't need a dress in another size. I need a *body* in another size.

I sighed as I looked at myself. I was almost six feet tall and 118 pounds. Too tall for the petites, too thin for the misses sizes. The dreadful magenta number I had on at that very moment fit me around the bust and shoulders but was so short it barely made it past my crotch.

I thought back to my adolescence, to the years when I towered over the boys and was, therefore, ostracized by the "in" group and never invited to their makeout parties. I was gangly and awkward and I hated myself, even though my father kept assuring me that tall was beautiful. As I grew older, I came to terms with my body. Sort of. I told myself I was willowy, statuesque, model-ish. Not model-ish like Cindy Crawford or Claudia Schiffer; model-ish like those homely types you see in the more avant-garde fashion magazines and think, How did *they* ever get to be models? Over time I discovered that, while I wasn't beautiful, I did have a certain attractiveness; that if I spent enough money and shopped at the right stores I could not only find clothes that would fit me; I could find clothes that would flatter me.

The Perky Princess, however, was not such a store. Its merchandise was ridiculously flashy—loud colors, shiny fabrics, lots of gowns with spaghetti straps; merchandise for women who change clothes six times a day and parade around cruise ships in an attempt to impress people they'll never see again.

But beggars can't be choosers, as they say. I couldn't spend the next three days in the skirt and blouse I'd been wearing since six o'clock that morning. No, I had to buy something at the Perky Princess. I ended up with three god-awful dresses that were much too short and made me look like a cross between a hooker and a middle-aged woman who can't adjust to the fact that she's no longer a "chick." The best news was that the boutique had a small sporting goods section and, even more miraculously, a pair of running shoes in my size.

I bought the sneakers, some shorts, and a couple of *Princess Charming* T-shirts, fled the store with all my belongings, and headed for the elevator. I pushed the UP button. The elevator arrived almost immediately, and when it did, I stepped inside, faced front, and illuminated the button marked DECK 8, all without even noticing that there was someone else in there with me. It wasn't until the doors of the elevator kept opening and closing owing to some momentary mechanical problem that the person revealed himself.

"Try pressing the CLOSE DOOR button."

I jumped when I heard the voice. I'd been so lost in thought (What would everyone on the ship think of me in my Perky Princess purchases?) that I hadn't even considered the fact that I would most likely not be riding to the eighth deck alone. Not on a ship with 2,500 passengers.

The voice belonged to a young man, who was leaning against the back, mirrored wall of the elevator. He was sandy-haired, pony-tailed, and in his early-to-mid-twenties, and was dressed in blue jeans, Reeboks, and a very colorful Hawaiian shirt.

I nodded and did as he suggested, pressing the CLOSE DOOR button. After a few tense moments, the elevator finally began to ascend.

"Been shopping?" said my companion as he eyed me.

"Yes, the airline lost my luggage," I explained.

"Bummer," he commented. "Total bummer. You probably took this cruise so you could veg out, get mellow, the whole enchilada, and then they lose your bags and you're fucked, right?"

"That's it exactly," I said, sensing I was in the presence of a dude. A dude with a 'tude. I pressed the DECK 8 button again, just in case I'd forgotten to.

"Hey, that's cool," said the man.

"What is?" I asked.

"That we're on the same floor, Deck 8. It's cool when you meet someone in a totally random way and then it turns out that your living spaces intersect."

I smiled at the alleged "coolness" of it all as we continued to ride up together.

"I'm Skip Jamison," he volunteered. "From New York. *City,* that is."

"Elaine Zimmerman," I said. "And you're right: our living spaces do intersect. I'm from New York too. City, that is."

"I knew it. Your energy is very Manhattan," he said. "Very 'Don't touch me.' "

"Thank you," I said, not knowing what else to say. "Are you a veteran of these cruises?" Something about Skip suggested that he might be. Perhaps it was the shirt.

"No, I'm a total virgin. Normally I'll hop an Airbus when I have to go down to the islands, but I really needed to chill out this time. So I said to myself, 'Fuck the flying. Take a cruise.' Sometimes you need a meltdown before doing business in the Caribbean. The pace is nice and slow there, nice and mellow, and if you're not used to it, it can sort of freak you out."

"You do business in the Caribbean?"

He nodded.

"What kind of business?" Drug deals, probably.

"I'm an art director with V,Y&D. One of my clients is Crubanno Rum, and when the spirit moves the client, the spirit moves *me*. So here I am, on my way to scout locations for a photo shoot."

I was stunned. This guy, this *child*, held a position of responsibility at Vance, Yellen and Drier, the big ad agency? He was actually an art director working on an account as important as Crubanno Rum?

"It's amazing that V,Y&D lets you take a seven-day cruise down to the Caribbean to scout locations for photo shoots," I said, knowing that Pearson & Strulley would never have paid for my cruise, never mind let me take a leisurely seven days to get to a job.

"I had some vacation days coming," Skip said. "Plus I told them I could use a creative time-out. Recharge the batteries. Get my butt in gear. How about you? First cruise or what?"

"First cruise," I said. "I came with two of my friends."

"That's too cool," he remarked.

"Too," I responded, glad that Skip wasn't responsible for advertising copy as well as photo shoots.

"Maybe we'll all get together sometime," he offered. "Are you and your friends into music?"

Oh, no. Not another disco king. I wasn't over Lenny Lubin yet. "It depends on what kind," I said tentatively.

"New Age. Yanni, John Tesh, Andreas Vollenweider. Laid-back sounds are my thing, basically. They're good for my head."

I knew how laid-back Andreas Vollenweider was. The Weather Channel often played his "sounds" as background music during the local forecasts, particularly when the forecasts involved a violent storm.

"I'm a Beatles fan myself," I said, recalling the adoration I had felt toward Paul McCartney as a teenager, probably the last time I had adored any man.

"Hey, that's cool," said Skip. "I have nothing against oldies groups. If you and your friends want to hang out in that lounge where they have all the jukeboxes, give me a jingle. I'm in Cabin 8067."

I'm sure Skip was expecting me to reveal my cabin number, but

I did not. Instead, I wished him a pleasant trip. When the elevator left us off on Deck 8, we each said, "Nice to meet you"; then I went my way and he went his. I waited for him to disappear into his stateroom before I stopped at mine and opened the door. Let my friends give strange men an open invitation to do them bodily harm. *I* was not about to.

And speaking of my friends, Pat and Jackie practically doubled over with laughter when I emerged from my cabin at twenty after six in my Perky Princess creation, a heavy, gold, long-sleeved dress with tassels.

"Listen," I silenced them, "if Scarlett O'Hara could wear living room drapes out in public, I can wear this."

We took the elevator down to the Palace Dining Room, an enormous space that was the very antithesis of "intimate." It was decorated entirely in dusty rose, a shade that achieved a brief popularity in the eighties. The carpet, the upholstered chairs, the tablecloths, the napkins, everything was the same dreary shade of pink, except the giant crystal chandelier that hung from the center of the ceiling and the equally giant ice sculpture that sat in the center of the dessert table. (It was in the shape of the ship's logo, the crown and the shoe.) There was nothing remotely nautical about the room, and aside from the occasional pitch and roll over the ocean, I had to keep reminding myself I was even on a ship.

We showed the head waiter the little Cruise Convenience Cards we'd been given as ID and he informed us that we were to be seated at Table 186 for the duration of our cruise.

Table 186, it turned out, was a table for ten.

"Good God," I said as we followed the head waiter past dozens of tables to ours. "Every night is going to feel like a Bar Mitzvah."

We were not the first to arrive at Table 186. Already seated were an elderly couple from Akron, Ohio, who, we were soon to learn, were celebrating their sixty-fifth wedding anniversary; a dewy-eyed, twentysomething couple from Fayetteville, North Carolina, who had chosen the *Princess Charming* on which to honeymoon; and a middle-aged couple from Short Hills, New Jersey, who simply *had* to get away while their 6,000-square-foot house was being renovated. The tenth person had yet to show up. I chose to cast my lot with him or her and sat down next to the empty chair.

After a second or two of awkward silence, we went around the table counterclockwise, introducing ourselves, first names only, just like at a twelve-step meeting.

"I'm Jackie," Jackie said, sounding disappointed that we'd been put exclusively with couples.

"And my name is Pat," said Pat with a little finger wave.

"Elaine," I said, with the enthusiasm of a prison inmate.

We all stared at the empty seat next to me, then moved on.

"Brianna," said the young newlywed, who looked as if she were at her high school prom. Her long brown hair was swept up in a chignon, except for the little tendrils that hung down around her baby face, and she wore a corsage on her right wrist. After she told us her name, she gazed adoringly at her new husband in eager anticipation of the utterance of his name.

"Rick," he grunted, then squeezed her arm, nearly crushing the corsage. He was a bruiser, that Rick. Buzz haircut, thick neck, huge chest. A football player, no doubt. Or perhaps a member of one of those militia groups.

"Dorothy. I'm eighty-six," said the spry little white-haired woman to Rick's right. I guessed she had volunteered her age along with her name so we would all go, "You're eighty-six? That's amazing!" But nobody did. She looked eighty-six and then some.

She turned to her right, to her husband, a stooped, wizened creature with a large, Gorbachevesque wine stain on his bald head, and roused him from his nap.

"What is it?" he shouted. He was very cranky and would stay that way for the next seven days.

"They're waiting for you to say your name, dear," Dorothy said gently but loudly into his left ear.

"My what?" he said, cupping the same ear.

"Your name," she repeated without the slightest trace of impatience. She winked at us and whispered, "He doesn't hear so well. He's eighty-nine."

"The name's Lloyd," he bellowed, then went back to sleep.

"Gayle," said the woman to Lloyd's right. "With a *y* and an *e,* not an *i.*" She was extremely petite, which made the immense diamond ring on her right hand stand out all the more, and she was outfitted in a very chic little black cocktail dress. Her accessories included a diamond tennis bracelet and diamond stud earrings. In addition to all the diamonds, she was a redhead and therefore made me think of the redhead for whom my father had abandoned me and for whom he had undoubtedly purchased diamonds instead of supporting his family. This did not predispose me toward liking Gayle.

"Kenneth," said Gayle's husband, winding up our little game. He was of average height, weight, and table manners. After introducing himself, he tossed several of his business cards at us. He was a stockbroker, it appeared, or rather, according to the business cards, an "asset manager." Either way, he was doing all right if he could afford all the rocks Gayle was flaunting, not to mention the Armani suit he was sporting.

"Where's our mystery guest?" said Dorothy, pointing to the empty chair. She addressed the question to me, as if she thought I knew the missing person.

I explained that I was with Jackie and Pat and didn't know anyone else on the ship. (I didn't think my brief exchanges with Henry Prichard, Albert Mullins, Lenny Lubin, and Skip Jamison counted.) I added that perhaps the person who had been assigned to our table had asked to be changed to the eight-thirty seating, something I had thought of doing before deciding to leave well enough alone. You have to pick your shots in life, I knew. I was more interested in leaning on the purser's office to find my luggage than I was in getting them to switch us to the later seating.

I was about to put my handbag on the empty chair when an extremely attractive man appeared and parked himself there.

"Sorry I'm late, everybody," he said as he held up his hand in a gesture of apology.

Our eyes met, and as hopelessly clichéd as it sounds, I felt a surge of electricity charge through me—a jolt that literally made my brain short out. The feeling was thrilling and terrifying and thoroughly absurd.

What on earth is this? I asked myself as I tried desperately to regain control. It couldn't have been love at first sight, because I didn't believe in love at first sight. And it couldn't have been lust at first sight, because I was the least lusty person on the planet. Furthermore, very handsome men left me cold, not including my adolescent fantasies about Paul McCartney. Remember the old rock 'n' roll lyric: *If you want to be happy for the rest of your life, never make a pretty woman your wife?* Well, I took it seriously—in reverse: If you want a husband who won't cheat on you, don't marry one that looks like John F. Kennedy, Jr.! Not that my ex-husband, Eric, was such a beauty, and look what a cad and a bounder he turned out to be. Still, fortune cookie-ish or not, it was my firm belief that if you picked a man that women found irresistible, you'd be more than likely to have your share of heartache.

No, this guy is far too good-looking to interest me, I thought, as he sat there in his slightly frayed but freshly laundered light blue Ralph Lauren shirt, khaki slacks, and brown loafers, a vision of preppiness. He had a thick head of hair that was dark and wavy with little glints of gray, sky-blue eyes that dazzled behind a pair of tortoiseshell glasses, a straight nose, a square jaw, gorgeous teeth, juicy lips—well, you get the picture. As for his body, he was lean and wiry, yet broad shouldered, strong. And he was very tall—six-five or so. A cross between Michael Crichton and Clark Kent. Perhaps *that's* what I'm feeling, I decided. I'm simply identifying with this man's *tallness.*

And yet, there was also a sense that he was familiar to me somehow; that we had met before. But as he pulled his chair closer to the table and placed the napkin on his lap, I tried to imagine where we could have met and how, and couldn't.

All nine pairs of eyes were on him as he cleared his throat and introduced himself.

"I'm Sam Peck," he said, setting off another roll call, this time with last names.

"Jackie Gault," she said as she tried not to drool. Sam Peck wasn't the beefy type she favored, but he wasn't chopped liver either, particularly if you were as ravenously hungry as Jackie was.

"Pat Kovecky," said Pat, who smiled in Sam's general direction but was unable to make eye contact with him.

"Elaine Zimmerman," I said with a slight quiver to my voice that betrayed the jumble of emotions I was feeling. The fact that I was feeling anything but apathy toward a man was a miracle.

"Brianna Brown. I mean [giggle] Brianna *DeFabrizio*," said the newlywed, who had momentarily forgotten she was one.

"Rick DeFabrizio," said the groom, glaring at her for not acknowledging that she was *his* property now, and then nibbling on her ear in a gesture of forgiveness.

"Dorothy Thayer," said the eighty-six-year-old.

Silence.

"Wake up, dear. They want to know your name again," she told her husband.

"They want to know WHAT again?"

"Your name."

"Lloyd!"

"Your last name too, dear."

"Lloyd Thayer!"

"Gayle Cone. That's C-o-n-e, not C-o-h-e-n." Gayle's expression was deadly serious this time, as if it were imperative that people not mistake her for a Jew.

"Kenneth Cone," said her husband with a little chuckle. "Cone. Like the baseball player."

"You mean *David* Cone," Jackie said. "The pitcher."

"That's the one," Kenneth chuckled again. "No relation though." He sounded regretful, as if he wished he were a famous, shiny star too. Ironically, he *was* shiny: shiny, slicked-back hair; shiny, manicured nails; shiny, crisp-new money. In fact, both of the Cones gave off a kind of eighties-style, nouveau riche aura. They seemed the sort of people who'd made it big during the Reagan era, survived Black Monday, and were now into conspicuous consumption in a thoroughly guiltless, clueless way.

"Good evening, everybody. My name is Ismet and I'll be your waiter for the cruise."

Great, another name to remember.

Ismet announced that he was born and raised in Turkey, had worked for Sea Swan Cruises for seventeen years, and was supporting a family of thirty-two. And then, he told us the specials.

"Each night we will have a different theme in the Palace Dining

Room," he explained. "Tonight is French Night. May I recommend the coq au vin?"

"What did he say, Dorothy?" asked Lloyd.

Dorothy reported to her husband, word for word.

"What the hell's cockavan?" demanded Rick, the newlywed from Fayetteville.

His bride, Brianna, leaned over, kissed his cheek, and said very diplomatically, "I think it's chicken, honeybun. In wine sauce."

"Then why didn't Ishmael or whatever his name is just say so," Rick scowled, as if Ismet had deliberately shown him up in front of the womenfolk. Unlike Lloyd, who was merely out of sorts, Rick appeared to be one of those disaffected white American males who takes his inadequacies out on foreigners.

While we were all perusing the menus Ismet had handed us, the sommelier joined our happy group.

"Hello, hello, everybody. I'm Manfred, your wine steward," he said, pressing his hands together in the manner of a supplicant and then bowing deeply. He was positively resplendent in his red coat and silver tasting paraphernalia. "To whom may I bring a bottle of wine this evening?"

Brianna and Rick said they were sticking with their sodas. Gayle said she and Kenneth had already enjoyed a bottle of Dom Perignon in their stateroom and were, therefore, "satiated, alcoholically." Jackie said she wanted her usual Dewars and water. Pat said the Miami Whammy and piña colada she'd had earlier were quite enough for one day. And Dorothy said she and Lloyd had given up booze the same year they'd given up eating dinner any later than six-thirty. That left Sam Peck and me. We raised our hands—simultaneously. Manfred scurried over with the wine list, which he placed on the table between us, apparently mistaking us for a twosome.

"Now that's what I like to see: a couple with an appreciation for the grape," he beamed, obsequiousness oozing from every pore. "And such a lovely couple you are, too."

Sam turned to look at me, peering over his eyeglasses, presumably to inspect the woman with whom he had just been erroneously linked. I wondered what sort of women he preferred and how I measured up in my gold dress with the tassels.

"We're . . . um . . . not together," I told Manfred when Sam didn't correct him right away. I didn't want this Adonis to feel as if he'd been saddled with me by an unctuous, matchmaking cruise ship employee.

"No, but there's no harm in sharing the wine list, is there?" Sam said offhandedly, as if he were a very bored world traveler who was often forced to make conversation with simpering females. His voice was flat, accentless, leaving me no hints as to where he was from. All I knew with any certainty was that he had great cheekbones.

"No . . . no harm. I can take a look at . . . well, unless you want to see it first and then . . ." I was actually stammering. I was so disoriented, so flustered, that I was behaving like some tongue-tied groupie—and just because this man, this Sam Peck person, was sitting so close to me, was addressing me, was suggesting we share the goddamn wine list.

It occurred to me suddenly, with shocking clarity, that I didn't have the vaguest notion how to talk to or even relate to a man in whom I was interested. "Be yourself," everybody always says when this sort of thing crops up. "Be yourself and he'll love you for what you are." I wasn't so sure about that. In the movies, women in my situation tend to behave in one of two ways: they either act as awkward and foolish as I was acting, or they make themselves seem the epitome of coolness, indifference, smart-aleckyness. Where was *my* smart alecky side when I needed it? I thought, willing myself to slip into the "Don't touch me" mode Skip Jamison had referred to.

"Why don't you just order a bottle for both of us," Sam said almost impatiently, as if he were assigning the task to a flight attendant on some interminably long trip. But then he added, "Are you in the mood for white tonight? Or are you a red person?"

I was a red person, all right. I couldn't remember the last time I blushed, but there I was, flushing and sweating like a heart attack patient. Jackie and Pat were looking at me as if they couldn't believe what they were witnessing.

"What about a Merlot?" I blurted out before I'd even glanced at the wine list. Actually, I *was* a red person. I had started drinking red wine the minute they released that study saying two or three glasses a day kept the cardiologist away.

"Good choice," Sam said, with the barest of smiles. I had the feeling he was laughing at me, at my uneasiness. He was probably used to women turning to mush in his presence.

Eventually, Manfred brought our wine and Ismet brought Jackie's scotch and then we gave the waiter our dinner orders—for all six courses. I tried to concentrate on food, but I could only concentrate on Sam, on his nearness, on the subtle, citrusy scent of his cologne, on the fact that, since he was a lefty and I was a righty, our arms made contact every time we each reached for the bread basket.

Of course, there were other dynamics going on at the table. In between visits from the ship's photographer, we all attempted to make chitchat with the perfect strangers we were being compelled to sit with. At a table of ten, it's difficult to engage everyone in the same conversation, so we kept breaking off into little groups, not including Brianna and Rick, who kept to themselves, feeding each other, nuzzling each other's body parts and generally making it clear that where they really wanted to be was back in their stateroom, Doing It.

At one point, after the entrées had been served, Gayle and Kenneth were telling Jackie and Pat about the bathroom tiles their interior decorator had ordered for their newly renovated master bath (when you're on a cruise, you tend to stay away from subjects such as health care, the budget deficit, and the O.J. Simpson verdict for fear of coming to blows with people you'll have to sit across the table from for the next seven nights). Dorothy and Lloyd were concentrating on their sole meuniere, which meant that Sam and I were left to talk to each other.

I broke the ice. "How's your steak au poivre?"

He didn't answer right away. Gee, he really is aloof, arrogant, full of himself, I thought. Then I realized that I had caught him in the middle of a bite. When he finished chewing, he took a sip of his wine, swallowed, and said, "Let's just say I've had better beef at Burger King."

"That good?"

He nodded. "How about your veal cordon bleu?"

I rarely ate veal, particularly veal layered with ham and cheese, but I had taken as little time to study the menu as I'd taken to check out the wine list. It wasn't important what I ate or drank that night;

it was only important that I didn't spill any of it on myself or Sam.

"How's your veal?" he repeated, as if I were a dullard.

"My veal." I paused, wracking my brain to think of something memorable to say, something that would get a rise out of Mr. Big Chill. "Actually, it has the consistency of a snow tire I once owned."

I got the rise. For the second time, Sam peered at me over his glasses, but this time he smiled too.

"So," I asked, feeling encouraged, "what do you do for a living?" The old reliable.

"I'm an insurance agent," he said, returning to his meal.

"Really?"

"You seem surprised. What did you think I was, a trapeze artist?"

"No. It's just that I've never met an insurance agent who didn't try to sell me insurance. I've been sitting next to you for a whole half hour and you haven't once used the words 'term,' 'annuity,' or 'non-smoker discount.' "

He looked up from his food and flat-out laughed. "So you've been hanging on my every word, is that it?"

"Every other."

He laughed again. My heart leapt. "Tell me about you," he said. "What do you do back in . . . wherever you live?"

"I'm in public relations. In New York."

"Ah, an image consultant." His tone was mocking. "Who do you work for?"

"Pearson & Strulley. I'm an account executive."

"You specialize in fashion accounts, is that it?"

"No, why would you say that?"

"Your dress." He appraised the gold tasseled number. "It's so . . . so . . . cutting edge." There was enough sarcasm in his voice to cut through my rubbery veal.

"The airline lost my luggage," I said. "This dress was the best the Perky Princess had to offer. This and the two I'll be wearing over the next couple of nights."

"I can hardly wait." He sipped his wine. I sipped mine, my *third* glass, which was one glass more than my normal dosage. I knew I'd regret it later, at about three o'clock in the morning when the heart-burn would kick in, but people were always preaching about how you were supposed to stop projecting and stay in the moment. At that moment what I wanted was a third glass of wine.

As I watched Sam wrestle with his steak, I wondered why a guy like him was taking this cruise by himself. He was more than presentable, and he had a credible, albeit banal, job. So where was the girlfriend? The wife? The best buddy from the office?

"You said you're a PR person," he mused, nodding his head at me. He was definitely thawing out. "And you're on vacation this week, is that it?"

"Yes. Pat and Jackie and I decided to take a cruise together. We've been friends for several years."

"That's nice. I travel so much I've lost touch with a lot of my friends."

"I didn't know insurance agents traveled that often. Is this cruise business or pleasure?"

"Strictly pleasure. I'm a tourist for a change. Like you and your friends."

"Why a cruise?"

"Simple. Ships don't have wings."

"Excuse me?"

"I have a major aversion to airplanes and haven't flown in years. The last flight I took was a puddle-jumper between two little towns in the Midwest. There was a bad snowstorm and the plane was shaking like a son of a bitch. I said, 'That's it. Never again.' When I travel for business, I drive or take trains. But it's cold up north in February. I needed a little sun and sand and Caribbean atmosphere. Hence, the cruise."

"By yourself?" It slipped out. I hadn't meant to pry.

"Yes, but I stopped asking my mother's permission to go places by myself a number of years ago."

"You know what I meant."

"Sorry. Yes, I'm traveling alone. I'm not seeing anyone at the moment. I figured, why not sail the high seas solo?" So Sam was unattached presently. I tried to look unphazed by the revelation. "Actually, I enjoy traveling alone," he went on. "You can do what you want, when you want, without having to worry that you're neglecting the other person. Do you know what I mean, Arlene?"

"Elaine."

"Sorry."

"That's all right. *Stan.*" I couldn't resist.

"Sam."

"Sorry."

"I'll bet." He smiled again. Now I don't want to make too much of his smile, because he was fabulous looking even when he wasn't smiling. But on those rare occasions when he did smile, it was down-right impossible not to melt. I kept asking myself, What's this guy doing on *my* cruise? At *my* table? I wasn't a big believer in luck, but for some reason I felt as if I'd won the lottery without ever having played it.

There was a brief silence as we chewed our meat. Or attempted to.

"Tell me more about your work," I prompted.

"*My* work? Come on, the insurance business isn't nearly as glamorous as public relations." He was mocking me again, but I didn't mind. At least I had his attention.

"You have disdain for public relations, is that it?"

"No, I just don't know much about it. Enlighten me."

"What do you want to know?"

"Tell me about your clients."

"Is this a setup or are you really interested?"

"I'm really interested."

I wanted to believe him. So I told him about Dina Witherspoon, the onetime actress/sex kitten who, because she had the temerity to turn sixty, was now endorsing arthritis pain medication; about The Aromatic Bean, the chain of cappuccino bars whose twenty-nine-year-old chairman drank only chamomile tea; about Mini-Shades, the company that manufactured sunglasses for small children and household pets. Sam proved to be a terrific listener. He laughed when I made jokes and became serious when I became serious and asked smart questions about the media instead of the usual, "Is Katie Couric as nice in person as she is on TV?" I was starting to loosen up and enjoy myself, and I assumed Sam was too. But then Ismet came along with the dessert cart, inquiring whether any of us wanted anything, breaking the spell.

Everybody started talking about chocolate mousse and crème brûlée and how much weight people gain on cruises, which prompted Gayle to reveal that she and Kenneth had a personal trainer who had just landed a bit part in the next Jean-Claude Van Damme movie.

The remaining minutes at the table were a blur, as Ismet hurried us along so he could set up for the eight-thirty seating. As we were all leaving the dining room, Sam mentioned something about checking out the show—according to the schedule of activities, the evening's entertainment consisted of a comedian, an opera singer, and a man who walked on hot coals in his bare feet—and then going to bed. The thought of Sam going to bed inspired me to ask, "Which deck are you on, Sam?"

The minute the words were out of my mouth, I laughed at the irony of them. I, who wouldn't give my deck number to the ship's chaplain.

"Are you all right?" Sam asked. My question hadn't exactly been a knee slapper.

"Yes," I said, still laughing. "I'm fine."

He looked at me quizzically, then said, "Deck 7."

"One floor down from me. I'm on Deck 8," I volunteered. Happily.

"Well," he said, not reacting to my announcement, "I guess I'll see you tomorrow. Have a good one." And off he went.

I stood there for a few seconds, watching him from behind. He was a tall, commanding presence as he strode through the hall, past the herd of other passengers on their way into the dining room. It wasn't until he was well out of sight that Jackie grabbed my arm and asked me if I was drunk.

"Why would you ask that?" I said.

"Because you were flirting with that man," she said. "I've known you for six years and I've never seen you flirt with a man."

"I was flirting?" I asked. "I thought I was only being friendly."

"Okay. So you were being friendly. I've known you for six years and I've never seen you be friendly to a man."

"That's not true," I said defensively. I turned to Pat. "Is it?"

She nodded.

"Oh, look," Jackie said, pointing to the wall opposite us. The photographs the ship's photographer had taken earlier that day were displayed there. "Let's go find ours."

We searched through the hundreds of shots on the wall until I finally spotted one of Jackie, Pat, and me. I lifted it from the display case, while my friends looked for the duplicates we had instructed the photographer to take.

Stepping away from the crush of people, I studied the photograph. There the three of us were, standing arm-in-arm on the gangway, moments before we crossed the threshold of the *Princess Charming*. My vision wasn't the greatest, since I'd left my bifocals up in the stateroom so as not to call attention to my advancing years, but I could see that the photo was a pretty good one. (None of us were blinking or doing something funny with our mouths, for example.) I could also see that we were not the only ones in the picture. Hovering in the background, just over our shoulders, was Sam Peck.

4

We all said we were too tired to go to the show. It was still early—eight-twenty or so—but it had been a long day and we wanted to pace ourselves. This was only the first night of the cruise, after all. There were six more to get through.

Instead, we ended up in Pat's stateroom. We could tell that Kingsley had been there, as the bed was turned down and there were two chocolate mints on the pillow. Pat lovingly placed the mints in the tote bag she had designated for souvenirs. The other thing we noticed was that her soiled blouse had been picked up to be dry-cleaned, just as Albert Mullins had promised it would be. He had telephoned her room a scant ten minutes after she had unpacked, told her to hang the blouse outside the door of her cabin, and said he would take care of the rest.

"Looks like Albert's a man of his word," Jackie said. "Plus, I think he's got the hots for you, Pat."

Pat giggled. "You think everybody's got the hots for everybody. You even suggested that Elaine was interested in that man at our table. *Elaine,* of all people."

I couldn't very well take offense. Like Jackie, Pat had never known me to be interested in a man.

"You saw her. She *is* hot for him," Jackie insisted.

"Why are you two talking about me as if I'm not here?" I said from the chair in the corner of the room. Pat and Jackie were sitting next to each other on the bed.

"Well? Aren't you hot for Sam?" Jackie asked.

"Of course not. He was a decent dinner companion, that's all."

Usually, I shared everything with my friends. But for some reason I was too reticent to blab about the huge crush I'd developed on Sam. To tell Pat and Jackie how I felt, to say it out loud, to let the words hang in the air, seemed downright scary to me. What if they made fun of me? What if they tried to talk me out of my feelings? What if Jackie wanted Sam for herself? What if? What if? What if? But the worst "what if" of all was: What if I let myself fall for Sam, have a shipboard romance, do the whole "Affair to Remember" thing, and then he turned out to be a louse?

I decided to deflect the attention away from myself by encouraging my friends to talk about the men in *their* lives. But since there *were* no men in their lives, they ended up talking about their ex-husbands.

"Peter's really gone off the deep end about the nursery," Jackie was saying. "He never shuts up about wanting to expand. He talks about his 'vision' for the business. Vision, my ass. He just wants me out so he can run everything himself and look like a mogul to his cutie-pie new wife, speaking of a vision." Jackie rolled her eyes. Trish, Peter's second wife, was Miss Junior League. She never went anywhere without her pearls, her velvet headbands, or her impeccable manners. She was always syrupy sweet to Jackie when they ran into each other, and Jackie, who was not much on etiquette, always gave her the finger. Behind her back, of course.

"At least you have an idea of Peter's *needs,*" Pat offered, trying out her favorite new word. "You know what they say, Jackie: Forearmed is forelorn."

"Forewarned, Pat," I said.

"Right. What I mean is, even now, after all these years, Bill doesn't communicate with me, doesn't tell me what he wants. And of course, during our entire marriage, he never explained how I was lacking, so there was no way for me to know what or how to change."

"What makes you think it was *you* who was lacking?" I asked, wishing that Pat thought more of herself, that we all thought more of ourselves. Women are always accused of malebashing, but the people we most often bash are ourselves.

"You're right, Elaine," said Pat. "It wasn't that *I* was lacking or that *Bill* was lacking. It was that Bill was busy being a doctor and I was busy being a mother and there was no common ground."

"But the children you were busy being a mother to were *his* children," I pointed out. "How much common ground does a guy need?"

Pat shook her head. "I didn't pay enough attention to him," she said. "I didn't."

"Why, because you didn't greet him at the door every night in some slinky Victoria's Secret number?" Jackie said with disgust. Jeans and a T-shirt were her at-home attire.

"No, because I didn't show enough interest in his career," Pat said. "I was too busy carpooling."

Jackie and I had no way of identifying with the conflicts full-time mothers face, but we could easily appreciate the fact that there was only so much energy to go around. How were you supposed to deal with this kid's gym class and that kid's piano recital and still act fascinated by your husband's diagnosis of some eighty-year-old woman's gallstones? I felt for Pat. For Bill, too.

"Back in the sixties, Peter and I used to talk about having kids," Jackie mused. "But we were kids ourselves. 'Flower children.' Christ, who knew we'd end up making a successful business out of goddamn flowers."

"Who knew," Pat and I said in unison, like a Greek chorus.

"The nursery became our kid," said Jackie. "The problem is, joint custody isn't working out. At least, not for Peter."

"Perhaps you should find out what's really behind Peter's striving, what he's really thinking and feeling," Pat suggested.

"Let me tell you something about men," Jackie said, as if she were an authority. "If you ask them what they're really thinking and feeling, they get that glazed look, like they don't have a clue what you're talking about, like it must be some hormonal thing you're going through. The truth is, men just aren't that deep."

"You don't think so?" asked Pat.

"No, I don't. Women are always wasting their time trying to get inside a guy's head, to understand his 'essence.' Well, hello? He doesn't have one."

"If you think men are so shallow, Jackie, why are you always talking about having sex with them?" I asked.

"I'm not always talking about having sex with them," Jackie maintained. "Sometimes, I talk about falling in love with them, about having what I used to have with Peter. Again."

"But Peter left you," I pointed out. "What's so wonderful about falling in love with the sort of man who leaves you?"

"Not all men leave their wives, Elaine," said Pat. "You mustn't assume the worst all the time."

"I know," I conceded. "But I didn't even love Eric, and it was still like a stick in the eye when he slept with that low-rent Elizabeth Arden. Imagine how much it would have hurt if I *had* loved him? I'd be crazy to fall in love. Any woman would be."

I was trying to talk myself out of my obsession with Sam Peck, I knew. But the truth was, I was pretty far gone already—and after only one meal with him. I was at that silly stage in a relationship where all you want to do is say the guy's name, drop it casually in conversation, use it to illustrate a point, let it roll off your tongue in as many ways as you possibly can. *Sam Peck. Sammy Peck. Samuel Pecking Order. Sam and his Peckeroo.* Still, I resisted even mentioning his name to Jackie and Pat. I felt too raw, too exposed. It was too soon.

"It's not crazy to want to fall in love," Jackie said, defending her position. "If you've had love once, you want it again. It's only natural. I look back on my marriage and I remember that the early years with Peter were really fantastic. So I say to myself, 'Jackie, at the very least, you can have really fantastic early years with some other guy.' "

"What happens when you get to the later years?" I said. "Why go through the early years with somebody, through the courtship, the chase, the hunt, or whatever you want to call it, when it's inevitable that the good times won't last? Why waste all that energy?"

"Because you don't know at the outset that the good times won't last," said Pat. "It's not a certainty that relationships fail."

"Fifty percent of them do," I said.

"Fifty percent of them don't," Pat said. "Bill and I may be divorced and he may be upset that he has to spend all that money to support an ex-wife and five children, but I still don't think of our marriage as a failure. I really don't."

"That's because you and Bill had *fantastic early years,*" Jackie said, driving home her point. "I'm telling you, if you had them once, you want them again."

"Where does your whole bit about men not having an essence fit in?" I challenged.

"I was talking about the later years, not the early years," Jackie explained, as if it were obvious. "You don't go looking for a man's essence until the good times are over. It's when he starts planting himself in front of the TV after dinner and can only manage a grunt when you ask him a question that the 'essence' thing crops up because you're desperate to understand why he isn't the way he was when you were first together."

I laughed ruefully. It all seemed so hopeless.

"So, even after all the heartache, you still want to fall in love," I said, shaking my head at Jackie.

"Sure. Or at the very least, find a steady sex partner," she said, taking us full circle.

"Be careful what you wish for," I warned. "There's something to be said for waking up in the middle of the night, walking into the bathroom, and *not* finding the toilet seat up."

"There's also something to be said for waking up in the middle of the night, turning over in bed, and finding a man's arms around you," she countered.

"Not if the reason you're waking up in the middle of the night is because the man whose arms are around you is snoring," I retorted.

"Elaine, you're impossible," said Pat.

"I'm not impossible," I said. "I'm just incapable of finding true love."

She smiled affectionately. "You're perfectly capable of loving someone. You just haven't found the someone."

"Who says I will?" I said.

"Who says you won't?" she asked.

I considered the question, then stood up from the chair and stretched.

"I don't know about you two, but I feel like taking a walk on the Promenade Deck," I said, needing time alone with my thoughts about Sam. "A little fresh air might do me good."

"I feel like getting into bed and watching TV," said Pat.

"And I feel like calling Henry Prichard's room," said Jackie, suddenly very perky, "to see if he wants to meet me for a drink."

"I thought you were tired," I said.

"I thought *you* were," she said.

She walked over to Pat's phone, picked up the receiver, and asked to be connected to Henry Prichard's room. "He said he had the six-thirty seating at dinner, so he could be back in his room by now," she whispered to us, cupping her hand over the mouthpiece. After another second or two, Henry answered his phone. Pat and I listened as Jackie went right ahead and invited him to join her in the Crown Room for a drink. Apparently, after a brief back-and-forth, he accepted because when she hung up, she turned to us and pumped her fist like a ballplayer who'd just hit a home run.

"He said he was in the casino when he remembered that he hadn't taken his pills," she said, explaining why Henry was in his stateroom when she called. "At the very second his phone rang, he was trying to decide if he should go back to the casino or go to bed."

"Pills?" I said, my imagination immediately focusing on the diseases from which Henry Prichard might be suffering. Communicable diseases.

"Yes, Elaine," Jackie sighed. "Antibiotics. He said he's getting over a sinus infection. I've had one too, but naturally, I didn't do anything about it."

"I guess Henry takes better care of himself than you do," I said. "Even so, are you sure you're ready to spend time alone with him?"

"Alone? There are over two thousand people on this ship!" she laughed.

"Jackie's a big girl, Elaine," Pat said.

I nodded, thinking I'd like to see how Pat was going to react the first time Lucy, her only daughter, went off with a man she barely knew.

"Well, I'm outta here," Jackie said, opening the door to the cabin.

"Have fun," Pat called out to her.

"Don't let him sell you a car," I added.

———

Before heading down to the Promenade Deck for my evening stroll, I stopped briefly in my stateroom to get the blazer I'd worn on the plane. I threw it over my shoulders and walked toward the elevator. When I got there, Skip Jamison, the boy wonder of advertising, was standing there adjusting the rubber band around his blond ponytail. He was not alone: there was a large group of Japanese people waiting for the elevator too.

"Hey, we've gotta stop meeting like this," said Skip in between chomps on his chewing gum. "It must be karma or something."

"Hi, Skip. Where are you off to?" I asked, hoping it wasn't the Promenade Deck.

"The library," he said. "They've got one on Deck 3. I thought I'd do a little Deepak Chopra, if they carry his stuff. I'm really into the mind-body thing. How 'bout you?"

"Absolutely," I said. "I've always felt the mind and the body go hand in hand." I suddenly thought of Jackie having an after-dinner drink with Henry Prichard and wondered if her mind was going hand in hand with his body.

As if reading *my* mind, Skip asked where my friends were.

"One's in her cabin, watching TV. The other's with a new friend, having a drink."

Skip touched my arm. "And you?"

"Me?"

"Yeah, where are you—"

The elevator arrived. We all stepped inside. The Japanese people pressed DECK 5, where the casino was located. Skip pressed DECK 3, the library floor.

"Elaine, babe. Which deck do you want me to hit for you?" asked Skip, who was standing right next to the panel of buttons.

"Oh. Sorry." Babe. "Would you mind pressing DECK 6?" I said.

He did as I asked. "Going for a walk on the Promenade Deck, is that it?" he speculated. "To check out the stars?"

"Yes," I said hesitantly, sensing that Skip might change his mind about the library and want to join me for a little stargazing.

I was right. He said, "That's a cool idea. Mind if I come?"

"Ordinarily, I wouldn't," I said, "but I'm meeting someone there.

A man from my table at dinner." Well, it wasn't a total lie. Sam would be with me. In spirit, anyway.

"Hey, that's cool," said Skip, looking disappointed despite his up-beat tone. "I'll catch you later then."

The elevator stopped at Deck 6.

"Enjoy," said Skip as I got off. "Treat this night like it's your last."

Now that's an odd thing to say, I thought. And then I guessed that one of the hallmarks of Deepak Chopra's work was probably the old carpe diem thing.

"Thanks, Skip," I said as the elevator doors were closing. "You too."

When I stepped out into the night, onto the Promenade Deck's Astro-Turfed surface, I was immediately struck by the stark contrast between the air inside the ship, which was recycled and stale, and the air outside, which was fragrant and fresh. When you spend even a few hours inside a ship, with its boutiques and restaurants and wall-to-wall amenities, it's easy to forget there *is* an outside. But there was no mis-taking how achingly beautiful a night it was—clear, sultry, sensual.

A row of lounge chairs, as well as a running track, extended along the perimeter of the deck. It was about eight-forty-five by the time I showed up, and there were far more loungers than runners.

I wandered toward the rear of the ship, hoping to find a secluded spot where I could stand beneath the stars, which were out in force, as was a perfect, crescent moon. After several minutes, I found a to-tally deserted corner, directly over the stern of the boat. I took a deep breath and drew myself up to the railing, then looked down at the swirling waters below. A soft, salty breeze played with the ends of my hair as I watched the ocean churn with the wake the engines of the *Princess Charming* were stirring up. I inhaled again, more deeply this time, letting the sea air fill my lungs, clear my head. My mind and body were in sync. Deepak would have approved.

This is why people should go on a cruise, I thought dreamily as I took another breath and exhaled slowly, indulgently. Not for the six-course meals. Not for the duty-free shopping. Not for the lectures on napkin folding. For this. For the luxury of being able to stand on the deck of a ship in the middle of the ocean on a starry, moonlit night. As the TV commercial says, it *is* different out here. There's nothing but you and the vastness of the sea, nothing but you and infinity. The sensation is thrilling and intimidating and totally unlike any other. My life in New York seemed suddenly not to exist. My mind was fixed only on the present, only on the sights and sounds and impressions of those moments.

When I'd first thought of going out onto the Promenade Deck, I'd intended to exercise, to walk off my dinner, to compensate for not having had time to run my usual four miles that day. But I just stood there, my hands on the railing, my skin tight and tingling in the salt air, my thoughts melting, one into the other.

It wasn't Sam who came to mind first, which surprised me. It was my father I conjured up; not the phantom father I hadn't seen in years, but the young man I'd adored as a child. He had wavy dark hair like Sam's, but he wasn't nearly as conventionally handsome—or as tall. Still, I had thought him the most magical creature on earth, as he alone had the power to sweep me into his arms and make me feel like a princess. He was a pharmacist, and he worked at a drugstore not far from our home in New Rochelle. But dispensing prescriptions was only one of his talents: he sang better than Julius LaRosa, danced better than Fred Astaire, told better jokes than Milton Berle. At least, *I'd* thought so. Unfortunately, his many talents also included romancing women who were not his wife—a fact I probably could have lived with if only he hadn't left, if only he hadn't gone away to the redhead's house, if only he hadn't become the father of another little girl, a counterfeit daughter to sweep in his arms, sing to, dance with, treat like a princess. If only.

Oh, give it up already, I scolded myself, as I always did when the hurt and anger began to well up inside me. That was then. This is now. Live your life.

I swallowed the lump in my throat, gazed down at the sea, and watched the water bubble up as we motored down to the Caribbean. I couldn't take my eyes off the ocean. It was hypnotic, like staring into a fireplace with a roaring blaze going. I allowed myself to think of Sam then, to focus on his face, the way he moved, the things he said, the things he didn't say. I let myself get hopelessly sticky and sentimental as I wondered if he liked me, had found me interesting or entertaining or pretty, had formed any opinions about me at all. I closed my eyes and imagined an entire identity for him, the way you do when you meet a man who intrigues you and you don't know much about him. I gave him a fictional mother and father, a few siblings, a steady girlfriend in college, an ex-wife, maybe two. And then, I gave him me. I actually pictured us together over the course of the cruise, permitted myself to believe that love wasn't an illusion, that men could be faithful and true, that happiness was possible, even for me.

I was having a wonderful time picturing and imagining and fantasizing when my concentration was broken by the sound of a voice on the PA system.

"Ladies and gentlemen. Dis is your captain speaking."

It was Captain Svein Solberg, Mr. Personality. It was nine o'clock on the dot, and as advertised, he was giving us the second of his twice-daily reports on our position and the weather. Apparently, we were somewhere near the Bahamas, several hundred miles from Puerto Rico, and traveling at seventeen knots.

"Da veather is fair," he reported, obviously looking up at the same clear sky I was, "vith very little danger of rain. Barring any unforeseen problems, ve anticipate smooth sailing for da entire cruise."

Very little danger. Smooth sailing. For the entire cruise.

I pondered the captain's words. Could things really go smoothly from here on out? Was it okay to let go of my relentless worrying for once in my life? Was it time to relax and enjoy myself?

"Why not?" I whispered to the seagull that kept circling overhead. "Why not?"

As I stood on that deck of the ship, watching the seagull soar, I felt a sense of adventure and excitement I hadn't felt in years. It's only the first night of the cruise, I told myself. *Anything* can happen over the next six days. Anything.

I thought of Sam again. It didn't matter that I had spent all of two hours in his company, that he was a blank page at that point. What mattered was that I wanted him in a way that was frightening and wonderful.

"Why not?" I said out loud this time. "Why the hell not?"

Day Two:
Monday, February 11

5

The phone in my cabin rang at 7 A.M., jolting me out of a deep sleep.

"Yes?"

"This is your wake-up call," a male voice explained.

"My—?"

"Yes, ma'am. You instructed us to phone you at seven o'clock, and it's seven now."

"Oh, right. Sorry. I completely forgot." Before I went to bed, I'd called the purser's office and asked to be awakened at seven so I could go running first thing in the morning. It had seemed like a good idea at the time. How was I to know that I would be up all night because my stateroom was located directly underneath the ship's "Teen Disco" and that the bass from the music they were playing would render me a human vibrator? If you've ever lived next door to a construction site where the jackhammer is the tool of choice, you know what I'm talking about. I honestly thought my teeth would fall out. "Thank you for the call," I told the wake-up man.

"You're very welcome and have yourself a pleasant day, Mrs. Zimmerman."

Mrs. Zimmerman. "I will. You too."

I washed, dressed, and was ready to go by seven-twenty, eager to take advantage of my first full day at sea, hopeful of seeing Sam. Unfortunately, the first person I saw upon bounding out of my cabin, into the hall, was Mr. Lube Job.

"Lenny!" I whispered, not wanting to wake the other passengers.

"What are you doing here at this hour?" When Jackie, Pat, and I had first met him at the mustering at the Crown Room, he had told us—bragged to us—that his room was on Deck 9, the so-called Commodore Deck, where all the fanciest cabins were. So why would he be standing around at seven-thirty in the morning in the hall of Deck 8? What's more, he was still wearing the same clothes from the night before.

He laughed, assaulting me with his booze breath, and nodded toward the cabin two doors down from mine.

"Didn't I tell you lovelies I was a swinger?" he grinned, teeth clicking, bracelets clanging. "I went to the show last night, got lucky, and ended up with the dollface in 8026."

"Gosh, that *was* lucky," I said, trying to share his enthusiasm. What was lucky was that, given his age and lifestyle, Lenny didn't die in the saddle.

"Where are you off to?" he asked, not bothering to notice that I was wearing running shorts and running shoes and was, therefore, very likely going running.

"The Promenade Deck," I replied.

"All alone? What about your friends?"

"They're probably still asleep."

"In their cabins?"

"No, in the engine room."

Lenny laughed. "I just thought maybe they got lucky too," he said, nudging me in the ribs. "You never know where people will spend the night on cruises like this, huh?"

"No, you never know," I agreed as I tried to sidestep away from Lenny, who was literally blocking my path.

"I'll tell ya what *I* know," he said, sticking his hairy, bejeweled chest in my face. "I was on my way back to my room to shower, but I just might pay another visit to 8026. Stamina's my middle name, you get what I'm saying, honey?" He nudged me again.

"I sure do," I said, nudging him back just enough to slip past him. Feeling extremely sorry for the dollface in 8026 if Lenny Lubin was her idea of a good time, I took off for the elevator.

———

The weather was glorious, and as I stepped out onto the Promenade Deck, into the brilliant sunshine and warm, tropical air, I experienced the same sense of adventure and possibility that I'd felt the night before.

There were quite a few passengers doing laps around the running track, I discovered: some jogging, some walking; some young, some old; some wearing headphones, some wearing those seasick patches people stick behind their ears. I tightened the laces on my new sneakers, did a few stretching exercises, and set off on the track.

Boy, this sure beats the FDR Drive, I thought, comparing the scenic route that the *Princess Charming* afforded me with my daily run on the Upper East Side of Manhattan, which was fraught with garbage trucks, exhaust fumes, and muggers. Yes, I could get used to this, I decided as I sprinted past a pretty white sailboat that was making its way down to the Caribbean.

I was on my fourth or fifth lap on the track, working up a nice sweat, when I turned to my left and noticed that Sam Peck was running up alongside me. He was about to pass me, but then he recognized me and slowed down.

"Hey," he said between breaths as he kept pace with me. "Look who's here."

Yeah, look, I thought. I wasn't wearing a drop of makeup, my hair was pulled back into a sloppy ponytail, and my perspiration-soaked T-shirt was hanging out of my shorts. I looked like an unmade bed. Sam, on the other hand, was a vision. His blue eyes were as entrancing as the color of the sea; his dark lashes and dark hair were shiny, lustrous; his legs were long and tapered, yet muscular too. I could easily imagine them draped around mine.

"Hi. How're you doing," I said, trying to sound casual as we trotted next to each other.

"I'm doing fine, thanks. Mind if I tag along with you?"

"Not at all." Mind?

"I didn't figure you for a runner," said Sam in that cool, detached way he had.

"What did you figure me for, a trapeze artist?" I asked, throwing back his remark from the night before.

He laughed. "Score one for Elaine."

So he remembered my name. Score two for Elaine.

"I run four miles every morning," I explained, still processing what I considered to be a compliment.

"Before work?"

"Yes. I get up at five and run until six-thirty. I'm in the office by eight."

"I'm impressed. I'm not nearly that disciplined. I just run when I can, in between business trips, to keep myself in reasonably good shape."

I should be in such reasonably good shape, I thought as I stole a quick glance at Sam's hard, flat stomach.

"You said last night that you do a lot of traveling for business," I said as we chugged along, "but I don't remember you mentioning which insurance company you work for."

"Dickerson Life Insurance."

"Dickerson Life Insurance?"

"Yeah, up in Albany."

"I've never heard of it."

"Albany?"

"No, Dickerson Life Insurance." He was teasing me again.

"They're a publicly traded company. I've been with them for fifteen years," he said.

"Fifteen years. That's a long time to do anything," I said. "At least, that's what people tell me. I've been in public relations for sixteen years."

"I guess we're a couple of lifers."

"I guess so. What made you go into the insurance business in the first place?"

"My father was an executive with Travelers. He's retired now, but insurance must be in my genes."

I wouldn't mind being in your jeans, I thought, shocked by my emerging lasciviousness.

"What about your mother? Did she work?" I asked, refocusing.

"Yeah, but she was a ballerina. I couldn't see myself in a tutu, so I went with the insurance business."

"Probably a wise choice."

"But let's get back to you," said Sam. "You're at your office by eight, you work a full day, and then what?"

"What do you mean?"

"What happens after work? What do you do for fun?"

"I do what most single career women in Manhattan do for fun: I either work late at the office, nuke a frozen dinner at home, or go out for dinner with other single career women and put the tab on one of our expense accounts."

"What about men?"

"What about them?"

"Aren't there any in Manhattan?"

"Sure, there are men in Manhattan. But they're either married, married to their jobs, or married to their mothers."

"That bad, huh?"

"Worse."

Sam laughed. Score another one for my team.

"You said last night that you're divorced," he went on. He was much chattier than he'd been the night before. I found all these questions extremely flattering.

"Yes, I am divorced," I said.

"Are you still in touch with your ex?"

"Only when he calls to verbally abuse me. About a week ago, he issued his first death threat."

"Doesn't sound very chummy. Did you take his threat seriously?"

"Hardly," I scoffed. "Eric is in the funeral home business. His expertise is in dealing with people who are already dead. He wouldn't know how to actually *cause* someone to be dead. He'd need a manual. Or he'd have to hire someone else to do it for him."

"Why would he want to kill you at all?" Sam asked, moving away from me slightly.

I smiled. "Don't be alarmed. I'm making it sound more dramatic than it really is. I do that sometimes."

"Then tell me the real reason your ex is so angry at you."

"Eric had an affair with Lola, the makeup artist who worked for his funeral homes. There was an ugly divorce. A few months later, I started doing PR for his chief business rival. Eric wasn't happy about it. I think it's a macho thing with him at this point. Men don't like to be shown up by a woman, an *ex-wife* in particular."

"People don't like to be shown up by people. Period."

"True, but I think it's especially galling for a man to be outdone by a woman who doesn't have to lie or cheat or offer up her body—a woman who uses her talent and ingenuity to accomplish her goals."

Sam smiled. "Wow. You must be terrific at public relations. You talk like a press release."

"Thank you."

"Positive spins aside, I think death threats from a former spouse are a little extreme. I, for example, have only threatened to break a woman's kneecaps."

I laughed. "Was this woman your ex-wife? I don't think you mentioned last night at dinner whether you'd ever been married."

I had turned to look at Sam when I'd asked the question and so I saw the sudden blankness, the detachment, the aloofness—the same look he'd arrived at the dinner table with the night before—return to his expression. It was as if a curtain had descended across his handsome face, obscuring the teasing, intelligent eyes, the wry, sexy smile, all of it. I waited for him to say something, to answer my question, but he just continued to run alongside me, silently, staring straight ahead. It was awkward, to say the least. I was about to rush in to fill the dead air, to ask if he'd gone to the show last night, played the slot machines in the casino, anything, when he finally spoke.

"I was almost married," he said, so softly the words were barely audible.

Oh, I get it, I thought. Sam Peck is one of those men who can't commit, can't stand intimacy, can't pull the trigger; the type who's out the door the minute the woman hears wedding bells. And he's ashamed to admit it.

"You don't have to talk about it," I said, looking out over the ocean as we ran. I tried to sound nonchalant, but I was crushed, figuring that if I *were* to fall in love with Sam, the relationship would never go anywhere, never be more than a clichéd shipboard romance, certainly never get to the living-together stage or, God forbid, the altar. Wait! Perhaps I can change him, I thought, falling right down into the pit into which scores of women throughout the ages have fallen—that insane fantasy where we allow ourselves to believe that we and we alone can cure his addictions, smooth the rough edges of his personality, convert him into our very own Prince Charming. It's so tempting to believe such things, but look what happened when I'd tried to convert Eric from a frog into a prince: I ended up with a frog who turned into a weasel.

"My fiancée died a week before our wedding."

Sam said something, but I couldn't hear him over the din of the ocean. I turned to look at him.

"What was that?" I asked. His eyes were sorrowful, haunted. "I didn't—"

"The woman I was supposed to marry died right before the wedding. About two years ago."

I was stunned. Sam Peck had had a fiancée? A fiancée who died? How? Why? Under what circumstances? I was dying to ask, was flooded with questions, but said instead, "Oh, Sam. I'm so sorry." And I was. Sorry for Sam. Sorry for the woman he was supposed to marry. Sorry I was always so quick to prejudge, to assume the worst about everything and everyone.

"Thanks," he said. "The first few months were hell, but I'm rebounding. Slowly but surely."

"Is this cruise part of the healing process? The fact that you're taking time off from work, I mean?"

"All the traveling I do helps. I'm never in one place long enough to dwell on anything. And I'm certainly not in one place long enough to get a serious relationship going with someone else."

"I understand," I said and nodded, a small lump forming in my throat. Poor Sam. Poor *me*. If Sam got a serious relationship going with me, that would make me a transitional woman and who wanted to be one of those? But in time, with patience, perhaps—

"I didn't mean to drag the conversation down," said Sam, his face brightening a little, the curtain beginning to lift. "I'd much rather listen to you tell one of your stories. You make me laugh, Elaine. Did you know that?"

"No. Well, not—"

"You do," he said. "That stuff you told me about some of your clients last night at dinner was great material."

"It was all true."

"And you know what else?"

"No."

"You're tall."

"You noticed that."

"Yeah, and it's a relief. Usually, I have to look down at women when they're standing next to me. Way down. We're talking nose bleeds here."

"But your nose doesn't bleed with me, is that it?"

"That's it."

It wasn't: "I love you, Elaine." But we were getting somewhere, I thought.

Our conversation drifted away from ourselves and we talked about Jackie and Pat, the Caribbean, the *Princess Charming*. I asked Sam if he had gone to the show last night.

"I went for a half-hour or so, in time to catch the guy who walked barefoot on hot coals."

"Was it fun?"

"Not exactly. The guy's manager forgot the coals, so they had to use briquets."

"And people think the entertainment on cruise ships is amateurish."

"Actually, tonight's show could be even better entertainment," he said with his tongue in his cheek. "They're having an Elvis revue. Six Presley lookalikes will sing 'Love Me Tender' and the audience will vote on which one did the best impression of The King."

"Sounds deadlier than watching Captain Solberg on the *Princess Charming* Channel."

"Oh, you're a fan too?"

I nodded enthusiastically. "I love his weather reports. He could be the next Willard Scott."

Sam laughed.

We made more small talk, but it's hard to run and talk without getting a little winded, so at some point we stopped the chitchat and just ran together. Out of the corner of my eye I could see that people were observing us as we ran, assuming we were a couple. And this time, I didn't shrink from the assumption. There are worse things than being linked with Sam Peck, I thought. Much worse things.

At eight-thirty, we called it quits.

"Time for breakfast," Sam announced. "Want to join me?"

An invitation. I was thrilled. But duty called: I always checked in with my office first thing in the morning when I was out of town. Yes, I was nursing a serious infatuation with Sam. But men came and went; my job was my anchor, my security.

"Thanks, Sam, but I've got to go back to my cabin to phone my office."

"Are you kidding? Those ship-to-shore calls are ten dollars a minute. Why not wait until Wednesday when we get to San Juan?"

"Money's not an issue. My expense account will pay for it."

"Fine, but why are you calling your office? You're on vacation, remember?"

"I call my office every day. In case there's a problem with one of my clients."

"Pearson & Strulley is a huge PR firm. Can't someone else there handle your clients while you're away? Like your assistant?"

Obviously, Sam didn't understand how indispensable I was to Pearson & Strulley.

"My assistant is wonderful. An absolute gem," I said. "Her name is Leah and she's from Jerusalem, and before she came to work for me she was a soldier in the Israeli army. I figured that if she could survive the conflict in the Middle East, she could survive me. I'm not an easy person to work for."

"I guessed that, somehow."

"She's incredibly organized and approaches even the most menial task as if it were a military maneuver. Best of all, she loves to work. The woman puts in almost as many hours as I do."

"Then why not let her cover for you while you're away?"

"Leah is not an account executive," I said. "Perhaps someday she'll grow into the position. With a few more years under her belt. Under *my* tutelage." I was laying it on a little thick, but I wanted to impress Sam. The truth was, Leah was more than capable of doing my job, which is why I called the office even when I was on vacation: to make sure she hadn't stolen my job.

"Well, I'm starved," said Sam. "If you change your mind, I'll be in the Glass Slipper."

"The what?"

"That's the name of the café by the pool. They serve buffet breakfasts and lunches. Sure you won't join me?"

I shook my head. "I'll see you later though," I said, moving away from Sam but not wanting to. "At dinner."

"At dinner," he said, pushing his eyeglasses back up the bridge of his nose with his index finger. They'd kept sliding down during our run.

"At dinner," I repeated with a little wave as I backed inside the ship. When I *was* inside, out of Sam's sight, I mimicked Jackie and pumped my fist in triumph.

"Yessss," I said, feeling as if I'd truly scored a victory. I had never imagined that I would meet a man on the ship, a man as good-looking and personable as Sam Peck. And yet that's exactly what had happened. I wasn't just an anonymous passenger to him now, some divorcée he got stuck with at dinner. I was Elaine. The one who made him laugh.

Suddenly, the cruise was looking better and better to me. I was actually glad that Jackie and Pat had suggested it.

I was inserting my key into my cabin door when I heard some-one coming out of the stateroom two doors down from mine: 8026. I was dying to catch a glimpse of the "dollface" who had so en-thralled Lenny Lubin, so I stood there for a few seconds, pretend-ing to fumble with my key, and waited for her to appear in the hall.

Come on, where are you, honey? I don't have all day, I thought as she seemed to be taking her sweet time.

Finally, someone emerged from 8026, but not the someone I had pictured. *He* was in his nineties and in a wheelchair, and while he was in pretty good shape for a ninety-year-old, he was no dollface. I rushed over to help him maneuver the wheels over the door's threshold, and he thanked me and told me I reminded him of Susan Anton. I thanked him and told him he must have an excellent mem-ory because hardly anyone remembered Susan Anton.

When I got inside my stateroom, it hit me that Lenny had lied about what he was doing on Deck 8 so early in the morning. The question was: Why?

Immediately, my overactive imagination kicked in, and I began to assign all sorts of sinister motives to Lenny's appearance in our hall. Perhaps he wasn't the benign old lecher he made himself out to be. Perhaps he was involved in some kind of conspiracy.

Oh, boy, there I go, I thought, chiding myself. As my friends were well aware, I believed deeply in conspiracies—the Russians killed JFK, the Mafia killed RFK, the cops framed OJ, and all the rest. It was all part of my unfortunate mind-set that, when push came to shove, people weren't to be trusted.

I laughed at my own idiocy. Lenny Lubin was a harmless lush, who wanted everyone to think he was a stud. So he probably made up all that stuff about the dollface in 8026 because he couldn't face the fact that he hadn't gotten laid in years.

I felt for Lenny. I hadn't gotten laid in years either.

Of course, there was still the question of why he had chosen a stateroom on *our* hallway to lie about. But I didn't have time to play Agatha Christie. It was nearly nine o'clock and I hadn't even placed my first call to the office.

I took a quick shower and was about to call New York when Pat knocked on the door. She was on her way to breakfast, and was then planning on having a haircut, a facial, and a manicure.

"Are you booked for lunch?" I asked.

"Sort of," she said. "Somebody did ask me to join him."

"Him? Who?"

"Albert Mullins. The one who insisted on having my blouse dry-cleaned."

"The bird watcher."

"Yes. He called first thing this morning and invited me to meet him at the Glass Slipper around noon."

"What did you tell him?" I asked, picturing Pat wrestling with the decision.

"I said that I'd probably be eating with you and Jackie but that he was welcome to join us. Now it turns out that Jackie is under the weather."

"What's wrong?"

Pat shrugged. "She woke me up this morning, asking if I had anything for a bad stomach. You know how Bill always likes me to travel with a healthy supply of stomach medicines."

"Yes, Pat. I know. But tell me more about Jackie."

"She said she had a nice drink with Henry Prichard, that they stayed in the Crown Room until about ten-thirty and then went to bed."

"Together?"

"No." Pat giggled. "Jackie said Henry was the perfect gentleman."

"She must have been devastated."

"Elaine. In any case, now she's got these terrible cramps and episodes of nausea and she feels dizzy too."

"It must have been something she ate," I reasoned. "Although she and I both had the veal and I feel fine."

"It's probably a bug of some sort. I ordered her some hot tea and dry toast from room service. I think she's resting now."

"Then I'll check in on her later. I really hope it's just a twenty-four-hour thing. She was really looking forward to this vacation, what with everything that's going on between her and Peter about the nursery."

Pat nodded. "I wondered if the stress of all that might be what's causing her symptoms."

"I guess we'll just have to wait and see. Listen, why don't I meet you and Albert for lunch at noon—and Jackie, too, if she's up to it? I've got a phone call to make now."

Pat agreed and went off to breakfast and then on to the ship's beauty salon. I hoped we didn't hit a patch of rough seas while she was having her curly blond locks snipped. Talk about a bad hair day.

I closed the cabin door behind Pat, pulled up a chair by the phone, and read the instructions on the card that was mounted inside the phone's headset. I gave the operator my credit card number, dialed my number at Pearson & Strulley, and waited for several seconds. Finally, the call went through, although there was a tremendous amount of static on the line.

At ten dollars a minute, there shouldn't be all this crackling, I thought while I waited for my assistant to answer the phone.

Eventually, I heard her voice—barely.

"Leah? It's Elaine," I shouted.

"Who?" she asked.

"Elaine. Elaine Zimmerman." It was the lousy connection, I told myself. They couldn't have forgotten me already.

"Elaine. I can hardly hear you."

"That's because I'm in the middle of the Atlantic Ocean." I paused and waited for a wave of static to clear. "So, is anything going on with my clients?"

"Yes. Plenty."

"What? Tell me."

"Which do you want first: the good news or the bad news?"

"You've worked for me a long time, Leah. You know the rules."

"Right. Sorry. Bad news first. Dina Witherspoon was arrested for shoplifting a gold bracelet from the jewelry counter at Neiman Marcus. The SEC is investigating Mini-Shades for securities fraud. And a Santa Monica man is suing The Aromatic Bean for $2.5 million, claiming the cappuccino he spilled on his arm caused second-degree burns."

I couldn't believe it. I was gone twenty-four hours and what happened? A public relations nightmare! *Three* public relations nightmares! Nightmares that would be next to impossible for me to contain from my stateroom on the *Princess Charming!*

"Are you there, Elaine?" asked Leah.

"Unfortunately," I said after waiting for more static to clear. "You mentioned that there was good news. What is it?"

"That you can relax and enjoy your vacation, because I'm taking care of everything here."

"You are?"

"Yes. Harold promoted me this morning. I'm an account executive now."

Harold Teitlebaum was the group vice president of Pearson & Strulley, the man to whom I reported. He hadn't mentioned anything to me about wanting to promote Leah. Not a word.

"I don't think I heard you," I said, hearing her perfectly.

"I said, Harold promoted me. I'm not your assistant anymore."

I took a minute to let all this sink in. A ten-dollar minute.

"I'm happy for you, Leah, but Dina Witherspoon, Mini-Shades, and The Aromatic Bean are *my* clients," I said, wanting to make it quite clear to this Israeli Eve Harrington that I was still in charge.

"Oh, absolutely. I'm only covering for you until you're back from vacation. Then, Harold will assign me my own clients. He says he's already got a few in mind."

"Harold's been a busy boy," I said dryly.

"You sound angry, Elaine."

"Angry?" I didn't feel angry, exactly. I felt left out, shut out, out of the loop. I was stuck on a ship in the middle of nowhere and couldn't come to my clients' rescue or my own. "I'm fine. Just fine," I said from between clenched teeth.

"Listen, Elaine. I've really got to go. Harold wants me to fax Liz Smith a press release explaining that Dina Witherspoon wasn't shoplifting that gold bracelet; she was only *lifting* it, to see how heavy it was, and it happened to fall into her bag without her realizing it."

Harold wanted *Leah* to fax Liz Smith a press release? About *my* client?

"Oh, I almost forgot," Leah added before rushing off to do my job. "You had a call from your ex-husband first thing this morning."

"Eric? What in the world did he want?" As I've already indicated, Eric and I were not one of those divorced couples that made even the slightest attempt at cordiality.

"It was a little strange," said Leah. "He said he heard you were taking a cruise."

"Sure, he heard I was taking a cruise. I told him the last time he called to yell at me."

"He said he wanted to confirm your trip."

"Confirm it? That is strange, even for Eric. Why would he give a damn about my travel plans?"

"I have no idea. But what's even stranger is that when I asked him if he wanted you to return his call when you got home from the cruise, he started laughing."

"Laughing?"

"Yes. As if I'd said something hysterically funny."

"But Eric never laughs. He spends most of his time with corpses and they're not known for their witty repartee."

"Well, I'm sure you and he will figure out whatever has to be figured out. In the meantime, I really should get back to work."

"While I sit here playing shuffleboard, you mean?"

"Face it, Elaine. You're on a cruise and I'm in the office. Which of us is in a better position to handle things here?"

She was. But still.

"I'm in complete control," she said, as if I was supposed to find that reassuring instead of threatening. "Now, run off and have fun."

"But I really think *I* should be the one to—"

"I can't hear you, Elaine," she interrupted as the static returned to the phone line.

"It's just as well," I said and hung up.

6

At ten-fifteen, I called Harold to discuss his unilateral decision to promote my assistant. But when the call went through, *his* assistant told me he was in a meeting. I gave her the ship's phone number as well as the number of my stateroom and asked that he call me back. He did not. At ten forty-five, I called again and was told Harold was in another meeting. At eleven forty-five, I called a third time and was told Harold had gone to lunch. All the while, Kingsley kept knocking at my door and asking when he could make up the room. Each time I said, "Later," and each time he said, "No problem." At eleven-fifty, I put Kingsley out of his misery and vacated the cabin.

My first stop was Jackie's room. The DO NOT DISTURB sign was hanging outside, but when I put my ear to the door, I could hear that the television was on, so I knocked lightly.

"It's Elaine, Jackie," I said. "I just wanted to see if you were alive."

I listened for some signs of life and was relieved when I heard a rustling of sheets, then a shuffling of footsteps. After a few minutes, Jackie appeared, holding her stomach and grimacing in pain.

She was, obviously, not well. Her skin had a yellowish tint and her eyes were milky. Even her short, spiky blond hair looked wilted. I had never seen her in such bad shape, not in the six years we'd known each other. Because she worked outdoors, she'd always had a healthy, ruddy complexion and seemed the antithesis of the fragile flower. Not that she took great care of herself. She ate junk food and drank more than most women I knew and had smoked a pack of Marlboros a day until four years before, when she'd given up cigarettes for biting her nails down to the cuticles. She'd have an occasional hangover and her back acted up every now and then, but she gave the impression she was immune to colds and flus. "I'm too mean for those germs," she'd laugh when the subject would come up. I'd always believed her. Until now.

"Don't look at me like that," she groaned, flipping off the TV with the remote control. "I feel horrible enough already."

"Do you think you're seasick?" I asked.

"Me? Peter and I used to go deep sea fishing. Besides, you can barely feel the waves on this ship. Half the time I forget I'm even on the water."

"Then what do you think is the problem?" I asked, gently taking hold of her elbow and guiding her back to bed.

She smiled weakly. "You tell me, Elaine. You're the hypochondriac. What's the disease of the week?"

"Actually, there *was* a cruise ship where the passengers got Legionnaire's Disease."

"Yeah, well. What I've got isn't that exotic. It's just your basic gotta-run-to-the-bathroom-every-five-minutes bug. Or maybe I ate something that didn't agree with me."

"But you felt fine at dinner," I pointed out, "and when we were up in Pat's room. Were you okay when you were having a drink with Henry?"

"Sure. This thing didn't hit me until about two o'clock this morning. And then, boom."

"Well, why don't you lie back and I'll tell you a bedtime story," I said, fluffing her pillows.

She shook her head. "Your stories are always about those criminals you call clients, or how this bitch at Pearson & Strulley is trying to steal that bitch's job. I don't think I'm up to one of those stories."

Well, that ruled out my telling Jackie about Leah. "All right. Instead of my telling you a story, why don't you tell me about your drink with Henry?"

"It was nice," she said. "No big fireworks or anything. Just nice to sit and hang out with a guy. A guy I'm not business partners with."

"What's he like?" I asked. "He seemed very outgoing."

"He is. He's a sports fan and we talked about baseball, basketball, football, and hockey."

"What? No bobsled racing?" I was not a sports enthusiast, even though I ran every day. Sports were frivolous, as far as I was concerned; running was medicinal.

"No, but we did spend ten minutes or so on bowling. Henry has his own ball and shoes and is in a league."

Just then, Jackie winced in pain.

"More cramps?" I said.

She nodded and held her breath for several seconds, waiting for them to pass. "What were we saying?"

"How you and Henry talked about sports," I reminded her.

"Right."

"Listen, you're probably exhausted, Jackie. Why don't I let you rest, so this bug can work its way out of your system. I'm supposed to meet Pat for lunch—"

"Lunch. Ugh. I can't even think about food."

"Sorry." I stood up. "Can I go down to the ship's infirmary for you and get some Kaopectate, Immodium, anything?"

"Pat's already given me her entire supply of Dr. Bill's samples. I think they were part of her divorce settlement."

"That's more than I got from Eric. But then I didn't want anything from Eric. Not even a free coffin."

"But I bet you *do* want something from Sam Peck."

"Who?" The remark caught me completely off guard. I had trouble swallowing.

"Come on, Elaine. I saw the way you looked at him last night."

I walked toward the door. "I'll check on you later," I said, avoiding having to address the issue.

"Okay, but you know how paranoid you are about catching things," she warned. "The next time you come, you'd better wear a surgical mask."

"I'll see if the Perky Princess sells them," I said, blew her a kiss, and left.

———

I made it to the restaurant right at noon, just as Captain Solberg was giving the first of his daily orations over the PA system. The Glass Slipper, as it was called, was on Deck 11, the Sun Deck, where the ship's two swimming pools were located. It was a café with an informal ambiance, a place where it was perfectly acceptable to stand on the buffet line in bare feet and a soaking wet bathing suit and drip all over your fellow passengers. (I was not wearing a bathing suit, wet or otherwise, because my bathing suits were in the famous lost suitcase. I was, therefore, forced to wear yet another Perky Princess creation: a red, white, and blue caftan emblazoned with a gold sequined anchor.) As for the buffet itself, the offerings were cafeteria-style fare: hamburger patties as tender and juicy as hockey pucks; greasy french fries; mayonnaisy coleslaw; and a salad bar whose produce looked and smelled as if it had been decomposing in the hot sun for several days. I ended up heaping my tray with the only things I thought were safe: prepackaged Saltines.

I spotted Pat and Albert Mullins at a table for four overlooking the water. They were sitting across from each other, with Albert chatting and gesturing and Pat trying to eat and listen at the same time. Even from a distance, I could see that her trip to the beauty salon was a success: her wild, frizzy hair had been trimmed, shaped, tamed; her skin had been scrubbed and cleansed and toned into a rosy, post-facial glow; and her nails had been painted a snappy shade of coral. She looked as healthy as Jackie looked ill.

"Hi, you two," I greeted them.

Albert immediately rose from his chair with the rectitude of a soldier. I half expected him to salute me.

"Please, sit down, Albert," I said, sitting down myself, next to Pat.

Albert sat. "And how are you this fine afternoon, Elaine?" he asked.

"I'm swell, thanks." I turned to Pat. "But I just left Jackie's room. She's really sick."

"I know," Pat sighed. "I wish there was something we could do. Bill always took such good care of the children when they'd get stomach things. He knew how to make them more comfortable somehow."

I was tempted to point out that one of the reasons Pat divorced Bill was that in the last years of their marriage, he was rarely home, rarely there for his kids, sick or well; that perhaps she was allowing herself a little revisionist history. But I changed the subject.

"So, Albert," I said. "Seen any exciting birds yet?"

"They're all exciting to me, Elaine," he said as he took tiny bites of his hamburger, dabbing at the corners of his mouth with the napkin on his lap so as not to drip any ketchup—or grease—on himself or the table. Apparently, Albert's obsession with having Pat's blouse dry-cleaned was just the tip of the iceberg when it came to his fastidiousness. He had tucked another napkin inside the collar of his white T-shirt and had placed an entire stack of napkins beside his water glass, as backup. "I've seen pelicans and blue herons and seagulls, of course. Nothing you wouldn't expect to see out over the ocean in this part of the world. But I'm looking forward to tomorrow, when we get to our first port of call. I'm anticipating that there will be some very exciting species on that island."

Our first port of call was Isle de Swan, a two hundred–acre island owned by Sea Swan Cruises. Just off the northwestern coast of Haiti, it was an example of what had become a trend in the cruise industry: cruise lines buying large parcels of land from Third World and, therefore, cash-starved countries, developing these parcels, and converting them into stops on their ships' itineraries. They were good investments. The land was cheap and so was the local labor hired to wait on the passengers when they came ashore. We were due to arrive at Isle de Swan at seven-thirty the next morning.

"As I think I mentioned yesterday," Pat said in between forkfuls of coleslaw, "my ex-husband sometimes takes our children bird watching during the summer. I believe they've spotted red-bellied woodpeckers and hooded warblers, even a tufted titmouse."

The "tit" in titmouse caused both Pat and Albert a moment of extreme embarrassment, during which they each made a mad grab for their water glass and drank with intensity.

"Tell me, Albert," I said as I scarfed down my Saltines, "were you always interested in birds? Even as a young boy?"

"Yes," he nodded animatedly. "I wasn't much of an athlete. While the other boys were picked for the various teams in school, I became interested in birds. Why birds, I have no idea. I suppose I identify with them in some way. Or perhaps, it's that I live vicariously through them."

"What do you mean, Albert?" Pat asked.

"How many of us would like to escape our lives, our very selves, by simply spreading our wings and taking flight?" he said wistfully. "Birds can migrate from one breeding ground to another, follow the seasons. We humans are stuck with our lots, aren't we." It was not a question. "So I guess, in a nutshell, I envy the freedom birds have. But I must say, since I embarked on this cruise, I do feel as free as a bird. To be able to glide over the ocean like this, without a care in the world, is truly a joy. The Sea Swan people take care of absolutely everything for you—your meals, your entertainment, your companionship (he smiled at Pat)—and I don't remember ever being so utterly without responsibilities, obligations, problems."

My, another of Albert's impassioned speeches.

"You mentioned responsibilities and obligations. I wondered if you lived alone," Pat ventured, while I wondered what sort of problems Albert might be referring to.

He nodded. "I suppose I'm what's commonly known as a loner."

A loner, I thought, immediately associating the word with murder and mayhem. Well, why not? Every single time a guy arms himself with a rifle, climbs to the top of a tower, and shoots a parking lot full of innocent people, his neighbors turn up on the Evening News and describe him as a loner. Perhaps Albert's "problems" involved law enforcement officials.

"What about your family?" asked Pat. "Do they live in Manhattan? Or in Connecticut?"

"Actually, I have no family," said Albert. "Everybody's died off. It doesn't look as if I'm going to have any children—male or otherwise—anytime soon, so the Mullins name will probably end with me."

"Not necessarily," said Pat, ever upbeat. "You never can predict what will happen in life. My mother always said I'd never marry and have children—my sister, Diana, was the femme fatale when we were growing up and I was rather shy—but I not only married—a doctor, of all things!—I gave birth to five children, four of them boys."

"What does your mother say *now?*" asked Albert, sounding indignant on Pat's behalf.

"Oh, she and I have both come around in our thinking," Pat confessed. "She's starting to see that you can't put siblings in boxes and label them." She turned to me. "I actually worked up the nerve to say to her recently, 'You were wrong to plagiarize me all those years, Mother.' "

"Patronize, Pat," I corrected her. "She was wrong to patronize you."

"Yes, she was."

Albert nodded and pulled a packet of Handi-Wipes out of his pants pocket, then cleaned his hands thoroughly with the moistened towelettes. For all I knew, he showered after every meal.

"My mother was a bit of a patronizer, too, may she rest in peace," said Albert. I wondered if Albert's poor, deceased mother was the source of his money. A week on the *Princess Charming* wasn't cheap, and he didn't have a real (as in, paying) job, so I guessed that if he was the only surviving member of his family, he made his money the old-fashioned way: he inherited it.

We chatted a bit longer. Pat talked about her mother. Albert talked about his mother. I talked about my mother, even though she, like my father, was not one of my favorite subjects. She wasn't a horror or anything—she made terrific potato pancakes, for example. It's just that a part of me blamed her for my father's abandonment of our family. If she had been different somehow, more interesting or alluring, maybe he wouldn't have left us for the redhead. But who knew what made people do the things they did?

At some point, Albert asked our forgiveness, saying he had to go back to his stateroom to place a long-distance phone call. I was surprised. He had told us he was a loner. To whom do loners place long-distance phone calls? Maybe he's calling his stockbroker, I decided, given that, if my theory about Albert's finances were correct, there would be assets to manage. I suddenly thought of Kenneth Cone, the asset manager from Table 186, and considered introducing him to Albert. If they decided to work together, maybe I'd get a finder's fee or commission or something.

"Well," said Albert as he rose from the table, leaving a pile of soiled napkins in a heap on his plate. "I do hope you ladies have a pleasant day. A very pleasant day."

"The same to you," said Pat.

"Lunch was delightful, thanks to you both," he said. "I hope you'll convey my most sincere get-well wishes to your friend, Jackie." He paused, his mouth forming a mischievous grin. "Or should I say, 'to the third Blond Mouse'?"

Pat giggled, clearly flattered that Albert had not only remembered our nickname for each other but felt at ease enough with us to use it.

I wasn't flattered so much as puzzled. I didn't think we had ever told Albert our nickname. I certainly hadn't.

When Albert was gone, I related my phone conversation with Leah to Pat. "Harold is letting her handle *my* clients," I said, getting upset all over again. "What if it's the beginning of the end for me at Pearson & Strulley? What if they want new blood there? Younger blood? What if there's a blood bath and I'm one of the bathers?"

"I'm not a businesswoman or even an educated woman," Pat began. It had always bothered her that she hadn't gone to college; that she had worked and had babies while Bill climbed the ladder of higher education. "And I don't know the inside out of Pearson & Strulley," she went on. "But if you don't mind my saying so, I think you're overreacting."

"I don't mind your saying so," I replied. "Go on."

"All right then. It sounds to me as if your clients are in a pepper."

"A pickle, Pat."

"Yes, they're in a pickle and they need help. Fast. You're out of the country, so it's perfectly logical that your assistant, who has been trained by you and knows all the parties involved, would be chosen to manage the situation."

"You don't think Harold's trying to phase me out or anything?"

"Not at all. You still have your job. You're just on vacation. There's no reason to suspect that either Harold or Leah is out to get you. You're overreacting, Elaine. I hope you don't mind my saying so."

"I already told you: I don't mind," I said, minding. Once, okay. Twice, enough.

"Well, I think I'd better get going," Pat said after checking the time on her watch.

"Where to?"

"The cruise director is giving a lecture on duty-free shopping in the islands."

"Pat, I hate to burst your bubble, but duty-free shopping is an invention of the tourist industry. Trust me, you can buy the same stuff more cheaply at Costco."

"Really?"

I looked at her, so innocent, so trusting, so good.

"I was only kidding," I said. "You can get great bargains down here if you know what you're doing. That lecture sounds like a terrific idea."

"Want to come?"

I shook my head. "I think I'm going to buy a paperback, find a chair by the pool, and people-watch." *Sam*-watch more accurately described my plan.

"Then I'll see you later at dinner," said Pat. "Hopefully, Jackie will be up to joining us."

"Hopefully," I agreed.

After another attempt at reaching Harold, who was, supposedly, with a client, I bought a spy thriller by a British novelist I'd never heard of and went poolside, in search of an empty lounge chair—a mission not unlike going to the supermarket the day before Thanksgiving and trying to find a shopping cart.

Would you look at all these people? I said to myself as I gazed at the two thousand passengers stretched out next to each other—bodies of assorted shapes and sizes sizzling in the hot sun like rotisserie chickens on a spit. They didn't seem to notice that they had such little personal space that they were practically overlapping. They also didn't seem to mind the commotion coming from one of the two swimming pools. Apparently, there was a relay race in progress in which the six women positioned at one end of the pool were expected to grab—with their teeth—the balloons that were resting between the legs of the six men at the other end. Needless to say, every two seconds one of the balloons would pop in somebody's face and the explosion would cause participants and spectators alike to shriek with laughter. I considered throwing myself overboard or, at the very least, going back to my cabin. But I wanted to catch a glimpse of Sam. So I pressed on. I finally spotted what appeared to be the one chair on the entire deck that wasn't occupied—i.e., didn't have a person or a towel on it. I scrambled over to it, only to discover that it was broken.

I heaved a frustrated sigh and sat very gingerly down on the chair. It was only a little bent, I figured. Not a lethal weapon, by any means. I slathered myself with sunscreen, then scanned the crowd for Sam and was disappointed when I didn't see him. Still, it gave me a secret thrill knowing he was somewhere on the ship, that sooner or later we'd see each other again. I closed my eyes and fantasized about our reunion.

I must have looked terribly beatific because I heard a man's voice ask, "Meditating?"

I shielded my eyes from the sun, squinted, and saw that Skip Jamison was standing before me, his long blond hair hanging wet and loose around his shoulders. He had just come out of the pool and his bathing suit, a clinging, tight little black bikini, left nothing to the imagination. In other words, Skip had a substantial set of family jewels. I wasn't the only one to notice, either. Skip had two young women at his side.

"Yes," I replied. "I suppose you could call what I was doing a form of meditation."

"That's cool. Meditation's probably a good thing for you," Skip prescribed. "Chill you right out." He turned to the two women, who seemed irritated or annoyed or just plain bored that he was bothering to talk to a member of their gender, a member twice their age.

"So I guess I'll see you guys later? At dinner?" he said to Donna and Tori after introducing them to me and explaining that they were all assigned to the same table. The Young Singles Table.

"It's black tie," Tori reminded Skip. "Don't forget your tux."

"Me? Wear a tux?" He laughed. "I'm way too laid-back. Way."

"He's allowed to wear a regular suit," Donna informed Tori. "The instructions said: Black tie optional."

"Yeah, but tuxes are hot," said Tori. "They make guys look like movie stars."

"Or restaurant personnel," I interjected. "It depends on the cut of the tux."

Donna and Tori each gave me a butt-out face.

"Look, tuxes, suits, whatever. I'm not into that formal shit," said Skip. "I'm a casual guy and I've gotta go with that. Deepak Chopra says: Be comfortable in your own skin."

Donna and Tori looked at each other, shrugged, and went back to the pool. Skip picked up the towel that had been lining the lounge chair next to mine and wound it around his waist, obscuring the aforementioned family jewels. Then he stretched out in the chair.

"I think someone was sitting there," I said.

" 'Was' is the point," he said, getting comfy. "You know, it's pretty amazing how we keep running into each other, keep intersecting, isn't it?"

"Amazing." Actually, it is amazing how you're on a ship with a couple of thousand people and you keep running into the same two.

"What sign are you?" asked Skip.

God, I hadn't heard that line since the seventies.

"Scorpio," I said. "You?"

"Scorpio," he said, shaking his head and marveling at the coincidence of it all. "And do you know what else is amazing?"

"No, what?" I asked.

"That every time I run into you, you're alone. You told me you're here with two of your girlfriends, but whenever you and I see each other, they're not around."

"I didn't make them up, if that's what you're getting at," I said. "They exist. We just don't move in a swarm, the way insects do."

"Well, maybe I'll get to meet them before the cruise is over."

"I'm sure you will." I picked up the spy thriller I'd bought and opened it to the first page. "Do you mind if I read?" I asked, not wanting to be rude.

"Mind? No way. I'm just gonna lie here, shut the old lids, and cop some rays."

Skip pickled himself in the tanning oil that the former possessor of the chair had left behind, along with the towel, wished me "Happy reading," and closed his eyes.

I'd been reading and enjoying the warmth of the sun for a half-hour or so, tuning out the relay races, the tray-toting waiters, even the steel drums, when I happened to look up from my book and spot Sam. He was sitting several rows of chairs down from mine, reading a magazine. My pulse quickened.

Since he seemed engrossed in the magazine, I took the opportunity to indulge myself and stared unabashedly at him, studying every detail. And then, wouldn't you know, I was caught in the act—he looked up, straight at me. It was as if he had felt my stare, sensed that my eyes were on him. I was mortified.

I smiled sheepishly.

He smiled back, put his magazine down, got up from his chair, and walked over to me.

He was dressed in a pair of rumpled blue swimming trunks, his bare chest hard and flat and hairy. Furry, actually. Now, I know some women don't care for hairy men, myself having been one of them (if I wanted an animal, I'd get a pet, and all that), but I found *Sam*'s hairiness to be yet another source of wonderment. It was absurd.

"Elaine," said Sam, standing at the foot of my chair now. "How are you?"

"Fine, thanks. How are you?" I asked.

"Fine, thanks," he said.

God. We sounded like characters from *Dumb and Dumber*. I wondered why we were both acting so stiff and formal, after our rather peppy chat earlier that morning, and then I turned and noticed that Skip was sitting there, eavesdropping.

"Been getting some sun?" I said to Sam, posing yet another inane question. No, Elaine, he's been hot air ballooning.

Sam nodded. "And catching up on my reading." He kept waiting for me to introduce Skip, almost as if he thought we were "together." So I introduced Skip. He and Sam shook hands.

"Hey, man, don't I know you?" Skip asked Sam. "From the city?"

"Which city would that be?" Sam asked.

"New York. What other city is there?" Skip winked at me in that condescending way many New Yorkers have when they want to make people from other cities feel like hicks.

"There are a couple of others," Sam said dryly. "I work in Albany, for example."

Skip shook his head. "Christ, I swear I know you from somewhere. You don't have a twin in Manhattan, do you?"

"None that I know of," said Sam. "Maybe I've just got one of those ordinary, everyday faces."

Yeah, and I'm the spitting image of Michelle Pfeiffer, I thought.

"Do you two know each other from New York?" Sam asked Skip and me.

I answered. "No, we only met yesterday. In the elevator. Skip works in advertising and he's on his way down to the Caribbean to scout locations for a photo shoot for Crubanno Rum."

"That sounds like nice work if you can get it," said Sam.

"It is," Skip agreed. "The islands are a hot place to hang out. Really cool."

It was funny about the words "hot" and "cool." I never could figure out if they were supposed to be interchangeable or if they had different meanings, too subtle for the over-forty set to comprehend.

"So how do you two know each other?" Skip asked Sam and me.

"Elaine and I are tablemates," Sam explained. "Table number 186. Early seating."

Skip looked from Sam to me and back to Sam. Then he nodded his head in recognition. "So *this* is the dude from your table."

"The dude? What are you talking about?" I said.

"You know. The dude from your table," Skip repeated. "The guy you were gonna meet on the Promenade Deck last night. To check out the stars."

God, I suddenly remembered how I had lied to Skip about that, just to get rid of him.

"Uh, no. That was someone else," I lied some more.

"A man from our table?" Sam asked, looking skeptical.

"Yes," I said. "Lloyd Thayer."

"You met Lloyd, the eighty-nine-year-old, on the Promenade Deck last night?"

"That's right. Dorothy came too. They both wanted to take a

walk and I said I'd go with them. In case they couldn't see in the dark or something."

"That was considerate of you," Sam said.

"Very spiritual," Skip agreed, then turned to Sam. "She fools you, this Elaine. She's got a soft side *and* a very 'Don't touch me' thing. Which is totally New York, believe me."

"I believe you, Skip," Sam smirked. He was getting a kick out of being treated like a hayseed. "Now I hate to run, but I've got an appointment in five minutes."

"An appointment?" I asked, praying "appointment" wasn't a euphemism for "date."

"Yeah. With the ship's barber."

"Oh." I smiled with relief. "They must be having a special on haircuts. Pat had one today too."

"I didn't hear about any specials," said Sam, "but you know what a small town Albany is. Can't get a decent haircut there to save your life. I figured I'd try the guy here on the ship, since the brochure says he comes to us straight from Manhattan."

I laughed. Skip didn't. I don't think he realized his leg was being pulled.

"See you at dinner, Elaine," said Sam. "Good meeting you, Skip."

And he was gone.

I was staring after him, replaying our conversation, when Skip said, "I'm not crazy about Sam's vibes."

"What do you mean?" I asked.

He shrugged. "There's an energy there. A different kind of 'Don't touch me' thing than yours. His is more of a 'Don't fuck with me' thing."

"You just don't trust him because he's getting a haircut," I smiled, regarding Skip's long, golden, surfer-boy locks. When I was his age, I didn't trust men who got haircuts either. "But thanks. I appreciate the warning."

7

The afternoon was uneventful. I checked on Jackie, who was still feeling rotten, and Pat took ballroom dancing lessons— she had always yearned to become proficient in the marengue, she said. I also tried to reach Harold again—three times. The first time, his assistant said he was on another call. The second time, she said he was away from his desk. The third time, she said he had left for the day. Harold was avoiding me, obviously, but he wouldn't get away with it; I had his home number.

Dinner that night, as Donna and Tori had pointed out to Skip, was the first of two of the *Princess Charming*'s formal evenings. The travel agent had briefed us about these black tie affairs, and as a result I had packed two simple but elegant dresses, which would be of absolutely no use to me now, since they were stuck in the baggage compartment of some 757. So, on went another Perky Princess purchase: a short, white, sleeveless, sequined number that overemphasized my skinny arms and legs and made me look like a cross between a Roaring Twenties flapper and an extremely shiny stork.

Pat and I ordered Jackie some chicken soup from room service and sat with her on her bed, encouraging her to eat.

"I'd rather have a scotch," she said, but nevertheless finished the entire bowl of soup.

"Maybe tomorrow," said Pat.

"No 'maybe' about it," Jackie countered. "I'm not missing another day of this cruise if I have to crawl onto that Isle de Swan."

"Thatta girl," I said, admiring Jackie's pluck.

"I don't know," said Pat, shaking her head at Jackie. "If you're not better in the morning, I think we should take you to see the ship's doctor."

"The ship's doctor?" I said with alarm. "What if he's some quack whose medical training consists of a couple of weeks at the University of Calcutta?"

"Elaine," Jackie rolled her eyes. "It just so happens that Peter and I backpacked in Calcutta, in the seventies, and had a great time."

"Yes, but did either of you have to consult a doctor while you were there?" I asked.

"No," she conceded.

"There you go," I said.

"I think I should call Bill," said Pat. "I could describe Jackie's condition to him over the phone and he could tell us what to do."

"He's a fine doctor, Pat, but he won't be able to diagnose the problem long-distance," I pointed out. "Besides, you said you were going to wait and call his apartment on Friday, so you could wish Lucy a happy birthday."

"In case anyone cares what *I* think, it's time for you two to go down to dinner," said Jackie, nodding at the door.

"Are you sure you won't mind being here alone?" I asked.

"Positive. Tell everybody at Table 186 I said hi," she said and shooed us out.

Pat and I stepped out of her cabin and saw Kingsley maneuvering his housekeeping cart down the hall, in preparation for his evening "turn-down" service. As we walked by him, he smiled and said, "A gentleman passenger was asking about you."

"Asking about us?" I said.

Kingsley nodded. "He came by about ten minutes ago."

My heart danced as I wondered if it was Sam.

"What was this man wearing?" I asked.

"A tuxedo," Kingsley replied.

"That narrows it down," I said. Most of the men on the ship, Skip notwithstanding, would be wearing a tuxedo. If they didn't own one, they could rent one in the men's boutique, the Preening Prince.

"I probably shouldn't have said anything," Kingsley confessed. "The gentleman asked me not to."

"Come on, Elaine," said Pat, tugging on my arm. "Kingsley

already told us that he can't say any more. Let's go to dinner, all right?"

I shook off the suggestion, reached into my purse, pulled out a dollar, and handed it to Kingsley. *"Now* can you say any more?" I asked.

He smiled. "No problem. The gentleman was asking specifically about Mrs. Gault. The one who's sick."

"Henry Prichard," Pat and I said in unison.

"He didn't give me his name," Kingsley said.

I nodded. "That's okay, Kingsley. We know who it was."

And yet, why wouldn't Henry want us to know he'd been asking about Jackie? I wondered. And why wouldn't he just call her room and ask her directly how she was feeling? Come to think of it, how did he know she was sick in the first place? She hadn't emerged from her stateroom all day.

"Let's go, Elaine," said Pat, linking her arm through mine. "You know how Ismet likes us to be on time."

"You're right," I said, not wanting to miss a moment of Sam's company.

But Sam wasn't there when we arrived at Table 186. I pretended not to notice and sat down next to Dorothy Thayer. Pat took the empty chair to my left.

"Where's your friend?" Dorothy asked me after everybody said hello to everybody.

"He's not really my friend," I said. "I only met him last night at the table."

She smiled. "I meant your *girl*friend. The one who owns the nursery."

"Oh," I said, embarrassed that I was so taken with Sam that I had completely forgotten about poor, sick, electrolyte-depleted Jackie. "She's a little under the weather. We think it may be a stomach virus."

"What did she say, Dorothy?" Lloyd asked.

"She said her friend may have a stomach virus," Dorothy told her husband, whose black-tuxedoed shoulders were covered with dandruff.

"I wonder if it was something she ate at dinner last night," said Gayle, recoiling from her roll and butter. She looked quite opulent in her kelly green silk dress that set off her lustrous red hair. In keeping with the color of the dress, she had forsaken the diamonds for emeralds. Her husband, Kenneth, wore an Armani tuxedo and had a large, fat cigar in his mouth. Unlit, of course. It was all the rage among newly rich and successful men to have the finest in Cuban cigars flown in from Saint Martin or Saint Bart's or wherever contraband is flown in from, build a humidor in their basement (next to the wine cellar or exercise room or media center), and simply hold, chew, or suck on the cigar, the way men did in the fifties, only more so.

"I don't think so," I said reassuringly. "She and I both had the veal. It's probably a bug."

There followed a fairly lengthy discussion of the over-the-counter stomach medications currently on the market, including a debate over which was better at reducing acid buildup: Pepcid AC or Tagamet HB. And for some reason *that* led to a debate over whether one is to starve a fever or feed a cold. Even the newlyweds, Brianna and Rick, wrested their lips away from each other long enough to weigh in on the subject.

"At the first sign of anything, I load up on Vitamin C," Brianna shared.

"Vitamins are bullshit," Rick grunted. "You're wasting your money, honey bunch."

"I am not, sweetheart," said Brianna. "Vitamins really work. A lot of people take them."

"A lot of people think the government is their friend," said Rick. "A lot of people should wake up and smell the corruption." So I was right about Rick. It was entirely possible that he attended secret meetings dressed in combat fatigues along with other, similarly dressed individuals.

"I've been taking vitamins since eighth grade," Brianna said. "And I'm going to keep right on taking them, snuggle bunny."

"What did you say?" Rick stared at her as if he were seeing her for the first time. I guessed that she had never asserted herself before, never stood up to him, never contradicted his notion of his own male superiority—at least not in public. I also guessed that the honeymoon was over and so were the terms of endearment.

"Personally, whenever *I* feel a bug coming on, I run to the chiropractor," Gayle said. "It's astonishing how the manipulation of the vertebrae stimulates the immune system."

I looked at Kenneth, who was stimulating the cigar in his mouth, twisting it around, pulling it out, sticking it back in. I suspected that Kenneth didn't consult a chiropractor when he was feeling poorly; he sought out women of the Heidi Fleiss variety.

Lloyd was in the process of asking Dorothy what was being said when Sam finally showed up.

"Sorry I'm late, everybody. Again."

He pulled out the chair next to Pat and sat down.

He was a striking figure in his formal clothes—the tall, lean body, the dark, wavy, newly trimmed hair, the crisp white shirt against the lightly tanned complexion. He looked as wonderful in a tuxedo as he did in running shorts and swimming trunks, a man for all wardrobes. I had to remind myself to breathe.

"You must like making grand entrances," I said, leaning over Pat to talk to him.

He shook his head. "I'm just one of those chronically late people," he explained. "I'm never on time, no matter how hard I try."

I'd always detested chronically late people, but I quickly made an exception in Sam's case.

"So," he said, glancing at the empty chair to his left. "Is Jackie up in her stateroom waiting for the CNN sports report to come on?" Apparently, they had discussed her passion for sports the night before, while I was discussing Smallbone kitchens with Gayle.

"No, she's nursing a virus," said Pat. "She didn't feel like coming down to dinner."

"Sorry to hear it," said Sam. "Has she taken anything for it?"

"We've already been through that, okay?" Rick snapped.

Sam laughed. "Sure. Far be it from me to bore you all."

Mercifully, both Manfred and Ismet descended on our table at that very moment. Manfred took our wine orders. Ismet told us the specials; as this was Italian Night, he was pushing the osso bucco.

"What the hell's ass-o buck-o?" Rick asked his wife, in the same hostile manner in which he had asked about the coq au vin the previous evening.

"You're Italian. You figure it out," Brianna said with a definite edge to her voice. Clearly, she had not gotten over their last little exchange.

"I'm *half*-Italian," said Rick. "On my father's side. But it was my mother that did the cooking. Like women are *supposed* to do."

"Are you suggesting that *I* should spend our entire marriage in the kitchen?" Brianna challenged. "Just because that's how your mother spent hers?"

"You got a problem with the way my mother did things?" Rick demanded.

Before Brianna could up the ante, Ismet queried the newlyweds about their dinner selections.

"I'll have the osso bucco," said Brianna, glaring at her husband.

"Just give me some spaghetti and meatballs, okay, Ishmael?" said Rick.

Ismet bowed and hurried off to fetch our orders.

Actually, the food was a lot better than it had been the night before, and I enjoyed every bite of my chicken alla romana. But mostly, I enjoyed talking to Sam—or rather, listening to him. After Pat told him all about her kids, he told us all about his brother's kids—six-year-old twin girls who visited him often in Albany. He seemed very attached to the children, a real doting uncle, but was refreshingly open about how daunted he was by the idea of raising kids of his own.

He'll make a wonderful father someday, I found myself thinking as he recounted his most recent Christmas with his little nieces. An honest, loving father. I knew full well that I was idealizing him; that, should he ever have kids, he could be as big a rat as my father was. But for the time being, I chose to buy the image of Sam as God, which is what happens when you're in the throes of blinding passion.

During dessert, while Pat was telling Sam about Bill and his work (there was talk of hiatal hernias and spastic colons and conditions that were not exactly appetite enhancers), Dorothy tapped me on the arm and asked if I'd ever been married.

"Yes," I said. "Briefly. I'm divorced."

She nodded sympathetically. "Divorce is so common in our society today, and I just can't understand it. Lloyd and I have managed to stay together for over sixty-five years—longer than our parents were alive."

"What's your secret?" I asked. "There must be something you two have learned about long and happy marriages that the rest of us haven't."

She smiled knowingly. "The secret to a long and happy marriage is sex, dear."

"Sex?" I said. I'd been expecting a sanctimonious little speech about trust and mutual respect and the need for partners to communicate with each other.

"Yes, sex," she insisted. "Lloyd and I still screw like bunnies."

I glanced over at Lloyd, who couldn't even guide his forkful of cannoli into his mouth. Half of it landed on the jacket of his tuxedo.

"He's an incredible lover," said Dorothy. Then she closed her eyes, either because she was getting in touch with some erotic memory or because it was past her bedtime. Her eyes remained closed for several seconds.

"Dorothy?" I asked.

She didn't answer.

"Dorothy?" I said again, nudging her gently this time. The thought crossed my mind that she might be dead.

"Yes?" she said finally, opening her eyes very slowly.

"Everything all right?"

She beamed. "Everything's wonderful," she said. "My husband and I are madly in love. Aren't we, Lloyd?"

"What did you say, Dorothy?" Lloyd shouted.

"I said, aren't we madly in love?" Dorothy repeated.

Lloyd didn't smile at his wife of sixty-five years, nor did he tell her he loved her. But in a gesture of unexpected tenderness for a man so crusty and cranky, he brought his hand up to her face and stroked her cheek.

"I told you," she giggled, winking at me.

"Yes, you did," I smiled, envying her.

———

After dinner, Pat, Sam and I decided to pass on the Elvis Presley revue and opted for the casino. We each got a bucket of quarters, found three slot machines that looked interesting, and hunkered down. Sam played one called Jackpot Jungle, Pat tried her hand at the Double Diamond Deluxe, and I worked the one called Super Joker. I'd never been much of a gambler, given that I was the type of person who abhorred risks, and yet there was something oddly thrilling about inserting that quarter in the slot, pulling the lever, and waiting to see if all the little apples and oranges and strawberries lined up the way they were supposed to. It was especially thrilling to win—even a dollar or two. All the lights on the machine would start flashing and the bells and buzzers would go off and the coins would come pouring out into your waiting hands. Still, all thrills aside, I couldn't imagine spending my days and nights at a slot machine and I wondered about those who did. As I surveyed the people in the casino that night, I noticed that many of them were women—women who sat, all alone, at a machine, cigarette in one hand, cocktail in the other, and played and lost and played and won and played and lost, and so on. Was this how they eased their loneliness, escaped a bad marriage, compensated for a humdrum life? Was gambling away a bucket or two of change a more socially acceptable type of rebellion than, say, running off to Mexico with a tall, dark stranger?

Speaking of tall, dark strangers, Sam walked over to my machine, leaned over, and said, "A bucket of quarters for your thoughts, little lady?"

I laughed. "My thoughts aren't worth that much, believe me."

"Enjoying yourself?"

"Sure. You?"

He nodded. "Although I think I've had it with the casino. I'd rather take a walk on the Promenade Deck. Want to join me?"

I checked my watch. It was eight forty-five. I had planned to go back to my cabin and call Harold. But the last time Sam had asked me to join him, for breakfast that morning, I'd said I had to call my office. I couldn't very well refuse him a second time by telling him I had to call my boss. Harold would just have to wait.

"I'd love to. Let's find Pat," I said, scanning the room for my friend. When I spotted her, she was still hovering over the Double Diamond Deluxe.

"Making a killing?" I asked her as she played her last quarter and had nothing but an empty bucket to show for it.

She shrugged with embarrassment. "I'm afraid I'm not very propitious at this," she said.

"Proficient, you mean?" I asked.

She nodded.

"Nobody is," Sam said reassuringly. "That's why they'll all be back here tomorrow. To try again."

"I feel better then," Pat sighed with relief.

"Listen, how about taking a walk on the Promenade Deck?" I suggested to her. "We can all work off Italian Night."

She glanced at Sam, then back at me. I knew what she was thinking: that three was a crowd. I also knew that she was being asked to make a decision, and I knew how long *that* could take. I tried to hurry her along. "What do you say, Pat? Will you come?" Sure, I wanted to be alone with Sam. But I despise women who dump their female friends the minute a guy enters the picture.

We waited as she deliberated. Sam was very patient. Finally, she said she wanted to go upstairs and check on Jackie.

"Are you sure?" Sam asked. "It's a beautiful night."

Pat smiled as she regarded me. This was a new situation for us, an entirely new situation. In the past, whenever the Three Blond Mice took a vacation, it was usually Jackie who met men, not me. Never me. Suddenly, the balance of our friendship had shifted. Suddenly, I was the one in heat.

"I'm sure," she said.

"Tell Jackie sweet dreams," I said. Pat left Sam and me alone.

"So? Ready for a walk?" he said.

"Ready," I said.

He put his hand on the small of my back, against the zipper of my dress, as he guided me out of the casino. His touch felt so exquisite that I literally shivered. I hoped he didn't notice how out of practice I was at being touched by a man.

When we got outside, onto the Promenade Deck, the air was breezy and warm, like the night before, but not as clear. There were masses of clouds overhead, obscuring the moon and the stars. As a result, the atmosphere was moody, mysterious, dramatic.

"Let's walk over there," Sam said, pointing toward the stern of the ship, where I had stood twenty-four hours earlier and watched the wake churning below.

I agreed and we walked toward the rear of the *Princess Charming*. Sam chose a secluded, out-of-the-way spot by the railing, sort of an alcove where the hull of the ship met the open deck area. It was dark and narrow and a little scary there, and if I'd been by myself, I would have been looking over my shoulder. But I was not by myself. I was with a man I liked. What was there to worry about?

"Cigarette?" Sam asked as the breeze blew a lock of his dark hair into his eyes. He combed it back in place with his long, tapered fingers.

"No, thanks. I don't smoke."

"Good. Neither do I."

"Then why did you ask me if I wanted a cigarette?"

"I don't know. I'm wearing a tuxedo and you're wearing a fancy dress and we're standing on the deck of a ship looking out to sea at night. It seemed like the kind of thing a really suave guy in this situation would say to a woman. That, or: 'Happy, darling?' "

I laughed. "You've seen too many Bette Davis movies."

"Guilty. But there's nothing like an old movie line when you don't know how else to get a conversation going."

"Don't tell me you're at a loss for words."

"No. I'm at a loss for the *right* words. You don't miss much, Slim. A guy's got to be real careful what he says around you." Slim. A nickname. No, it wasn't "beauty" or "beloved" but it was a damn sight better than "snuggle bunny." Actually, I rather liked it. I especially liked the way he said it. His tone was affectionate, playful, personal. "The truth is, I feel a certain pressure to keep up with you in the *bon mot* department," he admitted.

"Oh, God. Another man with a case of performance anxiety," I groaned.

He laughed. "Are you as hard on yourself as you are on others?"

"You bet. Except when it comes to my ex-husband. I'm harder on him than I am on anyone else."

"Ah, yes. You mentioned that you dislike him intensely. Thanks to Leah, the one who worked at his funeral homes."

"That was Lola. Leah is my assistant at Pearson & Strulley. Or at least, she was."

"What happened?"

"My boss promoted her today. Without bothering to tell me."

"You must be pretty pissed off."

I nodded. "But not as pissed off as I was about Lola. Eric used to say she was an artist when it came to dead bodies. It turned out she wasn't bad with live ones either."

"I'm sorry." Sam attempted to squelch a laugh.

"I wasn't being funny."

"But you are funny. The way you put things makes me smile. I can't help it."

I brightened. I loved it when he smiled. When *I caused him* to smile.

"Your friend Pat was telling me about her marriage at dinner tonight," he said, "how her ex-husband's medical career and her concentration on the children split them up. She still loves him, anyone can see that. And she's crazy about her kids and her house and her life in the suburbs. She sounded pretty content, except for Bill's not being around."

I was surprised that Sam would remember Bill's name—who catches every detail of their dinner companion's anecdotes?—and then I realized that Pat had probably invoked Bill's name seventy-two times in the fifteen minutes they were talking.

"She wants Bill back, plain and simple," I said. "She thinks if they get back together it'll be different this time; that they're older and wiser now."

"What do you think? Is she kidding herself?"

I shrugged. "They're older, we all are. But who knows about the wiser? Wisdom is sort of in the eye of the beholder, you know? If Bill comes back to her, Pat will think he's wiser. If she evolves into the kind of woman he wants to come back to, he'll think she's wiser."

"Thank you, Dr. Zimmerman."

"My pleasure."

"What about all the money he's been paying her in alimony and child support? His resentment over that will be hard to overcome."

"How would you know about his resentment?"

"Pat mentioned it."

"Oh. Well, he may resent the money he's been shelling out, but he's never missed a payment. He's been pretty good to those kids, from a financial standpoint."

"How about from an emotional standpoint? Is he there for them, other than taking care of them while Pat's on vacation?"

I shrugged. "He's a man."

Sam laughed. "Was that an answer of some sort?"

I laughed too. "Sorry. I had a father who wasn't there. Emotionally or otherwise, so I'm not exactly objective on the subject of men and fatherhood." I gave Sam the gory details.

"How about your mother? What role did she play in your father's unhappiness?"

"His *unhappiness?* Is that what you call his philandering?"

"Well, he obviously wasn't happy with your mother. Why else would he seek out other women?"

"Because . . ." I stopped. "How the hell do I know why men do what they do?"

"Easy does it, Slim. I was only suggesting that sometimes it takes two to break up a marriage; that maybe your mother wasn't Mother Teresa."

"No, she was better dressed."

He smiled. "Would you rather talk about something else?"

I nodded.

"What about Jackie?" he asked. "What went wrong in her marriage?"

"Peter found someone he wanted to be married to more than he wanted to be married to Jackie. Someone with money. Someone who puts sachets in her dresser drawers."

"I don't—"

"Sorry. Let me back up a little. Jackie and Peter met in college," I explained. "They were hippies. They lived off the land."

"And then Peter decided he wanted a woman who lived off a trust fund and put sachets in her dresser drawers?"

"Exactly. Peter's taste changed. In the old days, he was perfectly happy with a woman who wore overalls. He and Jackie got married, started J&P Nursery, and made a success of the place. Then he decided he would be happier if the woman he was married to wore pearls."

"But they still work together?"

"Yup. Professionally, they're a good partnership. *Were* a good partnership. Now Peter wants to make a veritable empire out of J&P Nursery and Jackie doesn't want to expand or be bought out of the business. Things are extremely tense between them at the moment. Which only goes to show that men are fickle creatures. You never know what they're going to do."

"No, Slim. You never do."

To prove his point, Sam did the most unexpected thing: he leaned over and kissed me on the cheek!

I was so startled, I could only stand there and stare at him, saying absolutely nothing. His lips were so gentle and soft and the gesture so sweet and unthreatening that, when he pulled back, I actually placed my hand on my face, on the very spot where his mouth had been, just to feel the warmth there. I was reminded of Lloyd Thayer; of the way he had stroked Dorothy's cheek and how the tenderness of the act had surprised me; of the fact that Lloyd and Dorothy had been married for sixty-five years.

"I guess I found a way to render you speechless," Sam laughed. "I killed you with kindness."

"You're full of surprises," I said, trying to recover. The last man who had kissed me on the cheek was Harold, my boss, the day he told me I was one of the most valuable members of his team. Of course, now I couldn't get him to return my calls. "Why did you do that?" I asked Sam, truly wanting to know.

He shrugged. "It was a reflex, an impulse. Don't you ever do things that are completely spontaneous?"

"Almost never."

"Well, I do. Besides, I didn't have to stoop that low to kiss you."

"Stoop that low to—"

"That didn't come out right. I meant, I didn't have to contort like a pretzel to kiss you, given that we're not that far apart in height."

"I see." For once, my tallness was coming in handy.

I was still absorbing what had happened when Captain Solberg's voice intoned over the PA system for his nine o'clock report.

"Good evening, ladies and gentlemen. Dis is your captain speaking."

Sam checked his watch and nodded. "He's right on time. Second night in a row."

"Ve are continuing our southeasterly track," Captain Solberg informed us, "past Cuba and den on to our first port of call, Isle de Svan. Ve vill be arriving tomorrow morning at seven-thirty and anticipate a beautiful day on da island. The temperature currently is seventy-eight degrees Fahrenheit and da skies are partly cloudy. Ve vish you a pleasant evening from da Bridge Deck of da *Princess Charming.*"

"I'm looking forward to this Isle de Swan," I said after Captain Solberg had signed off. "But how are they going to get all twenty-five hundred of us off the ship and onto the tiny island? There can't be a pier like there was in Miami."

"No, there isn't. They've got these tenders—they're like small barges that seat about a hundred people—and they shuttle you between the ship and the island. It can take hours to get everybody over and back. Since the ship only stays in port until four o'clock, I suggest you get in line early for the tenders if you want to spend more than ten minutes on the island."

"I thought you said this was your first cruise? You seem to know more than my travel agent."

"I bought a couple of those guide books that tell you about each ship. They rate the food, the rooms, the entertainment, all of it. The only thing they leave out is the company. They can't predict what your fellow passengers will be like."

"All right then. How would you rate the passengers on this ship?"

"Fishing, are we?" he smiled wryly.

"Of course I'm not." Of course I was.

"Okay. From what I've seen so far, I'd rate the passengers on the *Princess Charming* well above average. Very interesting."

"Oh, please. The people on this ship are about as interesting as a perfume seminar."

"I'm talking about you, Slim."

"Me?" He inched closer to me again. I involuntarily backed up. I was practically hanging over the railing.

"Yes, you," he said. "I've never met anyone like you."

"Come on. You don't even know me." My voice was high, squeaky, slightly hysterical. This was all so surprising. Wished for, yes. Fantasized about, certainly. But even my most vivid fantasies hadn't pictured things moving so fast.

"No," Sam acknowledged. "I don't know you. But I can't stop thinking about you."

Here comes the bullshit, I thought as Sam drew even closer. This guy probably shovels this line at women left and right. And after that nonsense about being at a loss for words. He could be a gigolo, for all I knew. One of those men who works cruise ships, trolling for single, unattached, wealthy women. Middle-aged women.

"I'm not sure *why* I can't stop thinking about you," Sam went on. "Frankly, you're as infuriating as you are funny. We've only spent a little time together, but each time we *are* together, I can't decide if you're a pain in the ass or the 'find' of the century."

"Well, why don't I just go back to my cabin and await your decision?"

"I didn't mean it that way. All I'm saying is that I didn't expect to enjoy this cruise, and now I am enjoying it. Very much. That was a compliment, Elaine."

"Thank you."

"You see, I wasn't in a vacation mood when I left Albany. I've been considering a career change and it's been weighing heavily on me."

"A career change? You mean, because of all the traveling you have to do?"

"Yes. That's a big part of it."

"But you said you enjoyed the insurance business; that it was in your genes."

"I did say that, didn't I."

I nodded. We were still standing very close together. We were standing so close together that, when I nodded, the tip of my nose brushed against his Adam's apple.

"Look, I don't want to bore you with my business problems," he said, pulling back suddenly. "I think this week's going to be a lot of fun. I'll worry about what happens after the trip after the trip."

Not me. *I* was calling Harold the minute I got back to my cabin.

"Now," Sam said, loosening his tie and unbuttoning his tuxedo jacket. "What do you say we lighten things up and head downstairs to the disco?"

"The disco? Why would we want to go there?"

"So we can dance, obviously."

"I'm not much of a dancer. I've been told that I lead."

"Nobody leads when you go disco dancing. You just step onto the dance floor and relax."

"I don't know how to relax."

"Sure you do." Sam took hold of my hand. It was the third time our skin had made contact. I was keeping track.

"I'm warning you," I said as he led me away. "Dancing isn't my thing."

"You'll have the time of your life," he said. "Trust me."

"I never trust people who say: 'Trust me.' "

" 'Never' is a long time, Slim."

8

The *Princess Charming*'s disco, like its restaurants and boutiques, was well meaning but tacky, with walls the color of Pepto-Bismol and black Naugahyde sofas. When Sam and I walked in, everybody was dancing to that overplayed song of several years ago, "Feelin' Hot! Hot! Hot!," which wasn't a disco song at all. It had a Latin beat and was better suited to Pat's marengue class. Presently, it was the basis for a Toyota commercial—reason enough not to want to dance to it, I thought.

Nevertheless, Sam dragged me out onto the dance floor, where I remained through a half-dozen numbers. At first, I felt terribly self-conscious. It helped somewhat that Sam was taller than I was; that *I* wasn't the one towering over everybody like the Fifty-Foot Woman. But I had no sense of rhythm, no connection with my own body, no patience for songs that lasted an eternity and consisted of lyrics like "Boogie oogie oogie."

"Relax," Sam urged. "Try."

"I am." I did. For me. I wiggled ever so slightly to the music, occasionally snapping my fingers and bouncing my head up and down for extra effect, and in spite of my initial resistance, I began to have fun.

Sam, it turned out, was a pretty good dancer for a white male. He was loose and graceful, especially given his height, and so very dashing in his black tuxedo. I wasn't the only one who noticed, either; several women were staring at him with their tongues hanging out.

Sorry, he's with *me,* I smiled smugly. The question was, *why* was he with me? In spite of his remark about not being able to stop thinking about me, about how he'd never met anyone like me, I couldn't help wondering what a catch like Sam Peck was doing with an uptight, bony ass like me. Were we headed for a romance, he and I? Impossible, I thought. Romances were a fiction, a plot device in books and movies. But then how to explain the fact that I was drawn to Sam in a way I'd never before been drawn to a man? That Sam seemed interested in me too? That even though I hadn't wanted to take a sea cruise, I was having the time of my life?

We danced until nine forty-five or until my hair frizzed, whichever came first. At some point, the deejay announced that it was "Karaoke Time!" The crowd applauded enthusiastically. I turned to Sam and said, "What does 'karaoke' mean, anyway? It sounds like some terribly contagious Asian disease."

"I don't have a clue," he said.

"And what's so wonderful about it? If people want to sing along with famous songs, let them do it in their car."

"I guess that means you won't be taking the microphone tonight," Sam smiled.

I shook my head.

Just then, the music started and people were lining up to take their turn at the microphone. The first tune was "Made in the U.S.A." and the first person to sing it was Lenny Lubin. Picture Jackie Mason doing Bruce Springsteen and you'll have a sense of what we had to endure. When Lenny was finished, the crowd cheered–because he was stepping down from the microphone, not because he was any good–and he came straight over to where Sam and I were sitting.

"Hey, am I a star or what?" he said, patting his orange hair to make sure it was still in place after all his gyrations.

"You were great, Lenny. Just great," I said.

"Thanks. Who's this?" he asked, nodding at Sam.

"Sam Peck," Sam volunteered. "Glad to meet you."

"Lenny Lubin. Lubin's Lube Jobs. If you're ever in Massapequa and need an oil change, stop in," said Lenny.

"Massapequa is in Long Island," I whispered to Sam. "Not too far from Manhattan."

"Thanks for helping this poor, lost, small-town boy through the highways and byways of life," Sam whispered back.

"What business are you in?" Lenny asked him.

"Insurance," Sam replied.

"Which outfit?"

"Dickerson Life."

"Dickerson? Never heard of 'em."

"Our headquarters are in Albany. I've been with them for ten years."

I looked at Sam. "You told me you've been with them for fifteen years."

"No, Elaine. I couldn't have said that. You must have me mixed up with Kenneth, at our table. He said he's been in the brokerage business for fifteen years."

I shrugged. I suppose I could have been wrong. But I wasn't usually, when it came to things people told me about themselves. I always listened intently when they volunteered the little details of their lives, because knowledge was power. The more you knew about people, the better you could protect yourself against them, should they turn out to be liars and cheats.

"Does this Dickerson write automobile policies? Homeowner? Flood? What?" Lenny asked Sam.

"All of the above," he said. "Our motto is: When you go with Dickerson, *in*surance means *a*ssurance."

"Very catchy," I said.

Lenny hung around for a few more minutes, asking me where the other two "lovelies" were. I told him. Eventually, he said he was going back to his cabin. He said he wanted to change out of his tuxedo into something more comfortable, so he could come back for some serious dancing.

"Want to stay? Go?" said Sam after we were free of Lenny.

"Go, I guess," I said. "I think I'm discoed out."

Sam helped me up. We were walking out of the disco when we ran into Henry Prichard, who was escorting a blond woman in a pale pink strapless dress. At first, he acted as if he'd never met me, even though we'd been introduced only the day before. And then, when I said hello and reminded him that I was Jackie Gault's friend, he actually said, "Jackie who?"

"Gault," I said. "You had an after-dinner drink with her last night."

"Oh, *Jackie,*" he said, nodding vigorously. He was still wearing the Pirates baseball cap. With his tuxedo. I suspected that his brief amnesia had more to do with staying in the good graces of the blonde in the pink strapless than it did with forgetting Jackie. After all, hadn't Henry come up to Deck 8, just before dinner, specifically asking about her? Isn't that what Kingsley had said? Or had Pat and I just assumed—

"I'm Sam Peck," said Sam, shaking hands with both Henry and his date, whose name turned out to be Ingrid. She was Swedish.

"Henry Prichard. Good to see ya."

Henry didn't even ask how Jackie was feeling, I noticed with disappointment. Or even say something innocuous like: "Give her my best regards."

"Enjoying the cruise?" I asked him and Ingrid.

"It's sensational!" Henry enthused. "Best thing I ever did. I swear to God, when I get back to Altoona, I'm gonna sell so many cars they're gonna have to let me win this cruise again!"

"How about you, Ingrid? Are you having fun?" I asked.

"Thank you. How are you?" she smiled.

Ingrid didn't speak much English but she was very pretty. I guessed that Henry wouldn't be talking baseball with *her.*

"How's the sinus infection?" I asked Henry, just to be polite. I remembered that he had told Jackie, the night before, that he'd come back to his cabin to take his antibiotics.

He looked at me blankly for a second or two. Then said, "Oh, that." He pressed his fingers on his cheekbones, underneath his eyes, and shook his head. "I'm better but I'm not home free. Still got that blocked head."

That's because you're a blockhead, I thought. I mean, this guy didn't seem to remember anything.

Eventually, I let Henry go on with his evening, vowing not to tell Jackie I'd even bumped into him.

"Aren't you the social butterfly," Sam said as we made our way out of the disco and walked toward the elevator.

"Me?"

"First, there was Skip. Then, there was Lenny. Now, there's Henry. Have you met all the single men on this ship in only two days?"

"All but two or three," I joked, hoping the question was evidence that Sam was jealous.

We strolled along the hall, a safe distance from one another, and stopped when we got to the elevator. Once there, we stood in silence for a couple of minutes, just the two of us, each waiting for the other to press the UP button, knowing that, once we got inside the elevator, we would have to determine which of our floors we would be going to and what we would do when we got there. We were living that excruciatingly uncomfortable moment when you're out with a man you've met on vacation and things are winding down and neither of you is sure how to end the evening or even if you *should* end the evening. Do you go to his room? Does he go to yours? Or do you each repair to your own room, leaving the other person wanting more? And if you *do* decide to call it a night right there at that elevator, *how* do you call it a night? Do you kiss? Shake hands? Flash the "Peace" sign? Do you stand there, the demure little woman, hoping the guy will direct the action? Or do *you* take control, knowing that whatever you do, you'll spend half the night second-guessing yourself?

All of this awkward silence was made more awkward by the fact that a squall had flared up outside and the ship was beginning to roll in a thoroughly unpleasant manner.

"Thanks for taking me dancing," I said finally, breaking the tension.

"You're welcome," Sam said.

"I had fun at the disco," I said.

"Sure you did." His blue eyes were skeptical.

"I really did. Trust me."

"I never trust people who say, 'Trust me.' "

I laughed.

"Are you going running tomorrow morning?" he asked.

"If this little storm we're having passes."

"Let's meet at the Promenade Deck at seven-thirty."

"I'll be there."

"And we'll have breakfast afterwards."

"I'd like that."

"I guess you and Pat and Jackie will be going over to Isle de Swan together?"

"If Jackie's feeling better. But you're more than welcome to come along with us."

"I would. Like to come along, that is." He paused, then moved closer to me. I could feel his hot, disco-charged breath on my hair. There was a faint scent of garlic, too. From Italian Night. "I guess it's pretty obvious that I'd like to see more of you."

"More of me?" How did he mean that, exactly? More of me, as in: more often? Or more of me, as in: with fewer clothes on?

"Yes, more of you. I told you before, I don't know quite what to make of you. You definitely require more study." He smiled over his eyeglasses.

"Sort of like a science project?" I asked, my breathing becoming shallower the nearer to me he drew. And the nearer to me he drew, the farther from him I shrank—strictly out of nervousness, you understand, and because I was so rusty at situations like this—until I backed right up against the elevator and inadvertently leaned on the UP button.

"Is something wrong?" Sam asked.

"Wrong? No," I said, unwilling to admit how off balance I was, how much I *longed* for Sam to kiss me. "I just didn't want you to think I'm easy."

He laughed. "No one could ever think you're easy, Slim."

"I get easier as you get to know me," I promised, hoping he wouldn't give up.

Reading my mind, Sam bent over and was about to press his lips to mine when the elevator arrived. Thanks to me.

We broke apart and glared resentfully at the elevator doors as they opened to reveal six or eight nuns. Needless to say, the romantic spell was broken.

Sam and I squeezed in among the sisters, pressed the buttons for our respective floors, and rode upstairs. We got to his floor first. Right before he stepped out of the elevator, he touched my arm and whispered, "See you in the morning."

"See you," I said back, hoping the nuns were pleased that Sam and I were ending the evening on such a chaste note.

Oh well, I thought. There were still five nights left.

Before going to my room (which was no small feat, as the boat's pitching and rolling made walking down the hall an adventure), I stopped at Pat's cabin for an update on Jackie's condition, but they both had DO NOT DISTURB signs hanging from their doorknobs. I figured they'd gone to sleep and would tell me how everything was in the morning.

Once in my stateroom I sank onto the bed, the covers of which Kingsley had expertly turned down, and realized that I was not the least bit sleepy. In fact, I was wired, antsy, restless. I felt like a high school kid who'd just come home from a hot date and was dying to share the juicy details with someone. The trouble was, there was no "someone."

It was a few minutes after ten. I flipped on the television and settled back to watch the news on CNN. The reception kept fading in and out, I assumed because of the squall, but I did catch a few of the stories they were reporting. There was something about interest rates. There was something about Prince William. There was something about hydroponic tomatoes. And just as I was starting to unwind, there was something about Dina Witherspoon getting arrested for lifting that goddamn bracelet from the jewelry counter at Neiman Marcus!

I shot up off the bed.

The picture on the screen was grainy and the sound was unclear, but there was no mistaking my client, surrounded by the media, as she was being led away in handcuffs from her Dallas hotel.

"I thought *you* were handling this, Leah!" I said out loud, incensed that Dina Witherspoon's reputation—and Pearson & Strulley's—had been placed in the hands of a neophyte, *my* neophyte!

Suddenly, the television reception fizzled out completely and the set went black. I wasn't sorry. Now I wouldn't have to watch stories about the scandals involving my *other* two clients.

That was it. I was calling Harold. He was a night person, I knew, and was often up until one or two in the morning. But I didn't care what time it was. This was my chance to remind him of my indispensability to the company; to make it perfectly clear that if *I* had been handling the Dina Witherspoon matter, her image would not have been splashed across television screens around the world as if she were a common criminal; that if my assistant was to be promoted, *I* should have been the one doing the promoting.

I weaved my way over to the phone, grabbing on to furniture so I wouldn't be tossed around by the ship's pitching and rolling. I lifted the receiver, gave the operator my credit card number, dialed Harold's home number, and waited. I was not surprised when the static on the line was even worse than it had been the day before, given the awful television reception. Still, I hoped the connection would clear just long enough for me to make my point with my boss.

I waited a few more seconds. The call was taking an awfully long time to go through. All I heard was buzzing and humming and crackling.

I wondered why Sea Swan Cruises even bothered to equip each cabin with a television and a telephone if both were so easily knocked out by a few rain showers. It will not shock you to learn that I can be just as irritated by inanimate objects that let me down as by people who do.

Several more seconds elapsed and the connection still hadn't been made. I was about to hang up and place the call again when I heard a man's voice very faintly. I assumed it was Harold saying: "Hello."

"Harold!" I yelled. "It's Elaine Zimmerman! I'm calling from the *Princess Charming!*"

In the way of a response, I expected something along the lines of: "Elaine, what a surprise." Or: "Elaine, get yourself on a plane and come home. Pearson & Strulley needs you." Or at the very least: "Elaine, what the hell are you doing calling me at home at this time of night?"

Instead, there was no response at all. Not to me, anyway. After I heard the man's voice, I heard another man's voice answering the first one. And then the first man said something back to the second one. It finally dawned on me that neither of these two men was Harold and that neither of them could hear me.

The phone lines must be crossed, I realized, remembering how the same thing had happened to me once in New York. I had picked up the phone in my apartment one Saturday night, intending to order Chinese food from the place around the corner, when instead of getting the owner of Pan Central Station, where they made heavenly moo goo gai pan, I got two Jamaican women arguing over which of them made better curried goat. I reported the problem to the phone company from a neighbor's apartment, and the repair person I spoke to said the line would be cleared within twenty-four hours. It wasn't. For two whole days, I was forced to eavesdrop on conversations that weren't worth eavesdropping on.

"Hello? Hello?" I said to the two men. "Can either of you hear me?"

They went right on chattering, as if I hadn't said a word, their voices tinny, garbled, annoying.

I was about to hang up in disgust when I heard one of the men tell the other man that the weather was nice and warm, the *Princess Charming* was much bigger than he had expected, and he was having a reasonably good time.

"I'm glad to hear it," the other one said. "I knew you'd see things my way."

Maybe it's a son calling his father up north to thank him for sending him on the cruise, I thought. Or maybe it's the father calling his son up north to thank *him* for sending him on the trip. The voices were so distorted I couldn't even guess at the ages of the men they belonged to.

Again, I was about to hang up when the conversation started to get interesting.

"So what line of bull have you been handing the other passengers?" asked the first man.

The other man's response was practically unintelligible, even though he was the one speaking from the ship, while the other one was somewhere in the States. His voice kept breaking up, and all I could make out was: ". . . not the problem."

"Then what is? You wouldn't have spent a fortune on a ship-to-shore call if there wasn't a problem," said the first man. "Sounds to me like everything's going according to plan."

". . . don't know if I . . . through with it."

"What are you talking about? Of course, you're going through with it. You don't have any choice, remember?"

". . . harder than . . . it would be. Now that I . . . her."

"Give me a break. She's a nightmare."

"She's not so . . ."

"You wouldn't say that if *you* had her for an ex-wife."

I giggled to myself. The remark reminded me of something Eric would say.

"You sure you want me to . . ."

"I've never been surer about anything in my life. What I'm not sure about is *you*. You've gotta stop calling me from the ship."

"Sorry. It's just that . . . needed . . . hear you . . . me again what a . . . she is."

"Open your eyes and see for yourself what a pain in the ass she is! She's right there on that fucking boat!" The man paused to collect himself. "Let me put it another way," he continued. "If you don't do the job, I'm going to go right to the—"

"Stop. I know."

Know what? Do what job? What was going on here, anyway? I sensed that whatever I had stumbled onto was infinitely more sinister than curried goat.

"So we're clear?" asked the man on land.

"We're clear," conceded the man on the ship. "I said I'll . . . it and I will."

I'll *what* it? I wondered with growing alarm.

"You're sure?" the other man asked skeptically, impatiently, wearily. "No more whining?"

"You heard me," said the passenger. "Before the *Princess Charming* is back in Miami, your . . . will be as . . . as this . . ."

Your *what* will be as *what* as this *what?*

"What'd you say, pal?" the other man asked. "Our connection's breaking up."

The man who was speaking from somewhere on the ship, somewhere on *my* ship, somewhere on my *floor* for all I knew, then replied: "I said, before the ship is back in Miami, your ex-wife will be as dead as this phone line."

There was one click. Then another click. And then the line *was* dead.

Day Three:
Tuesday, February 12

9

The *Princess Charming* pulled into our first port of call, Isle de Swan, at 6:30 A.M., an hour earlier than scheduled. The nasty weather of the previous evening had cleared, and the day had metamorphosed into a radiantly sunny one with light breezes and calm waters.

My view of the island out my porthole was obscured by the lifeboat—and by my inability to keep my eyes open, thanks to my second sleepless night in a row—but as I pressed my face against the glass, I couldn't help but be dazzled by the colors, the textures, the picture-postcard perfectness of the scene before me. The sturdy blue of the Atlantic Ocean had given way to the shimmering turquoise of the Caribbean Sea. The flat, uninteresting terrain of south Florida had yielded to lush, green vegetation, flowering plants so vivid in hue they seemed almost cartoonish, hills and mountains dotted with pastel painted houses, and beaches made of sand that looked (from the distance, anyway) to be as fine grained and cottony soft as any I'd ever seen. And then, a few miles away from Isle de Swan or maybe *many* miles away—it was impossible to tell—was the looming presence on the horizon of other islands: to the east, the Haitian mainland and its neighbor, the Dominican Republic; to the west, Jamaica and Cuba. It struck me then, rather belatedly, that the *Princess Charming* wasn't just a gaudy pleasure vessel, laden with food and booze and people who equated a good time with overindulging. It was also a conveyance, a mode of transportation, a method of ferrying you from the grayness of your everyday life to places of genuinely breathtaking natural beauty—and it did so in a leisurely, dreamy way that airplanes, with their brisk, impersonal, get-'em-in-their-seats, feed-'em-a-bag-of-peanuts, and-get-'em-down attitude, couldn't match.

Welcome to the Caribbean, I thought, allowing myself a smile. Welcome to paradise.

Unfortunately, my smile didn't last long. As I stared out my porthole that Tuesday morning, I quickly sank into the memory of the phone conversation I'd overheard eight hours earlier. I'd spent the entire night worrying about the call, obsessing over it, debating what to do about it, and had reached no solid conclusions other than to take a couple of Extra-Strength Tylenols for the excruciating headache all the worrying, obsessing, and debating had given me.

What I couldn't get over, couldn't stop replaying in my mind, was that I had heard a man, a passenger on the *Princess Charming,* agree to murder another man's ex-wife, a woman who was also a passenger on the ship. In other words, among the 2,500 badly dressed passengers on the Sea Swan's pride and joy, there were two people headed toward a terrible destiny: a hit man and a woman about to be hit.

Now I ask you: Even if you weren't as fundamentally paranoid as I was, even if you weren't prone to seeing danger and intrigue where none existed, even if you weren't a woman whose ex-husband despised her enough to want her dead, wouldn't the situation keep *you* up at night?

I'd tried to remain calm in my dark cubbyhole of a cabin as the hours ticked by. Midnight. One A.M. Two A.M. And so forth. I'd told myself I must have misheard the conversation between the two men. There was so much static on the line that, for all I knew, they could have been having a cozy little family discussion, saying "mother" instead of "murder" and "dad" instead of "dead."

Or maybe the subject was more nautical in nature, given the setting, and the men were merely saying "keel" instead of "kill."

Or better yet, maybe, instead of uttering the words "ex-wife," the men were actually saying "ex-cite," as in: "You'd better *excite* the people on that boat before it's back in Miami."

Yes, that was it, I'd decided at about three o'clock in the morning. Perhaps the man who'd been speaking from the ship was an entertainer of some sort—one of those talentless acts the cruise line employs for its shows—and the man on the other end of the phone was simply his agent, acting tough and tyrannical the way agents often do.

Good try, I'd sighed heavily at about three-thirty in the morning. Yes, there were plenty of vocabulary words that sounded like those I *thought* I'd heard the two men use. But one of my few physical merits, other than my miraculously high HDL level, was my exceptional hearing. Eric used to make fun of it, whenever he was out cheating on me with Lola and didn't want me to find out. He'd sneak into the apartment, late at night, and tiptoe around in his bare feet so his shoes wouldn't squeak against the hardwood floor. Just when he thought he was home free, I'd call out from the bedroom: "Eric? Where the hell have you been?" "Jesus, Elaine. You must have bionic hearing," he'd mutter, as if it were *my* fault that he was at that funeral parlor letting Lola massage him with embalming lubricants. "Your ears are so good you could hear a bird shit," he'd add for good measure if he was feeling especially guilty.

I did have excellent hearing, so the fact that I *thought* I'd heard the two men on the phone discussing the murder of one of their ex-wives probably meant that I *had*.

The next way I'd tried to calm myself during the night was to consider the possibility that, even though I *had* heard the men talking about murdering the ex-wife, they could have only been *joking*. Men were always joking about the women they used to be married to. They were always joking about women, period. They joked about how we either nagged them or neglected them; how we were either sexually insatiable or hopelessly frigid; how we either spent too much money on clothes and gyms and beauty salons or cared so little about our appearance that we let ourselves go; how we were such a *trial* to deal with, given the ever-fragile balance of our hormones. We were one big joke with men. Ha ha ha.

But if the two men on the phone were just joking about one of them killing the other one's ex-wife, why weren't they laughing during their phone conversation? Static or no static, I didn't catch even a single chuckle.

No, by four o'clock in the morning, I'd had to face facts: some poor, unsuspecting woman was about to buy the farm. And it wasn't a huge stretch to wonder if either Jackie or Pat or I was that woman. But would Eric really arrange to have me murdered? Would Peter hire a hit man to bump off Jackie? Would Bill, a man who had taken the Hippocratic oath to save life, actually pay someone to take Pat's?

Neither of the men on the phone sounded like any of our ex-husbands. But then, both of the voices were terribly distorted, because of the bad connection, so how could I really be certain who was who or what was what?

I kept asking myself: Why would anyone want to murder Pat, Jackie, or me? We weren't perfect, God knows, but we didn't deserve to be cold-bloodedly, premeditatedly killed either. Particularly not while we were on vacation, which would be the ultimate in nastiness, in my opinion.

Still, at about five o'clock that morning, I almost ran down the hall, pounded on my friends' cabin doors, and woke them up to warn them of the possible threat to their lives. And then two things stopped me. First, I reminded myself that Jackie and Pat already thought me a hysteric. The minute I'd open my mouth to tell them the tale of the two men on the phone, Jackie would roll her eyes and say in that husky, tough-girl voice of hers, "Elaine, give it a rest," and then dismiss whatever I said as paranoid bullshit. And Pat would put her hand to her mouth and start to giggle, thinking I was just being incorrigible, like a wayward child. The whole thing would be reduced to yet another game of Cry Wolf; I had spoken of so many plots and intrigues and conspiracies over the years that they no longer took anything I said seriously.

No, they'd never believe me.

And why ruin their vacation? Particularly when there wasn't a shred of evidence that any of us was the intended target of the hit man's hit. There were dozens of ex-wives on the ship, judging by the large group of desperate-looking single women in the disco the previous night. Maybe the two men were plotting to kill one of *them*.

I decided that the very least I could do was report the crossed-wires situation to the Purser's Office.

I picked up the phone at six-forty. The line was perfectly clear. I dialed the appropriate extension and got the same British woman

I'd spoken to on my first day of the cruise. When I told her what had happened the night before (leaving out the murder plot), she confirmed that the ship-to-shore connections had been affected by the bad weather, as had the television satellite reception, but that everything was fine now.

Not exactly, I wanted to say but didn't.

I was supposed to meet Sam on the Promenade Deck at seven-thirty, and although I was exhausted beyond belief, I wasn't about to pass up a chance to go running with him and eat breakfast together. But it was only six forty-five. There was still time to take action regarding the murder plot, and I knew exactly which action I would take: I would speak to Captain Solberg himself—discreetly, of course.

I washed, ran a comb through my hair, threw on my running clothes, and climbed the stairwell up to the Bridge Deck instead of waiting for the elevator.

The Bridge Deck was the level just under the Sun Deck, where the pools and the Glass Slipper café were located. The officers' area was at the bow of the ship, was surrounded by immense glass portholes (I guessed it was more important for the captain to be able to see the sea than it was for me), and contained all the *Princess Charming*'s navigation equipment. In other words, the Bridge Deck was the helm, the place from which the ship was kept on course, a sort of very large and cushy cockpit. There were modular sofas and framed lithographs on the walls and high-pile carpeting in a shipshape oceanic blue. But mostly, there were men standing around in crisp white uniforms, the gold stripes on their shoulders indicating their rank. One of them asked me what I was doing there at such an early hour of the morning. The Bridge Deck, it turned out, was off limits to passengers except during specially scheduled tours.

"I'm sorry to just barge in here like this," I said, "but it's urgent that I speak to the captain."

"Urgent?" asked the man, who introduced himself as the ship's first officer but didn't look a day over eighteen. He was Scandinavian, like Captain Solberg, and just as remote.

"Yes, very urgent," I said, unwilling to be deterred.

First Officer Nilsen shrugged and went in search of the captain.

While he searched, I paced, glancing at the radar equipment, the navigation charts, the framed plaques commemorating the awards bestowed upon the *Princess Charming* by the cruise line industry. Eventually, Captain Solberg arrived.

"Yes? How can I help?" he asked.

He was big and blond and craggy-faced, a Nordic Superman. Or maybe he just seemed larger-than-life because I'd seen him on television and heard his voice on the PA system.

"Is there someplace where we could speak privately?" I asked.

He arched his bushy golden eyebrows in what was, for him, a showy display of emotion.

"I won't take up too much of your time," I assured him. "But it is important. Urgent, as I told First Officer Nilsen."

Captain Solberg looked skeptical, but resigned himself to escorting me back to his private office, a rather messy place littered with faxes, charts, and Styrofoam coffee cups. He pointed to the visitor's chair. I sat in it.

"Now, vat is da trouble?" he asked, while he sorted through some of the papers on his desk.

I recounted the whole sorry story. Captain Solberg did not look up from his desk until I mentioned the word "murder."

"You are traveling alone?" was his response to my tale of intrigue.

"With my two best friends," I said. "Oh. I see what you're getting at. No, I'm not at all certain that one of *us* is the target of the hit man. We could be, of course. All three of us are divorced. But no matter who the intended victim is, she's a passenger on your ship and so is the man who is out to murder her. He must be stopped! Right away!"

In response, Captain Solberg didn't exactly jump up, sound the ship's whistle, and summon the passengers to our mustering stations. He remained seated and remarkably calm and asked, "Is dis your first cruise, Mrs.—"

"Zimmerman," I said. "Yes, it is."

"And you are feeling a little qveasy?"

"Queasy? No. I feel fine."

"Vat about da ex-husband? Miss him a little now dat you are at sea?"

"Miss Eric? Yeah, like I'd miss a migraine," I said.

"So you get headaches, Mrs. Zimmerman? Have maybe been in da hospital for da headaches?"

"No, no. I was just making a. . . . Never mind."

"You know, Mrs. Zimmerman, I have been a ship's captain for over tventy-seven years, and I have seen many women who come aboard da ship and feel sad, suddenly. Afraid. It's nothing to be ashamed of. Dat's vy ve have so many vonderful activities to keep you busy and happy. So you von't be lonely."

"Hey, vait a minute. I mean, *wait* a minute." I couldn't believe it. Captain Solberg wasn't buying a word I said! He thought I was just another lonely divorcée, a nervous Nellie, a hysterical female. Well, all right. So maybe I *was* all of those things. But that had nothing to do with the two men who were plotting to kill a woman on the ship! "I'm telling you the truth," I said, sitting up very straight in my chair. "I know what I heard, and a game of bingo isn't going to change that."

"So you don't care for bingo," the captain mused. "Vell den, ve have a lovely casino. It might be fun for you and your friends to gamble a little. Forget da troubles back home."

"I'm already gambling, Captain Solberg," I said hotly. "I'm risking my life by being a passenger on this ship. There's a killer on board and you don't seem the least bit concerned."

"Oh, I am very concerned," he said, looking about as concerned as a person relaxing in a hammock. "Vould you like something to drink? Some coffee? Or a little fruit juice?"

Jesus. This guy actually thinks I'm nuts, I thought. Or thirsty.

"Captain, you're in charge of the *Princess Charming*. Isn't that right?" I asked, starting over.

"Of course. And she is da finest ship on da seas, vith four main engines and six—"

"Yes, yes. I know," I said, cutting him off before he delivered his entire televised speech. "What I'm trying to confirm is that passenger security is your responsibility. Correct?"

"Correct."

"And you care deeply about your passengers' welfare. Correct?"

"Correct."

"And if one of your male passengers was about to murder one of your female passengers, *you* would have the authority to arrest the man and have him taken into custody. Correct?" I felt like Marcia Clark, for God's sake.

"No."

"No?"

"No. I cannot arrest one of my passengers for a murder dat has not taken place, Mrs. Zimmerman. If da crime were actually committed, den I could do something. Not before."

"But if you can't do anything until the crime has been committed, it'll be too late," I insisted. "A woman will have been killed."

Captain Solberg rose from his chair, looming above me in his white uniform like a huge glass of milk. He lumbered over to my chair and helped me up. Then he opened one of his desk drawers, reached inside, and handed me a small package, prewrapped in cellophane and stamped with the *Princess Charming*'s charming logo.

"Here, here," he said in a soothing tone. I assumed he meant: There, there. "Ve hope you enjoy da cruise."

I studied the see-through package he had bestowed upon me. A parting gift. It contained several discount coupons to any of the ship's nine lounges, a free week's use of the health spa's StairMaster, a pass to the movie of my choice, and a packet of Dramamine.

"Try not to vorry so much," said Captain Solberg as he ushered me out of his office. He was not the first person to tell me not to worry so much, but he was the first person to tell me from a cruise ship on which a potential murderer was running around loose.

"I'll try," I said, clutching the package to my chest.

Emotionally and physically spent, yet looking forward to meeting Sam and going for a run, I walked to the elevator and pressed the DOWN button. When the elevator arrived, there was Skip Jamison standing inside. Again.

He was wearing another in his collection of colorful Hawaiian shirts, along with white shorts and a pair of Reeboks, and he was very involved with the music that echoed through the headphones of his Sony Walkman. In fact, he was so busy humming and nodding his head and snapping his fingers to the beat that he seemed not to notice me at first.

"Hey, it's Elaine. Cool," he said finally as we were descending, and lifted the headphones off his ears.

"Oh, hi, Skip," I said, still consumed with thoughts of hit men and ex-wives. "What are you up to?"

"Just getting in touch with my music on my way down to breakfast," he said cheerfully, tapping his feet to whatever song he'd been listening to.

"Well, don't let me interrupt," I said. "I'm not really awake yet, so I won't be very good company."

"I get it. You need your space. That's cool," he said. "I'll go back to my tunes." He placed the headphones over his ears and turned the volume up.

I smiled, wishing I could be so carefree. Then Skip shouted something at me, the way people always do when they forget they're wearing headphones and don't realize they're shouting.

"Great song," he yelled as he gave me the thumb's-up sign. "Eric Clapton's unplugged version of 'Layla.' "

I nodded absentmindedly.

"A classic rock 'n' roll tune," he roared over the guitar riff ringing in his ears. "But then, I love 'em all. All the really cool songs, especially the up-tempo ones."

That's nice, I thought, wishing Skip would shut up already.

"A lot of my friends think I'm way too top-forty in my taste," he went on.

"But you told me you liked the more mellow, New Age artists," I said, making conversation, reluctantly.

"What?" he yelled.

"I said, you told me you liked the New Age artists," I replied, much louder, thinking they could probably hear us in San Juan.

"Yeah, I like them too," Skip shouted. "I'm pretty much across the board when it comes to music. Classics. New Age. Top-forty. All the hits."

"Cool," I said.

"I guess you could call me a hit man," he said. "A fucking hit man."

I spun around to look at him. Was it possible that *Skip* was the man who was plotting to kill the woman on the ship? Dear sweet, laid-back Skip? He couldn't have needed the money to do the hit—he was an art director at a major ad agency, an agency known for its bloated salaries. Still . . .

"Skip?"

"Yeah?"

"Were you by any chance in your stateroom last night? At about ten o'clock?"

"Yeah, I was reading. Why?"

"Just curious," I said.

The very instant the elevator arrived at the Promenade Deck, I mumbled a tight "goodbye" to Skip and hightailed it out of there.

10

"**H**ey, hey, slow down," Sam cautioned as he saw me rushing out of the ship, onto the Promenade Deck. "The deck's still slick from last night's rain. You could fall and break one of those stilts of yours."

Stilts. The boy who lived next door to us when I was growing up always called my legs stilts, and I would cry myself to sleep over it. Now, Sam had just referred to them in the very same way, and I was thrilled.

He was stretched out in one of the loungers, his own stilts hanging over the end of the chair. He'd been waiting for me, as I was the one who was late for a change.

I stopped, caught my breath, and relaxed. "You're right. I *was* in a hurry. I just didn't want to be late for our date."

I rarely used the word "date," first, because I rarely had dates, and second, because I'd always equated dating with bungee jumping in terms of risk level. But its goofy, adolescent connotation felt appropriate somehow, especially after Sam and I had practically kissed on the lips the previous night—if not for the arrival of the elevator. With that near-kiss under our belts, we had moved our relationship up a notch, taken it to the "dating" level, acknowledged that, since the cruise lasted only seven days, we'd better get going if we wanted anything to happen in the romance department. That's one of the odd aspects of vacations; they last a finite period of time, and if you meet someone you like, you have to do away with some of the rules of the road and accelerate the getting-to-know-you process.

My fears about The Phone Call faded, at least temporarily. Sam looked so handsome sitting there, so benign in his T-shirt and running shoes, so un-murderer-ish.

Still, before he and I went running together, before things advanced any further between us, I *had* to ask him the question I had just asked Skip. I had to know if there was any chance that *he* could have been the one that made the call.

I inquired casually, "I was wondering, did you spend the rest of last night in your cabin? After we left each other?"

He peered at me over his eyeglasses, a wry expression on his face.

"No. I partied with the nuns we met in the elevator," he replied. "They were a wild bunch, let me tell you."

"Come on. I'm curious," I said.

"A couple of dances at the disco and you're keeping tabs on me already?" he teased.

"Of course not. I just want to know if you tried to watch TV in your stateroom last night and got the same awful reception I did."

"Oh. No, I didn't even turn the TV on. As a matter of fact, I didn't go back to my cabin until eleven-thirty or so."

"You didn't?" I sighed with relief. Not that I'd really suspected Sam of being the hit man.

"No. When I got off the elevator, I realized I wasn't ready to go to bed. I felt restless, excited, like a kid."

"I know. Me too."

"So instead of going to my cabin, I turned around and came back out here."

"To the Promenade Deck?"

He nodded. "I thought maybe I could calm down a little, sort things out."

"Oh, you mean, about the career change you've been wrestling with?"

"That was part of what was bothering me."

"What was the other part?"

He smiled.

"Wait. I know," I grinned, full of myself. "You were trying to decide whether I'm a pain in the ass or the 'find' of the century. Wasn't that the other dilemma?"

"It was."

"And did you come to any conclusions?"

"I already told you, Slim. You require further study. Much further study."

"I see. And the career change? Did you sort that out?"

He shrugged. "Not entirely. The problem is, my heart's just not in my work anymore. Ever since my fiancée . . ." He stopped, as if debating whether to say more, reveal more.

"Go on, Sam. Please," I urged. I wanted to hear about her, wanted to know what had happened to her, wanted to know if Sam was still in love with her.

He adjusted his eyeglasses, pushing them back toward his head with his index finger. "My career hasn't meant as much to me since Jillian died," he said. Jillian. A lovely name. "I'm not as driven now. I don't feel it's the end of the world if I'm not on time for things, if I don't show up in the city where they send me. I don't care as much about any of it since she's gone."

I nodded, picturing Sam trying to cope with the death of his fiancée, particularly with such a demanding travel schedule.

"Would you really feel differently if you went into a field other than insurance?" I asked. "When you lose someone you love, the emptiness is with you no matter how you earn your living."

"True." He looked at me, his eyes such a deep, intense blue behind the glasses. Then he said, as if in response to a question, "I'm over her. I really am. It's the experience I'm having trouble . . ." He stopped again.

"The experience?" I asked. "You mean, that Jillian died only a few days before you two were to be married?"

He nodded solemnly. "That and the fact that I—"

"You what?"

He shook me off this time. There would be no more questions, I sensed. Sam wasn't like the people who spill their guts to the complete strangers they meet on vacation; he was more reserved about his personal history. He had a story to tell, that much was obvious, but he wasn't ready to tell it. Not to me, anyway. Not yet.

"Hey," he said abruptly, as if forcing himself to lighten his mood. "What do you say we go for a run, have something to eat, and get over to Isle de Swan before the day's over?"

"Sure, let's get started," I said. And after a few stretching exercises, we did.

Sam and I ran our four miles, had a quick breakfast in the Glass Slipper, and decided to meet over on the island, instead of trying to hook up and ride the tender together. I wanted to check in with Pat and Jackie to see what they had in mind for our visit to our first port of call.

When I got to Deck 8, I found both of my friends glued to the television set in Pat's cabin, watching the cruise director on the *Princess Charming* Channel as he described the activities available to us on Isle de Swan. They were both dressed in T-shirts and shorts, their *Princess Charming* tote bags filled with their bathing suits, sunscreen, books, etc.

"Jackie," I said, heartened to see her up and around. "Are you feeling better?"

"Better enough to take a five-minute ride over to one of those beaches out there," she said, nodding at the porthole. She still looked pale, weak, not herself. "If you think I'm gonna sit in my room while the two of you are out there playing 'Baywatch,' you can forget about it."

"But to spend hours in the hot sun when you've just . . ." I didn't finish the sentence. I knew I was being a nag. Instead, I gazed out at Isle de Swan through Pat's porthole. Since hers was minus the lifeboat, the view of it was unobstructed and absolutely glorious. You could easily see the vibrant pinks and purples of the bougainvillea blossoms, the cream-colored sandy beaches, the blues and greens of the shimmering, clear water.

"I'll be okay," Jackie said. "If I'm not, I'll take the tender back. No big deal."

"All right. So what's the plan?" I asked. "Do you both want to go to the island now?"

Jackie said a quick yes. Pat replied that she had to telephone Albert Mullins's stateroom first, to coordinate their schedules. I had forgotten that both she and Albert had signed up for one of the cruise's excursion packages–a series of drawing lessons or "art safaris," as they were called, led by an acclaimed artist from South Florida named Ginger Smith Baldwin. At each port of call, the ten to fifteen people in Baldwin's group would be trooping to a designated site, given the necessary art supplies, and then receive instruction on how best to capture the mood. Their tableaux could then be brought home and either framed and hung or simply shared with friends and family, the way one shares snapshots or videos. Since I was severely artistically challenged and Jackie was more interested in water sports than watercolors, Pat was taking the series with Albert.

"He's looking forward to drawing birds," Pat explained as she dialed his extension.

I went back to my cabin to take a quick shower and change, then rejoined the others in Pat's room.

"We're meeting Albert and the rest of Ginger's art class at the elevator on Deck 2," she explained.

We took the elevator down to the second level of the ship and waited in the loading area, along with at least two hundred other passengers. One of them was Henry Prichard. Another of them was Ingrid, his fetching friend from the previous evening. If Jackie was disappointed that Henry had attached himself to another woman while she was in her cabin fending off stomach cramps, she didn't let on. She simply turned to Pat and me and said stoically, "Looks like the car salesman got away."

"I'm sorry, Jackie," I said. "I know you had hopes for the two of you."

"I had hopes of getting some action, that's all," she said. "I guess that's the deal with these cruises. You're out of commission for one day and there's another babe to take your place. But hey, Henry's not the only guy on this ship. I'm not throwing the diaphragm overboard just yet."

"That's the spirit," I said, patting her on the back, which made her cough, unfortunately.

"Has the bug moved to your chest?" Pat asked her. "I hear some congestion in your lungs."

"I'm fine," Jackie said, waving both of us off. "Now, where's the rest of your art class, Pat?"

Pat looked among the throngs of people and spotted Albert. She waved. He bowed. We made our way through the crowd over to where he was standing in line for the tender.

"A very good morning to you all," he said, doffing his tan safari hat. He was also wearing a T-shirt and shorts, and had both a camera and a pair of heavy binoculars dangling from braided cords around his scrawny neck. One wrong move and he's going to choke himself, I thought.

"Good morning, Albert," said Pat. "Are you ready to create a work of art today?"

"Most certainly," he said in that arch, fussy, faux-British manner of his. "I've never tried to express my feelings for birds in terms of the visual arts, but I'm game to give it a go!"

Pip pip.

Standing a few bodies away from Albert was Gayle Cone, from Table 186. She was wearing a chic little sundress over her bathing suit, carried a Prada bag instead of the *Princess Charming* totes we were all toting, and had substituted her diamonds and emeralds for ivory, her idea of the perfect, islandy accessory, I presumed, the animal rights activists be damned.

"Kenneth and I have a Baldwin," she gushed to Jackie and me, while Pat chatted with Albert.

"So? My mother and father have a Steinway," Jackie countered.

"No, no. I wasn't talking about a piano, darling. I was talking about an oil painting. By Ginger Smith *Baldwin*. We bought it last year at a gallery in *Soho.*" Gayle shook her head at Jackie, as if she couldn't believe someone could be so hopelessly out of touch. "And now I'm actually signed up for her series of art safaris! Can you stand it? My friends in New Jersey will be green, absolutely green!"

"What about Kenneth?" I asked, not seeing him anywhere. "Isn't he going over to the island today?"

"Oh, he's already there," she explained. "We operate on entirely different schedules, Kenneth and I. I suppose that's why we've been together so long. He stays awake until all hours of the night and then gets up and goes gallavanting at the shriek of dawn. I tell you, the

man never sleeps, whereas I'm out like a light by nine-thirty or ten."
She paused, pulling us closer, drawing us into her confidence. "I've
been taking melatonin," she whispered. "I know it's an unregulated
hormone and I'll probably grow a beard or something, but it makes
me sleep like a dead woman. Kenneth could tap dance on the ceiling and I wouldn't move a muscle."

A dead woman, I shuddered, reminded once again of the dreaded
phone call. At least Gayle didn't have to worry about the hit man,
since she wasn't an ex-wife. She and Kenneth had been married just
once: to each other.

"Anyhow," she said, "Kenneth's probably out there snorkling or
scuba diving—don't ask me which is which—or baking on the beach.
We're going to meet for lunch. After my art class with Ginger."

Speaking of Ginger, a striking woman bearing a name tag that
read GINGER SMITH BALDWIN appeared. She was dressed in sandals,
cut-off blue jeans, and a tie-dyed T-shirt. Wavy reddish-brown hair
flowed down her back. Long, triangular-shaped, silver-and-turquoise
earrings hung from her earlobes. And she had eyes as blue as Sam's
and dimples that framed her friendly smile. She was both attractive
and approachable, nothing like the brittle artiste I had envisioned
when Gayle had spoken of her.

She introduced herself to the small group that had huddled
around her and asked for their tickets, verifying that they had each
paid for the series of art lessons.

"Ticket?" she asked me.

"No. Sorry. I'm not signed up," I said. "I can't even draw a stick
figure." Maybe because I'd always thought I looked like one.

Ginger was understanding. "Art isn't about perfection," she said
with a throaty laugh. "It's about expressing yourself, putting your
emotional response to a scene on a canvas or sheet of drawing paper.
When I work, I let the picture tell *me* what I should be doing. Sometimes I put people in my paintings—stick figures, even—and sometimes I end up scrubbing them out. I really believe that art is a matter
of addition and subtraction. You have to bring in the groceries before you can take out the garbage, you know?"

No, I didn't know. But I liked Ginger Smith Baldwin immediately
and thought: Why couldn't I have had an art teacher like this woman

when I was in school, instead of the boring old fart I was stuck with?

I wondered if Ginger had a PR agent and whether she'd consider becoming a client of Pearson & Strulley. I made a mental note to write her one of my famous "pitch" letters when I got back to New York. I was sure I could book her on the weekend edition of the "Today" show, at the very least.

The tender ride to Isle de Swan took about five minutes. When the bargelike ferry arrived at the island's little dock, a battalion of Haitians helped the two hundred of us off the boat and pointed us in the direction of the beaches. That's what Isle de Swan was, it turned out: a maze of beaches, some rocky and windswept and more suitable for painting or reading than swimming or sailing; others wide and sandy and heavily populated with lounge chairs, sun-bathers, and waiters carrying trays of rum drinks. There was also a cluster of boutiques in the center of the island, sort of a Caribbean version of a mall. Each shop sold essentially the same merchandise—native crafts such as wooden voodoo masks, brightly colored ce-ramic pieces, and anything in batik.

Ginger's group went to the northernmost beach on the island, a rugged promontory that overlooked both the sea and another smaller island known as Bird Heaven. Albert *was* in heaven when he caught his first glimpse of a roseate spoonbill.

Jackie and I waved goodbye to Pat, Albert, Gayle, and the oth-ers, and went off to a beach called Jewel Cove, where you could rent Hobie Cats and wind surfing equipment and snorkling gear—Jackie's idea of heaven. I plunked myself down in a lounge chair, under the shade of a large palm tree, while she went in search of the person in charge of the water sports concession. It was about eleven o'clock by then. Almost time for another meal.

I squelched my hunger pangs, stretched out with my paperback spy novel, and scanned, first the beach, then the water, for Sam. I didn't see him. Instead, I spotted that hot new twosome, Henry and Ingrid, diving in and out of the sea like dolphins, and Skip Jamison, standing ankle-deep in the water in his tight black bikini and hav-ing a mind-body experience with his tablemates, Donna and Tori. I

also saw Dorothy Thayer, who had brought along some of the crois-
sants that were served at breakfast and was tearing them into little
pieces and feeding them to both the seagulls and her husband,
Lloyd. And then there was Lenny Lubin, out there in the water, right
smack in the middle of all the swimmers, climbing repeatedly onto
a wind surfing board and then slipping off again. Poor guy. His wind
surfing was as pathetic as his karaoke singing.

As I watched Lenny make a fool of himself, I remembered that
when Sam and I were about to leave the disco the night before,
Lenny was about to leave too: to go back to his room and change
out of his tuxedo, he'd told us. It dawned on me that it could have
been *Lenny* who'd made the phone call to the ex-husband who
wanted his former wife dead. He had the opportunity, as they say
on those cop shows. But then so did Skip. So did hundreds of other
men on the ship, for all I knew. Even Henry, who could easily have
left Ingrid for a quick trip to his cabin to "take his pills," could have
had the opportunity. And what about Albert who, while we were all
riding over to the island on the tender, happened to mention that
he had turned in early the night before, at about nine-fifteen, to be
exact? He wasn't my image of a hit man, but what experience did I
have with hit men?

Jackie came back to tell me that all the water sports equipment
had already been rented, so she was going swimming.

"You're still pretty weak, don't forget," I cautioned.

"Elaine," she growled. "I didn't come all the way down here from
the frigid Northeast to just *look* at the water, ya know?"

She went down to the sea, dove in, and swam for close to a half
an hour. When she reappeared at our chairs, she looked absolutely
worn out.

"Was it really necessary to be Esther Williams today?" I said. "You
don't look so hot."

"To tell you the truth, I don't feel so hot," she admitted, then qual-
ified the statement. "Actually, I *do* feel hot. I think I've got a temperature."

I reached over and felt her forehead. She was definitely feverish.

"That's it. We're going back to the ship," I said, packing up my
tote bag.

"Shit," she moaned. "I really needed this vacation, Elaine. You don't know how much."

Her lower lip quivered.

"What is it?" I asked.

"Nothing. I hate whining," she said, trying to shrug off whatever was bothering her.

"You won't be whining if you tell me. You'll just be telling me."

She smiled weakly. "It's just the whole thing with Peter," she said. "The way he's been pressuring me about the nursery. What really gets me is that he wants to make the place his little kingdom and yet he's hardly ever there now. I swear, he's turned into this fucking little yuppie who dresses up in a bowtie and suspenders and drives his Beemer into the city for meetings."

"Meetings? Who with?"

She shrugged. "I don't have a clue. We barely talk anymore. Maybe he's seeing plastic surgeons about getting his dick enlarged."

I laughed. "Even when you're sick, you're sick, Jackie."

I patted her hand. Her skin felt hot and clammy, even though she was shivering.

"You know, I hate to cut you off if you're up to talking, but maybe Henry Prichard isn't the only one who should be on antibiotics," I suggested. "The ship's doctor could start you on something, and you'd be feeling better in twenty-four hours. Then you could really enjoy the vacation."

"All right, already. I hear ya," she said. "I'll go to the damn doctor." She started to get up, but was so dizzy she fell back into the chair.

"Tell you what," I said, concerned about her. "Let me find Pat, tell her what we're doing, and then we'll go straight to the doctor, okay?"

"You'll miss the beach barbecue," Jackie said.

"I'll live," I said, hoping I would. Hoping all three of us would.

I trudged over to the beach where the members of Ginger's art group were busily interpreting the scene before them; some using colored pencils, others paintbrushes. Albert, I noticed, was doing a rendering of the stork that he had spotted through his binoculars over on Bird Heaven. The drawing looked exactly like one of my stick figures.

"Sorry to interrupt," I told everybody, then knelt down where Pat was seated. Her creation was more abstract than Albert's; it was a series of blue lines and pink squiggles, and it reminded me of Lucy Kovecky's pictures that were always magnetized to the door of the family refrigerator.

I told Pat that Jackie had a fever and that I was taking her back to the ship, to the doctor on board.

"I should come with you," she said, putting down her pencils.

"I think I can handle this one alone," I said. "You stay here and create."

She giggled, then whispered, "Albert says I have the makings of a real Renault."

"Renoir," I corrected her. "Renault's a car."

"I guess he didn't realize," she said. "If I didn't know better, Elaine, I would think he's becoming rather attached to me. Imagine."

"Imagine," I smiled.

"Unfortunately, the person I want to become attached to me is Bill," she sighed. "But in the meantime, Albert's a nice companion. We're going hiking together after our art class. Unless, of course, you want me to help with Jackie?"

"I may not be anyone's idea of Florence Nightingale, but I can at least get Jackie back to the ship," I assured her. "Have fun."

"I will."

I walked Jackie back to the tender and helped her on board. We had to wait fifteen minutes in the hot sun while the cruise staff loaded more passengers onto the boat. When we finally shoved off, we were a full house.

So much for Isle de Swan, I thought as we motored away from the island. I hoped things would go better in San Juan, our next stop, where, at the very least, I'd be reunited with my suitcase.

We were several hundred feet away from the *Princess Charming* when another tender was being launched, taking an additional two hundred people over to Isle de Swan, just in time for lunch.

"Hey!" someone called out from the other boat as it was passing ours.

I turned to find the voice and there was Sam, standing against the railing and waving at us.

"Where're you headed?" he yelled, looking disappointed that we were going in opposite directions.

"Jackie's not feeling well so we're going to the doctor," I called out to him.

"Can't hear you!" he shouted.

"Jackie's not . . ." I stopped when I realized that between the diesels of the two tenders, the steel drums, and all the people noise, he'd never be able to hear me. "See you at dinner," I yelled, waving goodbye, heavy with a sense of missed opportunities. I'd always thought the expression about two ships passing in the night was a bunch of romantic crap, but at that precise moment it really resonated. "Goodbye!" I called out again, draping myself over the railing. "Until tonight!"

"Oh, brother," Jackie muttered, shaking her head at me. "So I was right about you and this guy."

I lowered my head and nodded, like a guilty kid.

"You're completely shitfaced over him, is that it?" she asked, incredulous.

"I think so, Jackie," I confessed. "God help me, I think so."

11

I had expected the ship's infirmary to be a modest little affair, reminiscent of the one at my summer camp—a white room, smelling of rubbing alcohol and furnished with a couple of rickety chairs, a scale, tongue depressors, and adhesive tape. But the *Princess Charming*'s infirmary was more like the Mayo Clinic—a big-city, state-of-the-art hospital complete with examining rooms and operating rooms and a full-fledged pharmacy.

"I think we've just wandered onto the set of 'ER,' " Jackie said after we got off the elevator on Deck 1 and found ourselves in the midst of a medical wonderland. There were people everywhere—ailing bodies draped across the chairs and sofas in the large waiting room; nurses bustling about, taking pulses and temperatures and insurance information; ship personnel of various ages and afflictions, stopping in for treatment and/or gossip. Even Captain Solberg, our fearless leader, passed through, "to pick up da prescription for Prozac," he said matter-of-factly after nodding a cautious hello at me and introducing himself to Jackie.

"So that explains it," I mumbled once he was out of earshot.

"Explains what?" asked Jackie.

"Why he acted so unconcerned when I went to see him this morning. He's not dispassionate, just depressed."

"You went to see him this morning? What for?" said Jackie as we approached the front desk to sign her in. I gasped when I saw that there were twenty-four names ahead of hers. The nurse in charge,

whose ID tag read WENDY WIMPLE, R.N. and who was British, esti-
mated that there would be a two-hour wait.

Good God, I thought. At least when you're at a restaurant and
they tell you you're in for a two-hour wait, you can have a drink at
the bar.

"So why did you go to see the captain this morning?" Jackie repeated once we were signed in and seated. I was grateful that she
was still lucid, given how feverish she was.

"Oh, it was just a problem I had with one of the male passengers,"
I said, sticking to my decision not to tell her or Pat about the murder plot. "I felt I should report the person."

She rolled her eyes. "Oh, here we go," she sighed. "Elaine and
her intrigues and conspiracies."

We sat together in that waiting room for what seemed like an eternity, and I came to understand more fully why they call such places
waiting rooms. I looked around at the other people waiting. From
what I saw and heard, they were suffering from everything from sun
poisoning and food poisoning to heart disease and kidney failure.
I'm telling you, the place was packed with physical wrecks, and
Jackie was one of them. As time wore on, she became more feverish, alternated between chills and sweats, didn't even have the
strength to razz me. And she showed virtually no interest in inter-
rogating me about Sam, for which I was grateful. I have to admit,
there was a teensy weensy part of me that resented her for keeping
me away from him.

At one point, the nurse called out the name of yet another patient
that wasn't Jackie and directed the person toward the examining
rooms. I glanced at my watch and saw that it had now been over
two hours since we'd signed in. Enough was enough. I approached
the desk and asked how many people were in front of Jackie and
how long it would be before her turn would come.

"There are seven people in front of her," Nurse Wendy Wimple
said crisply. "I'd say she could be waiting another forty-five minutes
to an hour before seeing the doctor."

"*The* doctor? You mean, there's only one? For all these people?"

"There is only one here at present," said Wendy, whose manner
was as starched and stiff as her white uniform. "The backup doctor
is on call."

"Then *call* him," I suggested. "The sooner the better."

I looked over at Jackie, who had chosen that very moment to lapse into a delirium. Suddenly, she was moaning and waving her arms in the air and speaking in an odd combination of pig latin and iambic pentameter.

"Can't you see my friend needs help?" I shouted as I banged my fist on the reception desk. "She's out of her mind with fever."

"How do you know it's the fever?" the nurse asked from between pursed lips. "We've treated several psychiatric patients today."

"Look here, missy. I don't know where you received your nurse's training, but you don't have to be a medical genius to figure out that that woman over there"—I pointed to Jackie—"is sick. *Physically* sick. Now if you won't take her inside to see the doctor, I'll—"

"You'll what?"

"I'll . . . I'll . . ." I was stumped. This wasn't Manhattan, with a hospital on every block, so I didn't exactly have leverage here. And even if there were another hospital within swimming distance, we'd have to get there and sign Jackie in, and then the wait would start all over again.

"I'll . . . I'll report this to the editor of *Away from It All,* the most popular travel magazine in the States," I sputtered. "I'm in the public relations field. I can easily leak the information that if you're a passenger on the *Princess Charming* and you're unfortunate enough to get sick, you'd better bring along your own doctor, because you'll never live to—"

I didn't finish my sentence because in the middle of my tirade, out walked the doctor.

"Is dere a problem, Vendy? I could hear da commotion from all da vay down da hall," he said, seeming concerned but not angry.

Another Scandinavian, I thought as I regarded him. He was stockier than Captain Solberg—quite roly-poly, in fact—but blonder, fairer, gentler. Perhaps it was his voice that suggested a certain caring and compassion. It was soft, low, without an authoritative edge.

"I'm sorry, Doctor—"

"Johansson," he offered, shaking my hand after removing his white latex gloves. "Dr. Per Johansson."

"Nice to meet you," I said. "I'm sorry about the way I spoke to your nurse, but my friend over there"—I pointed again at Jackie—"has

been waiting over two hours to see you, and her condition is dete-
riorating rapidly."

"Vat are her symptoms?" he asked as all the other patients in the
waiting room watched with keen interest. There wasn't much else
in the way of entertainment; the magazine selection wasn't the best.

"Well," I began. "It started early yesterday morning with terrible
stomach cramps and . . ." I paused. "Why don't I just go over there
and bring her to you," I said.

Before Dr. Johannson could escape, I ran over to where Jackie was
sitting, dragged her to the desk, and, propping her up like a department store mannequin, said, "Take a look at her, Doctor. She's
a sick puppy."

Dr. Johansson looked puzzled. "Puppy?"

"Oh." I smiled. "No, I know you're not a veterinarian." I hesitated
for a second or two. "You're *not* a veterinarian, are you?" You never
could tell with ship's doctors.

He smiled back, a good sport, and said he wasn't.

I nodded, relieved. "What I meant was, my friend has a high fever.
Feel."

I took hold of Dr. Johansson's hand and placed it on Jackie's forehead. "See?"

He arched an eyebrow and looked rather sternly at the nurse.
"Let's get her into da examining room, Vendy. Right avay."

"Yes, Doctor," Wendy acquiesced. She took one of Jackie's arms,
Dr. Johansson took the other, and together they led my friend away,
down the hall.

Famished and figuring the examination would take a while, I
dashed up to the Glass Slipper for a quick snack. But it was three-
thirty by this time and the café was closed.

"How about just a roll and butter?" I begged a busboy who was
wiping down one of the tables. "Please?"

He smirked, probably thinking I was one of those insatiable,
orally fixated passengers who can't go five minutes without a *nosh.*
I reached into my *Princess Charming* tote bag, opened my wallet, and
handed him a five-dollar bill, the smallest change I had with me. His
smirk disappeared and he hustled back to the kitchen and returned
with a pastrami on rye and a glass of iced tea. I thanked him, sat

down at the table he'd been cleaning, and ate and drank while he wiped.

At about four o'clock, I watched from the Glass Slipper as the *Princess Charming* pulled out of the harbor at Isle de Swan. Next stop: San Juan at one o'clock the following afternoon. Somehow, the idea of heading toward a major city—the capital city of a country with genuine diplomatic ties to the United States, a place with several hospitals to choose from—was comforting. Needing to be comforted further, I thought of Sam then, wondered how he had spent his afternoon on the island, wondered how it would feel to see him again at dinner. I couldn't wait.

I went back downstairs to the infirmary. Jackie was still in with Dr. Johansson, Nurse Wimple told me, so I sat down, picked up a dog-eared, three-year-old copy of *People* magazine, and waited. I was trying to involve myself in a story about Oprah Winfrey's latest adventures in dieting when Pat appeared—battered, bruised, and limping!

I jumped up from my seat and rushed over to her. She was not alone; Albert Mullins was holding her by the left elbow.

"What happened?" I said.

"I had a little accident," she said, grimacing in pain. Her chin had a nasty cut on it. Her right arm was scraped and bleeding. And her right ankle was very swollen.

"What kind of an accident?" I asked, directing the question to both Pat and Albert. "When I left you two, you were in Ginger's art class, creating."

"Yes, and it was a thoroughly enjoyable experience," Albert volunteered, "made even more so by your friend's delightful company."

"Swell. What happened after the art class?" I said impatiently.

Pat started to answer, but her bruised chin clearly made it difficult for her to move her mouth to speak, so Albert filled in.

"We had the lovely lunch that the ship provided," he reported. "Chicken legs dipped in a rather pungent—"

"Forget the menu, Albert. I want to hear about the accident," I said.

"Yes, yes. Of course," he said quickly. "After lunch, Pat and I decided to explore the island a bit on our own—I was *so* eager to spot a double-crested cormorant, you see—and we took a little hike south in the direction of Elizabeth's Refuge."

"Where?"

"Elizabeth's Refuge, an island landmark. It's in the brochure, Elaine."

"I didn't read the brochure, Albert."

"Well, then. Allow me to explain. When Christopher Columbus and his ilk were laying claim to the West Indies, one of the ships ran into a violent storm and washed up on the shore of the island that is now Isle de Swan. A local woman named Elizabeth was the proprietress of a stone tavern along the very stretch of rocks where the ship came aground. Legend has it that she rescued singlehandedly the ship's captain and crew, and her tavern was thereafter rechristened Elizabeth's Refuge. It's a derelict building now, of course, but still a thrilling historical monument to the courage and bravery—"

"The accident, Albert. Get to the accident."

"Yes. The accident." He looked at Pat with a mixture of guilt and sympathy and continued. "We were climbing down the rather steep and narrow stone steps leading away from the building when a large group of sightseers were on their way up to the area. Pat was walking directly in front of me—I had her in view at all times, I assure you—but she was either distracted by the people in the group and wasn't watching where she was going, or she was inadvertently shoved by one of them. It was quite a crowd, you see. In any case, she ended up twisting her ankle, missing a step, and falling down onto the hard, unforgiving stonework. I feel terribly responsible, really I do. First came that unseemly business when I spilled the drink on her blouse. Now comes this regrettable, utterly preventable fall while she was on *my* watch! I'm beginning to think your friend isn't safe around me."

I'm beginning to think so too, I thought, wondering if it were even remotely possible that Albert was the hit man and Pat was his intended target. Suppose he had meant to kill her and botched the job? He *was* a complete dip-shit. It was easy to imagine him screwing up. On the other hand, he was seriously clumsy; he'd said so himself in the midst of his stirring apology over the Miami Whammy incident.

He could have nudged Pat down those stairs—accidentally—and then been too ashamed to admit it. And Pat herself wasn't exactly Connecticut's answer to Ginger Rogers. During her marengue lesson the day before, she had stepped on the instructor's toes so often that he had handed her over to the assistant instructor, on whose toes she had also stepped. I was probably overreacting, the way Jackie and Pat always claimed I was.

Pat suddenly groaned in pain, as if to remind everyone that she had come to the infirmary for medical attention, not to listen to Albert and me chat.

I wrote her name on Nurse Wimple's sign-in sheet—there were twenty-six names before hers—and helped her over to the seating area.

I'll never see Sam again, I thought, figuring Pat's wait would be even longer than Jackie's and I'd miss dinner, just as I'd missed lunch.

"I think we can handle things on our own now," I told Albert. "You don't have to stay."

"But I feel honor-bound to remain by Pat's side until we learn the full extent of her injuries," he protested.

"Pat will give you a call," I said. "When she's up to it."

"As you wish," he said, bowing and then setting Pat's *Princess Charming* tote bag, which he had been carrying for her, on the floor. He took hold of her left hand, the uninjured one, and pressed his lips to it. "I bid you a speedy recovery."

"ThkyouAlbt," Pat said, her sore chin forcing her to speak as if her jaw had been wired shut.

"You're most welcome, my dear," he said and left.

I turned to Pat. "Did he push you down those stairs?"

"Albt?"

"Yes, Albert. He said you might have been 'shoved.' "

Pat shook her head gingerly. "Mybe. ButnotbyAlbt."

"How do you know? He said he was walking right behind you. Isn't it possible that he was the one who did the pushing and shoving? To hurt you?"

"WhywldAlbtdothat?"

"I don't know." I sat there ruminating on the current state of Pat's relationship with Bill, trying to imagine why a man of his intelligence would hire someone like Albert to murder his ex-wife. Finally, I asked, "You told Jackie and me that Bill called you on the phone, just before we left for the cruise, and said he wanted to see you."

"Hedid."

"Did he ever say *why* he wanted to see you?"

"Hetoldmehemissesthekids."

"But he sees the kids on his regular visits. And he has them for this whole week, while you're away."

"Iknow."

"Did he say anything else the last time you spoke to him?"

She nodded. "Thehousetoobig."

"He said the house in Weston is too big?"

She nodded again.

"The bastard. What does he expect you to do? Move yourself and his five children into a tiny apartment? So he won't have to pay the mortgage anymore?"

Pat shrugged. "Can'ttalk. Hurts."

"Sorry." I squeezed her good arm. "Listen, Jackie should be coming out any minute, and once she's finished with the doctor I'll ask him to take you next. He seems like a very nice man."

"SodoesAlbt."

"The jury's still out on Albert, Pat."

She was about to disagree with me when Dr. Johansson emerged. He came right over to us, took a quick look at Pat, and said, "Vat happened to dis one?"

I explained.

"Vat a shame," he commiserated, lifting Pat's tender ankle in his large, experienced hands and giving it a cursory examination. "Ve'll x-ray it, but I think it's just a sprain. Ve'll clean up da bruises, ice da ankle, and she'll be good as new in no time."

I breathed a sigh of relief. One down, one to go. "What about Jackie?" I asked Dr. Johansson.

He furrowed his brow and said, "Ve took some blood, a urine sample, and a culture, to see if dere's a bacterial infection, but da main thing is, I vant her to stay here overnight. Maybe even two nights."

"Stay here? You have beds?" I asked.

Dr. Johansson smiled. "Come. I'll show you."

He instructed Nurse Wimple to take Pat back to one of the examining rooms while he escorted me on a behind-the-scenes tour of the ship's infirmary. "Dis is vhere ve do some of da surgeries," he said as we passed one of the operating rooms. "Ve can do everything from open-heart surgery to setting a broken leg. Da other doctor does cosmetic surgery for some of da passengers. Dat's vhy he's not here dis afternoon; he did four face lifts dis morning."

I shook my head in amazement. It had never occurred to me that people took cruises to have face lifts. But then, it had never occurred to me that cruises had hospitals.

"Dis is da lab," Dr. Johansson said proudly as we walked by a room in which four white-gloved and white-coated technicians sat hunched over vials of blood. "And den dere are da patients' quarters." He stopped when we got to a section of the infirmary where there were several private rooms, most of them filled. In one of the rooms lay Jackie, propped up in bed, an IV needle in her arm and one of those dreadful, white-and-blue-dotted gowns on her body.

"Can I talk to her?" I asked.

"Of course. Ve're only keeping her as a precaution," Dr. Johansson said reassuringly. "Until ve get her fever down and can figure out vat she's got. Just don't tire her. She's very veak."

"I won't," I promised. "And thank you, Doctor. Very much."

"You're very velcome," he said. "Now, I'd better go and take a look at your other friend."

I nodded, wondering how *I* had managed to stay out of harm's way and how long my luck would last.

12

"**J**ackie? Can you hear me? It's Elaine," I whispered, standing beside her hospital bed.

"Of course I can hear you. I'm sick, not deaf."

I smiled. "You gave me quite a scare in that waiting room," I admitted. "But you seem better already. Maybe this Dr. Johansson knows what he's doing."

"He's very thorough, I'll tell you that. He asked me a million questions—whether I'd eaten any bad shellfish, been bitten by a deer tick, come in contact with any poisonous—"

"Poisonous what?" I interrupted. Could Jackie have been poisoned? Did Henry Prichard plop something into her drink the other night when she wasn't looking? Was *he* the man on the phone and *she* the ex-wife he'd been hired to kill? I was off and running again.

"Poisonous substances," she continued. "I told him I work at a nursery, where we've got the occasional bag of toxic chemicals. As I said, Dr. Johansson's very thorough."

"I'm glad," I said, pulling myself back to reality.

"And you know what?" she said. "He's a sports fan."

"Jackie, how on earth do you know that?"

"Because when he got through asking *me* a million questions, I asked *him* a few. Like where he was from, how he came to be a ship's doctor, the basics. He's Finnish, born and raised in Helsinki, did his medical training in London, was divorced about ten years ago, and decided to take the job with Sea Swan Cruises when a buddy of his, a doctor who used to work for the cruise line, retired."

I laughed. "Sounds like Dr. Johansson wasn't the only one doing the examining. You even managed to find out he likes baseball?"

"Not baseball, Elaine. He's from Finland, for Christ's sake. He skis."

"Well, I'm delighted that you and Dr. Johansson both ski," I said. "That'll give you something to talk about while he's lifting your hospital gown and pressing that ice-cold stethoscope to your chest."

She smiled.

"He did ask me not to stay long," I remembered. "I should probably get going."

Jackie nodded glumly. "I can't believe this happened on our vacation."

"I know," I said, taking her hand and patting it. "But there will be other vacations, other trips together. We can go where we want to go, do what we want to do."

"Mamas and the Papas. Nineteen-sixty-something. Peter liked that song."

"Bully for Peter." Could *Peter* have hired Henry Prichard to murder Jackie? I wondered. So she wouldn't be able to stand in the way of his plans for the nursery?

I had to stop this. I was driving myself crazy. It was probably some other woman whose ex-husband wanted her dead. I made up my mind that the very instant I got to San Juan—well, the very instant after I retrieved my lost luggage in San Juan—I would contact the authorities there, tell them the story, and hope that they would be more inclined to take action than Captain Solberg had been.

"The important thing is for you to get well," I told Jackie.

"I guess so. Just think of me every now and then, when you and Pat are out there partying."

"I don't think Pat's going to be doing any partying," I said, then reported on our friend's travails on Isle de Swan. "At least, not tonight."

"Poor Pat," she said. "Send her my love, okay?"

"I will. I'm sure she'll come to visit you in the morning. She just has to be off her feet for the next few hours."

Jackie smiled.

"What?" I asked.

"With Pat and me out of commission, that's two less single women at the dinner table tonight. Which means *you'll* have Sam all to yourself, girl. Go for it."

Kingsley helped me get Pat into her stateroom, onto her bed, after Dr. Johansson had taped her ankle, cleaned and bandaged her cuts and scrapes, given her a healthy dose of Valium, and sent her on her way. I handed Kingsley my last five-dollar bill and sent him on his way.

"How're you feeling now?" I asked Pat when we were alone.

"A little woozy," she said, sufficiently woozy that the soreness in her chin no longer restricted her speech.

"Good. Why don't I help you undress, tuck you in, and let you sleep the pain away?"

She looked up at me, her eyes slightly crossed from the medication. Then she reached out her left hand and combed my hair away from my face, just like my mother did when I was little.

"I love you, Elaine," she said.

"I love you too, Pat," I said as I tried, first to get her T-shirt over her head, then to pull her shorts over her bad ankle. "Let me know if I'm hurting you, okay?"

"I love you, Elaine," she said again.

"I love you too, Pat," I said again and went ahead and undressed her. She was so out of it from the Valium that she told me she loved me several more times. "I know, Pat. I know," I said each time.

"No, you don't," she said dreamily as I helped her under the covers. "I never have the nerve to say what's in my heart. Have always been too shy. But you have been a wonderful friend to me, Elaine, a wonderful friend. You're so sophisticated and smart about everything, so pretty too. I wanted to tell you. I admire you as well as love you."

A lump the size of a meatball formed in my throat. I was thoroughly touched by Pat's declaration, Valium or no Valium. I leaned down and kissed her cheek.

"I didn't tell Bill I loved him for the longest time," she sighed, her eyelids fluttering and then closing shut.

"I'm sure he sensed it," I said softly as I turned off the lamp by her bed.

"I love Bill," she said and drifted off.

"I know," I said and closed the door behind me.

It was six o'clock by the time I got back to my stateroom—only a half-hour until dinner. I thought about trying to call Harold at the office but figured he'd be on his way home by then. I also thought about calling Leah, to find out how my clients were faring with their various legal problems, but decided my time would be better spent showering, dressing, and primping for Sam.

I hurriedly washed and blow-dried my hair, applied my makeup, and put on what I hoped would be the last of my Perky Princess purchases: a too-short white skirt and a peach-colored knit sweater emblazoned with two gold palm trees, one across each breast. Very tasteful. As it was Caribbean Night in the dining room and we were all told to dress in West Indian garb, I assumed my outfit wouldn't be any tackier than anybody else's.

Feeling naked without Jackie and Pat beside me, I walked into the enormous dining room, toward Table 186, my heart pounding as I scanned the table for Sam. Typically, he had not arrived yet.

"Hello, everybody," I said, taking the empty chair next to Kenneth Cone, who was dressed in white slacks and a lively, multicolored shirt, his brown hair slicked back in the current Eurotrash fashion, his complexion now a deep bronze.

"Elaine," he said, eyeing my palm trees. "Jackie and Pat coming?"

"No. Now they're *both* not feeling well," I explained. "Jackie's virus has landed her in the infirmary and Pat took a tumble over on the island today and sprained her ankle. She's resting in her room."

"What rotten luck," Gayle said in a tone that did not ring out with sincerity. She was wearing a pert little pink-and-green suit, more Palm Beach than Caribbean. Her jewelry this evening was sterling silver.

"Yes, it certainly is," Dorothy agreed. "None of us wants to have medical problems when we're away from home."

"What's that, Dorothy?" asked Lloyd. He and his wife were dressed in identical outfits: Isle de Swan T-shirts and blue jeans. Dorothy's jeans fit her perfectly. Lloyd's rode up so high the waistband was just under his armpits.

Dorothy turned to him and repeated what I'd said about Jackie and Pat, what Gayle had said about Jackie and Pat, and what she had said about Jackie and Pat.

"Tell them to get well soon," Lloyd bellowed in my direction. It was the first nice thing he'd said in three days.

"From us too," said Brianna, elbowing Rick, who grunted a less-than-heartfelt: "Yeah, right." Brianna wore a T-shirt that read CARIBBEAN QUEEN. Rick's T-shirt said JERK PORK. I couldn't have described him better.

Sam ambled along eventually, and apologized for being late as he always did. He was wearing the khaki slacks from the first night, along with a bright blue shirt that perfectly matched his eyes. He had gotten quite a sunburn on the island, I noticed, and the redness of his nose and cheeks made him look younger, like a little boy.

"Forget the sunscreen today?" I teased.

" 'Fraid so. I got off to such a late start that I had to rush to make the tender. I ended up forgetting the sunscreen *and* missing the chance to spend the afternoon with you. Why'd you go back to the ship so early?"

I related the whole, sorry saga.

"Can we get in to see Jackie after dinner?" he asked, seeming genuinely concerned about both her and Pat.

I shook my head. "The visiting hours at the hospital are over at six. We can see her in the morning though. After our run?"

"It's a date." Sam reached under the table and gave my hand an affectionate squeeze. My cheeks flamed the color of his.

Just then, Ismet showed up to recite the specials. His personal recommendation was the Caribbean lobster with white rice and pigeon peas.

Rick leaned over and said to Brianna, loud enough for all of us to hear him, "Did Ishmael just say they were making us eat pigeon piss? For all the money I'm spending on this honeymoon?"

"Pigeon *peas* are a staple of the Caribbean, sir," Ismet said, remaining polite in the face of Rick's persistent boorishness. "They're not very different from the peas you have in America."

"I hate peas," Rick grumbled. "Carrots too."

"Then have the lobster without the vegetable, honeybun," Brianna suggested delicately. It seemed that she was back where Rick thought she belonged: in the role of June Cleaver.

"Yeah, that's what I'll do," Rick told the waiter. "Bring me a lobster and some french fries, okay, Ishmael?" Ismet nodded while he noted the order on his little pad. "And don't forget the ketchup for the fries and some tartar sauce for the lobster, huh?"

Sam squeezed my hand again, as if to say, "What planet did this guy come from?" I squeezed his back, as if to say, "I don't have a clue, but I don't care because I'm with you." I was so smitten, it was sickening.

During dinner, while we all went one-on-one with our lobsters, sending fragments of meat flying and empty shells clattering, Sam chatted with Dorothy and I talked to Kenneth and Gayle—or tried to. The Cones and I had little in common, really. In addition to the fact that they were married and wealthy and I was single and a working girl, I didn't have an historic, architecturally important, 6,000-square-foot house I was redoing, had never heard of their interior designer, despite Gayle's insistence that his work was published in *"A.D."* several times a year, and was not even remotely interested in the challenge of preserving a building's integrity while tweaking it to the max with items from the *Sharper Image* catalog. At one point, Gayle went on and on about the house's dentil moldings, and all I could think of were teeth and scalings and many, many shots of novocaine.

Eventually, I gave up on Gayle, or vice versa, and attempted to draw Kenneth out, hoping he'd make conversation between chomps on his cigar. What I learned from him right away was that his marriage was a success because he and Gayle each understood their function and never strayed from it: his was to work; hers was to spend. He told me that he had been a stockbroker for several years at one of the big firms—Bear Stearns, Goldman Sachs, I can't remember which—and had done so well that he'd decided to set up his own investment business, first with a partner, then by himself.

"You don't mind working alone now?" I asked, knowing it would be a tough transition for me to go from a huge organization like Pearson & Strulley to an office of my own.

"No, I'm not much for the corporate Christmas party and all that," he said. "It's the trading I enjoy. I'm happiest when I'm buying and selling, watching the market, playing the game."

Some game, I thought, remembering the crash of '87.

"And of course, I'm happy making Gayle happy," he added, nodding at his wife, who was daintily trying to keep the peas and rice from sliding off her fork as it made its way to her mouth. "She's a little high-maintenance but you've gotta love her."

No, buddy, *you* do, I said to myself, imagining the bills Gayle piled up every month.

"Do the two of you have children?" I asked, as neither Gayle nor Kenneth had mentioned any.

Kenneth shook his head. "We've got three shih tzus." He pulled a photograph of the dogs out of his wallet and handed it to me. I nodded and said, "Awww, they're adorable," the way you're supposed to when you're handed a photograph of small dogs or small children. "Gayle was very eager for them, so I went along with it," Kenneth explained as he put the picture back in the wallet. "They're show dogs. Not inexpensive, obviously."

"Obviously."

"But at least I don't have to send them all to Ivy League colleges," Kenneth chuckled.

"That *is* a savings," I agreed.

"Anyway, they're Gayle's prize puppies. When she's happy, I'm happy."

I looked over at Gayle, at her jewels and her clothes and her perfectly coiffed red hair, and thought what a sucker Kenneth was. He worked his ass off so he could keep his wife in money and dogs? What did he get out of the deal? Not sex, judging by Gayle's description earlier in the day of their very different sleeping habits. And not respect; she barely paid any attention to the man. Then what? I wondered. Was it the trophy thing? Was her high-maintenance image a shimmering testament to his canniness about the stock market? To his abilities as a provider? To his masculinity? Who could tell with men?

I turned to study Sam, while Kenneth finished his lobster. I tried to imagine him and his fiancée—Jillian—in a lopsided relationship like Kenneth and Gayle's and couldn't. Sam was deeper than all that glitz and glitter, more down to earth. Never mind what Jackie had said the other night about men not having an essence. Sam Peck had an essence. I was sure of it.

After dinner, everyone coupled off, which, of course, left Sam and me to each other.

"So? What's your pleasure?" he asked as we stood outside the dining room, a violinist serenading us.

"What are my options?" I asked. It was only eight-thirty. Too early to turn in.

Sam took the schedule of evening activities out of his pants pocket, unfolded it, and read it to me. "Well, there's the show. Tonight's lineup is a fifteen-piece big band orchestra, a Glenn Miller type of thing."

"What else is there?" I asked. I'd heard enough renditions of "In the Mood" to last me a lifetime.

"There's Pajama Bingorama, where the best set of PJs wins five hundred dollars' worth of merchandise from the boutiques at Isle de Swan."

"I don't consider that an option. Go on."

"There's a demonstration by a couple of martial arts experts, a lecture on duty-free shopping in San Juan, and a Ping-Pong tournament."

"None of those jump out at me."

"Of course, there's always a moonlit walk on the Promenade Deck."

"You wouldn't be bored? I mean, since we did that last night?"

"You're not boring, Slim. Trust me."

"I never trust people who say—"

"Let's go," said Sam as he grabbed my hand and led me upstairs to the Promenade Deck.

It was a magnificent night—moonlit, starry, warm, fragrant. As the *Princess Charming* headed south to Puerto Rico, the sea was a gentle roll beneath us, a magic carpet ride taking us deeper into the

Caribbean. Sam and I strolled the deck, his arm at my elbow, until we reached the stern of the ship, where we stopped, in the identical spot we'd occupied the previous night, and grabbed hold of the railing. We each looked down at the tremendous wake below us and didn't speak for several minutes, entranced by the sounds and swirls the water was churning up.

"It's easy to forget how high up we are," I said finally, glancing at Sam. The breeze was making his loose-fitting blue shirt billow out like a sail.

"Fourteen stories high, according to the brochure," he said. "You're not afraid of heights, are you?"

"Not with the same intensity that you're afraid of airplanes," I teased.

Sam didn't smile or even respond right away. He just directed his attention back to the sea, almost as if I hadn't made the remark at all. Maybe he doesn't like to joke about his fear of flying, I thought. Or maybe he doesn't like me. As much as I'd hoped, anyway.

His expression had definitely turned serious, his body language tense. I wondered what was going on in his mind as he watched the waves lap against the side of the ship.

"Anything wrong?" I asked, trying to figure out what had changed Sam's mood. He'd been lighthearted and affectionate only moments before.

He shook his head but continued to stare at the ocean, rigid, fixed, only moving his index finger occasionally to push his eyeglasses back toward the bridge of his nose.

Fine. So he doesn't want to talk all of a sudden, I thought, assuming Sam's silence was just some Iron-John, man-communing-with-nature thing.

Then Captain Solberg's voice boomed over the PA system and brought Sam out of his funk.

"Good evening, ladies and gentlemen," said Svein. "Dis is da nine o'clock veather report and update of our current position. Da temperature is eighty-two degrees, da sky is clear—perfect for all of you who are interested in viewing da stars. Ve are traveling south at about tventy knots and expect to reach da pier in San Juan at our scheduled arrival time: von o'clock tomorrow afternoon. I vish you all a safe and happy good night."

" 'Safe' is right," I muttered, reminded of the hit man and his poor prey.

"What did you say?" Sam asked. "Something about safe?"

"It wasn't important," I said. "Just that I feel safe with you. Even fourteen stories high."

He smiled at me, his gloominess receding.

"Slim?" he asked.

"Uh-huh?" I said.

"Would you mind if I kissed you? I thought I'd ask this time, given last night's experience at the elevator." His tone was teasing, carefree again. I was relieved. Whatever had been bothering him wasn't me, apparently.

I inhaled deeply. I was prepared for Sam to kiss me this time. "No. I wouldn't mind at all," I whispered.

Sam drew his body next to mine. He tilted my chin up slightly, to place me in post position, and lowered his face. Lowered it. Lowered it. Lowered it. He *was* several inches taller than I was, but it seemed to take forever before his lips finally made contact with mine. And as his mouth made the excruciatingly slow descent onto my own, I kept wondering: Will his glasses get in the way of the kiss? Will my nose? Will he stick his tongue in my mouth? Do I let him? It had been so long since I'd kissed a man that I honestly couldn't remember who was supposed to do what. In the end, though, it all came back to me.

Sam's lips were buttery soft, juicy, succulent. He must have thought mine were okay too, because we kissed each other out on that Promenade Deck, under the moon and the stars and the sky, for two solid hours! I had never imagined that kissing could be so exciting. But it was—beyond anything I'd ever done in my life. Sam and I clung to each other—noses, chins, mouths, lips, tongues, everything moving as if part of a perfectly choreographed dance.

"Elaine," he murmured, during a rare break in the action. The mere utterance of my name at that particular moment—he had his face in my hair, next to my right ear—sent me into an absolute fever, and in response I kissed him with a ferociousness of which I had never thought myself capable.

"Yes," I murmured back. "Oh, yes."

Now, lest I leave the impression that all we did was kiss, I must

admit, for the record, that there was also a good deal of bodily grop-
ing, once our initial shyness wore off. We groped and fondled and
pressed against each other with barely a thought of who might be
watching or disapproving or getting a vicarious thrill.

So this is why people think sex is such a big deal, I thought at one
point—the very point, as it turned out, that Sam pulled away from
me.

"We've got a decision to make," he said, his lips raw, his cheeks
flushed with more than his sunburn.

"What kind of a decision?" I asked breathlessly.

"We can't stay out here all night, Slim," he said. "The question is:
Do we want to keep this going, in one of our staterooms, or pace
ourselves for the rest of the trip, give ourselves something to look
forward to?"

He's asking me if I'm ready to sleep with him, I realized, thinking it was an excellent question. On one hand, I was no spring
chicken and opportunities like this didn't come along every day. On
the other hand, we were only coming to the end of our third night
of the cruise. Sam and I would have a few more days to get to know
each other better. We could *ease* into a more serious sexual involve-
ment, wait until we were sure it was what we both wanted, avoid
doing something we might be sorry for later.

Yes, I decided, gathering myself together—my hair, my sweater,
my skirt, all of which were askew. We should hold off. Exercise self-
control. Wait another day or so before plunging in, so to speak. This
was the nineties, after all. People weren't supposed to just fall into
bed anymore.

I kissed Sam on the cheek and said, "Let's pace ourselves."

He nodded reluctantly but didn't try to talk me out of my decision.

He took my hand and we started walking back inside the ship.

This is the right thing to do, I told myself as I tried to settle down.
Sam's not going anywhere; he's stuck on this ship for four more days.
It won't kill him to wait a little longer. It won't kill me either.

Day Four:
Wednesday, February 13

13

The first thing I did when I woke up that Wednesday morning was rush to the mirror and look at my face, at my mouth, in particular. I examined it, ran my fingers over my lips, tried to recreate the exquisite sensations that kissing Sam had triggered throughout my body, attempted to put the evening in some kind of perspective. The fact that I had gone through over forty years of life without ever knowing such pleasure saddened me enormously. To have missed out in such a major way, to have trudged through all those weeks and months and years without meeting a man I'd even felt like kissing the way I'd kissed Sam, was tragic. But now I had met such a man. I had discovered what all the fuss was about. I had finally caught up to the rest of the world. I was so happy I actually cried.

I didn't have a lot of time to cry, though, because I was supposed to meet Sam on the Promenade Deck in fifteen minutes for our four-mile run. Afterward, we were going to visit Jackie.

I had called the hospital when I'd gotten back to my cabin the night before, to check on her, and the nurse on duty—not Nurse Wimple, thank God—had told me "the patient's vitals" were improving; that Jackie was still running a fever but was resting comfortably; and that Dr. Johansson had been in to see her after dinner and seemed pleased with her progress.

As for Pat, I knocked gently on her cabin door on my way to meet Sam at seven-thirty, but there was no answer. I guessed that she was still out cold from the Valium.

I rushed to the elevator, realizing that I had completely forgotten to comb my hair, when I found Skip Jamison standing there.

"You're up early," I remarked, as we were joined at the elevator by two elderly women in hair curlers.

"Today's my meeting with the folks at Crubanno Rum," Skip explained. "As soon as we get to San Juan, I'll be into my ad agency mode. Gotta get revved, gotta change my mind-set, ya know?"

"Sure," I said, remembering that Crubanno was based in San Juan. "Will you be spending the entire time with the Crubanno executives, scouting locations for photo shoots?"

"That's the plan. No fun and games today. Not for *moi.*"

"Just work work work."

"You got it. I guarantee I won't be having anything close to the kind of fun you were having last night. Man, you and Mr. Albany were really going at it."

"What did you say?"

"Hey, don't be embarrassed. I really think it's cool the way you give off that edgy Manhattan thing one minute and then turn it on full tilt when a guy gets you hot. You and Mr. Albany should videotape yourselves next time. Burn up the VCR, right?"

It wasn't just the familiar way Skip had spoken to me that upset me. Or even the fact that someone had seen Sam and me embracing. We hadn't exactly been discreet. No, I was bothered that it was *Skip* who had seen us; that he always seemed to be wherever I was; that he was like my little shadow, showing up at the elevator, hanging out by the pool, lurking, forever lurking.

"Listen, I'm happy for you, Elaine," he said when the elevator arrived and we started to descend. "You're doing just what you should be doing."

"What I *should* be doing?"

"Yeah. You should be making the best of these last few days."

"Making the best . . . of these last few days?" I stammered as a thin line of perspiration formed above my upper lip.

"Yeah, of the cruise. If I were you, I'd make them the best fucking days of my life."

The women in the hair curlers frowned at Skip's crude language. I frowned too, but for a different reason. I'd been so wrapped up with Sam that I had actually forgotten about the hit man for a few hours. But now I wondered: Was Skip really an art director at a major advertising agency or was that just a cover? Could art directors at major advertising agencies be hit men too? Had Eric, that dopey, anal-retentive, tight-sphinctered ex-husband of mine, actually hired Skip to kill me?

No, I told myself as I got off the elevator on the Promenade Deck. If Eric wanted to kill me, he would have done it years ago. Not only that, he would have done it himself, instead of hiring someone else to do it. Eric had trouble delegating, as the people who worked for him knew well. It was one of the very few things we had in common.

I hurried to the spot where Sam and I had agreed to meet. He was there, waiting for me.

"Good morning," he said, immediately pulling me toward him and kissing me.

God, here we go again, I thought as I felt my legs buckle. "We're shameless," I said between gasps for air. "Doing this in broad daylight."

"Want to stop?" Sam asked as he continued to kiss me.

"No," I said and locked my lips on his.

The next time we took a breathing break, Sam commented on my uncombed hair.

"It looks good that way," he said. "Wild. Untamed."

"Oh, please. It looks exactly the way it always looks when I don't have time to wash it, let alone comb it. It's so much trouble to keep up I should send it out to be dry-cleaned."

Sam laughed and said, "Come here."

He drew me into yet another embrace. We went at it for a few minutes more when I finally pulled away.

"Look, I'm as big a fan of all this kissing as you are," I said, "but I've got a full day ahead. I've got to run four miles, call my office, visit Jackie in the hospital, see how Pat's doing, go sightseeing in San Juan, find my lost luggage, stop at the police department—"

"The police department? What for?"

Damn. That had slipped out. I hadn't planned to tell Sam about the murder plot. Not when I hadn't even told my friends.

"I meant, the post office, not the police department," I said, tapping my forehead as if I'd simply mixed up my public servants. "I want to dash off some postcards. You know. Wish you were here, and all that?"

"But you don't have to go to the post office in San Juan. There's one on the ship. Deck 5."

"Oh. Well, that'll save some time right there. Thanks."

"You're welcome."

Sam was about to kiss me again when I pulled away and asked, "Does all this ardor mean that you've decided I'm the 'find' of the century as opposed to a pain in the ass?"

"It means that I'm coming closer to a decision," he said.

"When do you think you'll know for sure?"

"Soon." He grabbed for me.

Two can play coy, I said to myself as I evaded his grasp, waved goodbye, and darted onto the running track, leaving Sam in the dust.

We did our four miles, had a quick breakfast, and then went down to the hospital to see Jackie—or rather, I went to see Jackie while Sam waited outside. We had decided that, given how sick she was, she might not be ready for visitors she hardly knew. She had only met Sam once, after all.

When I got to her room, she was sitting up in bed, flipping through a copy of *Better Homes & Gardens* and muttering that she thought the pachysandra in one of the photographs looked wilted.

"Something tells me you're feeling better," I smiled as I approached her bed and bent down to give her a hug.

"Much," she said. "Per really knows his stuff."

"Per?"

"Dr. Johansson."

I arched an eyebrow. "So we're on a first-name basis with our physician, are we?"

"We are. He's a great guy. We really hit it off last night."

"That's right. The nurse mentioned that he had been in to see you."

"Yeah, he came by and we talked. It turns out, he's an American citizen, since his ex-wife is American. He's thinking of quitting the ship and setting up a medical practice in the States. He asked me where I was from and I gave him a real estate agent's speech about Bedford—how good the schools are, how quaint the village is, how close to New York City it is without being on top of it. He asked me if I thought *he* would like Bedford. I said it probably wasn't anything like Helsinki but it had its charms."

"There isn't much skiing in Bedford," I pointed out.

"I know," she said. "I told him that the only ski jumps in Westchester County are bad nose jobs. He thought that was hilarious."

I shook my head in amazement. "When I visited you yesterday, Dr. Johansson said you were very weak and that I shouldn't tire you out. How come he spent so much time with you?"

"He's the doctor. I guess he thought it was okay. He's got me on antibiotics, plus Tylenol for the fever, and I'm almost as good as new now."

"Jackie, that's great," I said, relieved. "Does he know what's wrong with you?"

"He said he thinks it's a couple of things: a stomach virus and a middle-ear infection, brought on by the sinus infection I never took care of back home. I'm still pretty dehydrated and I have to be on intravenous fluids for another day or so. But I'm gonna be fine. Thanks to Per."

"When does *Per* think you can leave the hospital? Or does he want you to stay here indefinitely, so he can keep a closer eye on you?" I teased. I was delighted that Jackie had become friends with Dr. Johansson. I had liked him almost immediately.

"Hopefully, I can get out of here in another thirty-six hours," she replied. "Let's see: that means I'll miss San Juan today and Saint Croix tomorrow, but I'll probably catch our last port of call. Nassau, isn't it?"

I nodded. "I'm sorry about all this," I said. "You must feel so cheated."

"I thought I would, but right now I'm just happy to be feeling better," she said cheerfully. "Now. Enough about me. Did you take my advice?"

"About what?"

"About Sam. I told you to have at him last night. Did you?"
I laughed.

"Is that a yes?" Jackie asked.

"It's a yes," I conceded, "although a more accurate answer is that we had at each other."

Jackie's eyes widened. "You mean you and Sam slept together?"

"No. We came close, but we decided to wait," I said, sounding like a horny but levelheaded teenager.

"Wait for what, for Christ's sake?" Jackie demanded. "Till your first issue of *Modern Maturity* comes in the mail?"

"There's still tomorrow or the next night," I said.

"Sure, but what about tonight?" she urged.

She had a point.

Pat was alert, conscious, still bruised and limping, but determined to carry on with the cruise. She said she intended to go with the other members of Ginger Smith Baldwin's art safari when the ship docked in San Juan, even if she had to go by wheelchair.

"I don't want you to spend time alone with Albert," I said, knowing he'd insist on being right by Pat's side before and after the art class.

"Why not? He's been so attentive," she said.

"Let him be a little less attentive," I suggested, picturing him pushing her off the pier in her wheelchair. "What if you skipped today's art safari and went sightseeing with Sam Peck and me? I'd like you to get to know him better, Pat."

"Elaine," she sighed. "Bill's the only man for me. You know that."

I laughed. Pat could be so Gracie Allen sometimes. "No, dear. *I'm* the one who's interested in Sam. I'd love it if you'd spend time with us. It would mean a lot to me. What do you say?"

She took her customary eternity to render a decision, agreeing to spend the afternoon with us, only after she telephoned Albert and made her apologies.

Fine, I thought. You talk to Albert while I go to the police station.

The *Princess Charming* motored into the port of Puerto Rico's capital city at one o'clock. I told Pat and Sam I'd meet them at Pat's cabin at two, figuring I would then have an hour to try Harold again at the office, check with the Purser's Office on my suitcase, and visit the local police.

Harold was unavailable. No surprise there. The purser had actually located my suitcase and was having it delivered to my cabin within the hour. Big surprise there.

Then came my adventure at the police station.

It was a five-minute taxi ride from the pier—a right turn, a couple of traffic lights, and there I was.

The first thing I did when I entered the station was to inform the officer on duty that I did not speak Spanish; that I was an American named Elaine Zimmerman; and that I was in trouble.

"What kind of trouble?" asked the officer, a nice-looking, middle-aged man named Ronald Morales.

"I'm a passenger on the *Princess Charming,*" I began, nodding in the direction of the marina where we had just docked.

"Ju were robbed when ju got off the ship?" Officer Morales asked, grabbing a pad and pen and making a few notes.

"No, nothing like that," I said. "It happened on the ship. While we were at sea."

He looked relieved that I would not be running back to America complaining about the crime in Puerto Rico and putting a dent in the country's tourist industry. "If ju were robbed on the ship, it's not my jurisdiction," he said. "Ju should talk to jour captain."

"I tried that," I explained. "Why don't I just tell you what happened and maybe you'll change your mind about helping me."

Officer Morales shrugged, and so I told him about overhearing the fateful phone call.

He smiled. "We hear a lot of stories about the passengers on those big cruise ships. They get a little bit crazy with the drinks, huh?"

"Well, you're always going to have your people who can hold their liquor and your people who can't, if that's what you mean," I said. "But the call I overheard didn't sound like a conversation between two partied-out drunks."

"I wasn't talking about the men ju heard on the phone," said the officer. "I was talking about ju."

"Me?"

He shrugged again.

"Look, I don't drink," I said defensively. "Well, except for the red wine. For my heart."

"Ju have a problem with the heart?" asked Officer Morales.

"No, but I will if nobody takes my story seriously," I said. "You don't believe me about the hit man, do you."

"I didn't say that. I only said there's nothing that I can do for ju." He paused, his expression softening slightly. "If the guy you're so worried about murders the lady here in San Juan, *then* ju come back to the station, okay?"

"I will if the lady isn't me," I said and headed back to the ship.

14

"**W**here've you been?" Sam asked when I finally showed up at Pat's stateroom a half-hour after we'd agreed to meet there.

"Unpacking," I lied. "Now that I have all my clothes, I can't believe how much stuff I crammed into that suitcase. Next time I'm traveling light."

"How do you like Pat's wheels?" Sam asked proudly, nodding at the wheelchair he had arranged to have brought to her cabin.

I regarded Pat seated on her special chair, her injured ankle wrapped and elevated on one of the foot rests. She was wearing a batik dress, which she had bought at Isle de Swan, and several native bracelets, also courtesy of one of the boutiques there. Her wild, frizzy blond hair protruded from beneath a wide-brimmed straw hat, yet another island purchase. Despite her bruises, she looked comfortable, relaxed, a seasoned, albeit slightly disabled, traveler.

"You remind me of a queen on a throne in that chair," I told her.

"I feel a little like royalty," she admitted with a giggle. "First the chair. Then the flowers."

"Flowers?" I asked.

She pointed to the enormous, utterly ostentatious arrangement on the dresser. I couldn't imagine how I'd missed it when I'd first entered the room. I glanced at Sam.

"Not me," he said, shaking his head. "I'm chivalrous, but not that chivalrous."

"They're from Albert," Pat explained. "Dear Albert. They arrived after I'd called to tell him I wasn't coming along on today's art safari."

"How thoughtful," I said. "And subtle."

"Albert is very solicitory," Pat said.

"Solicitous," I corrected her.

"There was a lovely card that accompanied the flowers," she added. " 'A get-well gift for a courageous lady,' it read."

"If I were you, Pat, I'd beware of geeks bearing gifts," I said.

Sam laughed. He had met Albert.

"I'm not kidding," I said. "Let's not forget that he may have pushed you down those stairs yesterday."

"Pushed her down the stairs?" Sam asked, then turned to Pat. "Is that what happened?"

"I don't remember exactly *what* happened," she said. "It's all so fuzzy now. There was a great crush of people."

"You see?" I said. "It could have been Albert."

"Elaine," Pat sighed. "No one is plotting to hurt me, least of all Albert."

"Look, Pat. Just do me a favor," I said. "Don't spend a lot of time alone with him, okay?" Within the span of only twenty-four hours, I had pinned the label of "hit man" on Skip, Henry, Lenny, and Albert. I was becoming obsessed.

"Well, I won't be alone with him today," Pat replied. "When I told him I wasn't taking the art safari, he said he wasn't either. Instead, he's taking the excursion to El Yunque."

"To El Whatie?" I asked.

"El Yunque is a 28,000-acre park, about a twenty-five-mile drive from here," said Sam. "It's the only tropical rain forest in the U.S. National Forest System and it's got 250 different species of trees, lots of hiking trails, and a bird sanctuary. Albert's probably going to see the parrots. They're a big attraction."

I turned to Sam. "You really are an expert on this cruise for someone who never took one before. Maybe you should be a travel agent instead of an insurance agent."

"It's all in the brochure," he reminded me. "The one you never deign to read. Which reminds me." He checked his watch. "Weren't we going sightseeing this afternoon?"

I glanced at Pat. "Should we place our fate in this man's hands and let him take us sightseeing?" I asked her.

"Yes, let's," she said enthusiastically.

Sam released the brakes on her wheels, pushed the chair gently through the cabin door, and off we went.

We decided to confine our sightseeing to Old San Juan, the charming, old-world section of the city that was close to the port where all the cruise ships docked. With its narrow, winding streets and huge crowds of tourists, wheeling Pat around was an adventure, but we were able to get to most of the monuments and historical sites without a problem. For example, we visited Casa de los Contrafuertes (aka the House of the Flying Buttresses), a building dating back to the early 1700s that currently housed a fascinating recreation of a nineteenth-century apothecary. We toured Casa Blanca, the house that was built in 1521 for Ponce de Leon before he went off to Florida in search of the "Fountain of Youth." And we stopped at the San Juan Cathedral, the sixteenth-century edifice in which de Leon's remains are ensconced in a marble tomb. I had been enjoying myself immensely until the "remains" thing forced me to refocus on the murder plot, this time with myself as the victim. It was a natural seque: Eric was in the remains business.

"Let's check out the shops," I suggested breezily, trying to jolly myself out of my morbid thoughts.

Sam and Pat agreed, so we wandered over to Fortaleza Street, Old San Juan's version of Worth Avenue. The street was jam-packed with shops, most of which sold jewelry at "rock bottom" prices to gullible cruise ship passengers. We went inside one of them, a shop with the no-nonsense name of The Jewelry Store, where Pat bought a gold pin in the shape of a dog for Lucy, whose tenth birthday was Friday. I bought Lucy a birthday present too—a gold locket in the shape of a heart. (My feelings for Sam had turned me into a romantic sap, not to mention impacted on my taste in jewelry.) As we were paying for the merchandise, I spotted Lenny Lubin at another counter, trying on dozens of gold chains. He had so many of them draped across his chest, he looked like an overtinseled Christmas tree.

We all exchanged hellos.

"Well, what do ya know. If it isn't the insurance agent and the three lovelies–minus one," he said. "And what happened to *this* lovely?"

"I took a little tumble yesterday at Isle de Swan," Pat explained.

"So you hurt that swell-looking gam of yours, huh?" he said, eyeing Pat's elevated leg.

"It's not so painful when I'm in the wheelchair," she reassured him. "Besides, I have a wonderful driver." She looked appreciatively at Sam. So did I.

"And what's with the other one?" Lenny asked.

"The other leg feels fine, thank you," Pat said.

"No, the other *lovely,*" Lenny said. "How long's she gonna be in the hospital?"

"How did you know Jackie was in the hospital?" I said quickly. I knew *I* hadn't told Lenny. I didn't think Pat had either.

Lenny shrugged his shoulders, which caused his chains to rise and fall. "Somebody on the ship musta said something to me about it. I got wind of it, that's all."

Or maybe you've been spying on Jackie, on all three of us, I thought, recalling the morning I'd caught Lenny lurking outside our staterooms, drunk and, supposedly, spent from his torrid night with the dollface.

"You know how people talk on cruises," Sam said to me, as a way of explaining how Lenny had probably heard about Jackie's hospitalization. "There's not much else to do on a ship but gossip. And eat."

"Yes, I'd like to," Pat said, entering the discussion.

"Like to what?" I asked.

"Eat," she said. "It's way past lunchtime."

"We could try that little café across the street," I said. "Just for a quick snack, so we won't spoil our appetite for dinner."

Sam nodded. "Lenny? Do you want to join us?"

Lenny looked absolutely flabbergasted that he had actually been invited somewhere.

"Thanks but no thanks," he said. "I've got thirteen more stores to hit." Hit. There was that word again.

———

We had a light snack in a pretty little café on the second floor of an art gallery. The food was delicious—much better than the *Princess Charming*'s—and the company even better. Sam and I made goo-goo eyes at each other every time there was a lull in the conversation, and Pat sat there beaming because I seemed so happy. The one negative occurred when Henry Prichard entered the restaurant, with Ingrid, and the only empty table was the one next to ours. I no longer suspected Henry of poisoning Jackie, but I still didn't like the way he'd been so friendly to her at first and then forgotten all about her.

Then came an even bigger affront: he'd forgotten all about Pat and me too.

When Pat leaned over to say hello once he and Ingrid were seated, he smiled but didn't acknowledge ever having met either of us.

"It was at the terminal in Miami," she reminded him. "On Sunday, the day we boarded the ship."

"Yes," I said. "I was using one of the pay phones in the terminal and you were talking on the phone next to mine. We finished our calls at about the same time and struck up a conversation. Is it coming back to you now?"

"Oh, sure. Absolutely," said Henry, flashing us a salesman's smile. His teeth looked very white against his tanned skin. "The sun must have melted my brain or something. How are you enjoying the trip so far?"

It was a thoroughly impersonal remark, without a word about where's Jackie or why is Pat in a wheelchair. It was almost as if the guy didn't want to remember having had contact with us—or didn't want to be *seen* having contact with us. Maybe he didn't want there to be a *link*. Maybe the person he was on the phone with that day in the terminal was the same person he was on the phone with the other night on the ship: one of our ex-husbands.

"Nice to see you again," Pat called out to him as we were leaving the café.

"Nice to see you too," said Henry.

Yeah, I'll bet, I thought.

We got back to the ship at about five o'clock, in time to visit Jackie, then shower and dress for dinner.

She was not alone when we got to her hospital room, nor was she receiving visitors at that precise moment. Dr. Johansson had the white curtain pulled around her bed and was, evidently, examining her. I laughed when I imagined them discussing the joys of downhill skiing while he searched her body for lymph nodes.

When he finished his examination, swept the curtain back, and waved us into the room, Jackie was sitting up in bed. The IV needle was still in her arm, but her color was much better and her eyes a lot clearer. Pat and I told her she was beginning to look like her old self again.

"Watch the 'old,' would ya?" she barked.

"You're hardly old," volunteered Dr. Johansson with an affectionate chuckle.

"I'm glad you're feeling better," Sam offered. "Pretty soon, you'll be back with your buddies."

"Yeah, but it's nice to know *you've* been filling in while I'm gone," she said, giving me a knowing look. "Per says I'll be out of here tomorrow, with any luck. I'm not supposed to get off the ship when we're in Saint Croix though, right, Doc?"

Dr. Johansson shook his head. "You'll be leaving da hospital to rest," he cautioned her. "Not to sightsee. Den maybe vhen ve get to da Bahamas, you can do da normal things."

"What's on your schedule for tonight?" I asked Jackie. There were no televisions in the hospital rooms.

"I'll be eating my first solid foods," she said. "If you consider Jell-O and chicken broth solid. Then the nurse will probably come around and take another vial or two of my blood. And if I'm a really good girl, Per will visit and tell me more about this ship. He's incredibly knowledgeable about what goes on around here."

"What goes on around here?" I asked with particular interest.

"Yes, do tell," Pat said.

"Well," Jackie began, "since Per has worked on the *Princess Charming* for so long, he knows all kinds of Trivial Pursuit–type things." Dr. Johansson smiled modestly. "Like: Did you know that the refrigeration department of the ship produces twenty tons of ice cubes a day?"

"No," I said, disappointed that the doctor's tidbits weren't of a more gossipy—i.e. useful—nature.

"It's true. And here's another factoid that'll knock you out," said Jackie, pulling a sheet of paper off the small table next to her bed and reading what was written on it. "The kitchen staff prepares about 25,000 meals each week, which includes three sit-down meals, room-service items, and midnight buffets."

"So cruises *are* a floating cafeteria," I said.

Jackie ignored me and went right on reading. "They serve about 90,000 eggs, 40,000 pounds of beef, 25,000 pints of milk, 165,000 pieces of bread, 230,000 cups of coffee, and—get this—20,000 piña coladas!"

"Yeah, and I'll bet Lenny Lubin will drink 19,000 of them," I whispered to Sam.

"What's more," Jackie informed us, "the ship's washing machines do about 290,000 pieces of linen—sheets, towels, pillow cases, table-cloths, napkins, etc. And that's just on a typical, seven-day cruise."

There's nothing typical about *this* seven-day cruise, I wanted to tell Jackie and all the rest of them. Not by a long shot.

15

"So this is the *real* Elaine Zimmerman," Sam mused, eyeing me, his mouth forming a sexy half-smile.

"No more Perky Princess gems," I nodded triumphantly. As I had previously announced to Sam, now that my luggage was back in my possession, I was appearing for the first time on the *Princess Charming* in my own clothes: a sleeveless black sheath and a white, double-breasted blazer. He was wearing a navy blue jacket with brass buttons, a fresh pair of khaki slacks, a light blue shirt, and a blue-and-white-striped tie. If I do say so myself, we were a handsome couple. A tall couple, anyway.

We were standing in front of the Crown Room, the lounge that had doubled as a Mustering Station the first day of the cruise. On this, our fourth night on the ship, the lounge was the setting for the Captain's Cocktail Party, which, other than enabling the passengers to meet and shake hands with Captain Solberg, was just another ploy to get us to buy drinks. Sam and I had decided to put in a brief appearance before dinner; Pat was tired from her outing in Old San Juan and had planned to have dinner in her cabin.

"You look terrific," said Sam, still assessing me. "So terrific I think I'll—"

He didn't finish his sentence. Instead, he grabbed me and kissed me. I did not resist.

I had been waiting all day to kiss him, and I couldn't miss his eagerness to kiss me. There was almost a hunger about the way he reached for me, a yearning. Was it possible that, in spite of his attractiveness and the fact that men who traveled all the time were the leading practitioners of the one-night stand, he hadn't been with a woman since Jillian? Had he somehow been holding out for me, just as I'd been waiting all my life for him?

"Sam. We're making a spectacle of ourselves," I laughed when we pulled apart after a long embrace.

"Can't help it. This is the first chance I've had to be alone with you all day." He held me at arm's length, letting his eyes roam approvingly over my body, his face full of lust. I felt–God help me–transformed. Ever since Sam had begun to lavish his attention on me, I *seemed* to myself to be softer, less brittle, as if I'd had my rough edges planed, smoothed, evened. I actually walked differently when I was around him, stood up straighter, didn't round my shoulders, smiled as I walked. Of course, part of the reason for the new and improved walk was that I felt less self-conscious about my height next to him. Sure, there were guys back home who were taller than Sam, but they were all with the New York Knicks.

"Listen, I want to thank you for being so nice to Pat today," I said. "Jackie too."

"It was easy. I like your friends," he said, still holding me around the waist.

"I'm glad," I said, thinking how important it was for the man in a woman's life to like her friends. And vice versa.

"How about taking a quick swing around the room, shaking hands with the captain, and then going to dinner?" Sam suggested.

Before I could disagree with the "shaking hands with the captain" part, Sam had taken *my* hand and swept me into the Crown Room. There was a short receiving line to meet Captain Solberg and suddenly Sam and I were on it.

"We don't want to actually *meet* the captain, do we?" I whispered. "I mean, do you stand in line to shake hands with the engineer of every train you take? Do I attend cocktail parties with the driver of the Hampton Jitney?" I didn't want Sam to know that I had already met Captain Solberg. Then I'd have to explain *why* I'd met him, and I wasn't prepared to do that. Not yet. Not until I was sure that Sam, unlike Pat and Jackie and Svein himself, wouldn't think I was delusional.

"Oh, come on," he coaxed. "It'll be fun to put the face with the voice that booms over the PA system at nine o'clock every night."

"But we've seen him on the *Princess Charming* Channel," I protested.

"Yeah, but you're in PR, Slim. You work with the media. You know people don't look the same in person as they do on TV. It'll be fun to see the guy up close and personal."

I couldn't talk Sam out of it. Before I knew it, he and I were next in line to shake the hand of Captain Solberg.

"Good evening. I hope you are enjoying da cruise. Thank you for sailing with Sea Svan," the captain said mechanically after Sam introduced himself.

"I'm having a great time," Sam said, moving me into the captain's view. "And so is my friend, Elaine Zimmerman."

"Ah, Mrs. Zimmerman," said Captain Solberg, recognizing me right away. "You are feeling much better, I see. No more murderer chasing you around da ship?"

"Murderer?" Sam asked, looking startled.

"I think it's the language barrier," I said breezily to Sam. "I was introduced to Captain Solberg yesterday morning and happened to mention that it must be *murder* to run a ship of this size. Obviously, he misunderstood the colloquial use of the word."

Sam bought it, but Captain Solberg regarded me exactly the way he had that morning in his office—as if he thought he was in the presence of a basket case. I knew in that single instant that I had just lost whatever credibility I might have had with him. In other words, if the time came when I *really* needed his help, I'd never get it.

Sam and I moved quickly through the receiving line, made our way out of the Crown Room, and rode down in the elevator to the dining room. We had forgotten we were still holding hands and murmuring romantic little inanities to each other when we arrived at Table 186.

The jaws of our tablemates dropped as we took the two empty chairs between Kenneth and Rick and sat down.

"Look! The tall one's got a boyfriend now, Dorothy," Lloyd said in such a discreet and tactful manner that half the people in the dining room turned around to stare.

"She's a grown woman, dear. What she does is her own business," Dorothy answered him, then winked at me. I winked back.

"I'm so happy for you two," Brianna cooed, then nudged Rick, who was munching on a hard roll. "Isn't it neat about Elaine and Sam, honeybun?"

Rick ignored her, trying not to get dragged into some hopelessly girlish conversation.

That left Gayle and Kenneth, but they didn't comment, perhaps because they wanted everyone to know they were too worldly and sophisticated to care about who was falling in love with whom on some cruise that catered to the Middle Class.

Gayle, for example, got very involved with the clasp on her oh-so-patriotic pin—a bejeweled American flag made of rubies, diamonds, and sapphires. She explained that she had chosen to wear the pin because tonight was American Night in the dining room.

Kenneth seemed more interested in launching into a speech on the vagaries of the stock market, although he did take a moment to ask how Jackie and Pat were faring.

"Much better, thanks," I told him. "Pat's recovering from her fall and Jackie should be out of the hospital sometime tomorrow."

"That's good news," said Kenneth, before going back to his discourse on puts and calls. I found talk of the stock market as boring as it gets, so I was grateful when Ismet appeared to tell us the specials.

"Tonight, in honor of your America the Beautiful, I am recommending the fried chicken and mashed potatoes," Ismet said, then glanced anxiously at Rick, who had never been a big fan of our waiter's recommendations.

But Rick surprised everybody by applauding when he heard Ismet's pick of the night. "Finally, something I can eat," he grumbled. Rick lived in North Carolina, where, presumably, he ate fried chicken and mashed potatoes several times a week.

Sam and I didn't even bother to consult the menu. We went with the fried chicken and mashed potatoes too, just to get the whole business over with. It was obvious from the way Sam was stroking my leg under the table and the fact that I was practically purring that food was the last thing on either of our minds. What was on our minds was sex, plain and simple. By the time dessert arrived, there was no question that *this* was the night we would sleep together. Why wait another day or two? I thought. Sam and I were adults. Single, unattached adults. We didn't have to ask anyone's permission to take off our clothes in the privacy of one of our staterooms and give free rein to our feelings for each other. It was right and normal and natural that we have sex. And I was a nervous wreck.

I don't remember how the food tasted or how much of it landed on Lloyd's dark blue sport jacket. All I remember is that I wanted dinner to be history so that Sam and I could create our own history.

Eventually, Rick and Brianna and Dorothy and Lloyd got up to leave the table. Sam and I were about to beat it too when Kenneth asked us if we wanted to join him and Gayle for the eight-thirty movie. We begged off, saying we'd already seen it. Much later, we realized that in issuing the invitation, Kenneth had never indicated which movie the ship's theater was showing.

Sam took my hand and we drifted wordlessly through the corridors of the ship. Past the photographers' display. Into the elevator. Up to Deck 7. Sam's floor.

My heart was thundering so loud in my chest I wondered if I was about to have a cardiac incident.

No, I told myself. You're about to have the time of your life.

We arrived at Sam's stateroom. He opened the door, flicked on the light, and beckoned me inside.

His cabin was exactly the same size and configuration as mine, I saw as he closed the door behind us. He even had a lifeboat hanging outside his porthole. The only difference between our rooms, other than that his was on a lower deck, was that his was not nearly as neat as mine. It wasn't just that Kingsley was a much more competent cabin steward than the one assigned to Sam; it was that Sam was not the compulsive person I was. *I* always hung my clothes in the closet the moment they were off my body (unless they were bound for the washing machine). Sam's clothes were all over the place—the shorts and shirt he'd worn during our afternoon of sightseeing were gathered in a little ball on the floor; several ties, which he must have decided against wearing to dinner that evening, were draped across the lamp shade; a couple of still-wet bathing suits were hanging on the knob of his bathroom door. The mess was quite a revelation to me, because whenever Sam appeared in public, he was neat and well groomed. I wondered if there were other things about Sam Peck that would surprise me.

"I guess Gordon didn't straighten up the room yet," he said. "He usually puts my stuff away when he shows up for the turn-down service."

"Don't worry about it," I said as Sam busily tidied up. "I didn't come here so I could give the place the white-glove test."

"Good." Sam threw the last of his clothes onto the floor of the closet and walked over to me. He encircled me in his arms, drawing our bodies exquisitely close. "Then let's talk about why you *did* come, Slim." His voice was low and soft and provocative. "I wasn't sure you would, to tell you the truth. Not after last night's rejection."

"I didn't reject you," I said. "I just thought we should wait another day or so. We hardly know each other. I'm not one for hopping into bed with strange men."

"So I'm less strange, twenty-four hours later?"

"No, I'm just more eager."

He laughed.

"Do you have any idea how good I feel when I'm around you?" he asked, beginning to kiss me—little pecks here and there, on my cheeks, my forehead, my neck.

"No. How good?" I said, letting his lips wander all over me, still more than a little overwhelmed that all this was really happening.

"So good I want to make love to you, Slim. Does that answer your question?"

"Yes," I moaned. "Yes."

Sam took my "yeses" as a cue to slip my white blazer off me. I was vaguely aware that he let it fall to the floor in a heap instead of hanging it in the closet, but I wasn't about to say anything.

Next, he unzipped my black dress, pulled it over my head, and let it, too, fall to the floor. And then he helped me out of my shoes and peeled my panty hose slowly and sensuously down my legs, off my feet.

I felt totally vulnerable, standing there before him, wearing nothing but my bra and panties. The last person to see me in my undergarments was a saleswoman at Saks, who, three weeks ago, had been rushing back and forth from my dressing room, frantically trying to outfit me with "cruisewear." But oddly enough, I didn't shrink from Sam's gaze, wasn't the least bit ashamed for him to see my body. I *wanted* him to look at me, to admire me, to be turned on by me. The very idea that I *did* turn him on was an amazing confidence booster.

"You're beautiful," he murmured. "Really."

Giddy with arousal, I took charge from then on. I removed Sam's eyeglasses and, with his help, his sport jacket, shirt, tie, socks, and shoes. And then I threw my arms around him and kissed him. Hard. Avidly. Greedily.

Sam was nearly naked now, except for his underpants. (They were briefs, not boxers, and they were, as they say in romance novels, "straining.") He reached out, lifted one of my bra straps off my shoulder and pressed his lips to the skin he had bared. I nearly cried with pleasure, having never in my life had my shoulder kissed.

To reciprocate, I ran my hands over Sam's hairy chest, nibbling on various spots, caressing them. Sam responded with low moans that eventually gave way to an actual: "Oh, Jesus."

He lifted my head up off his chest, crushed his mouth against mine, and kissed me with such force, such pent-up passion, that both of us were astonished by it.

Then we broke apart very suddenly, as if it had simultaneously dawned on us that we were still standing in the middle of the room when there was a perfectly good bed available.

Sam took my hand and led me toward the bed.

Well, this is it, kid, I said to myself as I swallowed hard. You're about to join that exclusive club of single, middle-aged, working women who actually have sex with men instead of attending support groups and whining about why they don't.

"I'd like to say something," I managed, just before we reached the bed.

"Tell me you're not changing your mind," Sam pleaded.

"No. It's . . . nothing like that," I said hesitantly. "It's . . ." I paused because I wasn't sure how to proceed, so out of the loop was I when it came to sex in the nineties. Or sex in this century, for that matter.

"Go on. What is it?" Sam urged.

"Okay. It's been a while since I've had. . . . Well, what I mean is, I haven't seen the need to. . . . The point I'm trying to make is that I'm not on the Pill or anything," I said finally, placing special emphasis on the "anything." So Sam would be sure to catch my drift. Why spend money on birth control or sexually transmitted disease preventions when I wasn't partaking, if you know what I'm saying?

"Oh. Is that all?" Sam laughed, looking very relieved. "I did come prepared tonight, but I completely forgot about it once we got going here." He laughed again. "I'm glad one of us is thinking clearly. I'll just step into the bathroom and wrap the rascal."

"Wrap the rascal?" Men had such cutesy ways of referring to their sex organs. "I'll be waiting."

As soon as he was out of the room, I reminded myself to relax. I was so excited about making love with Sam that I could barely contain myself. I almost felt guilty about feeling so happy, particularly when I thought of Jackie and Pat and the problems they were having—and when I thought of the poor, unsuspecting ex-wife who was soon to perish at the hands of a hit man. Life just wasn't fair, was it?

In an effort to work off some of my nervous energy while Sam was in the bathroom condomizing himself, I started to straighten up his cabin, picking up his clothes and either hanging them up or folding them on the chair. I was in the process of smoothing out his rumpled khaki slacks and sliding them over a hanger when something dropped out of one of the pockets.

I knelt down to pick it up.

It was Sam's wallet, a buttery, brown-leather Mark Cross model. I quickly debated whether I had time to give it an innocent little examination before he emerged from the bathroom. I wasn't interested in how much money he was carrying, you understand; I was interested in whether he was carrying a photograph of Jillian (still) and, if so, what she looked like.

I decided I had just long enough to search the wallet, recalling that it used to take Eric a few minutes to put one of those rubbers on.

Feeling like a prostitute rolling a John, I nevertheless unfolded the wallet and, as fast as my nimble fingers could manage it, began to riffle through its various compartments. Disappointingly, there were no photographs of the dearly departed fiancée.

Oh, well, I thought. Why make this scavenger hunt a total loss? While Sam is still in the bathroom, I might as well see what sort of credit cards he has, just to pass the time.

But the first card I lifted out of the wallet had me baffled, to say the least. It was a SkyMiles card. For members of Delta's frequent flier program.

I had a SkyMiles card. So did lots of people I knew. But Sam had told me that he never set foot on airplanes, that he was deathly afraid of flying, that he had taken the cruise because it was the only way he could get to the Caribbean. So what in the world would he be doing with a frequent flier card?

Then came another puzzle: The member's name on the SkyMiles card wasn't Sam Peck. It was Simon Purdys.

Simon Purdys?

I mulled this discrepancy over, calmly and rationally, and decided that Sam had probably grabbed a business associate's frequent flier card by mistake. Or maybe the unwitting swap had occurred on the ship. Yes, it was entirely possible that one of the passengers on the *Princess Charming* was named Simon Purdys and that, during the mad crush at the terminal in Miami, when everyone was opening their wallet and flashing their ID, Sam had somehow gotten stuck with Simon Purdys's SkyMiles card and Simon Purdys had gotten stuck with—say—Sam's Mobil gas card. It *was* possible, wasn't it?

As I cautiously flipped through the other credit cards in Sam's wallet—American Express Gold, MasterCard, Visa, Blockbuster Video—I saw that the name imprinted on every single one of them was Simon Purdys! So much for inadvertent swaps at the terminal.

What was going on here? Surely there must be a reasonable explanation. Sam didn't strike me as the type who would steal one of the other passengers' wallets. He was an insurance agent, not a thief. He earned a nice living, he'd told me. Besides which, he was Sam, honest Sam, a solid citizen, the man I was about to make love to.

I searched the wallet further, sensing I shouldn't, *knowing* I shouldn't, and ultimately discovered something truly damning—the one piece of plastic I couldn't reason away.

It was Sam's driver's license. Or should I say, Simon's.

There, in living color, on the left side of the license, was a photograph of Sam, his blue eyes twinkling behind the eyeglasses, his dark, wavy hair smooth and lustrous. In the center of the license, however, was the name Simon Purdys, along with an address, not in Albany, but in New York City. About two blocks from *my* apartment, as a matter of fact!

No wonder this guy looked familiar to me that first night at dinner, I thought, feeling dizzy, faint, nauseous, as I stuffed the cards back into the wallet and the wallet back into Sam's–Simon's–pants pocket. No wonder he looked familiar to *Skip* that day at the pool! Sam Peck was a total fucking fraud, a complete fabrication, an impostor!

I was absolutely devastated, completely shellshocked. None of it made sense. None of it. I could hardly let myself think about it. But I *had* to think about it.

I had heard two men on the phone, plotting to murder a woman on the ship, but I had never even considered that Sam might turn out to be a cold-blooded killer. I had never allowed that the reason he'd been romancing me was simply to get me alone so he could carry out the job he'd been hired to do. By *my* ex-husband!

My whole world fell apart in those moments, and the tears and the anger and the fear nearly strangled me. As I grabbed for my clothes and got dressed as fast as I could make my arms and legs move, I was consumed with feelings of betrayal, as if I had hurtled back in time to my adolescence. I was suddenly the gawky little girl again–the awkward child who was so needy she let herself love a father who lied to her over and over and then left her. History was repeating itself yet again.

So Simon Purdys is the hit man, I thought with a terrible, empty feeling in the pit of my stomach. He's the person Eric is *paying* to get rid of me.

I shook my head in disbelief, blinded by my rage, as I tried to make myself face the fact that the man with whom I was about to become intimate–the man with whom I had fallen in love!–had planned to seduce me before taking my life! To think that I had trusted this guy, this liar, this creature! To think that I had eaten dinner with him, gone running with him, let him befriend my friends, let him kiss me, was too much. It was all too much.

My hand was literally on the knob of the cabin door when Sam–or whoever he was–finally emerged from the bathroom. He had a white bath towel wrapped around his waist, covering his privates, but he was still erect, I couldn't help noticing. Unless, of course, it was a gun that was protruding from the towel. A gun equipped with one of those silencers.

"What are you doing?" he asked, feigning a pained expression when he realized that I was fully dressed and about to flee his little love nest.

"I'm escaping," I said, my voice choked with sobs. *"Mr. Purdys."*

He seemed surprised, hurt even. "How did you . . . I mean . . ." Pause. "I don't . . ." He stopped. What could he say? I had him.

"Just tell me one thing, Simon, or whatever the hell your real name is," I said, wiping my nose and eyes with the back of my hand. "Are you really in the insurance business?"

"Well, no," he admitted sheepishly.

"Pity," I said. "You could have sold me a life insurance policy and *then* killed me."

"Killed you? What are you talking about, Slim?"

"How dare you call me that," I snapped. "The only thing that's 'slim' are the chances that you and Eric are ever gonna get away with this."

"With *what?*" he demanded, the erection only a memory now.

I took one final look at his tall, lean body and handsome, lying face.

"With making me love you," I said and bolted out the door.

Day Five:
Thursday, February 14

16

I awoke to the cruel realization that it was February fourteenth. Valentine's Day. Swell.

I had spent half the night pacing my cabin, turning over in my mind everything Sam had said to me, replaying it in this new context, trying to piece together how he and Eric could have met and hatched their little plot. As if it wasn't devastating enough to my ego to learn that my ex-husband hated me enough to want me dead, I had to deal with the fact that the man I loved–the man for whom I had actually bought the sappiest Valentine in the ship's gift shop–wanted me dead too. Talk about a kick in the teeth.

What line of bull have you been handing the other passengers?

That's what the man on the phone (Eric) had asked the man on the ship (Sam) the night I'd overheard their conversation.

Of course, I now knew exactly what line of bull Sam had been handing us: the whole bit about being an insurance agent who was so afraid of flying he had to take a cruise. What a crock.

Open your eyes and see for yourself what a pain in the ass she is!

That was another thing Eric had said during the ship-to-shore phone call–a remark Sam had then spun to his own advantage in order to seduce me.

I can't decide if you're a pain in the ass or the find of the century, Slim.

Wasn't that the very line he had teased me with? In between nibbles on my earlobes?

God, he was disgusting. They both were. But you know what really galled me? That Sam would make up that sob story about the poor, sweet, dead fiancée. *Jillian*. Sniff sniff. I mean, really. Was I a sucker or what?

Well, they won't get away with it—either of them, I vowed. I knew I couldn't run to Captain Solberg with the fact that Sam wasn't who he'd claimed to be, especially since the captain had seen us together, arm in arm on that receiving line, only the night before. And I knew there wouldn't be any point in spilling my guts to the police in Saint Croix, where the *Princess Charming* would be docking within the hour; they would only blow me off the way the cop in Puerto Rico had. No, I would shut my mouth, keep to myself, take a time-out.

I wasn't even up to visiting Jackie in the hospital or checking in with Pat. I couldn't face my friends. Not when the man I'd told them I was crazy about ended up being my would-be executioner. There were some humiliations too unspeakable to share even with one's closest confidantes.

No, I wasn't talking to anybody. I would spend the day in Saint Croix thinking, assessing the situation, deciding my next course of action.

I washed and dressed purposefully, my mission to distract myself from my pain and suffering.

And then the phone in my cabin rang.

I became paralyzed.

It's Sam, I whispered. I know it is.

I let the phone ring and ring and ring, even though a tiny voice inside me wondered if it could be Dr. Johansson, calling to say that Jackie had taken a turn for the worse; or Leah, calling to ask my advice about handling the public relations messes my clients had gotten themselves into; or Pat, merely calling to wish me a good morning.

No. It was Sam, I knew instinctively. And he was calling for one of two reasons: either to tell me more lies, or to determine if I was in my cabin, alone, so he'd be free to come and kill me.

The ringing stopped. I exhaled, relieved.

I continued to dress. Then the phone rang again. And again I let it ring.

This went on two or three more times before I couldn't stand it anymore and took the phone off the hook.

Just after nine, as the ship pulled up to the pier in Frederiksted, there was a knock on my door. I froze until I heard Kingsley's voice outside my cabin.

"I have several phone messages for you, Mrs. Zimmerman," he called out.

"Oh, thanks, Kingsley," I said, stepping quickly into my shorts. "Would you mind just slipping them under the door for me?"

"No problem," he said and slid three envelopes underneath my stateroom door.

With trembling hands, I opened each one.

The first read: "Elaine. Please call. Simon."

The second read: "Elaine. I have to talk to you. To explain everything. Simon."

The third read: "Slim. Trust me. Sam."

Yeah, right, I laughed to myself. I trust you, Sam. You can't even keep your name straight from message to message.

I crumpled up the pieces of paper, tossed them in the garbage, and finished dressing.

And then I grabbed a sheet of *Princess Charming* stationery and wrote a note of my own: to Pat. I told her that I had plans to go sightseeing alone, that if she was feeling up to it she should go with Albert to whichever scenic spot Ginger Smith Baldwin had chosen for the day's art safari (I explained that I had misjudged Albert, was no longer suspicious of him, and felt perfectly comfortable with her spending time alone with him), and that I would see her later in the afternoon, in time to escort Jackie out of the hospital and up to her cabin. I also told her I loved her. In case something happened to me in Saint Croix and this was my last chance.

I stuck the note in an envelope, slid it under her stateroom door, and went ashore.

The Caribbean sun was as blinding as the steel drums were deafening as I rushed onto the pier, in search of a taxi.

"Welcome to Saint Croix, the largest of the U.S. Virgin Islands," said a smiling native woman who handed me a brochure extolling the virtues of Cruzan Rum, a local product which, said the brochure, was rated "Best" in a blind taste test conducted by *The Washingtonian Magazine,* that noted arbiter of rum.

I smiled back and asked the woman where I might find a taxi. She pointed to the minivans that were lined up at the end of the pier. "They'll take your tour group wherever you want on the island," she said cheerfully. "Shopping, sightseeing, even the Cruzan Rum Factory."

I thanked her but explained that I wasn't part of a tour group.

Her brow furrowed. I felt guilty. She was so sweet and pretty and I had just spoiled her Chamber of Commerce moment.

"But I'd still love to tour your charming island," I assured her, glancing across the pier at Strand Street, one of Frederiksted's most picturesque streets. It was lined with colorful, historic buildings, one of which housed a Kentucky Fried Chicken franchise.

She brightened. "You could join one of the other tour groups," she said, nodding at the minivans. "Otherwise, you'll have to pay extra. The drivers don't like to take a singleton." A singleton. "Just walk over and ask which tour group can accommodate an additional passenger."

"I will," I said, happy that I would be contributing even in a small way to the financial stability of such a lovely island.

I hurried over to the large fleet of minivans that stood ready and waiting to carry hundreds of cruise ship captives to various destinations throughout the day. In my haste, I nearly knocked down a "stilt man"—one of those native men who climbs onto a pair of wooden stilts, wears bright clothes, a straw hat, and a voodoo-like mask, towers over everybody on the pier, and provides terrific photo opportunities for tourists.

"I'm so sorry," I yelled up to the guy as he straightened his hat and mask.

"You must be from New York," he muttered. "Always in a hurry, New Yorkers."

I apologized again and walked, more slowly this time, toward the taxis, my heart heavy with the memory of Sam, of the morning he had called *my* legs "stilts" and I had nearly swooned with the romance of it all.

"Anyone have space for one more?" I called out to the minivan drivers. They all ignored me. Then a man stepped forward, introducing himself as Lully, and said he could squeeze me in with his group. I was doubtful at first, as Lully's "minivan" was a dilapidated old Ford Fairlane, but when I peered inside the car, expecting to see at least a half-dozen hot and sweaty tourists, I only saw two, a man and a woman. Relieved, I hopped in.

"Where y'all from?" asked both the heavyset man and his equally heavyset wife, between whom I was now sandwiched in the back seat of Lully's Fairlane.

"New York," I told the couple. "Manhattan."

"Well, how 'bout that, Mother?" The man nudged his wife, then turned to me to explain. "We went up to New York last Christmas, to see 'em light that big ol' tree at Rockefeller Center. We went to Radio City Music Hall and saw them Rockettes, too."

Mother frowned at the mention of the fabled dancers, then leaned over and whispered to me that she hadn't much cared for their leg kicks or their costumes, neither of which were very Christian, in her opinion. I told her I couldn't agree more.

I was attempting to bond with Mother, you understand, seeing as she and her husband and I were to be tourists together for the next few hours in an unairconditioned car that was badly in need of new shock absorbers.

"Mr. and Mrs. Frank Wicky of Hattiesburg, Mississippi," the man identified himself and his wife. "Glad to know y'all."

The idea of moping around the island by myself—or worse, running into Sam!—wasn't especially appealing. "Glad to know y'all too," I told the Wickys.

Lully drove us to Christiansted first, as Mother, who was also known as Agnes, approved heartily of the town's name. A bustling and very beautiful harbor, Christiansted had an actual "downtown" area, filled with business and government offices, elegant shops, and charming restaurants—all examples of the island's Danish architecture. (Saint Croix was discovered by Christopher Columbus, who was Italian, but it was the Danes who had the upper hand when it came to design, apparently.)

"Aren't we going to get out of the car and walk around?" I asked the Wickys. "Maybe have some lunch?"

"We take all our meals on the ship," Mother/Agnes confided. "They're already paid for."

"Besides," Frank chuckled, "we can see what we need to see from right here."

Yeah, sure, I thought sadly, knowing that many cruise passengers felt similarly. For them, seeing a port of call from the back seat of a taxi or through the porthole of one of the ship's lounges was a safe way to experience a foreign culture, a way to look but not touch or be touched. I gulped back tears as I remembered that Sam and I had spoken of seeing Saint Croix together, of strolling its streets and sampling its food and swimming its waters. When I let myself dwell on what might have been between us, the heartbreak was intolerable.

From Christiansted, we traveled west, past the University of the Virgin Islands and the Alexander Hamilton Airport and, of course, the Cruzan Rum Factory, eventually making our way back to Frederiksted. Once at the pier, the Wickys shook my hand and said goodbye. (Agnes added that it was a pleasure to meet a New Yorker who did not take the Lord's name in vain.) And then they walked aboard the ship. After a second or two, I realized that they were leaving it to me to pay Lully.

As I was reaching into my purse for the money, I suddenly said, "Lully, could I hire you and your car for just another half-hour?"

"Of course, missus," he said politely. "You want to do some shopping?"

I shook my head. "I want to do some crying."

I asked Lully to drive me to the loneliest stretch of beach within ten miles of the pier. He obliged. When we got there, he stayed with the Ford Fairlane while I went off to the sand, walking until I found a spot that suited me.

There, I sat down, legs crossed Indian-style, and stared out at the turquoise water, listening to the sounds of the waves and the seagulls and the more distant squeals of happy children. I had never been so depressed.

At some point, though, after wallowing in self-pity, I stood up, dusted the sand off my legs, and said out loud: "Never mind about your broken heart. Never mind that you married a man who considers murder a viable solution to a problem. Never mind about any of that. You're a dead woman unless you keep your wits about you. You had a good cry. Now dry your tears and get back on that ship."

I took my own advice. I blew my nose, pumped myself up for whatever was coming next, and summoned Lully to drive me back to the *Princess Charming*.

17

I returned to my stateroom at two-thirty, an hour and a half before the ship was to depart from Saint Croix and head north toward Miami. When I entered the cabin, I saw that several more envelopes had been slipped under the door.

I was tempted to throw them out without even reading them but then thought, what the hell. I'm on top of this now.

The messages were from Sam, basically telling me yet again that he wanted a chance to explain, that I owed him at least that much.

I was about to toss the notes into the garbage when I noticed that one of them was from Pat, alerting me that Jackie was being released from the hospital at three-thirty and that we should meet there to help her up to her stateroom together.

I was glad that I had gotten back to the ship in time. I'd been so wrapped up in my own little soap opera that I'd nearly forgotten that one of my friends was languishing in the hospital and the other was hobbling around on a sprained ankle.

I took a quick shower, changed my clothes, and rode the elevator down to the hospital. Jackie looked infinitely better than she had the day before. She was dressed and sitting on her bed when I arrived. Pat was there, too, minus the wheelchair. So, I was surprised to see, were the Cones.

"We stopped by to see how Jackie was doing," Kenneth explained. "We brought her a get-well gift too."

With a bemused expression, Jackie held up the small box from Little Switzerland, the swanky jewelry/crystal/fine china/perfume shop that had outposts not only on Saint Croix but on other islands in the Caribbean.

"Show Elaine," Pat urged as I stood there thinking how generous, albeit inappropriate, it was for the Cones to buy Jackie a gift, let alone one from a store with such expensive merchandise. I guessed their ostentatiousness knew no bounds. They'd met Jackie only once, after all, on that first night of the cruise, the only night she'd come to the dinner table.

Jackie took the lid off the gift box and carefully lifted out a crystal figurine in the shape of a garden hoe. I stepped closer so I could get a better look at it.

"It's lovely," I told the Cones. "And so thoughtful."

"Nonsense. We were out shopping anyway," Gayle said offhandedly. "We went down our list of people we felt obligated to buy souvenirs for—Kenneth's important clients, our dearest friends, our household staff, my hair colorist, my massage therapist, the dogs' therapist—and then Kenneth remembered that Jackie was getting out of the hospital today—and that she co-owns a nursery. When we saw the darling little garden hoe, we simply added her to our shopping list. Of course, we also bought a few things for ourselves."

I sighed and thought how simple life must be for people like Gayle and Kenneth Cone. Every day was Christmas.

"Now, I think we should let Jackie and her friends have some private time together," Kenneth said to his wife.

"Absolutely," Gayle agreed with him. "I have a manicure in ten minutes. We both do, Kenneth."

He nodded and off they went. Once they were gone, Pat and I got an update on Jackie's health.

"No fever, no stomach problems, no nothing. Just a little weakness in the legs," she told us.

"Where is Dr. Johansson?" asked Pat, whose own leg was much less swollen than it had been the day before; she was now hobbling around with the aid of a cane. As for the bruises on her chin and arm, they looked pretty scary but they didn't seem to bother her. "Shouldn't he be here to discharge you?"

"He already did discharge me," Jackie said. "And to tell you the truth, I'm gonna miss that sweetie's bedside manner. He says if I take it easy in my cabin for the rest of the day, I can hang out around the ship tomorrow and then go ashore the next day when we dock in Nassau. He asked me to have lunch with him there, if I'm up to it. Saturday's his day off."

"Jackie, you sound excited about it," I remarked. I was grateful that her vacation wouldn't be a total loss.

"Speaking of excited," she said, and smiled knowingly at me, "where's Clark Kent?"

I didn't answer, which she took to mean I didn't understand.

"Come on. I mean Loverboy. Your running pal. The insurance agent," she tried again.

"That's right, Elaine. I thought you were going sightseeing with Sam today," Pat recalled. "I was surprised when your note said you were spending the day on your own."

"Maybe Elaine was out buying Sammy boy a Valentine," Jackie quipped. "Or maybe she was getting her butt tattooed. With his name on it. That's the big thing with couples these days, isn't it?"

Pat turned the color of the red ribbon on Jackie's Little Switzerland gift box. I remained expressionless. I didn't know how to explain to my friends that I was no longer seeing Sam, without going into all the details.

"What's the matter, Elaine?" Jackie asked. "Did you and Sam have a fight or something?"

"Let's just say that I've changed my mind about him. He's not who I thought he was at all."

She looked at me with great skepticism. "Who the hell did you think he was?"

"I'd rather not talk about it," I replied. "In fact, I'd appreciate it if you two wouldn't mention his name again."

"Sure. Fine. Whatever," said Jackie, seeing I wasn't kidding. "Tell you what. Since it'll be awkward for you and old what's-his-name to sit at the same table at dinner, now that you've busted up, and since I'm back in the land of the living, thank God, why don't we all have dinner in my cabin tonight? Just the Three Blond Mice, huh?"

"That sounds like fun," Pat agreed.

"It sounds like heaven," I said, relieved I wouldn't have to go anywhere near Table 186.

We were back at sea, en route to Nassau, and the waters were rougher than they had been. Despite the ship's highly publicized stabilizers, she was rocking and rolling and tossing us around quite a bit. Undaunted, Jackie, Pat, and I ordered practically everything on the room service menu and staged an old-fashioned pig-out at the table Kingsley had wheeled skillfully into Jackie's stateroom.

"Looks like a party," he said, surveying all the food and booze we'd ordered. Per had advised Jackie not to drink alcohol, since she was still on medication, but she had ordered a scotch and intended to savor every sip of it. Pat and I had each chosen wine—a bottle of red for me, a bottle of white for her.

"It *is* a party," Jackie told Kingsley. "All-girls night. And we don't want any crashers. That means no turn-down service, no phone calls, no nothing. Okay?"

"No problem," Kingsley said. "When you're done with the table, just leave it outside your cabin."

"Will do," I said. "Thanks, Kingsley."

He waved, hung the DO NOT DISTURB sign on Jackie's doorknob, and left.

"Good man," I said, trying to convince myself that they weren't all bad.

Jackie ate every morsel of her own dinner and nearly all of mine too.

"I'm cured," she announced. "Per cured me. He's a medical genius."

"Bill is an excellent doctor as well," said Pat.

"Tell us about your day with Albert," Jackie suggested, getting Pat off the subject of Bill. "What'd you guys do in Saint Croix?"

"Well, after our art safari, we took a taxi ride to the Ghut Bird Sanctuary," she said.

"Why am I not surprised?" said Jackie.

"It was right in the midst of an exquisite rain forest," Pat continued as I tuned out. I just couldn't make myself care about the tropical birds

Albert saw or the raptures he went into when he saw them. And so I half listened but mostly I thought about Sam, or tried not to.

I think Pat was waxing poetic about some bird's plumbage (she had probably meant *plumage*), when I heard a rustling sound over by the cabin door and saw an envelope being slipped under it.

Assuming that it was yet another message from Sam—and that Kingsley was merely being efficient in slipping it under Jackie's door instead of mine, given that I was having dinner in her room—I tiptoed over to the door, grabbed the envelope, and stuffed it surreptitiously into my pocket.

I'll read it later, I thought. No point in spoiling the evening with more of Sam's ramblings. He was *my* problem, not my friends'.

The party broke up about nine, and I weaved my way down the hall to my cabin just in time to hear Captain Solberg's nightly weather report. I had barely stepped inside my room when there was a knock at the door. I assumed it was Pat or Jackie, since we had literally just left each other.

I opened the door.

"Let me have five minutes to explain. Just *five* minutes."

It was Sam. Gee, it's really a shame that he's a hit man, I thought as I regarded him. It had been Country & Western Night in the dining room, so he was wearing blue jeans and a denim shirt. All that blue made his eyes only more devastating. I despised how attractive he still was to me.

I tried slamming the door in his face, but he was stronger than I thought and he was easily able to muscle it back open.

"Fine. I'll just give Security a jingle," I said coldly, moving toward the phone.

"Slim, look," he said, following me inside the cabin. "I really think you're overreacting here. I understand how you could feel lied to, confused, betrayed. But the way you've been avoiding me, refusing to even speak to me, is a little—"

"Hello?" I said into the phone, ignoring Sam's speech. "Yes. I'm calling to report that a man has broken into my stateroom and is harassing me. That's right. My cabin number is—"

We were cut off. Sam had placed his finger on the cradle of the phone.

"Oh, so you're going to kill me now? Is that it?" I said with a sneer.

"Kill you? What the hell's gotten into you?"

He looked genuinely bewildered by my remark. Which only proved what a terrific bullshit artist he was, as far as I was concerned.

"Just five minutes," he bargained. "If you don't want to talk to me after that, I swear I'll never bother you again."

"Never bother me again? What would Eric think of that?" I scoffed.

"Eric? Your ex-husband? What's he got to do with this?"

God, he was good. Maybe acting was the right career for him, not killing poor, defenseless ex-wives. He could win an Oscar with that innocent act.

"Five minutes, Slim. Just five minutes," he said again.

I *was* mildly curious about what he would say, how he would explain the Sam Peck–Simon Purdys bit, never mind the rest of it.

"Five minutes," he repeated, sensing he was getting somewhere.

"All right," I said finally, taking the dare. "But not here."

"Wherever you say then."

I considered the situation. I wasn't about to spend even five minutes alone with the man. That would be much too risky, I knew. The question was: Where on the ship *would* I feel safe with him?

"It'll have to be in a very public place," I mused. "With *lots of people* around."

"Name it," Sam said, his confidence building.

I walked over to the dresser, picked up the ship's schedule of events for that evening, scanned the listing, and lit on the perfect place for Sam to plead his case.

"We'll meet in Her Majesty's Lounge on Deck 3," I told him.

"Her Majesty's Lounge is a piano bar," Sam pointed out. "They have a couple of Ferrante and Teischer knock-offs performing. I doubt there'll be much of a crowd."

"They're not performing there tonight, according to this activities sheet," I said. "It says the ship's food and beverage manager is giving a lecture in Her Majesty's Lounge—an event that's sure to be *very* well attended."

"Why? What's the subject of the lecture?"

"Napkin folding."

18

I insisted that Sam and I take separate elevators to Her Majesty's Lounge on Deck 3. God forbid that we should take the *same* elevator, that it would be crowded, and that my body would be forced to brush up against his.

As luck would have it, my elevator got to the third deck a few minutes before Sam's. So I went straight to Her Majesty's Lounge, which, I discovered, had been set up to resemble a classroom instead of a bar, with several rows of chairs facing a lectern. There were close to seventy-five people in the room, and every chair but three was occupied. I quickly appropriated one of them and put my purse on the one right next to it, saving it for the man who'd been hired to murder me. Talk about bizarre.

The speaker standing at the lectern, the ship's food and beverage manager, was a woman named Ashley Bliss. When I arrived, she was in the midst of explaining that, although the art of napkin folding might look tricky, it was, in fact, a remarkably simple skill to master. She went on to say that there was no better way to create an atmosphere for a dinner party than to design one of the "soft sculptures" she was about to demonstrate to us.

"Select the fold to suit the mood, I always say," she said jauntily as she fingered the sample napkins that were resting on the lectern. "And be sure to remember that while napkins made entirely of synthetic materials may be the easiest to clean, they do not hold a fold the way linen, cotton, or even cotton-synthetic blends do. But the *most* important thing I want to stress before we get started here tonight–and I do mean stress!–is: Always fold your napkins *before* your party guests arrive, while you still have time and don't feel *stressed!"*

Everyone applauded, including me. This was riveting stuff, let me tell you.

Sam slipped into his chair, just as Ashley was beginning to discuss the Basic Ring Fold and the fact that its versatility and "gentle contours" made it the design of choice for a casual supper.

"We can't talk here," he said and was instantly "shushed" by the people sitting in front of us.

"We'll just have to whisper," I whispered, then glanced at my watch. "You asked for five minutes. If I were you I'd get started."

Sam smiled. "You're beautiful when you're angry."

"Oh, please. Enough with the movie lines," I hissed, relishing the compliment in spite of myself. "Just get on with it, would you?"

I couldn't even look at Sam. Just sitting so close to him, trying not to breathe his scent, was hard enough. So I fixed my gaze on Ashley, who was folding a napkin into a triangle, point facing upward, demonstrating the aforementioned Basic Ring Fold. I watched in awe as she brought the left corner of the napkin up to meet the top point and then repeated the process with the right corner, folding the lower left edge in to meet the centerline, repeating *that* process with the right edge to form a kite shape, folding the napkin back along the centerline, and holding the folds in place, pulling the bottom of the napkin through a napkin ring and shaking the folds out into little fans. "See how easy?" she said, receiving a thunderous applause.

"My real name is Simon Purdys and I live in Manhattan. On the corner of Eighty-fifth and Third," he said in a hushed tone.

"I already know that," I snapped. "I checked out your driver's license while you were in the bathroom getting ready to . . ." I shook my head when I remembered that I had nearly let this homicidal maniac enter my sacred temple.

"I'm not in the insurance business," he went on, not even addressing the issue of why I had been riffling through his wallet. "I'm a travel writer. For *Away from It All* magazine."

I snickered. "And I'm the articles editor for *Playboy.*"

My reference to *Playboy* triggered more shushing and a couple of dirty looks.

"It's true," Simon whispered. "I'm doing a story for the magazine on cruises. For the past month and a half, I've sampled every damn cruise line there is: Carnival, Royal Caribbean, Norwegian, Celebrity, you name it. Sea Swan is my last assignment. In other words, Slim, I'm here on the *Princess Charming* on business. And when I travel for business, I don't use my own name—ever. If the people who run cruises, hotels, and resorts find out I'm there to cover them for a national travel magazine, they fall all over themselves to give me VIP treatment and I don't get the real story. So I use aliases. A lot of travel writers do. This time, I happened to pick the name 'Sam Peck.' As in 'Peck's Bad Boy.' I've certainly lived up to the name in *your* opinion, haven't I?"

I didn't respond for several seconds, preferring to listen to Ashley finish discussing the Sea Wave, a fold in which the napkin achieved a ruffled look, suitable, she said, for a Sunday brunch. Was this Simon Purdys telling the truth? I asked myself, wanting to believe him but afraid to. Could he be a writer for *Away from It All?* I'd read the magazine every now and then but only rarely taken note of the bylines. I'd never had a client in the travel industry, so I'd never needed to get to know travel writers, take them to lunch to pitch them a story, any of that. Still, if this guy were really just a travel writer pretending to be an insurance agent so he wouldn't get VIP treatment from the cruise line, why hadn't he told *me* the truth? We had grown so close in such a short time. Why, I wondered, hadn't he *trusted* me with his real identity?

"I was *going* to tell you," he said, reading my mind. "I was going to tell you everything last night. After we'd made love."

The "made love" incited more shushes and dirty looks, especially from Ashley.

"I'm afraid I'll have to ask the couple in the back to step outside to finish their conversation," she called out from her lectern as she was beginning her demonstration of the Buffet Bundle, a napkin fold that held silverware in a nifty little package.

"Come on, let's get out of here," Simon said, grabbing my hand and pulling me out of my seat.

"If you two would like to see the rest of the demonstrations, simply turn your in-cabin television sets to the *Princess Charming* Channel at six o'clock tomorrow morning," Ashley offered in a conciliatory tone. "They'll be replaying my entire lecture."

"Okay. Now what?" I said when we were outside in the corridor.

"Have a seat," said Simon, pointing to the floor.

"Here?" I asked.

"You wanted to talk in a public place. Well, this is a hall. Halls are public places. People will be walking past us by the dozens, so you won't have to be alone with me. And you won't have to get your dress dirty." He took the sheet of paper containing the evening's schedule of activities out of his shirt pocket, unfolded it, and spread it onto the floor, indicating that I was to sit on it. I sat on it. He sat next to me—a little closer to me than I would have liked. Either that, or he did not sit close enough. I couldn't decide which.

"So. Where were we?" I said, trying to pick up the thread of our conversation.

"I was saying that I was going to tell you about being a travel writer for *Away from It All*—"

"If you're a travel writer for *Away from It All*," I interrupted, "then what was that whole song and dance about your conflict over your career? You told me you were wrestling with a job change, remember? Or was that just part of the insurance-agent-who's-afraid-to-fly bullshit?"

He shook his head. "The part about the career conflict was true. I have been considering a job change. Actually, I quit the magazine last year, but I have a very persuasive editor. She offered to pay me twice what I was making, so I came back. Don't get me wrong—I love writing and I love traveling. But I want a life. I'm forty-five years old. The novelty of flying off to some exotic foreign country every other month has worn off. I actually took the cruise assignment as sort of a no-brainer—a few weeks where I could try to figure out what the hell to do with myself."

"If any of this is true—and that's still an 'if,' " I said, "I can't figure out why you didn't tell *me* who you were. I'm a big girl, not to mention a PR person who's had more than a little contact with magazine writers. I would hardly have gone straight to the public address system and announced your real identity to everyone on the ship, for God's sake."

"The more involved we became with each other, the tougher it was for me to tell you, Slim," he said. "I didn't expect to get attached to anybody on this cruise. I didn't expect to get attached ever again, if you want to know the honest truth."

" 'Honest truth' is a redundancy, as any *journalist* would know," I said huffily. "Frankly, I don't think you could spot an honest truth if it hit you in the face."

He straightened his glasses over the bridge of his nose as if he *had* been hit in the face. "Oh, okay. I think I get it now," he said, nodding his head.

"Get what?"

"Get what all this anger is about, this overreaction. You want to know about Jillian. If I fabricated her too."

"The thought has crossed my mind in the past twenty-four hours," I replied. "Before that, whenever we'd be alone together and you'd descend into your—how should I term them?–'sad silences,' I'd assumed they were because of Jillian. Because you missed her. Because she died just before you two were to be married. But now that your story turns out to be a lie, who knows? You didn't say *how* she died or under what circumstances. So maybe the sad silences were just a little method acting on your part, to keep yourself from getting bored on yet another Caribbean cruise. Maybe Jillian is really one of those twin nieces of yours that you mentioned at dinner the other night. Or come to think of it, maybe 'Jillian' never existed at all."

Simon gazed up at the ceiling before answering, as if hoping for divine intervention. Then his eyes met mine. "You were wondering if Jillian existed, and I was wondering how I would explain her to you." He paused to collect himself. I remained unmoved. "Jillian Payntor more than existed; she was the center of my life, my whole world," he began, then paused again to clear his throat. "She was a lawyer. An assistant prosecutor in the Essex County Prosecutor's Office. When I met her, she was on a hot streak, hadn't lost a case in two years. No one wanted to argue against her—least of all me." He smiled, apparently at the memory of their love spats. "She was the sister of a friend of mine at the magazine," he went on. "A photographer named Jason Payntor. Jillian and I were the lucky beneficiaries of Jason's matchmaking." He smiled again, this time at the memory of the First Date, no doubt. "Neither of us was looking for a serious relationship—I was always traveling, she was always trying cases—but we hit it off literally right from the start. There was no question in either of our minds that we would be together for the rest of our lives."

Sort of the way I'd felt about you, I thought with a heavy heart.

"She gave up her condo in Montclair, moved into my apartment on Eighty-fifth Street, and commuted to New Jersey," Simon continued. "Since I didn't have to commute, my part of the bargain was cooking her dinner whenever I was in town."

He cooked her dinner, I mused, wondering what was on the menu at their place. Eric had made me dinner once: borscht. I'm allergic to beets, but he had forgotten.

"How long did you two live together before you decided to get married?" I asked, still unsure if I was buying any of the story.

"A year and three months. We were happy, Slim. Our schedules were hell to coordinate, but we made it work. We were determined not to be one of those two-career couples where it's: 'Dinner tonight? Check with my secretary.' We were about as close as two people can be."

I nodded dully, remembering how Eric and I were about as close as two people who were suing each other.

"We picked a wedding date in May," Simon recalled. "Then came a glitch. Jillian couldn't take a honeymoon until the following October, because of a big case she'd been assigned. There was no way we were putting off getting married, so we opted to do things backwards: have the honeymoon *before* the wedding. The magazine was sending me to the British Virgin Islands ten days before the ceremony. It seemed like the perfect solution to have Jillian come along."

"What happened next?" I said, hanging on his every word now and hating myself for it.

"We had an incredible time," he said, his voice becoming lower, softer, more wistful. "Jillian loved to sail and so did I. Toward the end of the trip, when we were staying at a place in Virgin Gorda, we chartered a thirty-eight-foot sloop, had the hotel pack us a picnic lunch, and sailed out of the harbor."

"I've never been to Virgin Gorda," I said, suddenly feeling the need to insinuate myself into the story. "I hear it's very romantic."

"It's a pretty special place, kind of remote, the last safe harbor before you head out into the rough, open waters of the Atlantic. The North Sound is a haven for sailors, and the island itself is really lush—hills, coral reefs, cays, and islets, everything but crowds."

"No cruise ships there, I guess," I said, trying to picture Simon and his bride-to-be in paradise. I wanted to be able to picture Jillian, specifically. Picture how she had met her untimely end.

"No cruise ships," he acknowledged with a weak smile before proceeding with the story. I could tell by the way he closed his eyes, then inhaled and exhaled deeply that he was preparing himself for the hard part, the bad part. "Jillian and I were both experienced sailors so we took the boat all the way out to Anegada, the so-called 'shipwreck island,' " he said, struggling a bit. "The weather was clear when we left the harbor, and we had a brisk sail over to the island." He stopped again, working his jaw muscles. "Later that afternoon, while I was down below checking the charts and Jillian was at the helm, a sudden, violent squall struck. The boat was knocked down, and before Jillian could react, the mast hit the water."

"The boat capsized?"

"No. It was slammed onto its side at about a ninety-degree angle."

"My God. You must have been terrified."

"There wasn't time to be terrified. As I was thrown across the cabin, against the galley counter, I heard Jillian scream. I charged through the hatch, into the cockpit, and she was gone."

"Gone? What do you mean 'gone'?" My own heart was racing as I tried to imagine the scene.

"She'd been swept overboard, Slim." The words came slowly, as if he could barely get them out, as if each one triggered a numbing pain that could never be eased. I'd experienced my share of psychic pain, but I'd never endured a trauma like the one Simon was describing.

"If only she'd been wearing a harness," he mumbled, shaking his head. I didn't know what a harness was in sailors' parlance, but I assumed it was meant to keep a boat's occupants hitched to the boat.

"But surely she was a good swimmer," I said, figuring Jillian was good at everything.

"We were in the middle of a bad storm," he said impatiently. "The swells were over ten feet high. Swimming didn't have anything to do with it."

"Sorry."

"After the boat had righted itself, I searched the waters for Jillian, trying not to panic. It seemed like forever until I finally spotted her. She was fighting frantically to stay afloat. I was relieved to see she was alive, but I knew that if I had a prayer of moving close to her, I had to get the boat under control and turn it around. With the wind and rain beating the shit out of my body, I dropped the sails, which had been flapping around like crazy. Then I started the engine, completely forgetting to secure the jib sheets and allowing them to get tangled in the propeller. Do you understand what I'm saying, Elaine?"

"Not exactly."

"I'm saying that in a single second, the boat had no sails and no engine. It was dead in the water, totally disabled."

"Disabled," I nodded, spellbound.

"I kept looking for Jillian, would spot her off in the distance, and then lose her again. The surging waves took her one way and me and the boat another, and before I knew it, she and I were half a mile apart. I had never known such powerlessness. It was like I was living one of those nightmares where you can't get where you have to go no matter what you do."

I nodded again, having had such dreams.

"I scrambled down below and radioed for help," Simon pressed on, "knowing damn well that even if the charter company did send a rescue boat, it would come too late for Jillian. Then I went back up on deck yet again, searching for her, becoming elated when I finally located her. But that was to be my very last glimpse of her. I actually had to stand there and watch as Jillian Payntor, my wife in every way but a marriage license, got smaller and smaller and smaller until I couldn't see her anymore."

Simon had been tearing up as the story moved to its inevitable conclusion, but now he was crying openly, quietly, removing his glasses to wipe his eyes with his hands. I didn't know what to do, I really didn't. Part of me wanted to reach out and encircle him in my arms, rock him, console him, tell him everything was all right because *I* was here now and *I* would love him just as much as Jillian had. The other part of me wanted to run back to my cabin, afraid, not for the first time, that I might be in the presence of a pathological liar as well as a hit man, a sociopath who simply made up stories—the more melodramatic, the better—because he couldn't help himself.

"I kept shouting to her, begging her not to leave me," Simon said, gulping back tears. "I shouldn't have panicked and started the engine before securing the sails. I shouldn't have let that propeller get jammed. I shouldn't have let either of us go out on a boat we weren't familiar with. Shouldn't have. Shouldn't have. I *should* have saved her, but I just couldn't pull it off. I failed, do you understand that? I was on my goddamn honeymoon and I let the love of my life drown."

Well, that did it, of course. Nobody was *that* good an actor; Robert De Niro couldn't have been more convincing.

I fell apart right there in that hallway, pulling Simon to me and holding him tightly, tenderly. "It wasn't your fault," I said, choking back my own sobs as I stroked his dark hair, patted his back. It was bad enough to feel abandoned by the person you loved most in the world, I knew. But to believe that you let the person die, that you could have saved their life and preserved your own happiness, was so torturous I couldn't fathom it. "There wasn't anything you could do," I said softly. "I know you must miss Jillian terribly, but she died in an accident. A tragic accident. You weren't to blame. You must know that."

"I should have been able to save her," he said, shaking his head. "It was my responsibility."

Why was it his responsibility? I wanted to ask. Because he was the man and men were raised to believe it was their job to save women? He'd said that Jillian was an experienced sailor, not to mention an accomplished professional woman. She must have seen the squall coming and should have warned him about it. Why was it *his* fault that she died?

I pulled a packet of tissues out of my purse. I handed Simon a bunch of them and kept a few for myself. We cried together for several minutes. People walking in the hall slowed down as they went by us, like rubberneckers on a highway. At one point, a woman whispered to her husband, "They probably came in second in tonight's Big Bucks Bingo."

That broke the sadness and the strain, and Simon and I actually laughed.

"What is it that they sing in those cruise commercials?" he asked wryly. "Ain't we got fun?"

I nodded and squeezed his hand.

"I'm sorry I didn't tell you who I was," he said after a long silence. "I had every intention of telling you. Last night."

"I believe you," I said. And I did. Almost.

"That's a relief," he said wearily. "Now. Maybe you can tell *me* something."

"Sure. What?"

"Why were you going on last night about your ex-husband and me plotting to kill you?"

I was so ashamed. "Oh, that," I said casually. "It must have been the medication."

"Medication?"

"Yes. I'd gotten a tiny case of sun poisoning, so I took an antihistamine pill yesterday, even though it warns you on the package that one of the active ingredients can make some people delusional." And *I'd* had the nerve to accuse *Simon* of lying! "Just forget all that. I didn't know what I was talking about." I wasn't ready to tell him about the hit man and the ex-wife. Not until I was absolutely, positively, one hundred percent sure he wasn't involved.

"Look, what do you say we call it a night?" He extended his hand and helped me up off the floor. "I haven't talked about myself like that in a long time. I'm kind of worn out."

"I understand," I said, pretty worn out myself.

We walked to the elevator and waited for it to come and take us to our staterooms. Before it arrived, Simon looked at me, his expression so poignant it nearly broke my heart. He cupped my chin in his hand, studied my face, and said, "May I make a suggestion?"

"Sure."

"I say we each get a good night's sleep and start fresh in the morning. The ship will be at sea tomorrow, before stopping in Nassau on Saturday afternoon. Why don't we go for our morning run, spend the day together, and pick up where we left off? I'd really like that, Slim. You?"

"Well, I wouldn't mind a night to let everything you've told me about yourself sink in," I said, cursing myself the minute I realized I'd said "sink."

"You seemed to like me when I was an insurance agent," he smiled. "Do you have anything against travel writers?"

"Only that they get to go to the best places for free while the rest of us have to pay through the nose," I said. "But I'll try to keep my resentment in check."

"I appreciate that."

The elevator came. Simon held my elbow and walked me inside. We each pressed the buttons for our respective decks. When we arrived at his, he leaned over, kissed me on the cheek, and said goodnight.

" 'Night," I said, then rode up one more floor to my deck. The moment the elevator doors parted, I took off down the hall to my stateroom. I had a phone call to make. An urgent phone call that would confirm once and for all whether Simon Purdys was who he said he was.

I hadn't had much success in the past reaching Harold Teitlebaum, my boss at Pearson & Strulley. But I was determined to make contact with him this time—not to bawl him out about promoting Leah, but to ask him about Simon. Harold was a veteran of the public relations game; there wasn't a single media person he hadn't rubbed shoulders with. If Simon Purdys wrote for *Away from It All* magazine, Harold would not only know him, he'd know everything about him except his mother's maiden name—and maybe he'd know that too.

I gave the operator my credit card number for the ship-to-shore call, then Harold's home telephone number, and waited, crossing my fingers he'd be home. After several seconds he answered.

"Harold!" I said excitedly.

"I don't want to hear about it, Elaine," he said, probably anti-cipating a harangue about Leah. Harold was used to my harangues, which was probably why he had avoided my calls up to now. "I've got enough to deal with here. All hell has broken loose this week."

"I know. I know. But I'm not calling about Leah. At least, not tonight."

"What is it then? You've fallen in love with some shipboard Casanova and you're calling to tell me you're quitting your job and running off with him to Antigua?"

"The *Princess Charming* doesn't stop in Antigua." Well, he was right about the first part. "Actually, I'm calling to ask if you're familiar with any of the people who write for *Away from It All* magazine."

"Elaine. You know better than to ask me that. There isn't a na-tional magazine writer I'm *not* familiar with."

"Of course, Harold. You're the best. But I was wondering if you knew this particular writer."

"Who?"

"Simon Purdys."

I held my breath while I waited for Harold to respond.

"Sure. The tall one with the dark hair. The one whose fiancée, the lawyer, died in a sailing accident."

I started laughing. It was an odd reaction, I admit, given that there was nothing the least bit funny about Jillian's death. I was just re-leasing my anxiety, all my pent-up fears about Simon. And I was laughing because I was happy, I realized. The man I'd fallen in love with wasn't a hit man after all.

"Elaine? You all right?" Harold asked as I continued to laugh—at ten dollars a minute.

"I'm fine," I said. "Finally."

"Listen, about the Leah thing, she was pushing for a promotion and the kid knows what she's doing, thanks to you, so I figured what the—"

"I'm fine," I repeated. "About Leah, about the promotion, about everything."

"I'm not so sure. You don't sound like yourself," he said. "You sound relaxed. For you."

"I *am* relaxed, Harold. Especially after speaking to you." I smiled. "See you back in the office next week."

I hung up, wrapped my arms around myself, and danced around the cabin, feeling utterly liberated. Simon hadn't lied to me. He was honest and good and true.

Of course, there was still the matter of the man on the ship who *wasn't* honest and good and true—the *real* hit man—but I wasn't going to worry about him anymore.

For the first time since we'd left Miami, I anticipated getting a good night's sleep.

I took off my dress and was hanging it in the closet when I remembered the envelope that had been slipped under Jackie's stateroom door while she, Pat, and I were having dinner. I had stuffed it in the back pocket of the dress, so I wouldn't have to tell my friends what was going on between Simon and me. But now that everything was all right between us, now that he wasn't a murderer and I wasn't his target, I whipped it out of the pocket and tossed it in the garbage.

Boy, Simon must have been really desperate to reach me by the time he wrote that one, I giggled as I continued to undress. I'll bet he poured out his heart to me, told me how much he cared for me, said something really mushy and wonderful.

The more I thought about the note, the more curious about it I became. I fished the envelope out of the garbage, tore it open, unfolded the piece of *Princess Charming* stationery, and began to read.

The first thing I noticed was that the handwriting on this note was dramatically different from the earlier ones Simon had barraged me with.

Sam was a lefty, and his writing had that lefty slant, the sort of unruly scrawl you can barely decipher. But whoever wrote the note I now held in my hand had a very neat, legible script, each letter arched and graceful, particularly the capital *T*'s, which were finished off with a little curlicue. No, this was the work of a calligrapher—or at the very least, someone with beautiful penmanship. It didn't take a genius to figure out that Simon wasn't its author.

The second thing that struck me about the note was that it was a nursery rhyme—or should I say, a very twisted spin on a nursery rhyme. It read:

Three Blond Mice.
Three Blond Mice.
See how they run.
See how they run.
They took a cruise like many an ex-wife,
Trying their best to escape from strife.
But *one* of them's going to lose her life.
Poor Blond Mice.

Day Six:
Friday, February 15

19

"**I** need to talk to you," I told Simon when he showed up at seven-thirty for our run on the Promenade Deck.

"So we're not mad at me anymore? We're making fun of me now?" he asked with a self-deprecating laugh.

"Making fun of you?"

"Of all those messages I had the steward slip under your door yesterday. I think I wrote 'I need to talk to you' on every single one of them."

"This has nothing to do with those messages," I said gravely. "It's *this* message I want to talk to you about."

I pulled the gruesome nursery rhyme out of the pocket of my running shorts and handed it to Simon.

He'd only read the first line when he looked up at me. "Three Blond Mice? Isn't that the nickname you and Pat and Jackie call yourselves?"

"Yup. Read on."

He did. When he got to the "One of them's going to lose her life" part, he looked up again. "Obviously, someone on the ship has a bizarre sense of humor. Who wrote this?"

"I don't know, Simon, but whoever he is, he was hired by my ex-husband and he's going to kill me before the ship is back in Miami."

"Slim." He rolled his eyes, reminding me of Jackie whenever she thought I was being a Drama Queen. "You've got to stop taking those antihistamines."

"I'm not taking antihistamines. I just made all that up because I didn't want to tell you the truth."

"About what?"

"That I thought you were a hit man and Eric hired you to murder me."

He stared at me. For much too long. I prayed he wasn't rethinking his affection for me.

"Look, I really need to sit down with you and explain everything," I said as calmly as I could manage. "Could we skip the run this morning? Please?"

He shrugged. "Your stateroom or mine?"

"Yours. The hit man is probably hiding in mine."

"Okay. Here's the story. From the top," I said as soon as we got to Simon's cabin. He sat on the bed. I paced. Without realizing it, I also began picking up various articles of his clothing that were lying on the floor.

"I wasn't expecting company," he apologized, clearly amused by my compulsiveness as he watched me fold a T-shirt here, smooth out a pair of pants there. "But you know, Slim, the cruise lines are always looking for cabin stewards. Maybe you should apply for the job."

"Maybe I should. Now do you want to hear the story or not?"

"I want to hear the story."

"All right. On the second night of the cruise, at about ten o'clock, I placed a ship-to-shore call from the phone in my stateroom. To Harold Teitlebaum, my boss at Pearson & Strulley."

"Because you were pissed off that he promoted your assistant without discussing it with you first?"

"You have quite a memory."

"You say things that are hard to forget. Or maybe it's the *way* you say them."

"Thank you." I assumed it was a compliment. "Anyhow, there was a storm that night, as you may also remember."

"I do. The ship was really pitching and rolling."

"Right. The television in my room wasn't working and I wondered if the phone would go out too. But I decided I'd take my chances and try to reach Harold. It turned out that the phone lines were crossed and I ended up overhearing a ship-to-shore conversation between two complete strangers. At least, I thought they were."

"You knew them?"

"I'll get to that in a second. At first, all I could make out was that they were men. Their voices were distorted because of the lousy connection—one of the voices kept breaking up, in fact. But the more they talked, the more obvious it was that the man on the ship had been hired by the man on shore to murder the man on the shore's ex-wife, a passenger on the ship."

"Run that by me again?"

"The two men were plotting a *murder,* Simon. The guy on shore wanted the guy on the ship to kill his ex-wife—and do it before the *Princess Charming* was back in Miami."

"That's incredible," said Simon, adjusting his eyeglasses, focusing his attention on me more intently. "What did you do?"

"I called the Purser's Office to report the crossed phone wires. Then I went straight to see Captain Solberg. I told him that a woman on board his ship was the intended target of a hit man."

"What did he say?"

"He said I should take a Dramamine."

"No, really. How did he react?"

"I'm serious. Talking to the guy was a total waste of time. I explained to him that a crime was about to be committed on *his* ship and he said he couldn't take action unless a crime had already *been* committed. And then he suggested I go play bingo."

"Jesus. No wonder he made that crack about murderers when we were on the receiving line at the Captain's Cocktail Party. He probably didn't believe a word of your story."

"Neither did the police in Puerto Rico. But *you* believe my story, don't you, Simon?"

"Sure. The only thing I don't understand is why you automatically assumed that Eric and I were the men you overheard on the phone and that you were the one we were out to get."

"I hate to admit this, but I have a tendency to automatically assume things, particularly regarding threats to my health and well-being. It's a quirk of mine. A very *minor* quirk though." I felt it was important to be honest with Simon, but I certainly didn't want to scare him away.

"That explains why you thought *you* were the ex-wife the men were plotting to kill. It doesn't explain why you figured *me* for the hit man. I wasn't exactly menacing you, was I?"

"No, you were romancing me."

"Oh, now that makes everything crystal clear." His tone was heavy with sarcasm.

"You were romancing me, trying to get me alone," I pressed on. "But it was when I stumbled on the not-insignificant fact that Sam Peck was really Simon Purdys that I decided you must be the hit man. I thought, this guy's traveling under an alias *and* he's been spending a lot of time with me. I put two and two together and found you guilty."

"I'm not sure I would have leapt to that precise verdict."

"That's because you *knew* you were using an alias. You also knew why. But I didn't have a clue that you were on assignment for *Away from It All,* remember? I was just some poor, unsuspecting shnook who fell in love with you the first night of the cruise."

The words popped out of my mouth before I could reel them back in, and I was so embarrassed I nearly hid my head inside Simon's green polo shirt, the one I'd been folding and was about to put away in his dresser drawer.

I had already told him I loved him, of course, on the night I'd stormed out of his cabin, the night of our aborted lovemaking. But that time, it had been less of an admission and more of an angry parting shot. Now, I had actually gone and revealed my true feelings for him. And all before we'd even exchanged home addresses and telephone numbers!

He pulled me onto the bed next to him and kissed me. It was a long, passionate kiss, and while I certainly enjoyed it, I didn't know if it was an I've-fallen-in-love-with-you-too kiss or a consolation prize.

"Go on with the story," he said after we pulled apart.

"The story. Right," I said, regrouping. "Once I found out that you were a travel writer, not a hit man, I figured it's got to be some other ex-wife on the ship who's in big trouble. But then I read this note."

I unfolded the nursery rhyme and read it again, shaking my head in rage and disbelief. "I'm telling you, Simon," I said angrily. "If Eric so much as even *thinks* he's gonna get rid of me while I'm on vacation, he's—"

"Whoa. Whoa. Whoa. What makes you so sure that Eric is behind the note?"

"He's the only ex-husband I have."

"No, I mean: What makes you think *you're* the 'Blond Mouse' that's referred to in the rhyme?"

"The fact that the note was slipped under *my* . . ." I stopped, remembering that it had been slipped under *Jackie's* door.

I told Simon about this, my voice trembling, my palms cold and clammy. "My God," I said, the situation growing clearer now, even deadlier. "So *Jackie's* the ex-wife the hit man's after. That rotten Peter is having her killed. I had a hunch there was something sneaky about—"

"Not so fast," Simon interrupted. "Your cabin steward knew that all *three* of you were having dinner in Jackie's room. It wasn't a secret. It's more than likely that the person who wrote the note knew you all were there too, especially if he's been keeping close tabs on things. He could have intended the rhyme for any one of you. The envelope wasn't addressed to anyone by name, was it?"

"No."

"So there's no way we can say for sure which of you three he's after," Simon confirmed. "The only thing we *can* say for sure is that he's definitely after one of you."

I flew into his arms, knocking him down onto the bed, probably knocking the wind out of him too.

"Should we tell Pat and Jackie?" I asked him. "I haven't said a word to either of them up to now. Jackie just got out of the damn hospital and hasn't had five minutes of fun on the trip. And Pat? How on earth is she going to handle a conversation about the possibility that her precious Bill may be planning to have her murdered? She actually thinks they'll get back together someday! Not only that, she abhors violence or even any talk of it. She told me she wanted to be the first on her block to get a television set with a V-chip. Of course, she called it a T-chip."

Simon shook his head, seeming genuinely confounded as to how to deal with the situation. Or was it a flicker of fear I saw in his eyes? For me. For us.

We sat back up on the bed.

"Hey," I said. "Don't panic, please. You're the only person on this ship who's heard the story and believes it, the only person I can depend on now. You have to help me save Jackie's life or Pat's life or, God forbid, mine."

I knew full well what I asking. I was calling on a man who had spent the last two years torturing himself about not being able to save his fiancée's life—imploring someone who was already wracked with survivor's guilt, who already considered it a crime against nature that he hadn't rescued a woman—to participate in yet another rescue operation. But the operative word here was "participate." I was looking for him to share my burden, not carry it. I wanted to share everything with Simon, because I loved him. And whether he knew it or not, whether he was ready to admit it or not, he loved me too.

"Remember, we'll be partners in this," I said, trying to clarify my position, make him more comfortable. "We'll be helping *each other* solve the murder plot. It won't fall on your shoulders alone to fix things, won't be your responsibility."

"But it should be my responsibility," Simon demanded, exhibiting the sort of macho behavior that I'd already given him permission to shed. Why can't men understand that, as much as we appreciate their interest, we don't require that they singlehandedly save the day? That it's not their *birthright* to save the day?

"Simon, I—"

"Look, Slim. You were very amusing and entertaining the way you told the hit man story—almost as if it were just another dinner table anecdote—but you and I both know that the guy who wrote the note means business. I don't want anything to happen to you on this cruise, okay?"

I hugged him tightly. "Nothing's going to happen to me on this cruise," I said resolutely. "How can it? I've got a famous travel writer on my side."

"A famous travel writer, my ass," he scoffed. "When I told you my real name, you'd never heard of me."

"I know," I said apologetically. "For most of my life I've had tun-

nel vision; if it wasn't expedient for me to know something or someone, I didn't. I just didn't realize the seriousness of the problem until
I took this trip."

"And now?"

"Now, I see that my rigid view of the world has hurt me more than
helped me, particularly when it comes to my emotional life." Aw,
what the heck, let it all hang out, I told myself, the way people often
do when they're convinced they're about to die. "For example, I
have a father I've refused to speak to since I was a teenager and a
half-sister I've never even met. I shut them both out, pretended they
don't exist. But who knows? If I make it off this ship in one piece, I
just might venture out of the tunnel."

Simon held me, stroked my hair, rubbed my back, murmured soft,
soothing things to me. "I know," he whispered at one point. "I've
been in kind of a tunnel myself."

We remained in each other's arms for a long time, both aware that
we were living the proverbial calm before the storm. It was Simon
who finally pulled away.

"If we're going to nail this hit man, we'd better get started," he
said after taking a deep breath and standing up straight and tall, his
body language that of a man on a mission. "There are only two full
days of the cruise left. We don't have a whole lot of time to waste."

"No, we don't," I agreed.

He sat back down on the bed when he realized we still needed to
come up with a plan for catching the creep.

"Can you think of any men you've met so far, any guy on the ship
who's been hanging around you or your friends or acting suspi-
ciously?" he asked.

"There are a few who keep turning up. It could be a coincidence,
obviously, but on a ship this size, it's been uncanny how often I've
run into them. I can't speak for Pat and Jackie. God knows who's
been lurking around them. But we might as well start somewhere."

I gave him thumbnail sketches of Henry Prichard, Albert Mullins,
Lenny Lubin, and Skip Jamison. He listened, then said, "Is there any
connection that you can think of between one of these men and either Eric, Peter, or Bill? Something that would link any of them to
one of the ex-husbands?"

"Not off the top of my head, but I'll give it some more thought while I'm having breakfast with Jackie and Pat," I said.

"Good. And while you're doing that, I'll make a few phone calls and try to verify that these men are who they say they are. It won't take long to find out if Skip Jamison is really an art director at Vance, Yellen and Drier; if Lenny Lubin really owns a business called Lubin's Lube Jobs in Massapequa, Long Island; and if Henry Prichard is really a salesman at. . . . Which car dealership is he with?"

"Peterson Chevrolet," I reminded him. "In Altoona, Pennsylvania."

"Thanks."

"That still leaves Albert Mullins though. He doesn't have a job, as far as I know. It'll be tough to check him out, won't it?"

"Maybe," Simon acknowledged, "but we can at least confirm that he lives in Manhattan and has a weekend place in Connecticut. That is, if he's listed in both phone directories."

"Hardly anyone's listed anymore. We're all trying to hide from those telemarketers."

He smiled. "I'll give it the old college try anyway. Look, after I make the calls and you have breakfast with your friends, you'll need to fill me in on all three of your ex-husbands. What sort of men they are; who their friends are; what they do in their spare time."

"I'll tell you whatever I can," I said, gazing at Simon with a mixture of love and gratitude. Sure, *I* could have made the phone calls he said he'd make, ask the questions he suggested I ask, snoop around the ship trolling for clues. I'd been on my own for most of my adult life and had managed pretty well, in spite of my "quirks." I was a can-do person, someone who got things done, a big achiever. In the six years since my divorce, I'd supported myself, created a nice little social network, even learned how to change a flat tire. Yes, I had my moods and my fears and my loneliness, but I'd gotten along very capably, and I'd been, if not ecstatically happy, then moderately so. I certainly didn't expect to fall in love, never gave it a thought. I had my future all planned: I would work hard at my job, take vacations with my friends, watch the Academy Awards on television, that sort of thing. But you know what? It was *better* now that

Simon Purdys was in my life. Much better. I'd be an out-and-out liar if I said that having a man to adore, confide in, trade wet, sloppy kisses with, was anything less than fabulous, wonderful, a miracle.

Yes, a miracle, I thought as we set about trying to prevent a murder. That's exactly what it was.

20

After leaving Simon's stateroom, I rushed back to mine, hoping to catch Pat and Jackie before they went roaming around the ship like lambs to the slaughter. Fortunately, they were still in their cabins. I suggested we all go up to the Glass Slipper café for breakfast, knowing that while I was keeping my friends occupied, Simon would be checking out Skip, Lenny, Henry, and Albert.

"Let's have Bloody Marys to celebrate my recovery," Jackie said after we had forged our way through the buffet line, been seated at a table next to the kitchen (the only table left), and asked by a waiter if we wanted anything to drink. It was a busy morning in the Glass Slipper. Sensing that their vacation was winding down, many passengers had gotten up extra-early so they could pack away a nice, hearty meal, snare a lounge chair around the pool, and soak up their second-to-last day of UVA rays.

"I think I'll skip the Bloody Marys and have herbal tea," I said, wanting to keep a clear head.

"Oh, loosen up, Elaine," said Jackie. "It won't be as much fun unless we all get sloshed. Just think: We'll be Three Shits to the Wind."

I laughed. "You two go on ahead. I'll stay with the tea."

"What's the matter? Was there a story on the news this morning about the health hazards of tomato juice?" Jackie tweaked me. It was heartening to see that she was back to her old self.

"Actually, the story was about the piece of celery they stick in the tomato juice as a stirrer," I countered. "According to the latest research, when you bite into a stalk, you run the risk of getting a string caught between your teeth that you can never floss out."

It was her turn to laugh. "Pat? What about you? Want to toast me with a Bloody Mary?"

"That would be detectable," she replied.

"Wrong. Vodka doesn't stay on your breath the way scotch does," Jackie said.

"I think she meant delectable," I pointed out. "Didn't you, Pat?" She nodded.

The waiter, a strapping young man with a long, dark braid, waited patiently through our back-and-forth, then wrote our beverage orders on a pad and left.

"So," Jackie said, turning to face me. "Let's hear what really happened between you and Sam Peck, Elaine. Feel like talking about it now?"

"Actually, I'm delighted to report that Sam and I"—I had to remind myself that he was still *Sam* to them—"have patched up our differences and are seeing each other again."

"Elaine! That's wonderful news," Pat said, clapping her hands. "He seems like such a nice man. He certainly was very kind to me the day we all went sightseeing in Puerto Rico."

"He *is* a nice man," I agreed.

"With a very nice ass," Jackie chimed in. "So is it love or what?"

"I can't speak for him, but as I told you on the tender coming back from Isle de Swan, Jackie, I've never felt like this about anyone."

"Good God. She really has flipped out," Jackie said, nudging Pat. "When's the wedding?"

I scoffed but secretly wondered the same thing, although what was really weighing on me at that moment was what sort of information Simon's phone calls had uncovered and whether any of it would lead us to the hit man.

I fielded a few more questions about my relationship with "Sam," trying not to gush. Eventually, we ate breakfast and discussed our plans for our last full day at sea. There seemed to be only two things on the agenda. Jackie had an afternoon checkup with Dr. Johansson, and Pat wanted to call Bill's apartment to wish Lucy a happy tenth birthday.

"I propose that the three of us spend the day together," I said. "We can buy souvenirs, get pampered in the spa, go to the lectures, do the whole cruise ship bit. We haven't had enough quality time on this vacation, just us Blond Mice." The hit man wouldn't dare strike if we stuck close to each other, I figured. There had to be security in numbers.

"Done," said Jackie, high-fiving me.

"We could start with the two of you coming back to my stateroom while I call the children," Pat suggested. "They're probably waiting by the phone now. I'm sure Lucy is. Gosh. I can't believe she's ten years old today."

"Let's do it," I said, the thought of families and children and birthdays reminding me of a much simpler, safer time.

Ever since the divorce, Bill Kovecky had lived in a rather modest (for a fancy-shmancy doctor) three-bedroom apartment in the Murray Hill section of Manhattan, having given up his more lavish place when he agreed to fork over a sizable chunk of his income in alimony and child support.

Pat was giggly and excited at the prospect of placing her first ship-to-shore call and even more excited at the prospect of speaking to Bill, who, she assumed, would answer the phone since he had taken the week off to be with the children.

Jackie and I sat on the bed while she gave the operator the number at Bill's apartment.

"Hello? Hello?" we heard her say when the call went through. "Is that you, Bill? Oh, it's you, Dennis, sweetheart. You're getting to be so grown up you sounded just like your father. Yes, dear. I'm calling from the ship. Yes, it's exactly like the one on TV. Are you having a good time in New York? He took you to a hockey game? And to a museum? And to Planet Hollywood? My, that must have been fun. Honey, these calls are very expensive and I do want to speak to the other kids too. Yes, I'll see you Sunday. I miss you bunches."

Pat made kissing noises into the phone, then spoke to her other three sons, making kissing noises to them too. Finally, Lucy came on the line. She received a stirring rendition of "Happy Birthday" *and* the kissing noises.

"Ten years old," Pat mused to her daughter. "That's right, you're almost a teenager now. Yes, Aunt Jackie and Aunt Elaine are right here in the room with me, and they send their love. I will. Now tell me, sweetheart. What's your father planning for your special day today? Lucy? What is it, sweetheart? Why are you crying?"

Pause.

"What do you mean he's not there?" Pat went on, looking upset. "He left the apartment early this morning? To ride on an airplane? Then who's staying with you and the boys? Mrs. Who?"

"Uh-oh. Sounds like Dr. Bill flew off on another medical mission," I whispered to Jackie. "You'd think he could have waited until *after* Lucy's birthday."

"Why should this day be different from all the others?" she said. "According to Pat, this kind of stuff went on throughout the marriage."

"So he didn't leave a number or say where he was going?" Pat was asking Lucy. "Well, I'm sure he just forgot to, dear. And when he comes back, you'll have a real birthday celebration together, okay?" She had her game face on, but she was devastated, we could tell. She had convinced herself that Bill had changed, that he was no longer putting his career before his kids, that he wanted his family back. And now he'd gone off and left the children in the hands of a housekeeper, probably so he could participate in some conference on irritable bowel syndrome.

I went to Pat and asked her if I could talk to Lucy, just for a minute. She handed me the phone.

"Hi, cutie," I said. "It's Aunt Elaine. Happy birthday."

I told Lucy about the special present I had bought her in Old San Juan, which seemed to cheer her up, and she told me she wanted to come and stay at my apartment the next time she was in New York. I said of course she could stay at my apartment, as long as she didn't bring along her brothers and their raging hormones. She didn't understand my remark but thought it was funny, and by the time I handed the phone back to Pat, she was laughing.

As she and her mother were saying goodbye, I began to wonder about Bill Kovecky, about what had made him leave town in such a big hurry. I'd never met him, so I didn't have any firsthand knowledge of him, but I couldn't help asking myself: What kind of man flies off on a business trip the day of his only daughter's birthday? What kind of man agrees to take care of his five children while their mother is away and then goes away himself?

I'll tell you what kind: the kind that isn't to be trusted. I didn't know who wrote that nursery rhyme that was left under Jackie's door, and I didn't know why he wrote it. All I knew at that moment was that it was possible—just possible—that Bill Kovecky had taken a flight out of New York so he could jet down to the Bahamas and rendezvous with the writer of the note . . . to oversee Pat's murder personally.

21

The minute I got back to my stateroom I called Simon.

"What'd you find out?" I asked breathlessly when he answered.

"Not a whole lot," he said. "Lenny does own a business on Long Island called Lubin's Lube Jobs. Skip is an art director at V,Y&D. Henry sells cars at Peterson Chevrolet in Altoona. And Albert is listed in both the Manhattan and Ridgefield, Connecticut, phone directories."

"Damn."

"The only moderately curious thing that came out of all my calls was that when I dialed Albert's two numbers, I got recordings saying they'd been disconnected and that no further information was available."

"Who disconnects their phones when they're only going away for a week?"

"I had the same thought. Maybe Albert isn't planning on coming back. Maybe once he does the hit, he's taking his money and moving to Mexico or something."

"But why would a person like Albert Mullins have to kill people for a living?" I asked. "He's already got two residences and enough money to travel the globe in search of Snowy Egrets."

"Maybe Albert's two residences are the spoils of past hits," Simon suggested. "Or there's another possibility: He's not the hit man."

"Or there's a third possibility: He is the hit man but he isn't in it for the money."

"You think he murders other men's ex-wives just for kicks? Because he has a grudge against women?"

"God knows. There are enough misogynists around. Actually, I was thinking that the hit the hit man's supposed to pull off on this ship might be his *first;* that he could be sort of a fledgling hit man; and that he's only doing the job because he was forced into it."

"When did you come up with all this?"

"When I started to mull over the phone call I overheard between the two men that night. If memory serves, the ex-husband seemed to be pressuring the guy on the ship. I got the distinct impression that the hit man was having second thoughts and had only placed the call to his 'employer' to back out. It was almost as if Bill or Peter or Eric—whichever of them is behind this—had something *on* the guy that was making him feel obligated to go through with the job."

"You didn't tell me any of this before."

"I didn't?"

"No, Slim. You didn't."

"Sorry. Is the information important?"

"It could be."

I gave Simon a report on my morning with Pat and Jackie, in particular on Bill's rather sudden departure from New York. "I'm betting that Bill and Albert are in this together," I said. "Albert leaves town as if he's never coming back. Then Bill leaves town without telling anyone where he's going. What's more, Albert becomes Pat's devoted servant from the first minute we step onto the ship. Is his attentiveness toward her the real thing or is he all over her like a cheap suit because he's simply following orders? From *Bill?*"

Simon sighed. "I don't know. There's no way to know."

"You're not giving up, are you, Simon?"

"Of course not. As a matter of fact, I spoke to Captain Solberg about this whole mess."

"You what?"

"I know you already talked to him, but that was before you got the nursery rhyme."

"What did he say?"

"You mean *after* he offered me discount coupons at several jewelry stores in Nassau?"

"No. Not that again."

"He was so unresponsive and I was so frustrated that I ended up blurting out my real name and the fact that I was on assignment to cover the ship for the magazine."

"Oh, Simon. You said that traveling under an alias is how you get a true picture of the places you write about."

"I've already gotten a true picture of the *Princess Charming,* believe me. What I need now is for Captain Solberg to investigate the threats that have been made against a woman on *his* ship. I thought that by telling the guy I was doing a story for *Away from It All,* I might get a rise out of him."

"Did you?"

"Not in the way I'd hoped."

"Why? What did he do?"

"He asked if I'd brought along a photographer from the magazine and if he or she would mind shooting him from his left side, his good side."

"Great. Another Barbra Streisand. Is that all he said?"

"No. He told me the same thing he told you: He'll only investigate a murder *after* a murder has been committed."

"Jerk."

"Gee, thanks."

"Not you. Captain Solberg."

"Oh."

"Listen, Simon. I suggested to Pat and Jackie that we spend the day together—just the three of us. I think it's important that we stick close, given the situation."

"I understand. But I'll miss you today."

"I'll miss you too." I made kissing noises into the phone, the way Pat did.

"We'll see each other at dinner though," said Simon.

"And maybe after dinner, once Jackie and Pat are back in their staterooms with their doors locked, you and I can repair to my room and try one more time to solve this puzzle."

"I had the same idea."

"Simon, I really want to thank you for helping me," I told him. "It's such a comfort to have someone to share all this with."

"I haven't helped you at all," he said. "Not yet anyway."

"Oh, yes you have," I assured him. "You believed me. That means a lot."

"I'm glad. Now *I'd* like to make a suggestion, Slim."

"Sure. Go ahead."

"I think I ought to spend the night with you tonight. In your stateroom. As a precaution."

I didn't answer.

"Are you there?" he asked.

"Yes. I'm just processing what you said."

"I want to protect you, Elaine. I won't sleep at all knowing you're alone in that room with a murderer running around."

"That's very sweet of you, Simon. It's just that the last time we planned to spend the night together, in *your* stateroom, it didn't go very well. I'm still having flashbacks."

He laughed. "Look, I'll sleep in the chair or something. We won't even touch each other, if you don't want to. But I really would feel better if I could watch out for you, that's all."

I was extremely touched by his desire to watch out for me. The only person who had ever watched out for me was me.

I pictured Simon on the phone in his stateroom, so earnest, so considerate. My being in jeopardy was probably forcing him to relive the whole Jillian nightmare.

"Of course you can sleep in my room," I said, not exactly making the sacrifice of the century. "You don't snore, do you?"

"Only when I fall into a very deep sleep," he said. "But don't worry: I don't expect to."

Pat was still riled up about Bill's leaving the children with a housekeeper, but she agreed to spend the day with Jackie and me as planned. Our first stop was Her Majesty's New Age, the ship's women-only health spa. Jackie was having the dead cells on her face exfoliated. Pat went for the bath in freeze-dried seawater and seaweed. And I booked a forty-minute session with the reflexologist. Reflexology, for the uninitiated, is a form of foot massage in which varying degrees of pressure are applied to specific parts of the feet to alleviate imbalances, weaknesses, or blockages in the body. I didn't believe in reflexology any more than I believed in bathing in seaweed, but I figured it couldn't hurt.

I was wrong. My reflexologist, a serious Slavic woman named Nadia, began with my left foot.

"Ouch!" I said after she'd ground her finger into the middle of my big toe.

"For da pineal gland," she informed me. "Must do to clear da head and sinuses."

"My head and sinuses are perfectly clear," I said. "How about going a little easier on me, okay?"

This time she pressed deeply into the heel of my left foot. Again, I cried out in pain.

"For da sciatic nerve," she explained. "Also fixes da hemorrhoids."

"That's very interesting, Nadia, but I don't have hemorrhoids, thank God."

She ignored me and began kneading the center of the sole of my left foot. Instead of torturing me though, it tickled something wicked.

"Hey," I giggled, yanking my foot away from her. "What part of the body were you unblocking that time?"

"Da heart," she said, grabbing hold of the foot, determined to continue. "I can feel dere's a little blockage but I can cure—if you be quiet and let me do."

I let her do.

My session with Nadia ended just as Jackie and Pat were wrapping up their spa adventures.

"Now what?" I asked them. "A little skeet shooting?"

"My ankle's still sore," said Pat, who'd been hobbling around pretty well with the aid of her cane. "I wouldn't mind doing something more sedentary."

"Same here," said Jackie. I kept forgetting this was her first full day out of the hospital. I wanted to keep her safe from the hit man, but I didn't want to tire her out.

"Something more sedentary," I mused, scanning the schedule of the day's activities. "What about the Perfume Seminar?"

They liked that idea. So off we went to the Perky Princess boutique, where folding chairs had temporarily replaced racks of clothing and were arranged in a little circle. We sat down. Within a few minutes, a heavily made-up woman named Veronica joined our group, introduced herself as the ship's onboard perfume expert, and began to pass vials of different fragrances around the circle. She spoke, we sniffed. The experience, while not wildly entertaining, was pleasant enough—especially when Veronica got to the vial of vanilla. She explained that, although vanilla wasn't perfume, per se, it was considered by French women to be *the* fragrance of choice. It certainly smelled better than those infuriating inserts that perfume manufacturers stick into upscale magazines these days.

Smelling the vanilla made the three of us hungry, so our next stop was the Wine and Cheese Appreciation Hour. There, we sampled wines and cheeses from all over the world—at least the ones we could reach. The event drew so many passengers looking to scarf down some free food and booze that we could barely get near the table where the food and booze were.

Over the course of the day, we also attended an Art Auction (one of Ginger Smith Baldwin's oil paintings was being sold, and Kenneth and Gayle Cone, who were gaining a reputation around the ship as quite the big spenders, were the highest bidders); an ice carving demonstration (we were shown how to chip the ice into the shapes of various farm animals); and the ship's version of that all-time TV favorite "The Dating Game." (The contestants, most of them elderly women, were asked what most appeals to them in a man. They said, "A Living Will.")

As we went from activity to activity, Pat pocketing souvenir after souvenir, I kept marveling at the fact that we never once ran into Albert, Lenny, Henry, or Skip, even though the ship was at sea the entire day and there was nothing for them to do except make the rounds of the activities, just as we were doing. Of course, Albert could have been in the ship's movie theater, where they were showing Alfred Hitchcock's thriller *The Birds*. Lenny could have been holed up in any one of the ship's nine cocktail lounges. Henry could have been holed up in his stateroom with Ingrid, or vice versa. And Skip could have closeted himself away in the library with yet another Deepak Chopra tome.

At four-thirty, Jackie had her checkup with Dr. Johansson, so Pat and I accompanied her to the hospital. Remarkably, when she signed in with Nurse Wimple, she was not made to wait among the fifty or so other patients but ushered right into one of the examining rooms.

"I think Dr. Johansson really likes Jackie," I told Pat as we sat together in the waiting room. "He certainly seems to be giving her preferential treatment."

Pat was deeply involved in a recipe in *Redbook*—something involving bread crumbs and canned cream of mushroom soup—and didn't respond. But, I suddenly thought, if Dr. Johansson has a female patient he likes and plays favorites with, maybe Dr. Kovecky does too. Maybe Billy boy has a lady friend. Maybe that's why he hired a hit man to kill Pat.

Jackie came out of the examining room looking flushed and excited.

"Per says I'm doing fine," she said. "He doesn't want me staying up late tonight but he still wants to take me to lunch in Nassau tomorrow and show me around."

"At least *you'll* be safe," I said without thinking.

"Safe?" she asked.

"I meant, in case you have a relapse."

It was British Night in the Palace Dining Room and Ismet was recommending the steak and kidney pie.

"Listen, Ishmael, you can leave the kidneys off my plate and just bring me the steak, okay?" said Rick. "And make it medium rare, huh?"

The rest of us ordered the beef Wellington.

"Elaine! You aren't worried you'll get Mad Cow Disease?" Jackie stuck it to me.

"Mad Cow Disease is the least of my problems right now," I said.

She looked puzzled but went on with her conversation with Kenneth Cone, who had sat down next to her after arriving a few minutes after his wife did.

Simon and I were sitting next to each other too. It was still such a thrill every time I saw him again. In spite of the thorny problem that was hanging over our heads, I felt so lucky that he was in my life—for however long my life lasted.

"How are you enjoying the cruise?" I asked Dorothy, who was seated on Simon's other side.

"It's been wonderful." She smiled, her eyes twinkling. "Like a second honeymoon."

"What did she say, Dorothy?" Lloyd asked.

"She wanted to know if we were having a good time on the cruise," said Dorothy.

"What did you tell her?"

"I told her we've been fucking like newlyweds."

All conversation at the table came to a temporary halt.

"Did I say something out of line?" Dorothy asked, playing innocent. She was a devil, that Dorothy.

"Your language is a little saltier than Kenneth and I are accustomed to," Gayle sniffed.

"What did she say, Dorothy?" asked Lloyd.

"She said that she and her husband don't have sex," was Dorothy's response.

"Good grief. The old witch has sex on the brain," Gayle muttered. "If she still *has* a brain at her age." Obviously, Dorothy had struck a nerve.

"I hate to break it to you, dear," Dorothy said to Gayle, "but *you're* going to be eighty-six too someday, God willing. All that money you flaunt can't change that."

"I guess the white gloves are off now," I whispered to Simon, who was amazed by the exchange that had erupted. Jackie was trying to keep a straight face. Pat was trying not to faint. And Rick and Brianna began arguing with each other and were, therefore, oblivious to all of it.

"Oh, so it's my money you're envious of, Mrs. Thayer," Gayle said coolly, her tiny, surgically enhanced nostrils flaring. "I thought it was my manners you coveted."

"I'm sure Mrs. Thayer didn't mean any harm," Kenneth appeased his wife, as was his role in the marriage, apparently. Hoping everyone would settle down, he turned back to Jackie, with whom he'd been discussing the next day's stop in Nassau. He asked her what the three of us were planning to do during the few hours the ship was docked there. She told him she didn't know what Pat and I were planning to do but *she* was spending the day with Per Johansson.

"Who?" asked Kenneth.

"The doctor who took care of me when I was in the hospital," she explained. "He's from Finland, originally, but he's been working for Sea Swan long enough to know his way around the ports of call. I couldn't ask for a better tour guide."

Kenneth arched an eyebrow, as if he were surprised or amused that Jackie had struck up a friendship with Dr. Johansson.

"What are you and Gayle going to do in Nassau?" she asked.

"What we do back in New Jersey," he said resignedly. "We're going shopping."

After dinner, Jackie, Pat, Simon and I sat in the atrium and talked for an hour or so before Jackie announced she was ready to call it a night. Pat said she was tired too. We all took the elevator up to Deck 8 together, the unspoken assumption being that Simon and I would say our goodnight in private, in my stateroom.

"Do me a favor, both of you," I said to Jackie and Pat as we all stood outside their cabins. "Double lock your doors, okay?"

"Elaine," Jackie sighed.

"There was a robbery right down the hall from us," I lied. "I wasn't going to say anything because I figured neither of you would believe me."

"We don't, but we'll double lock our doors anyway," Jackie agreed.

Pat nodded. "I wouldn't want the thief to take all the souvenirs I've collected."

"That's the spirit," I said.

I kissed my friends goodnight, wishing that the hit man would chicken out and let the three of us live to be at least as old as Dorothy Thayer.

22

"**S**o tell me about Eric," Simon asked after we'd settled into my cabin, he in the chair, I on the bed. We had determined that my assignment was to furnish him with short biographies of the ex-husbands.

"I'll start with his parents," I said. "The mother came from money and lorded it over the father. But the father was the one with the business sense. It was his ideas and her dough that made Zucker Funeral Homes what it is today. Eric simply stepped into a good thing."

"You mentioned the other day that he's been making abusive phone calls to you, ever since you did public relations for his business rival."

"Yes. Eric isn't one to keep his anger all bottled up inside. He's a yeller and screamer. He's compulsively neat and organized, as I've told you, but he gets totally out of control when he's mad. A major Type A. He rants and raves and shuts up, then rants and raves all over again. His father is like that too. They're a couple of heart attacks waiting to happen."

Simon pursed his lips. "Eric just doesn't sound like our man," he said. "Why would he arrange to have you murdered because of a PR campaign you did almost six years ago? If he's such a hot head, he would have had you murdered back then. Or is there something you did more recently to slight him, Slim? Think."

I thought for a minute, then shook my head.

"All right. Tell me about his friends, the guys he hangs out with on the golf course or wherever."

"He doesn't have any friends. And he doesn't play golf."

"He must do something when he's not working."

"Yes. He cleans out his closet. Every single weekend. It's a thing with him."

"No wonder you married him. Let's move on to Jackie's ex-husband," Simon said. "Give me the story there."

"Well, as I think I've told you, Peter and Jackie met in college, at Penn State."

"Right. You said that Jackie was from Pittsburgh. Is Peter a Pennsylvania native too?"

"Yes, but his family moved to New York when he was a kid. Why?"

He shrugged. "Henry Prichard's from Altoona. I'm grasping at straws."

"I know. Me too. After Peter and Jackie graduated from college, they got married, moved to Vermont, and bought a farm there. It was the sixties, and people were into buying farms in Vermont, remember?"

He nodded.

"The problem was, they didn't make a dime off that farm. They had all the butter they could churn, but they couldn't pay their mortgage. Then, Peter's parents were killed in a plane crash, and Peter, an only child, inherited their place in Manhattan. It offered Peter and Jackie a way to get out from under their debts in Vermont, so they sold the farm and moved into the apartment. Peter taught a course at the New School. Jackie worked in a florist shop."

"How did the nursery in Bedford come about?"

"Unlike Eric, Peter's a very gregarious fellow. A natural networker. Someone he knew knew someone else who knew someone else who wanted to be a partner in a nursery in Westchester. Peter and Jackie had some money left from Peter's inheritance, and they ended up going into business with the man."

"We don't know the name of this person?"

"No, but it doesn't matter. Apparently, he was stung by a bee while he was pruning some rose bushes and died instantly. Personally, I never go anywhere without my EpiPen Auto-Injector."

"Did this poor guy leave his share of the business to Peter and Jackie?" Simon asked.

"Yes, and they renamed it J&P Nursery and made a huge success of it. Jackie was the workhorse. Peter was the schmoozer. The combination was great for the business but lousy for the marriage. He was always out there hustling, while she was always out there hoeing or whatever she does. And while he was out there hustling, he met Trish, the present wife."

"How did he meet her?"

"The same way he met the business partner that died: through a friend of a friend of a friend—a rich friend. I'll tell you one thing: For a guy who used to be a hippie farmer, he sure made a smooth transition into a capitalist. Jackie says he wears suits now. With suspenders."

"That *is* cause for alarm."

"What's alarming is Peter's ambition. He wants control of that nursery, and Jackie is an obstacle—as long as she's alive."

"Okay. Let's suppose that Peter's the ex-husband we're after. Who's the hit man? That's the question that needs answering now."

"It could be one of his laborers at the nursery," I suggested. "Maybe the guy's an illegal immigrant and Peter threatened to send him back to the old country if he refused to kill Jackie."

"Maybe." Simon rubbed his eyes. He looked exhausted, defeated. He knew as well as I did that we were just playing a guessing game, just wasting our time. Neither of us was a detective, or even an amateur sleuth, and all we had to go on were a garbled, ship-to-shore phone call and a nursery rhyme.

"Is it worth talking about Bill Kovecky at this point?" I asked. "I've pretty much told you his story, especially how he bolted out of New York so suddenly and left his kids the way he did. I still think he could be our bad guy and Albert could be his henchman. The only thing that throws a monkey wrench into that theory is that Pat still loves Bill. He must have *some* redeeming qualities."

"Listen, Slim, I need a break from all this," said Simon, slumping in the chair. "Could we turn on the TV or something? Just to clear the cobwebs a little?"

"Sure." I jumped up from the bed and switched on the television. Larry King was just winding up an interview with Demi Moore. She was discussing the perils of having money, fame, and a fabulous body.

I reclined on the bed. Simon remained in the chair. It took me a few seconds to realize how silly that was. Why should he be uncomfortable, while I was stretched out like a queen? Especially when the reason he was in my room was to watch over me, to be my bodyguard?

"Simon. Why don't you lie down next to me?" I patted the bed. "It's okay. Really."

"Are you sure? I know you weren't crazy about having a sleepover date when I first brought it up."

"I know, but that was only because of the last time we were . . ." I stopped. Water under the bridge. "Now, of course, we're much too consumed with this hit man business to even consider having sex. Isn't that right?"

"Absolutely," he said, getting up from the chair and collapsing onto the bed, his body inches from mine. We were both completely clothed, but he was so close to me that I suddenly wanted him more than ever, despite what I'd just said.

I lay there, my heart beating, my lips burning, my loins aching, so tempted to tell Simon that I'd changed my mind and would be perfectly willing to make love to him. After all, we didn't know what tomorrow would bring, did we? *I* could turn out to be the ex-wife who got killed and then it would be too late.

Yes, I decided. We should take advantage of this time alone. It might be our last opportunity to have carnal knowledge of each other.

Without saying a word, without even glancing at Simon, I rose from the bed, took off my clothes, and hung them in the closet (I couldn't help it). Then, I turned to face him in all my naked lust.

"Simon," I said throatily.

He didn't move or speak.

"Simon?" I said less throatily.

No response.

I tiptoed over to my handbag, put on my bifocals, and inspected him more closely.

His eyes were shut. His body was still. And his mouth was hanging open at an odd angle, a tiny pool of drool accumulating on the pillow. Pretty soon, the snoring kicked in.

Some bodyguard, I thought, and slipped into my nightgown.

I turned off the television and the lights, climbed onto the bed as quietly as I could, and carefully wrapped myself around Simon. He stirred but only for a moment. Long enough for me to whisper: "I love you." Long enough for him to murmur: "I love you too."

Day Seven:
Saturday, February 16

23

Simon woke us both up at about seven, when he rolled over in bed and discovered, to his surprise, that his body parts were entangled in mine.

"Oh! Sorry!" he said with a start, extricating his arms and legs and then feeling for his pants and shirt. I couldn't tell whether he was relieved or disappointed when he realized that he was still fully clothed.

"Sorry about what?" I asked as I wiped the sleep from my eyes, hoping Simon wasn't turned off by my morning breath. I certainly wasn't turned off by his. On the contrary; my desire for him hadn't diminished one iota during the night. I found it incredibly exciting to wake up next to him, especially since what I usually woke up next to was my briefcase.

"Sorry about nodding out the way I did," Simon said. "I was supposed to stay up and watch over you."

"Hey, listen. These things happen. I'm still in one piece, as you can see."

He appraised me in my nightgown. "So you are." He smiled in a suggestive way that pleased me enormously. "Did I just pass out in the middle of a sentence or what? I honestly don't remember a thing."

"Not a thing?" I asked, wondering about our exchange of "I love you's."

"Zero," he confirmed.

I got up, padded to the phone, and dialed Jackie's cabin, then Pat's—to make sure that they, too, were in one piece. Thankfully, they seemed fine and were on their way to have breakfast together. Pat asked if Simon and I had shared a pleasant evening.

"Very pleasant," I answered.

"Oh, that's wonderful," she fluttered, then collected herself and got on with the business of the day. "About Nassau," she began. "We arrive at eleven-thirty. Jackie has made plans to meet Dr. Johansson at the hospital at eleven forty-five and then the two of them are going off somewhere. Albert has invited me to—"

"Why don't you and Albert spend the day with Simon and me?" I interrupted, afraid for Pat to be alone with Albert this late in the game. "It'll be fun—a double date."

"First you didn't want me to see Albert. Now you do. I was under the impression that you didn't care for him."

I don't, I wanted to say. I care for *you*. "Don't be silly. He's okay."

"Well, if you're sure. We'll have a foursome then. Where should we meet and when?"

I put my hand over the mouthpiece of the phone and asked Simon, the travel maven, where the four of us could rendezvous.

"Tell her we'll see them at Parliament Square, at the statue of Queen Victoria," he said. "When they come out of the ship, they should cross Rawson Square to Bay Street. Parliament Square, which is a cluster of historic yellow buildings with green shutters, will be right there."

I repeated all that to Pat and suggested that we meet around noon. After I hung up, I sat back down on the bed next to Simon.

"It's only seven-thirty," I said. "We have time for a run, if you feel up to it. You could go back to your room and change and I could join you on the Promenade Deck."

Simon shook his head.

"Okay. So we won't run," I said, figuring he was still worn out from all the whodunit stuff.

"I have the rest of my life to run," he said.

"Well, sure you do," I said, not understanding. "I just thought—"

He silenced me by taking hold of my hand and clasping his fingers tightly around mine. And then he looked deeply into my eyes and said with genuine drama, "The hit man could strike today—or at the very latest, first thing tomorrow morning. I may not be able to save you, Slim. Don't you get it?"

"Simon," I said, leaning over to kiss him. "We've already been through this: it's *not* your responsibility to save me. If it turns out that *I'm* the one the hit man's after, I'll give him the lecture of his life the second he comes within a foot of me. You probably thought I was shy and retiring, but that's just a pose I hide behind." I blinked demurely.

He laughed. "Well, if I can't save you," he conceded, "then the very least I can do is make love to you." He moved closer. "Right here. Right now. Before anybody tries to kill anybody."

Now there was an idea. "I accept," I said, delighted that he was seeing things my way. "Right here. Right now."

He undressed himself, never taking his eyes off me, even when he reached into his pants pocket for a condom. I couldn't help recalling that it was that innocuous piece of latex (or rather, Simon's disappearing into the bathroom to put it on) that had, only a few nights before, led me to believe *he* was the hit man and then to flee his cabin in tears.

There were no such histrionics this time. He simply slid the condom over himself quickly and efficiently, lifted my nightgown over my head, and let it fall to the floor on top of his own clothes, our garments commingling the way our bodies were poised to.

I can't believe this is finally happening, I thought, as Simon and I clung to each other—two tall, naked people whose legs were hanging off the end of the bed but whose other body parts were exactly where they were supposed to be.

Yes, it's finally happening, Elaine Zimmerman. Someone may murder you, but you're gonna go out with a great, big smile on your face.

Afterward, as we remained nestled in each other's arms, my body throbbing from all the activity it hadn't seen in years, I took my forefinger and traced the outline of Simon's face. Such a face, I marveled. Such a man. And such a lover! I had literally cried out with pleasure—and the people in the cabin below us had literally banged on the ceiling for me to shut up.

Simon seemed to enjoy himself too, judging by the way he said at the end, when it was over: "You're really something, Slim." I mean, that's a compliment when a guy says that to you, right?

There hadn't been any talk of love during our lovemaking—at least, not on Simon's part. *I'd* let a couple of "I love you's" slip out in moments of supreme ecstasy, but he had only moaned a few "Oh, Lord's."

So you'll wait, I told myself. There'll be time for him to utter those three little words. There has to be.

I was mulling over the question of why women, in particular, are so hung up on the I-love-you thing, when Simon said he was hungry. I started to get up, thinking he meant for us to have breakfast in the Glass Slipper café, but he pulled me back down onto the bed.

"I wasn't talking about food," he said, flashing me that sexy half-smile of his. "I was talking about this."

What came next was more satisfying than any whole wheat toast and decaf, let me tell you.

The *Princess Charming* pulled into Nassau Harbor at eleven forty-five, just a few minutes behind schedule. The sky was slightly overcast, the wind swirling a bit, but the air felt warm and soothing as Simon and I stepped off the ship, onto the wharf, into Rawson Square. Our ship was only one of several that was docked in Nassau that day, so the streets were packed with tourists chattering in a variety of languages. I worried that we'd never find Pat and Albert in the crowd, but Simon took my elbow and guided me across Bay Street and there, in the center of Parliament Square, next to the statue of young Queen Victoria, were my friend and her escort.

"Elaine! And Sam!" Albert greeted us enthusiastically. (Simon and I had agreed that he would remain "Sam" for the duration of the cruise.)

"Hello, Albert," I said warily, then hugged Pat and asked her how her ankle was feeling.

"Better," she said, still sporting her cane, "but I'm not up to running any marathons." Pat didn't run marathons even when her ankle felt fine. She didn't even walk vigorously.

"So: Do you two have any idea what you'd like to do today?" I asked her and Albert.

Albert nodded. "If we head west on Bay Street, we'll reach Chippingham Road."

"What's the big deal about Chippingham Road?" I asked.

"The Ardastra Gardens, of course," he said, as if I were hopelessly uninformed. "Where the tropical birds are." He checked his watch. "We've missed the eleven o'clock show, but we can certainly make the show at two o'clock."

"What sort of show, Albert?" Pat inquired.

"The pink flamingos," he said. "The sweet, spindly-legged creatures march together in a line. They perform three shows daily."

"Like lap dancers in Vegas," I mumbled.

"Actually, the flamingo is the national bird of the Bahamas," Simon told us.

"Right you are," said Albert. "And such beautiful birds they are. If we go to see them at two, that gives us a couple of hours to kill."

I wondered if Albert's use of the word "kill" had any significance.

"Ginger Smith Baldwin's art safari group is spending the afternoon on Paradise Island," Pat offered. "We could join them."

"I don't think so," said Simon. "Paradise Island's too far, if you want to make that two o'clock show at the Ardastra Gardens. We should probably stay in this general area. How about taking a look in the shops on Bay Street? They have incredible buys on watches."

"Do they," Pat mused. "I wouldn't mind buying the children new wristwatches as souvenirs, especially if the prices are that good."

"And then we could stop at the Shoal Restaurant on Nassau Street for their specialty of the house: the boiled fish and johnnycake," said Simon.

"My, you talk about this island as if you've been here before, Sam," Pat observed. "Have you?"

"No. I'm just a voracious reader of travel magazines," Simon said, winking at me.

"*Away from It All,* in particular," I teased, then linked my arm through his, still aglow from our morning intimacy. "Okay, Pat. What'll it be? A browse through the shops, fish and johnnycake for lunch, and then on to the dancing flamingos?"

She didn't answer immediately and I didn't push, given her well-documented slowness in making decisions. I turned to Albert. "What about you?" I asked him. "Any thoughts?"

"Whatever Pat wants to do is splendid with me," he said, combing his mustache with his fingers.

"Fine. Back to you, Pat," I said, trying not to let my impatience show. I mean, it wasn't as if we were deciding whether or not to go whale harpooning. "Pat?" I said again when she didn't respond.

I peered at her and realized that she probably hadn't even heard me. She was staring, trancelike, across the street, back at the wharf, in the direction of the *Princess Charming*. Her lower lip was quivering and her face was very flushed.

"Pat," I said, waving my arms in front of her eyes. "Are you with us? What on earth is the matter?"

"It's . . . it's Bill," she sputtered, clutching her right hand to her heart.

"What's Bill?" I said anxiously.

"Over there. I saw him. In the crowd." She pointed to the wharf.

"You saw him? Here in Nassau?" I said, taking her seriously. Pat didn't have the vision problems I had; *she* could read the newspaper without holding it three feet away from her face.

"Your ex-husband is here in Nassau?" Albert echoed, looking stricken.

"Yes, I . . . swear I saw him across the street, standing . . . among all those people." She pointed again.

I squinted in the hazy sun to see if I could spot Bill Kovecky. I'd never met him, but I'd skimmed through enough of Pat's photo albums and seen him pontificating on enough morning talk shows to pick the guy out of a lineup.

"Maybe you saw someone who only resembles Bill," I suggested, unsure of what to do. "They say we all have a double somewhere. Maybe Bill's is Bahamian." Bill Kovecky was so fair he was practically albino.

"I saw him," Pat said resolutely.

I believed her but didn't want to. Even after all my suspicions, I had trouble facing the fact that the father of my friend's five children was lurking in the crowd; that he had actually flown down to the last stop on our cruise in order to check up on his jittery hit man and oversee the job himself; that he and Albert had, indeed, conspired to murder Pat.

"I know it was Bill," she went on. "He was wearing his Alpaca sweater. His powder blue Alpaca sweater."

"He has more than one?" I asked. Alpaca sweaters went out with Perry Como.

Pat nodded. "I gave him the blue one for our second anniversary. He's kept it all these years."

"Mementos aside, what would Bill be doing here?" I asked, knowing the answer. God, maybe he'd even brought the girlfriend along.

"I couldn't begin to imagine," Pat said. "I suppose Nassau could be the site of one of those medical conferences he attends."

"That would be quite a coincidence," said Simon, who shot me a worried look. "Especially since he had your itinerary and didn't tell your kids that he was going to the same island their mother was visiting. On the same day."

Pat furrowed her brow, as if a horrible idea had just occurred to her. "Do you think he came because of some trouble with the children?" she asked us collectively.

"I haven't a clue," Albert sniffed, as if all this talk of Bill was getting on his nerves. "Frankly, my dear, your ex-husband is the last person I'd like to run into today."

"Oh, yeah? Why is that, Albert?" I pounced, hoping to intimidate the little shit into a confession. There was no doubt in my mind that if Bill was the mastermind of the murder plot, Albert was the hit man. Who else had been hanging around Pat for the entire cruise?

"Because . . . because . . ." He was blushing intensely now. "Because, if you must know, I was eager to spend the day with Pat–free of reminders of her former husband, a man whom she clearly reveres. You see, I'm interested in continuing my friendship with her when we return home–without interference from the good doctor!"

"Albert," Pat said, taken aback by his declaration. "Of course we'll continue our–"

"Don't listen to him, Pat," I interrupted. "He doesn't really want to continue your friendship when you get home. He's not even *going* home after the cruise. He's disconnected both his phones."

My outburst caused Albert's jaw to drop.

"Elaine," Pat sighed. "You don't trust anybody." She looked at

Simon for confirmation, but he was on *my* side. "Perhaps I didn't see him after all," she said, tears welling, disappointment written all over her face. She retrieved a tissue from her purse, dabbed at her eyes with it, then stuffed it inside the sleeve of her blouse. "Perhaps it was only that he and I used to talk of taking a vacation in Nassau, when we were first married, and never did. I'm probably just being a nostalgic fool."

"I don't want to hear another word about Bill!" Albert insisted, reaching for her hand. I grabbed her other hand. Neither Albert nor I would let go, and poor Pat became the object of our tug of war.

"Keep away from her, Albert!" I shouted at him. "We're on to you. On to the whole sick plan."

"Elaine! Albert! Stop this!" Pat cried as we continued to fight over her while Simon began to frisk Albert, who wasn't amused.

"What, may I ask, are you doing?" he said indignantly, trying to keep Simon away with little kicks of his feet.

"I'm looking for a weapon, buddy," said Simon. "Now hold still."

"Weapon?" Albert said, seeming revolted by the very notion. "I'm an ardent supporter of gun control!"

Simon stepped away from Albert after finding something in his pants pocket. "He's clean, except for the Swiss Army Knife," he told me in TV CopSpeak.

And speaking of cops, one was walking by at that very moment, although I couldn't exactly tell at first. Cops in Nassau dress very differently from cops in the States. As a reminder of the island's British heritage, they wear white jackets, navy pants with red stripes down the legs, and authentic pith helmets. Very colonial.

Simon waved him over.

"Is there a problem, ladies and gentlemen?" the officer asked, tipping the pith helmet. Cops in Nassau behave differently from cops in the States too.

"You could say that," I said, still hanging on to Pat, as was Albert. "This man"—I nodded at Albert—"has been hired by . . ." I stopped again, this time because Pat shouted, "Elaine, look! It *is* Bill!"

We all followed Pat's gaze across the square.

Sure enough, Dr. William Kovecky emerged from the crowd and was moving slowly and deliberately in our direction.

24

Bill Kovecky was shorter than he appeared on TV. When he stood next to Pat, both of them so pudgy and low to the ground, they looked like a matched set. Simon and I towered over them, and even wimpy little Albert seemed skyscraper-like in their presence.

Bill was also so fair-haired and fair-skinned that there was a translucent, otherworldly quality to him. Or maybe the Healer of Heartburn just needed some sun.

The third thing I noticed about him was that he *was* wearing a powder blue Alpaca sweater.

"Bill! What are you doing here?" Pat asked, wresting herself away from Albert and me.

"Whatever he says is a lie," I cautioned, inserting myself between Pat and her ex-husband.

"Ah, so this must be Elaine," Bill said dryly. "The one who thinks every man is the Antichrist."

"Now listen here, buddy," said Simon, sandwiching himself between Bill and me. "You're the one who's got some explaining to do."

"Yes indeed," Albert chimed in. "I was in the middle of a rather heated discussion with Pat's friends and now you've shown up–unannounced–and disrupted our afternoon. It's boorish behavior, if you ask me."

"I didn't ask you," said Bill. "I don't even know you."

I glanced at Simon. Either Bill and Albert really didn't know each other or they were brilliant bullshitters.

"Now if you'll all excuse me," Bill went on, trying to wedge his way around Simon, "I came down here to see Patricia."

"Yeah, you came down here to see her all right," I snapped, putting myself in his face. "To see her pushing up daisies."

"What is this woman talking about?" Bill asked Pat, who shrugged.

"You know exactly what she's talking about," Simon challenged, then turned to the police officer, who had been observing each of us without comment. I had a hunch the expression "ugly American" had occurred to him. "This man"–Simon pointed to Bill–"has conspired with this man"–he pointed to Albert–"to murder this woman"–he pointed to Pat.

"What?" shouted Pat, Albert, and Bill simultaneously.

"She looks very much alive to me," the policeman said nonchalantly, referring to Pat. "Are you all with one of the cruise ships?" As if that explained everything.

"All but one of us," I said. "We arrived this morning on the *Princess Charming,* never dreaming that Dr. Kovecky would actually appear at the scene of the crime!"

"What crime might that be?" asked the officer, removing the pith helmet long enough to scratch his head.

"Murder," Simon said. "I just told you."

The policeman smiled. "I think I understand the situation now," he said, nodding at us. "Many of the cruise ships offer Murder Mystery Shore Excursions. People say they're quite enjoyable. Some of you are actors, some are passengers, and you pretend a murder has been committed. The one who solves the puzzle wins a prize, isn't that how it works?"

Simon and I shook our heads and sighed.

The police officer chuckled. "I'll leave you to your fun," he said and took off.

We were back to square one.

"Would you mind explaining why you two told that cop I intended to murder Patricia?" Bill demanded of Simon and me. "And while you're on the subject, maybe you could throw in a line or two about my supposed connection to this man?" He meant Albert.

"You go first," I insisted. "Tell us what you're doing in Nassau."

Bill was about to tell us to go shove it, when Pat intervened. "Yes, Bill. What *are* you doing in Nassau? You left our daughter on her birthday. She was in tears when I spoke to her."

Bill suddenly looked chastened, sheepish. "I hate making Lucy cry," he said. "That's one of the reasons I'm here."

"Your logic escapes us," I said impatiently.

"Patricia," he said, glaring at me. "Must we talk in front of these people?"

"Yes," she said. "The sooner the better."

Bill inhaled deeply. "All right. If that's what you want."

"That's what she wants," Albert seconded Pat's request. His devotion was touching.

"The only flight I could get a seat on happened to be yesterday, Lucy's birthday," Bill maintained. "If I could have flown down here first thing this morning, I would have, but as I said, the flights were booked. And of course, if I'd tried to get on a flight later today, your ship would already have left Nassau. I told Lucy all this and she said she understood. She encouraged me to go."

"Lucy knew you were coming to Nassau?" Pat asked. "She said you didn't tell anybody where you were flying off to. The boys said the same thing."

"That's because it was supposed to be a secret," Bill said. "A surprise. All the kids were in on it."

"The *kids* were in on it?" I said, horrified that a man would involve his own children in their mother's murder.

"Sure. I explained everything to them," said Bill.

"Good. Now explain it to *us,*" said Simon. "What are you doing in Nassau?"

"Well," said Bill, "since I'm apparently not permitted a minute of privacy with Patricia . . ."

"That's right. You're not," I said.

". . . I came down here to talk to my ex-wife about our marriage," he said, "about the mistakes I made, about how I want another chance, about how I . . . miss my Patsy."

Patsy. And I'd thought the "Patricia" was a bit precious.

"Is that true, Bill?" said Pat, fanning herself with her hand, as if his statements had overheated her.

"Every word," he said. "I love my work. But I love my family too.

I just didn't realize how much until these past few months. Call it waking up. Call it coming to my senses. Call it whatever you like. The point is, I want balance in my life. I want *you* in my life, Patsy."

Pat grew silent. I think she'd gone into shock.

"She would have been home by tomorrow night," Albert said huffily. "You couldn't have waited until then to present your case?"

"Not that it's any of your business, Mr.—"

"Mullins. Albert Mullins. I met your *former* wife on the very first day of the cruise."

"Not that it's any of your business, Mr. Mullins, but I had a copy of Patsy's itinerary and I knew Nassau was the last stop on the cruise. I wasn't the best husband in the world when she and I were together, obviously. I figured that if I had a prayer of winning Patsy back, I had to show her I'm not the cold, detached doctor she divorced. The question was: *How* to show her? What sort of dramatic gesture could I make that would not only prove my sincerity but allow her to see a side of me she hasn't seen in years—the attentive, romantic side?"

Pat let a sigh escape, but that was about it.

He regarded her tenderly. "You and I had always talked about going to Nassau, remember, Patsy?" he said.

She nodded.

He continued. "I thought, what if I were to surprise you here, on the very island we'd planned to visit in the early days of our marriage? What if I were to whisk you away and convince you to take me back?"

"Whisk her away?" I said, still nervous on Pat's behalf.

He ignored me, having eyes only for her. "I booked us a room at Graycliff, Patsy. For the next four days. You can tell the ship you're flying back from here. It will be idyllic, just the two of us getting reacquainted."

Pat sighed again, this time wiping her now heavily perspiring brow with the tissue.

"What's Graycliff?" I whispered to Simon.

"It's an eighteenth-century inn and restaurant, just a short walk from here," he whispered back. "It's famous for its antique-filled rooms and 175,000-bottle wine list."

"You know, it really is handy to have a travel writer around," I said.

"What you're saying is that Graycliff is charming and romantic—the perfect spot for a reconciliation."

He nodded. "If Bill is telling the truth, he has anything but murder on his mind."

"Dr. Kovecky, you still haven't said why you've suddenly experienced a change of heart toward your ex-wife," Albert piped up.

"I thought I'd made myself pretty clear," said Bill, directing his remarks to Pat, not to Albert. "I was wrong. I was a fool. I would give anything if you would forgive me."

God, even *I* was ready to run off with Bill. Weren't those the words every woman who had ever been hurt by a man longed to hear? They were certainly the words Pat had longed to hear, and yet she didn't hurl herself into Bill's arms and say all was forgiven. Instead, she hung back, cocked her head, studied her former husband, still taking in everything he'd said.

"Won't you come with me, Patsy?" he said, extending a hand to her. "Let me take you to Graycliff. Give us time to talk, to work things out. Four days together. Think of it."

"I don't have to," she said finally, choking back tears. "I've thought of our being back together every day for the last six years."

Now it was Bill's turn to get choked up. "Have you?" he asked, his arms outstretched.

Pat responded by stepping into his embrace. They kissed unselfconsciously, never mind our prying eyes. And then Bill rested his head on Pat's soft, cushiony bosom.

She stroked his pale blond hair, what was left of it, tears streaming down her cheeks now. "I certainly have thought of our reconciling," she said. "But I've also thought of the things I could have done differently in our marriage, of the ways I could have been more involved in your career, for example. *I* allowed a lot of what happened between us to happen, Bill."

He nodded, just glad to be in her arms.

"I love you, have always loved you," she went on, "but we have a lot to work out. We can't just snap our fingers and have everything be back the way it was. I don't think either of us really wants everything to be back the way it was. There have to be changes on both our parts."

"I know," he murmured, suddenly bawling like a baby. God, men cried at the drop of a hat these days. "But we can make a start, can't we?"

"We'll make a start. That's exactly what we'll do," Pat determined. "We'll spend the afternoon together. At Graycliff. And then, when the ship leaves Nassau at five-thirty, I'll be on it, Bill."

He broke away from her. "You won't stay here with me for the whole four days?" he asked.

She shook her head. "Let's go slowly," she suggested. "That's what I want."

I almost applauded. Pat had actually said the words: "I want." She really had changed. She had stuck up for herself, for her needs. And she'd gotten her man back in the bargain.

"I love you, Patsy," said Bill.

"I know," she said, the picture of total bliss.

They started to walk away, hand in hand, when Pat hobbled over to me and whispered, "You see? I always said he would come back. I just didn't know it would be today!"

I hugged her. "Have a lovely afternoon," I said.

"You too," she said and hurried over to Bill.

As they walked off together, I heard him ask her about the cane and the limp and the still-scabby bruises on her chin and arm. She told him about her fall, and he launched into a lecture on strains versus sprains and contusions versus abrasions.

"See you back on the ship," she called, waving in our direction. "Don't let the *Princess Charming* leave without me."

"We won't," I called back, wiping away my own tears. I was overcome with feeling. Two feelings, actually. On one hand, I was ecstatically happy for Pat. On the other, I was absolutely terrified for Jackie and me. If Pat's ex-husband didn't want to murder her, then it had to be one of ours who wanted to murder one of us. A good-news/bad-news joke if ever there was one.

"I suppose I'll take solace in my dancing flamingos," said Albert, who was sulking.

"I'm sorry things didn't work out with you and Pat," I offered.

"Now you know why I invest so much emotion in birds," he said. "They don't run off with men to whom they were once married."

"I understand," I said. "Believe me."

Albert was about to leave us when Simon stopped him.

"I forgot to return this to you," he said, handing Albert his Swiss Army Knife.

Albert nodded.

"Just one question before you go," Simon said to him. "Why did you disconnect your phones in New York and Connecticut when you were only going to be away for a week?"

"So no one would rob me," Albert explained. "People are forever getting robbed when they take vacations. But not I. If a thief calls one of my numbers to check and see whether or not I'm home, he gets a recording saying that the number's been disconnected. He, therefore, assumes that the residence has no occupants. Hence, no jewelry or television sets to steal."

"That's brilliant, Albert," I said. "Very innovative. Thanks for sharing."

"Not at all," he said and left Simon and me to each other.

We had a leisurely lunch at the Shoal, browsed the shops, and hiked over to the Queen's Staircase, a famous Nassau landmark, according to Simon. Built out of a coral limestone cliff by slaves in the eighteenth century, its sixty-six steps were intended to provide a route between Nassau's downtown area and Fort Fincastle, an actual fort shaped like the bow of a ship.

"If we climb the sixty-six steps to the fort and then another two hundred or so to the Water Tower, we'll get a fantastic view of New Providence Island," Simon suggested.

"You've got to be kidding," I said, exhausted by the very idea.

"Or we can take the elevator," he said. "The view will be just as fantastic."

We took the elevator, rising over two hundred feet above sea level to the highest point on the island.

"Wow. This is gorgeous," I said as we stood together, holding hands, looking out over the most spectacular canvas of blues and greens and violets I'd ever seen. "I feel as if I'm on top of the world, literally."

Simon lifted my hand to his lips and kissed it. "So do I," he said. "So do I."

We held each other for several minutes, savoring our time together, unsure of the turn our lives would take next.

As we were making our way back to the ship, we ran into Jackie and Dr. Johansson on the wharf.

"Well, if it isn't Elaine and Sam," Jackie said cheerfully. "Did you guys have fun today?"

"It was interesting," I said wryly. "We were with Pat and Albert and you'll never guess who showed up."

"Albert's mother," she quipped.

"Not even close," I said.

"How about: Albert's long-lost ex-wife?" she tried again.

"Much closer," I said. "It was Pat's long-lost ex-husband."

"Bill? Here?" Jackie said with amazement. She turned to Dr. Johansson and gave him a very brief history of Bill and Pat's marriage, so he wouldn't feel left out.

"Yup. He flew all the way down here to surprise Pat," I explained. "He wants them to reconcile."

"Son of a gun. She always swore he'd come crawling back," Jackie said, slapping her thigh. "She must be in heaven."

"Fortunately, she's not," I said.

"What's that supposed to mean?" asked Jackie.

"Never mind," I said. "The important thing is that Bill and Pat are together now, at a romantic inn up the street. He had wanted her to spend a few days there, but she told him she wanted them to take things slowly. She's sailing home with us." I checked my watch. It was nearly five o'clock. Almost time to ship out. "She may even be back in her cabin already."

Jackie shook her head. "I can't believe Bill actually came around," she mused. "Miracles do happen."

I gazed adoringly at Simon. "They do," I said.

"I hate to interrupt, but I think ve should get you into some varm clothes," Dr. Johansson said, nodding at Jackie, who was wearing shorts and a T-shirt. "You only got out of da hospital a couple of days ago. Let's not push our luck, okay?"

"You're the boss, Doc," she said.

"Did the two of you go beachcombing?" Simon asked. Both Per and Jackie had sand all over their legs and feet.

"Ve vent just around da corner to da beach at Vestern Esplanade, near da British Colonial Hotel," said Per. "I arranged for da ship to prepare us a picnic lunch. Ve ate and valked and had a delightful afternoon."

Just then, there was a loud, insistent whistle from the *Princess Charming,* letting us know we would be departing Nassau within the half-hour.

"Another cruise coming to an end. Right, Per?" Jackie said, trying to sound carefree. I knew better. The look in her eyes told me that she didn't want the cruise to end; that, after being sick for most of her vacation, she had finally begun to enjoy herself; that the idea of going back to work with Peter wasn't especially thrilling.

"Yes, another cruise is coming to an end," Per confirmed. "Vonce ve leave da harbor here, ve'll be on our final leg of da trip. By tomorrow morning ve'll be docked in Miami and all da passengers vill be going home."

Maybe not *all,* I thought grimly.

25

The ship's farewell dinner was black tie. Jackie, Pat, and I convened in Jackie's cabin to admire each other's finery before taking the elevator down to the Palace Dining Room. Pat looked positively radiant, her afternoon with Bill a resounding success. She didn't go into details about their meeting, but she indicated that they had spent part of the time talking about solutions to their problems.

"What about the other part?" Jackie asked, winking at me.

Pat blushed. "We spent it . . . cuddling."

"Cuddling," Jackie nodded skeptically. "And did you practice 'safe cuddling'?"

Pat told Jackie to mind our own business.

"What about you, Jackie?" I asked her. "How was your day with Dr. Johansson?"

"Great," she said. "I was sorry it went so fast. Per's 'tour of duty,' or whatever you call it when you work on a ship, is up in May and he's planning a trip to New York. He said he'd call me, but you never know with men. Their 'I'll call you' is about as reliable as their 'I'll pull out.' "

I laughed, loving Jackie's coarseness, loving the fact that she was feeling so much better, hoping against all hope that Peter hadn't arranged to have *her* murdered.

It was weird, now that it had come down to the two of us. I didn't want her to die and I didn't want me to die, and the suspense of which of us might die was killing me. It was worse than watching

the last five minutes of the Miss America Pageant where the two fi-
nalists are crying and holding hands and wondering which of them
will win the title and go on to fame and fortune and which of them
will end up on the unemployment line.

"You know what I'd like to do before dinner?" I said to my friends.
"I'd like us to have our picture taken together by the ship's photographer—a formal portrait in our formal attire."

"Oh, yes!" Pat said enthusiastically. "I could have my copy
framed. It would make a wonderful souvenir."

Jackie approved of the plan too, so we headed down to the atrium.
When we got to the elevator, who should be standing there but Skip
Jamison. He was wearing one of those oh-so-hip tuxedos—the kind
that make men look like ministers instead of head waiters.

"Hey, it's Elaine," he said, "and her two best buds."

"Hi, Skip," I said. He pumped my hand and, after being introduced to Pat and Jackie, pumped theirs too. "I don't think I've seen
you since San Juan. How'd it go with the Crubanno Rum people?"

"Cool," he said. "We really bonded. Good chemistry all around."

"I'm glad," I said. The elevator arrived. It was packed with a large
group of women in sequins, but the four of us managed to squeeze
in anyway.

"I can't believe we're outta here tomorrow morning," Skip said,
shaking his head. "It seems like we just left Miami, doesn't it?"

"No," I said with complete candor. "It seems like we left Miami
a lifetime ago."

"Yeah? Which lifetime?" Skip asked.

I laughed. "This one," I said. "I'm not a big believer in reincar-
nation."

"I am," Skip said. "I was a croupier at a gambling casino in a past
life."

"How interesting," I said.

Skip got off the elevator on Deck 5, where the casino was located.

"If I don't see you again before we scatter tomorrow morning,
have a cool life," he said, and waved.

"You too," I waved back, trying to imagine how I could ever have
suspected Skip of being the hit man. He really was a mellow guy.
Too mellow for murder.

When we reached the atrium level, the three of us got on line for the photographer.

"I guess we weren't the only ones with this idea," said Jackie, observing the half-dozen or so people in front of us, all couples. "Take a look at the twosome saying 'Cheese' as we speak."

Pat and I glanced toward the head of the line, where Henry and Ingrid were posing for the photographer, their bodies locked in a tight embrace.

"I wonder if they'll see each other once the cruise is over," I said. "She's from Sweden. He's from Altoona. That's a tough commute."

"And think of all the money they'll have to spend on airmail stamps," Pat added.

"People don't write letters anymore, Pat," said Jackie. "They make long-distance phone calls. I bet Henry's already signed Ingrid up for that MCI Friends and Family thing."

I nodded, thinking how foolish I'd been to suspect Henry Prichard of being the hit man. He wasn't any more menacing than Skip. He was just a Chevy salesman from Pennsylvania who, since meeting Ingrid, probably had fantasies of moving to Sweden and selling Volvos.

Before long, it was our turn to have our picture taken. We climbed up on the little platform and stood together, holding each other around the waist and bracing ourselves for the flashbulb.

"Wait," said the photographer, lowering his camera suddenly. He was not the Australian we'd met the first day, but an American. "I'm gonna have to do a vertical. The tall one's screwing up the shot." He walked over and rearranged us so that I was standing in the middle, between my two friends. "There we go," he said, satisfied with our positions. "Smile, girls."

We smiled. He took the picture. I was pleased. No matter who the hit man ended up hitting, now there would be a record of the Three Blond Mice on the *Princess Charming,* alive and well and dressed to the nines.

"You can pick up your copies after seven-thirty tomorrow morning," said the photographer.

"Thanks very much," I said, handing the guy a dollar tip.

"Elaine, I'm shocked," Jackie said, arching an eyebrow at me as we made our way to the dining room. "You were the one who didn't want photographers near us that first day of the cruise, remember?"

"Yes, but now it's our last day," I replied. "Might as well live it up while we still can."

Simon was late for dinner as usual, but I saved a seat for him next to me. Pat took the chair to my left, and Jackie sat to Pat's left, next to Kenneth.

"How are you feeling?" he asked her, chomping on his cigar/pacifier while Gayle buttered her sourdough roll. He was resplendent in Armani once again, but it was Gayle who was the real show-stopper. Her dress was magnificent—a white silk sarong—and she wore a diamond pendant the size of Rhode Island.

"Physically, I feel fine," said Jackie. "Emotionally, I feel cheated. I'm finally ready to party and we're almost home."

"Almost but not quite," Kenneth pointed out. "You have the entire evening to party." He summoned Manfred, the wine steward, and said something in the man's ear.

"Of course, sir," Manfred bowed, then disappeared.

Just then, Simon arrived, looking so debonair in his tux. I wondered if my heart would always skip a beat whenever he entered the room or whether the thrill of seeing him would wear off in time, the way it had with Paul McCartney.

He said hello to everyone and sat down.

"You okay?" he whispered as he squeezed my hand under the table.

"So far," I whispered back.

Manfred returned with a chilled bottle of Dom Perignon and one fluted champagne glass. He placed the glass in front of Jackie, filled it, and rested the bottle in a nearby ice bucket.

"What's all this?" she asked Manfred. "I didn't order any champagne."

"Compliments of Mr. Cone," Manfred replied and bowed once again.

"You said you were ready to party," Kenneth explained to Jackie. "I thought I'd lend a hand."

Jackie seemed absolutely stunned by Kenneth's generous gesture. We all were.

"I guess the rich really are different," I whispered to Simon. "They throw their money around as if it's nothing."

"It *is* nothing. A bottle of Dom Perignon is chump change to people like the Cones," Simon said.

"I don't know how to thank you," Jackie told Kenneth.

"No thank-you's. Just drink up," he chuckled. "D.P. is too expensive to waste."

"You mean this whole bottle is for me?" she said.

"That was the general idea," he replied.

Jackie looked around the table. "Anybody else want some?" she asked us. None of us did. The consensus was that Jackie should celebrate to the max after what she'd been through. She shrugged, picking up the glass. "Well, in that case, here's looking at you, kids." She swallowed her first sip of the champagne and grinned, savoring the taste of the bubbly liquid. Then she took another sip. And another. Kenneth refilled her glass as she began chatting animatedly about her day in Nassau with Per Johansson.

I turned to Dorothy, who was sitting to Simon's right. "How are you tonight, Dorothy?" I asked. She and Lloyd were wearing paper party hats, along with their formal clothes. They looked very New Year's Eve.

"A little sad," she confided. "Lloyd and I have really enjoyed the cruise. At our age, it could be our final voyage."

I identified. "What was the highlight of the trip, as far as you're concerned?" I asked Dorothy. "Isle de Swan? Puerto Rico? One of the lectures?"

She shook her head. "The highlight was just being with Lloyd for seven straight days," she said. "At home, there are always distractions. The children. The grandchildren. The doctors' appointments. The grocery shopping. But once we stepped onto the ship, all that faded into the background. For a solid week, it's been nothing but sex, sex, sex."

"What did you say, Dorothy?" asked Lloyd.

"I said that this cruise has it all over the *Love Boat,*" she told her husband.

He patted her hand. She leaned over Simon and said to me, very pointedly, "When it's right, it's right."

I smiled, assuming she was talking yet again about her sex life.

"You're not following me, Elaine." She nodded her head at the two other wives at the table. Brianna was barely speaking to Rick, and Gayle was so bored she was picking lint off the tablecloth. "I'm talking about you," she said. "About your feelings for Sam. When it's right, it's right." She winked. "I've seen the way you two are, all that secret hand-holding under the table. I'm old but I'm not stupid."

"What did you say, Dorothy?" Lloyd asked her.

"I'll tell you later, dear," she said, as Ismet came along to announce the evening's specials.

"It is International Night in the Palace Dining Room this evening," said Ismet. "I am recommending the Wiener schnitzel."

"No way," Rick protested. "I didn't get all dressed up in this monkey suit to eat hot dogs."

"Wiener schnitzel is breaded veal, Rick," Brianna seethed.

"Then why didn't Ishmael say so, huh?" said her husband of only a week.

"Rick?" Brianna said.

"Yeah?" he said.

"Shut up," she said and told Ismet she would be having the veal.

While Rick brooded, the rest of us gave the waiter our orders. When Ismet departed, Pat began to pass around the "memory book" she'd bought in the ship's gift shop. It was a small, hardbound volume, the cover of which featured the *Princess Charming*'s logo and the date of our cruise, the inside of which was filled with blank pages.

"I hate to impose during mealtime, but I do hope that each of you will take a moment to write your address and phone number down in my little souvenir book," she said. "I think it would be lovely if we could all exchange Christmas cards through the years."

"Hey, Pat. I've gotta remember that memory book thing the next time I want a guy's address and phone number," Jackie said, slurring her words, her face flushed with the champagne.

She's getting smashed, I realized when I checked out the bottle of Dom Perignon. It was half empty, and we hadn't even had our first course yet. Obviously, Kenneth had been refilling her glass at regular intervals.

"Kenneth, would you or Gayle mind jotting down your address and phone number in my book and then passing it on to the others?" Pat asked, handing the book across the table to him.

He deferred to Gayle. "Darling? Do you want to do the honors?"

"No, Kenneth. You go ahead," she said, not bothering to stifle a yawn. "You have better penmanship."

Kenneth took a few minutes to scribble in Pat's book, then passed it on to Brianna, who scribbled in the book and passed it on to Dorothy, who scribbled in the book and passed it on to Simon, who scribbled some made-up address and phone number in Albany.

Ismet brought our dinners, Jackie polished off several more glasses of champagne, and Simon and I kept glancing at our watches, wondering when—and whom—the hit man would strike. We were fidgety now, on edge. We barely touched our Wiener schnitzels.

At one point, there was a loud commotion coming from a nearby table, and we all craned our necks to see what the trouble was.

"Look. It's Lenny Lubin," I said, nudging Simon. "He's so drunk, he probably doesn't even know he tried to unzip the dress of the woman sitting next to him."

"He probably doesn't feel that slap she just gave him either," said Simon.

"I think they're asking him to leave the dining room," said Pat, as we all watched the maître d' scurry over to scold Lenny. There was a heated exchange, which ended with the maître d' telling Lenny to go back to his cabin and sleep it off. "If you're still hungry in a few hours, there's always the midnight buffet," he consoled him. Lenny rose shakily from the table, staggered past us, and exited the room.

And I'd suspected *him* of being the hit man, too, I thought, marveling at how off-the-mark I was. Mr. Lube Job was too busy hitting on women to murder one.

Things settled back down after Lenny's departure. I leaned over and said to Simon, "Before Ismet comes by with the dessert cart, I'm going to make a quick trip to the Ladies' Room."

"I'll come with you," he said, getting right up.

"They don't usually let men in Ladies' Rooms," I pointed out.

"I'll wait outside," he insisted. "You're not going anywhere alone. We're down to the wire here, don't forget."

"I guess I was trying to," I admitted.

Simon and I excused ourselves and headed for the rest rooms. "I'll only be a minute," I said before opening the door to the Ladies' Room and discovering that there was a line, as there inevitably is in Ladies' Rooms. I considered leaving and coming back later, but nature really was calling so I stuck around until a stall became available—one that was operational, that is. Simon had been waiting about ten minutes when I finally emerged.

"Why is it that men can be in and out of public rest rooms in no time and women are forced to make a whole day of it?" I asked.

"That's one of life's great imponderables," Simon said and then kissed me on the mouth, suddenly, passionately.

"Ummm," I said. "Would you mind doing that again? I'll be more prepared this time."

He obliged.

"I want you to know something," he said when we broke apart. "In case anything happens, I mean."

"Yes?" I said eagerly, hoping Simon was about to say those three magic words.

"I want you to know that I . . . I'm grateful to you, Slim."

"Grateful?"

He nodded. "It sounds so trite, but you've brought me back to life. I didn't care about anything until I met you. Now, every day is an adventure."

"Simon, I'm happy if I've helped you. Really I am," I said. "But trying to prevent a murder from being committed on a cruise ship *is* an adventure. It's just possible that *I* haven't brought you back to life; that the high drama of the situation has brought you back to life."

He shook his head. "You're underrating your own specialness," he said. *"You* make every day an adventure. I love being around you."

"You do?"

"Yes."

Hey, love was love. Simon hadn't said he loved *me*, exactly, but I wasn't about to split hairs.

"We'd better go back to the others," I suggested. "If tonight's my last night on this earth, I'm not missing dessert."

We returned to the dining room and sat down at Table 186. I quickly noticed two things: that Ismet hadn't come along with the dessert cart yet and that both Jackie and Kenneth were not in their chairs.

"Where's Jackie?" I asked Pat.

"She said she was a little tipsy from the champagne and needed some fresh air," Pat explained. "She went up to the Promenade Deck."

"By herself?" I said, feeling my heart race and the moisture in my mouth dry up.

"Elaine," Pat smiled tolerantly. "Jackie will be perfectly fine. She wasn't that tipsy. Besides, she's *not* up there alone. Kenneth went with her."

"Oh, so that's where he is," I said, relaxing slightly. Kenneth wasn't a bruiser like Rick or a tall drink of water like Simon, but he could probably fight off the hit man if the need arose, I figured. Jackie would be safe with him, wouldn't she?

"My poor, deprived husband was dying to go on deck and actually smoke that cigar he's always chewing on," Gayle said, rolling her eyes as she fingered her pendant. "He said he wouldn't be gone long, though. He asked me to order him a fruit tart when or *if* Ismet ever shows up with that dessert cart." She frowned. "The help on this ship really isn't what it should be."

Gayle's remark led to a rather lively debate over the quality of Ismet's service and how much everybody should tip him. I listened but sat rigidly in my chair, clutching Simon's hand, waiting anxiously for Jackie to rejoin us.

"Elaine? Sam?" Pat said when there was a lull in the conversation. "Would you both like to have a look through my memory book while we're waiting for Ismet to bring the desserts? Everybody at the table contributed."

"That's nice, Pat, but we'll look through it later," I said, begging off.

She persisted. "You really *must* see the page where Kenneth wrote down the Cones' address," she said. "What a craftsman! He took an ordinary ballpoint pen and created a work of art! The way he scripted the letters." She shook her head in amazement. "He's as talented as those choreographers that do wedding invitations."

"Calligraphers," I corrected her.

She giggled. "Calligraphers."

Calligraphers. The word hung eerily in the air, like an organ chord in a minor key. There was no doubt in my mind that it had a special significance—a sinister significance. I knew I had used the word recently. In connection with the hit man, in fact. If only I could remember where or when.

And then, of course, it dawned on me. On Simon, too.

"Pat," he said tightly. "Give us the book. Right away."

Looking perplexed by our change of heart, she nevertheless handed the book to Simon. He set it down on the table between us and flipped to the first page, Kenneth's page.

Gayle and Kenneth Cone
Two Thistleberry Drive
Short Hills, New Jersey 07078

Simon and I looked at each other in horror. We didn't have to be handwriting analysts to notice that the capital *T*'s in the *Two* and the *T*histleberry, finished off as they were with distinctive little curlicues, matched exactly the fancy capital *T*'s that had caught our attention in the nursery rhyme—the nursery rhyme that had been slipped under *Jackie's* stateroom door.

"My God. I hope we're not too late," Simon said, bolting out of his chair and tearing out of the dining room.

"Wait for me!" I yelled, chasing after him.

"Where are you two going now?" Gayle called to us. "Ismet still hasn't brought the dessert cart!"

26

"**W**e'll take the stairs," Simon said when he saw that there was a swarm of people waiting for the elevator.

I nodded, even though the four-story hike up to the Promenade Deck would be a major undertaking in my Ferragamo sandals. I removed them.

"What do you think he's doing to Jackie?" I said as we raced through the corridors.

Simon didn't answer.

"What do you think provoked someone like Kenneth Cone to become a hit man?" I asked.

Still no response.

"Do you think Gayle is in on it too?" I tried again.

"Slim, let's find the damn stairwell and then worry about the rest of it, okay?"

"Sure."

We ran and ran and ran, frantically searching for a door with an EXIT sign, trying our best not to knock over all the old people in walkers.

We finally found the stairs and mounted them, several at a time. Dear God. Please let Jackie be all right, I prayed as we climbed.

Deck 2. Deck 3. Deck 4. Deck 5. Forget all that StairMaster bullshit. Try taking four stories at a gallop if you want a *real* workout.

By the time we got to Deck 6, Simon and I were both sweating profusely.

"Do you think they're still up here?" I said as we charged through the double doors onto the Promenade Deck.

"I don't know," Simon said breathlessly, "but we're about to find out."

We moved onto the running track, where he and I had spent such pleasant, carefree mornings together. The night was dark, with only a sliver of a moon, and the wind was bracing, as if to remind us that we were heading north, en route home to a frigid New York winter.

There was hardly a soul on the Promenade Deck, what with the six-thirty seating still in the dining room and the eight-thirty seating waiting to get in. As we made our lap around the track, we came upon a straggler or two, but for the most part the deck was deserted.

"Where could they be?" I said after we had just rounded the bow of the ship and hadn't seen any sign of Kenneth or Jackie.

"This is a big boat," Simon said. "They could be all the way back in the stern."

The stern, yes. A chill ran through me as I recalled the tight, narrow area of the ship where Simon and I had shared our first kiss. It was dimly lit and overlooked the churning, foamy wake created by the 75,000-ton vessel—a noisy wake that would certainly camouflage a woman's screams; a tumultuous wake that would carry a body out to sea so swiftly and violently that no one would ever find it.

We kept running, kept going, kept searching for my friend and her killer. The track seemed endless, our pursuit fruitless—until we finally got to the rear of the ship and spotted them.

Jackie was in Kenneth's arms, about to be tossed over the mahogany railing, her silhouette that of a bride being carried over the threshold if not for her flailing and kicking and beating on Kenneth's chest.

"Take your hands off her, Kenneth!" Simon shouted.

Kenneth spun around to see who had found him out. He seemed stunned, confused, uncertain.

"Put her down, Kenneth!" I pleaded with him. "You don't have to kill her. Whatever Peter's paying you, we'll double it!" What a sport.

"Peter isn't paying him anything," Jackie called out to us, appearing more indignant than traumatized by the situation, oddly enough. "Peter *blackmailed* him into killing me."

So I was right when I'd suspected that the hit man was being pressured into doing the job.

"Don't take another step!" Kenneth warned us, holding Jackie closer to the railing, seemingly prepared to drop her into the shark-infested waters if we did or said the wrong thing. "I'll kill her. I swear I will."

Now I understood why he had ordered the bottle of champagne for her at dinner, why he had tried to get her drunk: so she'd be less likely to resist.

But she *was* resisting, despite the Dom Perignon and her recent illness, and Kenneth was taking some serious shots to the shins.

"We've got to do something!" I said to Simon. "We've got to get her out of this!"

"I've got a plan," he said in hushed tones. "You keep Kenneth talking, keep him distracted. I'll do the rest." He started to back away from me, slowly, stealthily. When I was about to ask him what he was up to, he put his finger to his lips, indicating that I should just do as he'd instructed.

"So Kenneth," I said, trying to strike up a casual conversation with the man who had my friend's life literally in his hands. "Maybe there's a way to get Peter off your back *without* killing Jackie. For instance, you could call him tonight and tell him that the job was all taken care of. Then, the minute the ship docks in Miami tomorrow morning, Jackie could go and live in Newfoundland or someplace like that. Peter would never be the wiser."

Kenneth shook his head. "Forget about it. I'm not calling Peter."

"Okay. Then Simon could call him and pretend to be you," I suggested.

"Who's Simon?" Jackie said, momentarily halting her attacks on Kenneth's body.

"It's a long story," I said. "I'll tell you on our next vacation."

"Shut up. Both of you," Kenneth demanded, getting back to business.

"Kenneth," I said in my most soothing voice. "You're a stockbroker with a wife, three shih tzus, and a 6,000-square-foot house that's undergoing renovation. You don't need this shit. You really don't."

"You don't know anything about my life," he said, still dangling Jackie over the water.

"Only what you've told me," I said. "Is there more?"

He smiled wistfully. "It doesn't matter," he said. "There comes a time when it doesn't matter anymore."

"*You* matter," I said, flattering him. "The person who doesn't matter is Peter Gault. He's obviously got something on you, but if you turn yourself in, I'm sure the police will grant you immunity, or whatever it is they grant, and Peter will be the one they'll put away. The slimeball."

"You've got that right," Jackie agreed, "only I never knew how *big* a slimeball."

"Tell me, Kenneth," I coaxed, hoping to lull him into a confession. "How did you meet Peter and how did he talk you into committing murder?"

Kenneth wasn't biting, but Jackie piped up.

"*I'll* tell you," she said. "Kenneth spilled the whole story just before he announced that he was going to kill me."

"Go ahead," I said quickly, eager to hear everything before Kenneth snapped and threw Jackie overboard.

"They were introduced by a friend of Trish's, wouldn't you know," she said, "after Peter decided he needed a 'financial advisor.' " Her tone was mocking.

"I was an excellent financial advisor to Peter," Kenneth said defensively. "I put him in blue-chip stocks, T-bills, a nice mix of growth stuff. I made a bundle for him, but that wasn't enough. Nothing's enough with that guy."

"Isn't that the truth," Jackie said, speaking from experience. "To cut to the chase, Elaine, Peter got a statement in the mail from Kenneth's company one day—a statement with some other man's name and account number on it. Most people would have written the whole thing off as a clerical error, but not Peter. Why? Because the man whose statement he got by mistake was making more in the market than Peter was. A lot more. Peter was pissed, so he checked around and guess what he found out: the man didn't exist."

"Didn't exist?" I said.

"It was a dummy account," said Jackie. "It was set up as a front—a way to launder money from Kenneth's *other* business."

"What other business?" I asked, thinking perhaps Kenneth dabbled in the importing or exporting of gems, given Gayle's collection.

"Kenneth is the brains and bucks behind one of New York's most profitable prostitution rings," Jackie said.

"Escort services," he corrected her.

Prostitution rings? Escort services? Kenneth Cone? I was dumbfounded.

"Hooker operations," Jackie said, in case I needed yet another translation.

"I get the picture," I said, absolutely amazed. I had read about such things, of course—seemingly respectable, decent people engaged in illegal and rather seamy business ventures. Congressmen did it. Show business types did it. And let's not forget the Mayflower Madam. It was in mankind's nature to fuck up. Still, it confounded me every time it happened. I mean, Kenneth Cone had it all—money, a successful career as a stockbroker, an attractive if not hopelessly shallow wife—and yet he had to risk it all to be a pimp on the side. Just had to. As if life weren't fraught with enough risks.

"So Peter told you he'd blow the whistle on you unless you did his bidding, is that it?" I asked Kenneth. I was aware that Simon was lurking somewhere behind me but I was trying to concentrate on the task he had given me: to keep Kenneth talking and Jackie alive.

"What would *you* do?" Kenneth said. "Peter had me by the balls. He threatened to tell Gayle *and* the police if I didn't take this cruise and kill his ex-wife."

I wondered which Kenneth feared more: Gayle finding out about his scandalous activities and divorcing him, or law enforcement officials locking him up and throwing away the key.

"He wanted that nursery all to himself," Jackie mused. "What a psycho." She stuck her tongue out at Kenneth. "What a couple of psychos."

I was still processing the realization that I had sat at the same table with Kenneth Cone for seven straight nights, never suspecting that he was leading a double life or had a connection to Peter Gault, when I heard a loud whooshing sound behind me and then felt myself being knocked off my feet by a torrent of water. It was as if a dam had burst and now, suddenly, the water was rushing onto the deck. I looked for Simon and discovered that he had opened the valve that was meant to be hooked up to a large hose, in case of fire on the ship. It was a brilliant move, because the watery onslaught not only knocked me down, it knocked Kenneth down! He landed with a thud after slipping and sliding and trying desperately to regain his balance, dropping Jackie onto the deck in the struggle. All four of us were down, water gushing all around us, as we scrambled to stand back up.

"Don't even think about running!" Simon shouted at Kenneth, who was up, then down, then up again. "You're trapped on this ship, buddy. There's no place for you to hide."

Kenneth was not convinced. He managed to right himself, despite being ankle-deep in water, and sloshed his way toward the doors leading inside the *Princess Charming.*

"I'm going after him!" Simon yelled. He was clearly in a state of testosterone overdrive.

"Not without me you're not!" I said, dragging myself up out of the water, my hair and clothes a soggy mess. I glanced at Jackie, who was still on her back, floating.

"Sam saved my life!" she said, the weight of what had happened to her finally sinking in. "He did!"

I waded over to her. "Thank God you're all right," I said, out of breath from all the tumult. "We didn't know if we'd find you in time."

She cocked her head at me. "You two *knew* that Kenneth was going to try to kill me?"

"Listen, Jackie," I said, in a hurry to catch up with Simon, who was in hot pursuit of Kenneth. "You're okay now, right?"

"Sure."

"You don't need me to stay with you?"

"No."

"Good. I'll tell you everything later. Now, I've got to go and help Simon."

"Who is this Simon you keep talking about?" she asked.
"Later," I said.

Kenneth and Simon had a pretty good head start, but I caught a
glimpse of them sprinting toward the doors and ran as fast as I could
to at least keep them in sight. My thigh muscles were aching from
all the stairs I'd climbed and I had developed an enormous and very
painful blister on the big toe of my right foot, but it's amazing what
you'll put up with to rescue the man you love.

It quickly became clear to me that Kenneth was leading us on a
wild-goose chase—an arduous marathon that became all the more arduous because it was now well past eight-thirty, and the people from
the six-thirty seating had been let out of the dining room and were
roaming the ship, turning the hallways into obstacle courses.

First, Kenneth darted into the lounge where Jackpot Bingo was
just getting under way. Hundreds of passengers were seated in red
velour seats, tense with the possibility that they might hear *their*
number called out over the microphone—the number that would render them the winner of ten thousand smackeroos.

"Somebody stop that man!" Simon shouted as he pursued Kenneth across the stage that had been set up there, complete with a
giant, electronic bingo board.

No one made a move to stop Kenneth or help Simon. But several
people booed the interruption.

Kenneth's next mad dash was through one of the other lounges,
this one the setting for Ginger Smith Baldwin's final painting class.
Clustered around a table on which a large bowl of fruit rested, a half-
dozen people were trying to master the art of the "still life." One of
those people was Gayle Cone.

"Kenneth! What on earth happened to you?" she said as her husband bounded through the room in his wet clothes, Simon on his
tail and me bringing up the rear. "I ordered dessert for you, but you
never came back to the table."

"I wasn't hungry," he said as he ran right past her, knocking over
both the table and the bowl of fruit.

In and out he went, his next stop the meeting room where the cruise director was about to deliver a lecture on the disembarkation process.

"As you all know, you'll be leaving the vessel tomorrow morning in Miami," the cruise director was saying. "So this talk will cover baggage handling, customs regulations, airline flights and transfers, and of course, gratuities for members of our staff."

"Stop that man!" Simon yelled as the three of us stampeded through the room.

"Stop him from what?" asked the cruise director.

"From killing the passengers on this ship," I said, gasping for breath.

The cruise director laughed. "Now that's a funny bit," he said, "but you guys have the wrong meeting room. Stand-Up Comedy Night is down the hall and to your left."

Stand up, my ass. I wanted to sit down in the worst way.

Before I could explain what was going on, Kenneth had already taken off in search of another safe haven, Simon at his heels.

Oh, please, no, I thought when I saw that they were speeding through the nearby EXIT door and heading up the stairwell. I sighed, taking a couple of seconds to work the kinks out of my legs and feet, then climbed the stairs after them.

Deck 6. Deck 7. Deck 8.

For God's sake, I said to myself. Kenneth's going all the way to the top.

Deck 9. Deck 10. Deck 11.

Yup. Kenneth slammed through the doors leading to the ship's top level, home to the *Princess Charming*'s Glass Slipper café as well as her two swimming pools.

The deck was dark and deserted, except for the pools, which were lit up, and a pair of lounge chairs, which were occupied by a man and a woman engaging in sexual intercourse. When they heard us approaching, they hid under the towels they'd been using as blankets.

"My goodness! I never expected to see the three of you up here!" said the woman, peeking out from her towel.

"What did you say, Dorothy?" asked her companion.

I don't believe this, I thought.

Simon ignored the Thayers. "You've got nowhere to go now, Kenneth!" he shouted, wheezing from all the running. "This is the end of the line!"

Kenneth turned around to assess the situation, and in the process, he stumbled slightly. The momentary slow-down was all Simon needed to close the gap between them. He tackled Kenneth, right next to one of the swimming pools. They started punching each other, like a couple of drunks in a barroom brawl, and all I could do was watch in horror. I felt as impotent and helpless as Simon must have the day Jillian fell overboard during the storm. I had to do something, had to take action.

"Dorothy! Find a phone and call Security!" I screamed, loud enough so even Lloyd could hear me. With any luck, a handful of armed and very large men would arrive on the scene before it was too late.

"Of course, dear," said Dorothy, struggling into her clothes, grabbing a startled Lloyd by the arm, and scurrying off.

Kenneth and Simon continued to wrestle, grunting and cursing and threatening to do permanent damage to each other's manhood.

Suddenly, their fighting carried them right into the swimming pool, their bodies plunging into the water with a gigantic splash!

"Oh, no!" I screamed, louder this time, circling the pool to get a better look at who was doing what to whom. They were still under-water and I couldn't see anything but a big clump of black tuxedos. When they finally emerged, it was Kenneth who had the upper hand—more specifically, he had both his hands around Simon's head and was dunking him in the water, vowing to hold him down until he drowned!

At that precise moment, Captain Solberg's voice came over the PA system.

"Dis is your captain speaking," he said. "Vith your nine P.M. veather report. Da last von of da cruise."

You're telling me, bub, I thought, tuning him out as he went on and on about the temperature, the wind speed, the projected arrival time in Miami, and other matters that were totally irrelevant to me now.

I paced back and forth along the deck of the pool, pleading with

Kenneth to let go of Simon, promising him I wouldn't tell a soul about his call girl service, even offering to work part-time as one of his call girls, if he'd have me.

He didn't pay any attention to me. He was too busy trying to keep Simon's head underwater, trying to kill my brave, courageous sweetheart.

Well, he wasn't going to get away with it. Just then, my eyes lit on the pool skimmer mounted a few feet away in a storage area. I wasn't an expert on pool maintenance, being a city girl, but even I knew that a pool skimmer was basically a long pole with netting at the tip and that it was designed to rid pools of debris.

Kenneth Cone was debris, all right, and so I grabbed the skimmer, stuck it into the pool, and dragged the net across the surface of the water until I was able to ensnare Kenneth's head in the weave of the white fabric.

"Yesss!" I said when I hooked him.

He went berserk when he realized he was trapped in the netting. "What the fuck is this?" he snarled, pulling and tugging on the skimmer with one hand while continuing to hold Simon underwater with the other.

"You might as well call it quits," I said as Kenneth kept struggling unsuccessfully to extricate himself.

I counted the seconds, waiting for him to surrender, heaving a huge sigh of relief when I finally saw Simon's head pop out of the water.

"Simon!" I cheered as he gasped for breath, coughing up all the water that had accumulated in his lungs during the dunking. "Simon! Speak to me! Let me know you're all right!"

He couldn't speak, but he waved an exhausted arm at me.

It took another couple of minutes before he was able to focus on what had happened—particularly on the fact that I had Kenneth in my web, so to speak.

"Pretty clever, Slim," he said hoarsely as he watched Kenneth squirm inside the mesh of the skimmer. "You're really something."

I smiled, remembering that he had said the very same thing the first time we had sex. Unfortunately, I couldn't savor the compliment this time, since I was concentrating on containing Kenneth.

"Thanks, but I can't hold on much longer," I said, my grip on the skimmer weakening, my arms about to give out. "Do me a favor while we wait for Security to show up, would you, Simon?"

"Anything," he said wearily.

"Punch the guy's lights out so I can drop this damn skimmer, okay? I think one good shot in the nose ought to do the trick."

"I didn't know you were the violent type," Simon mused.

"I'm not," I said. "I'm just getting in touch with my masculine side."

He smiled, his handsome face a pulpy mass of bruises, his left eye almost totally closed.

He blew me a kiss, mustered all the strength he had in him, and then drew his fist back and pounded Kenneth right smack in the nose.

I heard a bone break. Oh, well.

Kenneth slumped, his body a dead weight. It was over.

"Nice one," I told Simon.

"A pleasure," he said, rubbing his knuckles.

While I lifted the skimmer out of the water and dropped it onto the deck, Simon grabbed hold of Kenneth's tuxedo jacket and pulled him to the shallow end of the pool, dumped him on the steps, and left him there.

"He's still breathing, isn't he?" I asked as I peered at our catch of the day. "We want him alive, so he can serve an extremely long prison sentence."

"He'll be fine," Simon assured me.

"I love you," I said as Simon emerged from the pool and wrapped his soaking-wet arms around me.

"I love you too," he said.

"You mean that?" I said. "I was afraid you'd be angry at me because *I* was the one who saved *your* life."

He laughed, and his laugh told me that he was finally free of the psychological burden he'd been carrying since Jillian's death.

"I love you," he said again, so there would be no doubt.

I smiled, feeling happier than I'd ever felt, more tuckered out too. "Listen," I told Simon. "The night wasn't a total loss for you in the It's-the-man's-job-to-save-the-woman's-life department. You didn't save mine but you saved Jackie's. One out of two isn't bad, right?"

"I love you," he said a third time, silencing me with a long and very convincing kiss.

We were in the midst of that kiss when four security guards arrived, accompanied by Captain Solberg.

"Vhere is da stockbroker who tried to murder da landscaping lady?" Svein asked. Apparently, Jackie had recovered from her near-death experience and told the captain everything.

Simon and I pointed to the still-out-cold Kenneth, whose body was draped across the pool steps, water lapping against the Armani tux.

After taking a quick look at him, the security guards had a little conference. Eventually, one of them radioed for Dr. Johansson, having determined that Kenneth required medical attention.

"Ve've already contacted da police in Miami," Captain Solberg said. "Dey'll take Mr. Cone into custody vhen da ship arrives dere tomorrow morning."

"What about Peter Gault?" I asked. "Have the police up in Bedford, New York, been alerted?"

"Yes, of course," said the captain, as if he'd been on top of the case from the get-go. "Mrs. Gault has nothing more to vorry about."

"I'm very relieved to hear that," I replied, then regarded Simon, who looked as if he'd just gone fifteen rounds with Mike Tyson. "Now, let's get you to the hospital," I said to him.

He shook his head. "Let's get me to bed. Yours."

"But you need a doctor, Simon," I insisted. "Your face looks like roadkill."

"Your love will heal me," he said through swollen lips. "It already has."

I linked my arm through his. "To bed then," I agreed, my own body about to collapse from exhaustion.

Propping each other up, we walked slowly away from Kenneth, from the security guards, from Captain Solberg, back inside the ship, down in the elevator.

We had arrived at Deck 8 and were ambling down the corridor to Cabin 8024, so tired we could barely lift one leg in front of the other, when I asked Simon, out of the blue, "Are you allergic to any-thing?"

"Penicillin," he said. "You?"

"A lot of things. I'll make you a list when we get home," I said. He nodded.

"What section of the Sunday *Times* do you like to read first?" I asked next.

"Travel," he said.

"Of course," I said.

"You?"

"The obituaries."

He nodded. We kept walking. Only a few more steps and we were there.

"Is your mother the type you have to visit all the time, the type who acts hurt if you don't?" I asked.

He nodded. "Yours?"

"Yes. But she loads me up with leftovers when I visit," I said. "She's a very good cook."

"Aren't you?" Simon asked.

"No," I admitted. "But I'm a very good microwaver."

He nodded.

"Well, that's all I need to know about you for now," I said as we had made it to my cabin at last. "The other things will come out as we go along."

"I thought you didn't like surprises," Simon remarked.

"I never used to," I said.

He nodded.

I inserted the key into the lock, opened the cabin door, and helped Simon inside.

Disembarkation

The M/S *Princess Charming* docked in Miami at seven o'clock in the morning on Sunday, February seventeenth. We were supposed to be off the ship by nine-thirty, and since Simon didn't leave my cabin until eight, I really had to hustle in order to shower, dress, throw all my clothes into my bag, and fill out the Customs form in time. When I had finally completed all my tasks, I stuck my head out the door, hoping Kingsley would either carry the bag out to the disembarkation area or arrange for a porter to do it. He was down at the end of the hall, wishing passengers a safe trip home. I caught his attention and motioned for him to stop by my cabin.

"Here's my suitcase," I told him when he arrived, smiling and full of good cheer. "And here's a little something for you." I handed him one of the windowed *Princess Charming* envelopes we'd been given specifically for gratuities.

"Thank you, Mrs. Zimmerman," Kingsley said, referring to the envelope, not the suitcase. "It's been a pleasure to serve you, and when you're planning your next cruise, think of Sea Swan." I would never forget Sea Swan. "I do have some bad news, unfortunately."

"Bad news?" I laughed. How bad is bad when you've just spent the last night of your vacation tangling with a hit man? "Go on, Kingsley. What is it?"

"It's your suitcase, Mrs. Zimmerman," he said. "It won't make it onto your plane back to New York."

"Why not?" I asked.

"All passengers were required to leave their bags outside their cabins by midnight," he explained. "With over two thousand people on the ship, we need several hours to sort the baggage and route it to the right airline terminal. Since yours didn't get onto the trucks, you won't have it back until tomorrow. Or maybe the day after." He braced himself for a tongue-lashing.

I shrugged. What did I care? I had lived without my suitcase for my first three days of the cruise. I could live without it for my first three days on dry land. Besides, I wasn't intending to actually *wear* any of the Perky Princess purchases I'd packed in the bag. Not to the office, anyway.

"No problem," I told Kingsley, who seemed relieved. He thanked me again for my patronage and my tip and took the suitcase wherever.

I cast a final, nostalgic look back at Cabin 8024—its puny porthole, its dorky decor, its lumpy bed—and I sighed. It was in this stateroom that I had made love to Simon, in this stateroom that I had discovered a part of myself I'd never dreamed existed.

"Thanks for the memories," I said out loud, grabbing my purse and my carry-on bag and heading down the hall.

I was to meet Pat and Jackie on Deck 2, near the Purser's Desk. Simon wasn't on our flight to New York, but he promised to join us at the Purser's Desk to say goodbye—as soon as he was finished with Dr. Johansson, with whom he'd had an appointment to clean up the cuts and bruises Kenneth had inflicted.

"Well, well. Here's our Elaine," Jackie said when I hurried over to my friends. "Our heroine."

There was an edge to her voice. I asked her if anything was the matter—other than the fact that her ex-husband and business partner had tried to arrange her death.

"She's upset that you didn't tell us about the murder plot when you first found out about it," said Pat. "Frankly, I'm a little muffed too."

"Miffed, Pat," I corrected her.

"Yes," she said.

"Now listen, you two," I said. "I'm going to ask you a question and I want an honest answer. If I had told you, a couple of days into the cruise, that I overheard two men on the phone talking about killing one of their ex-wives—and that I thought one of those ex-wives might be one of *us*—would you have believed me? Or would you have rolled your eyes and said, 'Elaine and her paranoia'?"

"I suppose I might have been a little skeptical," Pat admitted.

"Jackie?" I asked.

"No doubt about it. I would have rolled my eyes and said, 'Elaine and her paranoia,' " she conceded.

"I rest my case," I said.

"I'm sorry," she said. "I'm still trying to deal with what happened. I'm having a delayed reaction, I guess."

I hugged her. "You're entitled to feel a little shell-shocked. So are you, Pat." I hugged her too. "We've all been through quite an ordeal."

"You can say that again," Jackie nodded. "Poor Sam. I mean, *Simon*. Look at him."

We turned around to see Simon limping toward us. His face was covered with Band-Aids.

"Have a bad morning shaving?" Jackie teased him.

"Actually, I've just come from your friend, Dr. Johansson," he reported to Jackie. "He told me I'd be less likely to scare people if I wore the Band-Aids, but I'm not so sure." He laughed. "Oh, and he also told me to remind you that you can expect a visit from him in the spring."

Jackie smiled. "Thanks," she said. "Now at least I have *something* nice to look forward to when I get home."

"Are you worried that all the publicity about you and Peter and Kenneth will drive customers away from the nursery?" I asked, knowing how the media love a good scandal—and how fickle "loyal" customers can be.

"Sure I'm worried," said Jackie. "But there is a positive side to Peter being shipped off to jail: I'm in charge of the business. I'll be able to do things my way, without him—or Trish—breathing down my neck."

Simon patted her tenderly on the shoulder. He was fond of her, it was easy to see. Of both of my friends. "What about you, Pat?" he asked. "Any immediate plans?"

"Well," she began, a shy grin spreading across her face, "Bill has been invited to speak at a conference in New Zealand next month, and I'm going with him. In the past I would have said I was too busy with the children, but not anymore. I know they'll understand."

"Of course they will," I said, thinking how excited Lucy must have been that her father would be back in her life on a full-time basis. "What's Bill speaking about at the conference?"

"Diverticulitis," she said.

"Pat?" I asked. "I'm curious about something: Why is it that you mangle commonly used words but always get the medical terms exactly right?"

Pat considered the question, then said, "It might be the same phenomenon that occurs with stutterers. They stutter when they talk, but they don't stutter when they sing, you know?"

We all reflected on Pat's theory and couldn't think of any reason to refute it.

"I hate to break this up," Simon said, "but we've got shuttle buses to catch."

"I can't believe we're on different flights back to New York," I said, wrapping my arms around his waist and pulling myself closer to him. "What rotten planning."

Jackie and Pat winked at each other. "Let's give the lovebirds their space," Jackie suggested. "They probably want to say goodbye in private."

The two of them hugged Simon and said they hoped to see him soon, Jackie clinging to him for an extra second or two.

"Without you, I would be at the bottom of the ocean," she said, her voice choked with emotion.

"But you're not," he said softly. "You're on your way home and everything's fine."

"Thank you," she whispered and went with Pat to the Customs area, where I would meet them in another few minutes.

"Alone at last," said Simon, kissing me, his lips among the few parts of his face not obscured by the Band-Aids.

"I was just thinking," I said. "After seven nights at Table 186, eating dinner at my kitchen counter is going to feel a little strange. I bet I'll be so disoriented I'll sit there waiting for Ismet to tell me the specials."

"I could make the experience less disorienting."

"Yeah? How?"

"By coming over and eating dinner at your kitchen counter with you. You'll swear you're still in the Palace Dining Room."

"Only if you show up ten minutes late."

Simon laughed. "What time are you microwaving?"

"Seven-thirty."

"I'll be there at seven-forty."

"Perfect."